Dawn Starts in the West

To John & Kaye,
Thank you for your friendship and encouragement.

Dawn Starts in the West

L. Robert Pyle

Writers Club Press
San Jose New York Lincoln Shanghai

Dawn Starts in the West

All Rights Reserved © 2001 by L. Robert Pyle

No part of this book may be reproduced or transmitted in any form or by any means, graphic, electronic, or mechanical, including photocopying, recording, taping, or by any information storage retrieval system, without the permission in writing from the publisher.

Writers Club Press
an imprint of iUniverse.com, Inc.

For information address:
iUniverse.com, Inc.
5220 S 16th, Ste. 200
Lincoln, NE 68512
www.iuniverse.com

ISBN: 0-595-18302-6

Printed in the United States of America

This book is dedicated to my wife, Marilyn, and friends at FCC who encouraged me through the slow times.

Foreword

Christianity is not an occurrence but a journey. It begins even before we first meet Jesus Christ and continues until death moves us on to another realm. This story is an attempt to chronicle that journey. It is written a lot from memory and experience, some from study, a little from conversations with other Christians, and very little from Christian theory. Parts of it may strike a like chord in some. Parts may enrage others. It may even bore some who do not or cannot or will not see the spiritual significance of human life (If you are one of these, jump to the meeting in the forest in chapter 24.) In any case, it will not leave you untouched.

Whatever your reaction to whatever part of the book, I humbly request that you let Con, the hero of the book, Incor, Resig, Decev Croesus, Fourberie, Sarah, Rusty, Dugan, Pistis and Beatrice—but mostly, Cleato—lead you through the journey. Finish it, and I believe, you will not be the same as you were when you started it.

Introduction

O-Him stood on the parapet and looked down the long valley at the retreating army. Fires burned on both their flanks as they rushed away from his pursuing troops. They were rebels—enraged at the failure of their rebellion, determined to ruin O-Him's valley before they were finally cast into the lowest end.

His general, Mikhail, came up behind him. "As you said, My Lord, about a third of the forces deserted with Lu-for."

O-Him nodded but continued to watch the progress of Lu-for's army as it surged into the darkness. "Call back the Army. Let Lu-for go for now. The time to destroy him will come, but it is not now. He has some work to do for me first."

Mikhail frowned. "For you, Commander? I don't think Lu-for will be doing anything for you. He is so angry that he is trying to destroy all your work in the valley. Even now, he enters the City of Men."

O-Him sighed as if some great sadness overtook him. "So he does."

"Should we force him out of there and protect your people?"

O-Him shook his head. "Let him go. He has work to do for me there."

"Commander! I must…"

O-Him's hand came up. The general bowed and walked backward, out of O-Him's presence.

O-Him stared into the darkness, seeming to see something that none of his troops could see. He waited there on the wall for many minutes. Suddenly, a wail came from the direction of the City. It changed in timbre to a scream—the sound of millions of voices crying in anguish.

O-Him's shoulders hunched over and his brow creased deeply—as if he suffered a great pain in his chest.

Mikhail rushed up to him at the sound, then stopped and stared. Crimson blood ringed his brow, running down his forehead and through his pure white hair. Thick, ruby fluid dripped from his fingertips. Wounds in his wrists poured out more to follow what had already dripped to the stones. Blood pooled at his feet, running freely from holes in his ankles. Blood and water soaked the white linens around his abdomen and puddled on the stones like a bright pink lake.

Mikhail rushed to his commander and kneeled before him. Tears poured down his cheeks. "Oh, My Lord, I should never have left you. Lu-for has left a traitor in our midst and he has won through treachery what he could not gain by force."

O-Him looked at him through anguished eyes, then smiled. Slowly, he straightened himself to his full height. The blood dried. The wounds closed. In a few minutes, only the scars were left. "A traitor? Yes, but he has not won. We have."

Mikhail rose to his feet, then fell back to the stones. "I do not understand, Lord."

O-Him laughed. "You will, Mikhail. You will. For now, take your army and drive him out of the City. Cast him into the lower reaches of the valley. But do not destroy him. He yet has work to do that he does not know."

O-Him raised his scarred hand and dismissed him.

Mikhail rose, then bowed and turned quickly to the Army. "To Arms! We drive the rebel out!"

Chapter 1

"Dawn starts in the West"

It was a proverb of the Eastern Barriers. People on the Valley floor and the farmers of the Western Barriers didn't understand it.

In fact, they didn't understand much of anything about these mountains, thought Con Ataxia. He stood, at that moment, on a ledge overlooking a neighbor's field in the blackness of pre-dawn. His father's farm was high on the Eastern Barriers—higher than most others—as high as one could go and still grow enough crops to make a living. Con had stood like this a thousand times in his eighteen years, staring out over the Valley, waiting for the brilliance that was the source of the proverb.

If anyone of his neighbors had seen him there, they would have shrugged and moved on, for they themselves, had done it a thousand times. But no one could see his six feet and 180 pounds. No one could see the long, sand-colored hair blowing in the light breeze. No one could see his well-muscled arms, shoulders and chest—muscles developed since he was thirteen by hard, continual work in the thin soil of this high farm. Nor could they see the homespun shirt and leather britches, all made by his mother from things they grew on the farm.

No one could see him because he was miles from the nearest neighbors and because it was like pitch all around him. The sun was still below the crest of the mountains—which was why he was standing there.

On rare occasions, the farm work could wait. The lowing animals could tarry in their stalls. He rose on those days before his father, when the farm was still asleep. He would sneak out to his rock and gaze at the sight that had fascinated him and all the other farmers of the eastern mountains for so long.

"*Dawn starts in the West.*"

It seemed like a foolish thing to say. In fact, the people of the Valley ridiculed the farmers of the mountains for saying things like that—incomprehensible things that violated common sense.

"*Dawn starts in the West.*"

It meant to the eastern mountain people that things are not always what they first seem. When a magic act drifted through the small village and amazed people with sleight of hand, the farmers looked at one another and said, "Dawn starts in the West."

When the traveling peddler provided some gossip from the City about some shenanigans of the Rebels or the Army, where either side had won some battle through subterfuge, the farmers nodded and said, "Dawn starts in the West."

When the merchants of the City again and again promised reforms of Market so that the farmers would get treated better—a promise that was sure to be broken, and sure to result in a bigger chunk of the profits going to the merchants—the farmers glanced sideways at one another and murmured, "Dawn starts in the West."

Overhead, a million stars sparkled in the darkness. There was no moon this dawning, so the sky was inky between the pinpoints of brilliance. Con waited in anticipation, breathing lightly, not wanting to disturb the moment.

In the western sky, in a long line running north and south, near the horizon, a hundred new stars burst into being, spraying the eastern mountains with sparkles of bright, white light. Quickly, these grew into small suns, so radiant that it was hard to stare at the closest ones. They grew, like gigantic luminous balloons being inflated by the breath of a thousand angels.

Within seconds, the sun peeked over the rim of the Eastern barriers. Its bright, white light revealed the earthly suns to be the high, ice covered peaks of the Western Barriers, catching the very first rays of the ascending daystar and scattering them like incandescent raindrops across the face of the opposing mountains.

Dawn starts in the West.

Things aren't always as they first seem.

Con watched for a few minutes more. There was one more thing that he wanted to see but he would need to wait. Rapidly, the night line moved down the Western Barriers, first across the rocky faces, far above where men lived. Then, as the daylight battled the darkness across a long, straight front, a crazy quilt of small green and brown squares patched itself together down the side of the mountain—inch-by-inch revealed by the advancing forces of the rising sun.

Finally, the line reached the flat Valley floor and rushed eastward. Near the centerline of the north south valley, pricks of light shone on the dark side of the battlefront—scouts for the advancing army of light. The tall buildings of the City caught the slanting light rays first, showing up as these small lamps in the surrounding darkness. Con waited. This was a part of the dawning that fascinated him.

There was the City—thousands and thousands of men living in one place. All so close that one needed only to reach out. People lived and worked and ate and gave birth and grew old and died—and they never had to leave the presence of other people.

To a farm boy who had seldom seen more than one hundred people together at one time, except for Market, the concept was fascinating.

Con anticipated the next flash of light as the slanting rays caught the west wall of the city. From there, it would move rapidly across the enormous breadth of stone and whitewash that was this habitation of man. The City was twenty miles square—400 square miles of humans, markets, shops, tall buildings—some as much as four stories high.

People!

The idea always thrilled Con.

This week the thought was especially thrilling. This week was Market. Within a few days, he would be in the midst of it all for the eighteenth time—the first time as a man.

The line dividing night and day advanced, cutting the City in half—yet the City walls did not glow. The city buildings did not burst into white flame as they should have. The rest of the Valley, north and south, reflected the dawn. The City, though, remained in darkness—a big blob of darkness.

The line of night moved east, pacing the advancing light. It first stretched at the edge of the City, then pulled itself free, abandoning its trapped battalion, escaping to rush up the slope of the eastern mountains.

Con stared at the darkness that still covered the City, a chill running up his spine.

"Hey!"

He spun around at the sound. His father, Incor Ataxia, stood at the base of his rock platform.

"Do you think things get done by themselves? The day has started, boy. If we're ta leave this mornin', you gotta git to work."

"Pa, look at the City."

His father's mouth formed a big "O", then he nodded. "So that's what yer doin'."

He climbed up on the ledge and gazed out over the immense valley. "Yep, she's a looker. An' we'll be in 'er afore long."

Con spun around and looked at the City again. It was normal. The spires gleamed in the morning light. The white washed walls glowed in the effulgence of the bleached light of the sun. There was no hint of darkness anywhere in the Valley—except far to the south in the misty reaches of the Dragon's Citadel. It always seemed to be dark there.

Incor turned and climbed back off the ledge. "C'mon, boy. You got ta he'p me with this wagon. Yer ma ain't bein' a lotta he'p."

Incor walked away from the ledge—expecting, without looking back, that his oldest son was following in obedience, as he had done for eighteen years already.

Incor was a good four inches shorter than Con. He had the same sandy hair, although thinner on the top, revealing his scalp where the early Spring sun had already turned it pink. When he and Con sat next to each other they were very similar. Both had the thick forearms of farmers who handled tools every day. Both had the thick chest of a farmer who lived high in the mountains and lifted and threw bales and bales of hay and straw. Both had the tanned leather look to their faces and the back of their hands—Con's still looking like supple, well tended harness leather; Incor's like old leather left in the sun too long.

It was when they stood that the difference in height apparent. Incor had short, thick legs. Con had long, powerful legs, good for running.

They reached the bare farmyard. Incor pointed toward the milk cow's pen. "Let her to pasture, Con. Then he'p me hitch the team. We got to get movin' if we want to reach the City afore nightfall tomorrow."

The wagon was loaded—had been since the night before—with all the paraphernalia that was necessary for the family to live at Market. Cots, blankets, folded tables, poles, canvas, and trappings for their booth, baskets of food, and his father's farm books were all in place. In the center of it all was a place for Con and his ten year old, twin sisters when they weren't walking alongside the wagon. His mother, Resig and Hiram, Con's two-year-old brother, would sit on the seat next to Incor.

Resig, Hiram and the twins sat on the long, ramshackle porch that wrapped around the front of their single story house. The porch was supported on two-inch thick tree branches stripped of their bark. Rough wood planks made up the floor and, like the house, shakes covered the roof. Also like the house, the floor of the porch was set on pillars of flagstone stacked one on the other up to about eighteen inches.

Resig Ataxia stared at her men hitching the wagon. She was a thin woman in a gray, shapeless dress. Her black hair was streaked with gray and kept hidden under a broad, faded scarf. Wrinkles stretched from the corners of her eyes and her mouth was flat—expressionless as usual. If she was excited about her thirty-sixth market, she hid it well.

On her lap was Hiram, a ball of fat with smiling eyes and a thumb perpetually inserted into his mouth.

On either side of her, two little girls stood, dancing from foot to foot. Alternately, each leaned over and asked, "Is it time yet? Can we get on the wagon?"

They were skinny things with long thin legs and arms poking out of their homespun dresses. Each girl's long, dark blond hair hung in two side braids. Occasionally, one of them would flip one or the other of the braids to the back or front. When that happened, and the other saw it, she too, would flip the same braid to the back. Both of them constantly fingered one braid or the other, watching the progress of hitching and leaning over to ask their mother it if was time yet.

Incor stood from his work and yelled, "OK, mother, let's get a move on. We got two days a' hard travel and I don't want to get caught outside the City tomorrow night."

The girls exploded from the porch and climbed the side of the wagon. They disappeared into the load, then reappeared as two bobbing, braided heads. Con grabbed Hiram and held him while his mother climbed on top of the tall wagon. Then he handed him up.

His father climbed up the other side of the wagon and lifted his whip. "You climbin' up?"

Con shook his head. "Save the horses. I can walk as far as we're goin' today."

Incor nodded and snapped the whip over the lead horse's back. The team leaned into the harness and the wagon lurched into motion. Con watched it go then followed behind. The two braided heads popped up over the back of the load. Two skinny arms waved at him. Con smiled and waved back. Then they disappeared, moving to the front to watch the lane as it climbed the next rise.

Chapter 2

The Sun had already sunk behind the Western Barriers when Incor called out, "Thar she is. Ain't that a sight?"

For the last hour they had been traveling on flat road and the horses had slowed from the exertion of a day of pulling the heavy wagon. If they had not been coming down off the Easter Barriers for most of the day, they would not have made it as far as they did. In fact, the trip back would be much slower and Incor had marked a place high up the side of the hills where they would spend the night.

At his father's call, Con stood in the wagon and looked forward. A wall twenty feet high, painted bright white, blocked the road. For as far as Con could see in both directions that wall stretched, blushing like a pale rose in the last of the light. Along the top, parapets extended but they were just ornaments. There were no guards or soldiers patrolling the tops of the wall.

Directly in front of the wagon was a large gate. The thick, rough plank doors, hinged to open inward, were still wide open, waiting on the last of the farmers' wagons still trundling toward them. Con noticed that the setting sun was on their left. This was the Down Valley gate. It caught Con off guard. His father always went through the Up Valley gate.

Con tapped his father's shoulder and asked, "Why are we going in this way?"

Incor jerked his shoulder away from Con's hand. His face reddened. "Ain't your call to question me, boy. Jest 'cause yer of age don't give you no…"

Resig laid a hand on his leg and said, "He was jest askin', Incor. He didn't mean nothin'. 'Cause yer feelin' guilty ain't no reason to jump the boy."

Con's father glared at her but her gaze didn't falter. Soon, his eyes fell from hers and he stared ahead again, tapping the reins on the lead horses. "Still, the same..." he muttered.

Con slumped onto the wagon floor as it started to move again. His father looked back at him. "Stand up here, boy. I got to talk to you."

Resig looked at him, shook her head, and stared straight ahead again. Her jaw was set and her mouth described a thin straight line.

Incor rubbed his chin, then coughed. "Look here, boy. You know I always go in by the Up Valley gate. I think we all should. That way, the Market people can get us into our places in order, and everyone gets a fair shot the places in the square. It's best for everyone concerned."

Con nodded his head.

"And, look here. That straight road from the Up Valley gate to the Market is perfect for getting wagons and horses in order, now ain't it?"

Con nodded again.

"And you and me know that this way in from the south ain't straight. It requires a lot a' maneuvering to get a wagon in there and a lot a' maneuvering to get into the line goin' into the square."

Con nodded again.

"But I seen a lot of farmers—poor farmers, people what as don't want to work very hard and got poor farms and crops 'cause of it— make a mite a' money at market 'cause they got in the right spot at the right time. An' they all come in this south gate, ya' see. An' somehow they got in the line. I know I seen a few golds and silvers slippin' from hand to hand jest afore they got to get in afore me. So, I ain't stupid. I know how they ended up gettin' the prime spots when others had got there afore 'em at the north gate and shoulda' had the priority."

Con stared at the gate and said nothing. He could see where this was going. He knew that everyone said that we should all go in the Up Valley gate but he also knew that the successful ones often bypassed that way.

He had never thought of his father doing it. It seemed unnatural—a distinct change in the way his father thought and worked.

He looked into his father's eyes. Incor stared back as if he was expecting something—permission, acceptance, something—from Con. Con shrugged. "Maybe the only way to get ahead sometimes is to do the smart thing 'stead of what's expected."

His father nodded vigorously. "Yes, that's it exactly. That's what I been thinkin' since that last Market when that fat Rufus Gerryway ended up comin' a day late for Market but had a booth right next to ours. And he made a few Golds because he was there and not out on the fringes."

Resig's eyes flared and she turned away from her men. Incor maneuvered the wagon toward the center of the gate. Con gazed at the back of his mother's head and saw little tremors of anger there. Resig Ataxia was deeply honest—naturally honest. This deception angered and hurt her. Con immediately felt guilty for having agreed with his father.

Still, his father was right. It was done every year. Those who paid the bribes and took the crooked way to Market made out better on average than the ones who had done what was expected—done the honest thing. Why shouldn't his father do it? Why shouldn't they prosper instead of Rufus Gerryway, who never worked more than he had to.

The wagon wheels rumbled on the cobblestones of the entry road. Con glanced up at the sky. They were last to enter—and none too soon. Dark was settling on the countryside.

A guard stepped into the center of the road and held up his spear. "Hold up there, Farmer."

Incor halted the wagon. The guard, an overweight man in armor that was too small and barely held by its stretched leather straps, approached the side of the wagon. He touched his helmet and nodded toward Resig, then addressed Incor. "I've let through all the wagons on my list. Who are you?"

"Incor Ataxia from Ataxia Farms on the Eastern Barriers. I'm goin' to Market and I want to get there this way. What's the problem? Ain't this a public road?"

The guard pushed back his helmet, revealing a fleshy face covered with gray stubble. He scratched his cheeks with his outstretched thumb. "Well, it is a public road but this here gate ain't used normally for farmer traffic. You got to make special arrangements." He reached to his belt and shook a small pouch. It clinked.

Incor harrumphed. "Well, I ain't made no special arrangements and I don't think I'll make none with the likes of you, neither."

The guard smiled. "Oh. That the way it is? You come to sneak into the market line like a snake but you also think you're better than me and Pieto over there."

Another guard stepped into the ring of yellow light thrown by the torches burning on the sides of the gate. This one was a thin man. His armor was too large for him and it swung back and forth as he walked. He had a tremendous hooked nose on a pinched face. The over all appearance was of a turtle peering out of a iron shell.

Pieto reached up and grabbed a rope. As he pulled on it, the doors started to swing shut. The first guard trudged off toward the shutting gates.

Incor yelled, "Hold, there. I have to get through that gate."

The first guard looked at the western sky. Only a rim of light blue hung just at the tops of the mountains. All else was inky black. "Nope. Not tonight, farmer. This gate has to close by nightfall. City Father's rules, you know."

"So, how am I supposed to get in the City?"

Pieto cupped his hand and yelled in a high-pitched voice, "I think they keep the Up Valley gate open till midnight to get all you farmers in. If you push hard, you can just about make it." He bent over and laughed.

To retreat now and go around the City would put him last in line. Instead of getting a good position on the flagstones he would get the worst. Incor stewed. Resig snorted and looked out at the fields on their right. The twins began to sniffle. "Connie. Ain't we goin' to Market?"

Con said nothing. Seeing the trap his father was in, he did not want to become the scapegoat for the anger that was sure to break out in a moment. The lined and wrinkled back of Incor's neck was coloring—visible as a distinct darkening in the yellow light of the torches. Con knew the explosion was close.

Suddenly, Incor blew hard through pursed lips. Then he reached under the seat and pulled out a leather pouch. He shook it once. The first guard returned to the wagon and held up his hand. The gates quit moving.

Incor reached into the pouch and took out a few coins. He bent his wrist as if to toss the coins at the fat guard but the guard shook his head and pointed at his open hand. "Right here, farmer. Nice and gentle."

Incor's face glowed. Con stood up, knowing that his father was too proud to put up with such treatment. Fists would fly soon. Con reached back and picked up an ax handle.

Instead of jumping off the wagon and striking the guard. Incor leaned forward and placed the coins gently in the big, gloved hand. He straightened but the hand stayed in place. The guard shook his head. "Again, farmer. There are two of us."

Con wanted him to refuse. He wanted him to reach down and snatch the coins off the fat hand and kick out at the fat, slovenly face of the dishonest guard. He wanted his father to reclaim his self-respect. He leaned forward to tell Incor, but Incor leaned away toward the guard and dropped two more coins into the corrupt, demanding hand.

Resig wrapped her shawl around herself tightly and stared ahead. Con slumped down onto the bed of the wagon. Incor stared straight ahead, slapped the reins on the rumps of the tired horses, and ignored the guard who mockingly saluted as the wagon pulled through the gate.

"It was necessary," he mumbled. "You do what you got to do."

Con said nothing. Resig remained silent staring at the dark city street in front of them. The twins, still unsure of what was going on, pulled a blanket up around them and sat on a grain sack.

The wagon rumbled forward. Incor turned to his wife. "It was necessary."

She continued to stare straight ahead. He turned back to Con. "You do what you gotta'. Right boy?"

Con looked up at the immense, darkened city before them, thought of the three days of Market to come that would determine how they lived for the next year, and nodded once. He let his eyes seek his father's face again but the old man had turned his head toward the horses.

"Right," he heard his father mumble. "You do what you gotta'."

Just inside the gate, the buildings were few. On the left, a few two-storied, stone buildings stood. People draped themselves out the open windows and stared at the wagon as it moved past. On the right was an open dirt area scattered with stones, perhaps 100 feet long and 30 to 50 feet deep. In the center of that was a small white tent. Surrounding the tent were five or six people. Some stood and stared at the wagons, some sat on the ground, leaning against the tent, and reading. Yellow light flickered over the whole area, cast by burning lamps and lanterns placed in a wide circle every ten feet around the tent.

Con tapped his father. "What is this? Is this part of Market?"

Incor stared for a while, then shook his head. "Naw, boy. 'Pears to be the Army, though I can't tell which regiment. They're outa' uniform."

"Kinda' small for the Army. Don't they have a big place just inside the Up Valley gate?"

"Big place." Incor nodded. "Have a big recruitin' drive ever' Market—like some honest farmer was goin' to fall for that line." Incor quickly glanced at Resig and he frowned and fell quiet. Resig continued to hug herself in her shawl and said nothing.

It was quiet for a few seconds. Only the heavy breathing of horses and the rumble of the iron wheels on the cobblestones broke the gentle hiss of the torches and lanterns. The wagon in front of them stopped and Incor pulled his team to a halt. He turned to his son again. "Used to be that the regiments had a big presence at this gate. Tried to git all those usin' the south gate to quit it. Wanted them to change and join up with the Army. 'Course, the people who was usin' this gate wasn't exactly good candidates for no soldier's job. Else they wouldn'ta' been usin' this here gate."

Resig spoke in a low voice. "Does that include you now, Incor?"

"Woman, don't be gettin' on me about these things. I got the responsibility of feedin' you and these children. And it don't git no easier. I got to do what I see as best."

Resig snorted and turned away again.

"Con, your granddaddy on your mother's side, rest his soul, was a big man the Flame Throwers regiments. He had some officer position there. Did it most of his life. Your momma was part of that regiment when we got married. I joined up for a while. On'y, it jest didn't suit. I tol' her that I couldn't take the drills and such each week and we kinda' drifted away from it. I imagine one of 'em still has our names as soldiers somewhere."

Con stared at his father. He knew that his grandfather had been in the Army but no one ever spoke openly about it. His parent's service time had never been mentioned.

"So, these are here to recruit people?" Con asked as the Incor slapped the reins and jerked the wagon forward a few feet, only to stop again as the line ceased moving.

Incor glanced at the tent again. "Don't know what they want. If they are recruitin' they ain't doin' it like they used to. Ain't no bands. Ain't got enough for a parade. And they ain't got no platform for all the generals and such to speak from." Incor stared for a few minutes more then shrugged. "Beats me, Con. Can't see the regiment name."

Resig looked at the men and women around the tent then turned back to Incor. "They're militia. They ain't got no regiment."

"Militia! A'course! I heard the regiments had given up down here. On'y that militia would still be beatin' their heads ag'in this wall."

The wagon moved forward another ten feet. They were now about even with the tent. Con could see that there were six soldiers, if that's what they were. Two of them stood guard, carrying some kind of sword. Two more watched the road, but for what Con was unsure. The other two sat and read from a large book.

"Let's call one of them over. I'd like to meet 'em."

Incor slapped his leg. "T'ain't likely, boy. The one thing you don't do is let one a' them militia start to talkin'. You'll hear more about the Commander and that militia leader, Cleato, than you ever wanted to know. And you can't git rid of 'em. They're infernal pests."

Resig's head snapped toward Incor and her eyes blazed away. Even in the dim light Con could see the color in her cheeks.

Incor seemed to wilt, then said, "Aw, Resig. I was jest talkin'. I didn't mean you—or your brother."

Con stared at his mother. "You are a militiaman? And Uncle Proflig?"

Resig's eyes found Con's. There was a deep sadness there—deeper than normal. She shook her head. "I was in the militia—but I was never really a part of it. They require much more commitment to the Commander than I was willing to give. I quit attending militia drill just after your father and I got married. HE," she shot a glance at Incor, "didn't like the type of people who attended."

"And Uncle Proflig? He is still a militiaman. Boy, he sure doesn't act like somebody in the army."

"Not Proflig. Pistis."

Con stared. He had no Uncle Pistis—at least he didn't know of any Uncle Pistis.

Incor nodded. "You probably don't know him. Pistis quit comin' around when you were still a small boy." He glanced at Resig who was again staring hard at him.

"OK, I told him to quit comin' around. He couldn't leave well enough alone. Kept tryin' to get us back in the Army. Bah!"

Resig almost came off the bench. "Pistis only wanted what he thought was best. He never pressed you, Incor. He seldom even mentioned the Commander in your presence."

Incor held up one hand. "Enough, Resig. We had this fight 16 year ago. I don't want to do it ag'in."

She sank back onto the seat and wrapped the shawl hard around her again. It was quiet for a couple of minutes, then Incor shook his head, "I wish I had never come in this gate."

Resig mumbled, "I wish you hadn't, neither."

The conversation ended. Incor hunched over the reins. The twins lay down on the grain sack, hugging each other under their light blanket. Resig stared at the horses' rear, not seeing, Con thought, any of it. Con returned his attention to the tent and the militiamen.

None of them seemed to be greatly interested in the wagons. The ones on guard stared at the gate, not at the traffic. The others ignored everything except their own little group. As he watched, one of the readers closed his book keeping his place with a finger. He rose from the ground and walked toward the side of the tent. Stopping in the light but staring into the shadows, he opened the book, read something, then spoke. Con could see his lips move but could not hear what he said. A minute later, he nodded and returned to his spot on the ground.

There was a movement in the shadows. Slowly, a figure emerged from the darkness into the lantern light. It was a tall man. He was wrapped in a hooded cloak. The hood was up over his or her face, casting a shadow over the features. The cloak hung down and dragged on the ground, completely enclosing him.

The figure had extremely broad shoulders that could not be hid by the folds of cloth. He raised one arm and pointed at one of the soldiers. The cloth draped over and clung to the large muscles that worked like fluid. The large hand crooked a finger upward and the soldier rose from the ground and walked to him. A few seconds later, the soldier walked toward the wagon.

He stopped next to Resig, but looked over at Incor. "My Lord Cleato wants a word with the young man."

Incor's head popped up. He stared across his wife's lap at the top of the young soldier's head. "Be gone from this wagon and don't be botherin' honest farmers."

The soldier smiled. "If you were an honest farmer, sir, you would not be stopped in this lane at this time."

Incor's face flamed red. "You little…" He grabbed the handle of his whip but Resig touched his arm and stared at him.

"OK, Resig. OK. But I'll take no more sass from them."

The wagon in front started to move. Incor used the whip to wake up the sleeping horses and their wagon lurched forward. He turned toward the soldier again. "Be gone before I forget my wife's plea." He turned back toward the horses.

The soldier did not move. He stood and watched as the wagon lumbered away. Con stared after at him. The young man cupped his hands to his mouth and yelled. "There will be a message. Look for it."

Con shook his head. "I'll not need any messages from you. You mind what my father has told you. And don't be judgin' who is honest and who ain't."

The young man waved his hand and turned back toward the tent. Con's eyes swept the scene until they rested on the hooded figure once again. The lane twisted left and the wagon trundled into a shadow. The hooded figure stood still, facing the retreating wagon. It was as if he was staring directly into Con's eyes, even though Con could not see his at all.

The building cut off the yellow light from the tent and darkness fell.

Chapter 3

The morning dawned bright. The family had finally been assigned a spot (a very good spot) on the flagstones about midnight and had commenced setting up the booth. Four poles had been set at the corners of their assigned square. Rope was strung across the tops of the poles, and guy wires secured the poles to the flagstone paving. Across the ropes, fabric drapes were hung on the sides and rear of the booth. The front was left open. A wide board supported by several boxes on each end stretched across the front, separating the interior of the booth from the walking path. The wagon was at the rear of the booth and served as the living space for the family for the three days of Market. Privies were provided within a quarter of a mile, near the edges of the Market square. Water was available from the well at the center of the square.

The family finished setting up the booth by 2:00 AM and settled into a few hours of sleep before the Market began shortly after daybreak.

The Ataxia booth used blue drapes with an orange stripe along each seam. These were the family colors. All around them, similar booths were raised with various colored clothes, lining the winding paths where the merchants would wander later that morning. They recognized none of their neighbors. In years past, farms that were near them were often near them in Market—since they all had similar distances to travel and would arrive at the Up Valley gate about the same time. This year, since Incor had taken the alternate route, they were placed where their bribes could get them. Those around them probably also had come in from the south or were from farms very close to the City.

Incor seemed pleased. He bustled around the booth, smiling and nodding at his indifferent neighbors. He set his maps out on the table, whistling as he did. When he had them just right, he came to the rear of the booth to partake of the porridge then being scooped into bowls by Resig.

"This is the greatest spot we've e'er gotten," he said, smiling at his wife.

She said nothing but stared at the near empty pouch at his waist.

"Oh, Resig. Don't you worry. By the end of Market we will have that full and more. That was just a necessary investment and will pay off big—don't you worry."

Resig handed him a bowl and averted her eyes. She still did not speak.

Con sat on the tailgate of the wagon watching the interchange. He was uncomfortable with this new relationship between his parents. Never had he seen his mother so openly opposed to something his father had done. Normally, she was passive and supportive. Even when she had disapproved of something, she had forgiven quickly and was smiling and laughing with him within minutes. This new thing had been going on for days—perhaps a week.

Con wolfed down his porridge and jumped to the ground. A movement in the wagon caught his eye. From under the blankets on the straw mattress, four skinny legs and four skinny arms emerged. Then the twin heads popped out. His sisters, Melissa and Jennifer, sat up and stared around. Their sandy-brown hair stuck out at strange angles. Pieces of straw jutted out of the mass. The girls smiled and jumped up, their night dresses flapping around their legs. Con moved away from the tail gate and the girls rushed toward it, sounding like 600-pound oxen on the wooden floorboards. They were about to swing down when their mother caught their eyes.

"You two get dressed and get your hair combed before you jump down here. There are customers out there and I don't want them scared off by that sight."

The girls frowned and stomped back into the wagon. Rustlings, slaps, giggles, and flying clothes testified to their activities. Within a few minutes, they both were at the back of the wagon. Dresses of calico replaced the night dresses but nothing else seemed to change. Hair still danced on their heads to its own tune and was still covered with pieces of straw. Resig rolled her eyes and sighed, but she motioned the girls to come to breakfast.

"Melissa, you pull the straw out of Jennifer's hair. Jennifer, you return the favor. When you are done with that you may eat."

Con walked away from the scene, smiling. He had caught the hint of a smile on his mother's face as she scolded the girls. For good reason. The twins were the family clowns—and its treasure. The two girls could imitate anyone in the family or the neighbors—and often did, much to the embarrassment of their parents. They could sing and act—which entertained the family in the evenings. They could, also, bring sunshine in the darkest time with their gap-toothed smiles. They teased their older brother unmercifully. They were spoiled by an indulgent father. They were loved by everyone—even the toddler, Hiram. Their presence in the room would shut up the worst tantrum and have him laughing and coaxing them within minutes.

Con had no doubt that soon the two would work their magic and the rift between his parents would begin to heal—to be forgotten by the end of Market.

"I want to look around," Con said to his father.

His father nodded and bent over to place another colored square on his map—arranging it just so. "Be back within the hour. I need to teach something of haggling with these merchants. We will be seeing the big shots today. This location always draws them."

Con nodded back and walked out into the lane. He looked up to find the tower—a stone bell tower on one end of the square—to get his bearings then he started off to his left.

No actual goods were brought to Market. They weren't even grown yet. Harvest, in six months, would bring the goods into town. At Market the crops and livestock of the farmer were for sale while they were still in the field. The merchants bought at Market, speculating that the price would go up before harvest and they would make a profit, both on the goods and on their early investment. Supposedly it was done to insure the farmer had a market for his goods. Actually it only lined the pockets of the merchants a little thicker and cost the workers of the City more of their wages for food with no value being added.

Con stopped to admire the scene and listen to the confusion and noise that always emanated from this near riot. The merchants were flooding into the square now that breakfast was over. Each booth was outfitted like his father's with a table of some sort across the front. A farmer sat at each with a map of his farm laid out in front of him decorated with squares of stiff, colored paper, each color representing a different crop.

The merchants filled up the untidy aisles between the booths, roaming freely and glancing now and then at some board. If something caught their eye or they ran across a farmer with whom they had had previous good dealings, they stopped and the haggling began.

Food vendors mingled with the crowds, hawking their wares to farmers and merchants alike. Their cries, touting their choicest items, added to the excitement of the day.

The bargaining process was growing everywhere in the square. The din rose as Con stood there. For the next three days, this confusion, noise, bumping, yelling, cheating, honest dealing, every aspect of human relations would be going on in this square with thousands of people. Con smiled.

People!

Next to Con, a merchant suddenly yelled in anger. The farmer he faced screamed back in turn. The merchant spun on his heel and stomped off, almost knocking Con over. After five steps, he turned and yelled, "Five." The farmer's brown weathered face screwed up then relaxed. His gray head nodded once. The merchant beamed then rushed to clasp the other's hand. Both men laughed loudly as they shook on the deal.

The sun, reflecting on the bright colors of Market, stunned the eyes. Reds and blues on the pennants and women's dresses mixed with the browns and grays of the farmer's more somber work clothes. The merchants were dressed in the finest, most colorful clothes possible. It was as important for them to impress the farmer with their affluence and solvency as it was for the farmer to convince the merchant of the quality and quantity of his crops. Down payments would be given that day. The rest was due on delivery. If the merchant was insolvent, or went out of business, or did not have the cash to pay at harvest, the farmer was stuck with a crop and no buyer.

Con drifted between the booths, glancing at the maps, always watching the bell tower above the tops of the booths. Within an hour he was back at the Ataxia booth.

Incor stood at the front of the booth, talking to a merchant. He frowned at Con as he walked past. Con scooted around the end of the table and looked toward the rear of the booth. Con's mother sat there talking with two neighbor women. She caught his eye and waved him back to her. Con avoided that trap and walked to the back of the wagon.

Two sandy colored heads popped around the sides of the wagon. There was a squeal, then a two headed octopus wrapped all eight of its tentacles around Con's legs. He reached down and tickled the two girls until they fell to the flagstones laughing. Then he stepped out the snarl of limbs and went to the water jug.

Melissa disentangled herself from her sister and walked over to lean two elbows on the water table. She propped up her chin with her hands and said, "You're in trouble."

Con glanced at her and grimaced. "What have you two done now."

"Ain't us," chimed in Jennifer, who leaned against her sisters back. "It's you."

Melissa stood, turned to her sister, spread her legs, puffed her chest and said in her deepest voice, "Resig, if that Con has brought this trouble, I'll lace him." She wagged her finger slowly in her sister's face.

Jennifer, in turn, assumed the same straight-backed posture as her mother and said in an overly flat voice, "Oh, Incor."

Then they both laughed.

Con smiled. "What trouble?"

They turned to him and looked up at his face. Melissa answered, as she usually did. "An Army man was here, Con. Daddy said that if you was out there messin' with the Army when he tol' you not too, he was goin' ta lace ya', no matter how big you've got."

Con kneeled and looked the two in the eyes. "You ain't fibbin', are you? You know what I'll do if you're fibbin'."

Both frowned and Melissa spoke again. "We ain't. We seen him." She turned toward her sister who nodded vigorously.

Con's mind went back to the previous night and the hooded figure at the gate. "Was it that big man in the cloak that we saw last night?"

The girls glanced at one another with blank looks. Con realized they had been asleep. "Never mind. Was he a very big man with broad shoulders?"

Jennifer giggled. "Naw. He was just a little guy with spectacles. He didn't even have a uniform."

Con grinned, suspecting a trick. "Then how did you know he was a soldier?"

"'Cause he said so—real loud, too. Daddy's face got real red and he dragged the soldier back into the booth. Ever'body was lookin'." The girls giggled behind their hands.

The neighbor women left and Con's mother rose and waved him over. He drifted toward her.

She frowned at him. "Con, your father has a message for you. Some little man stopped at the booth just as the haggling started and announced at the top of his voice that he was from the Commander and wanted to see you. It was very embarrassing. Now, mind you. I think they have every right to follow what they believe. And I would be the first to say they got some excellent ideas. But, there is a time and place for everything and Market is not the time or the place. You better have a good explanation."

Con turned his hands out to his sides and shook his head. "I don't know anything about this. The only soldier I've ever spoken to was the one last night."

His mother harrumphed and turned back to Hiram. Con turned toward his father to find him glaring at him, holding a folded piece of paper in his right hand.

Con stepped forward. His father grabbed his arm and hauled him toward the back of the booth again. "What have you done? I let you out of here for one hour and you try to ruin me."

Con shook his head but Incor continued. "This is the first year that we have this kind of spot. Con, these people don't want to hear any of that soldier talk. I almost lost that sale because of that ninny showing up here."

Con shook his head again but Incor waved him quiet. "Don't you ever think about real things, boy. You're gonna ruin us with this foolishness."

Con stepped back and jerked his arm out of his father's grasp. He realized as he did that for the first time he was able to do so. Incor couldn't hold him. The shock of that revelation almost abated his anger. More calmly than he felt, he said, "I haven't done anything. The first and last time I ever talked with a soldier was last night. I haven't seen one anywhere around Market."

Incor stared at him. His cheeks were flushed and his hand was still in the position it had been when he held Con. Slowly he dropped his arm to his side. With a deep stare into Con's eyes, he nodded. "Just like 'em. They must a picked up somethin' weak in you last night and they was followin' up. Just like 'em."

He handed Con the paper. "You're an adult now, son. You got to make your own decisions. You do what you want with this." Incor turned back to his table and sat on the haggling stool. He turned his head back over his shoulder. "Jest make sure none of 'em show up here again."

Con walked back to the water table and sat on an upturned flour keg. He put the paper on the table, opened it, and smoothed it out. Instead of sentences, the paper was full of symbols and single words. At the top there was a symbol, like the sun. At the bottom, there was what looked like a cloud—drawn in pencil and very dark on the bottom, like a thunderhead. On the left side was the word BLOOD. On the right side was the word LAMB. Tying them all together were two thick lines, one vertical, the other horizontal. They crossed. There were arrows pointing up from the cloud to the lines and more arrows pointing from the top of the vertical line to sun.

Con turned the paper on its side, then upside down. Still, the symbols didn't seem to make any sense. He stared at it a little longer then started to fold it. Something caught his eye and he opened it again. This time, he held the paper out from him and glanced at it lengthwise. There in the cloud was a word. Con moved the paper around until it became clear: CON.

He walked back to his father and handed the paper to him. "What is this?"

His father glanced at the paper and then returned to his maps. "Same old stuff. They put it out all the time."

"What does it mean?"

Incor glance at it again "Boy, I was only in a regiment for a few months. These are all Army map symbols but I don't remember what each one of them is. I know its recruitin' papers, that's all. Throw it away."

Con looked around the area at the crowds. There were several men in the crowd as young as himself and younger. He looked back at his father. "Why me?"

"Don't be feelin' special. That's what they want. But they give these things to all the boys when they turn their majority. Wants to git 'em young, so's he can train 'em his way." Incor turned back to the front of the booth where a couple of merchants on horseback approached through the crowd.

He spun back suddenly. "And don't be askin' any of them soldiers what it means. That's why they do that—to git yer curiosity up. They jest want a chance to talk at you."

He turned again and greeted his customers.

Con turned toward the back of the booth. A loud, splintering crash spun him back to the front of the booth. The table top lay on the ground in two pieces. The maps and colored squares, so meticulously laid out a few minutes before, were scattered on the flagstones. A large being stood between the table pieces, a poleax with a half moon blade held before him in both hands. The noise of the square ceased. All bargaining ended as the crowds turned toward the scene.

Chapter 4

A similar being sat upon a horse just outside the booth. He carried a sword that was laid across the pummel of his saddle. He held the reins to the second horse.

They were both dressed in shiny, black, ankle length robes. Gold lacing was embroidered into the fabric, draping across the shoulders and appearing to hang like gossamer down their chests. The threads formed a five-pointed star. They had on sliver helmets with nose protectors that extended down to the middle of their faces. Their eyes were set deep in their heads so that one only caught a flash of reflected red as they looked around. Their hands had only three fingers and a thumb and they were large and hairy.

They stood and stared intently at Incor.

The one on the horse growled, "We've come for you."

Incor took a step backward and glanced from side to side. "Me. You can't take me. I've done nothin...."

The beast in front of him smiled, showing stubs of thick teeth, yellowed and broken. The beast spoke, though it was more like a rumble. "You took the bargain, Ataxia. Now, pay the price."

Incor stammered and looked around at the neighbors. None moved. "I've no bargain with you. Be gone from here."

The mounted being moved his head, staring first at the booth and then the others around it. "I think you did make a bargain, Ataxia."

Incor stepped back again, spreading his hands out palms to the rear, as if he was trying to hold back his family—or to protect them. He shook his head. "Not yet. You can't take me now. I jest got to Market. I jest got my first good place."

The being on the ground shrugged. "Now. Later. Believe me, Ataxia, its all the same."

With that, he threw his poleax back to his partner. In his other hand appeared an eighteen-inch dagger, edged on both sides. He quickly stepped forward and placed the tip of the dagger at Incor's neck.

"The rest of you stay back or we'll drag you all off."

The crowd stepped back and the being slammed his fist into Incor's jaw. Incor dropped to the flagstones like he was dead. The being threw him onto his belly, pulled his arms behind him. He wrapped them in a thin cord. With one arm, he lifted the limp form onto his shoulder. The whole maneuver took only a few seconds.

He snapped his fingers. His partner threw back the poleax. Without looking back, the first beast reached up and grasped the shaft of the weapon as it flew by. The dagger had disappeared.

Con, who had stood in shock, realized suddenly that they were about to ride off with his father. He screamed and rushed forward. A foot flashed out from under the robe, striking Con in the stomach. Pain exploded in his gut. It was like when the mule had kicked him two years before. Con fell to the ground.

He tried to rise but fell back, struggling for breath.

Someone in the crowd yelled, "Hooves. I seen it when he kicked the boy."

Someone else yelled, "Oh, Commander. It's Dragon Raiders."

The crowd slunk back. Con rose to his knees, trying desperately to breathe, to get up and rescue his father. The Raider flung Incor onto the back his horse and strapped him down. Then he turned to the crowd and lifted his robe.

Instead of feet, the being had two cloven hooves, like a stag elk. He let the robe drop back to the flagstones and laughed.

The other one frowned at him. "Git on your horse, Zorn. I don't want the Army showin' up while we're still here."

Con forced himself to his feet at that moment and charged toward the horses, screaming. The being called Zorn glanced at the charging man, sneered and lowered the poleax until its curved blade was even with Con's neck. Con, seeing the sharp edge in front of him, dropped to the flagstones and slid to a stop.

The one on the horse yelled at the crowd as Zorn mounted. "Ataxia is ours. Go about your business and just be glad it was not you we came for." Almost as an aside he sneered, "You certainly all deserve it."

The farmers and merchants in the square raised their hands up, palms forward. They bowed slightly at the waist as they backed away, clearing a path for the horses. Zorn sneered again and spat green phlegm on the stones. "Humans!"

The other snorted and screwed up his face as if a bad smell had just entered his bulbous nose.

They kicked the sides of their horses and ran them into the crowd, knocking over several people.

Con jumped up and started after them but a farmer grabbed him. "'Twill do no good, boy. They got him good. No one ever comes back from the Dragon."

"But, that's my father." He spun toward the crowd and looked at each one. They dropped their eyes to the flagstones.

"We can't let this happen. We have to do something. Call the Army. Call the City Father's."

None of the men looked up. Some of the women moved into the booth toward his mother making sympathetic noises.

One old farmer stepped forward. "Won't do no good, boy. There ain't nobody can git somebody back from the Dragon. Wunst they have gone that way, they's gone. Those that have tried has ended up in the same place.

"Now, look. I don' know you but I see you got a mother and brother back there. You got to think about them, now. You can't be runnin' after the Dragon, leavin' her to face this alone. You'll jest git killed and she'll have nothin' atall."

Heads bobbed up and down all around him and an encouraging murmur filled the square. The old man continued, "Now, it's a shame your daddy got took. But, like I always say, he probably brought it on hisself." The old man took a knowing look around the booth. "He shoulda' looked after his affairs better.

"Now, sell your crops, if you got any. If'n you need help doin' that, jest ask. I'll do the best I can for you. But, you'll find no one in this crowd willin' to chase down the Dragon Raiders to get a line jumper back."

Con stared at the old man, heat rising in his cheeks at the description of his father. He opened his mouth to argue when a groan from the crowd stopped him. Slowly the crowd separated as two men walked forward carrying some burden. Each one had something wrapped in calico rags stained with red draped over their arms.

Con's gut went cold and his knees weakened. Quickly he turned toward the booth, searching the corners, hoping to see two little sandy-headed faces peeking at him. His mother screamed. She started forward, then collapsed on the stones.

A man behind Con spoke. "They just stood there, holding their hands up, yelling for the Raiders to stop."

Con spun around. There, lying on the flagstones before the ruined booth, in blood soaked calico, were the broken bodies of two little girls; his two little girls; his sisters. Con dropped to his knees in front of them and stared, his mind refusing to take in the reality of what he saw.

The man who had carried them spoke again. "The Raiders didn't even swerve. They ran those terrible beasts right over the two young'uns."

Con looked up, tears blinding him, grief ravaging his chest. A noise, like a roaring wind, filled his ears until he could barely hear the crowd around him. Everything around him became bright white.

The other man spoke. "I'll swear, those Raiders laughed as they ran down the little ones."

Con rose from the ground. The girl's blood dripped from his hands and covered his tunic. He raised his hands, letting the blood drip down his arms. "Is this acceptable?" he screamed at the crowd. "Did these two also earn their fate? Is this what a line jumper earns?"

Many in the crowd hung their heads for they knew to answer yes was to condemn themselves. The others turned away, unwilling to deal with this reality, unwilling to face this consequence, unwilling to see.

Con stood over the bodies and cried. His clenched fists dropped to his sides and his chest heaved with his grief. Anger radiated out from his belly: anger at the Dragon; anger at the City; anger at the people that had been so fascinating a few hours before.

People!

He had been so enthralled with them. On the farm, he had seen people—masses of people working together—as the solution to his problems, to his quests—to this longing and emptiness that had filled him since his childhood.

People!

It had been in these desired relationships that all things could be fulfilled, all longings satisfied, all needs met.

People!

He stared at the crowds. The ones on the edge had returned to the business of Market. The others backed away, avoiding his eyes; avoiding the reality of the bodies lying of the pavement, avoiding the Ataxia booth. Within a few minutes, the crowd was gone. No one stood in the aisle. Con, his mother, his little brother and the bodies of his precious ones were alone.

No, people were not the solution.

People were the problem.

The heat of anger gave way to coldness. It was not an emotion. It was unemotion. It was not a feeling. It was no feeling. It began in his heart and spread through his middle—up into his chest and down his arms and legs. Finally, the coldness filled his head.

He looked at the bodies around him again. He heard his brother wailing in the back of the booth. The bodies of the two girls—his girls—lay in the their own blood on the dirty stones of Market..

Futility!

He glanced at the crowd surrounding booths and stalls and at the tops of the stone buildings on the edges of the square and finally, at the bell tower off in the distance.

Yes. Futility.

Con shook his head violently, trying to make the scene change. When he opened his eyes, it was all still there.

He snorted. That, too, is futility.

Dawn starts in the West

The Valley is as it is. It is not as we want it to be. It is not as it should be. It is as it is. Sometimes, at "Truth" times, we see that. Most of the time, we are fooled by our own minds, our own thoughts.

This, though, was a Truth time.

The Valley is as it is.

He dropped his hand again. Thick blood dripped from his fingers onto the flagstone and onto the crumpled white paper laying there, onto the symbols of cross and sun and storm.

A slight breeze stirred the drapes of the booth, blew the strands of sandy hair on the girls' heads, picked at the blood-stained paper, wobbling it, then scooting it along the stones out of the booth. There a sudden gust flipped it up and tumbled it down the cobbled path.

Chapter 5

The sun broke over the mountain peaks, sending streaks of light into the darkness on the valley floor. Con stood on his rock watching the City as the first golden rays exploded against its gleaming walls. Three weeks had passed since his sisters' death and the abduction of his father. The fields were green with the new crops. White, cotton-ball clouds scraped the tops of the Western Barriers, almost on the horizon from where Con stood. The rains would come this week like they had every week. The crops would grow. The summer sun would ripen them. Then the farmers of the fields would dip in their scythes and take the fruit that they considered their due.

Nothing had changed. The eternal cycle was still eternal.

Except, Con's father was somewhere in the lower valley, and Con's sisters were dead.

Nothing changed—yet nothing was the same.

The previous evening, just before dark, Con had entered his mother's room. She sat in the wooden rocking chair, hugging Hiram to her chest, as she had for the last three weeks, and rocked slowly back and forth. The little boy squirmed but Resig's grip was firm—almost fatal—on the boy. Con walked over to her and held out his hands.

"Give me Hiram," he said gently. "I need to talk to you."

She looked at him and hugged the boy closer. Then, with Con still waggling his hands at the boy, and the little boy wiggling to get to his brother, she loosened her grip. Con grabbed him and set him on the wooden floor. Hiram scooted away to the corner where his toys were stored and plopped himself down. Within a few minutes, he had his stuffed horse hitched to a toy plow and was plowing the bedroom floor.

His mother dropped her eyes to her folded hands in her lap. She didn't rock. She just sat. Con pulled a stool from near the wall, scraping it across the floor, and set it before her. He gently sat on it, hearing it creak at his weight, and leaned forward.

"Mother, it is time to do something."

Resig slowly raised her head. "I can't, Con. I just can't. I see their little faces all the time. I see their bloody little bodies crumpled in that filthy place."

"Mother, they are gone. They are dead. We can't do anything for them."

She wrapped her arms around herself, shook all over and began to sob.

Con touched her knee. "Mother. It is time to think about father."

Her head jerked up. Her cheeks were streaked with the tracks of tears. "Your father is gone. He run off with those killers."

Con shook his head. "No, he was captured by them. You have to remember that. He was captured by them. If he was captured, then he can be freed."

Resig shook her head violently. "He did this, Con. He as good as killed my little girls."

Con patted her knee again. She had said this over and over again on the trip home from Market. He had hoped she was over it. He sighed.

"Mother, what he did…." Con sighed. His arguments with himself over the last few weeks flashed through his mind. "…he did because he thought it was best for the family. He was wrong—but he was honestly wrong."

She glared at him. "What do you know? You just went along with him. Had we gone in by the other gate, we would all still be here. We might not have all the money of our friends on the lower farms but we would all still be here."

Con stood and walked to the window. He stared at the growing fields and gathered his thoughts. He knew what he needed to do. He simply did not know how to do it. Still staring out the window, he said almost to himself, "All of that is true. It is also true that he is still alive. We can't get the girls. They are gone. But we can get him."

He turned to his mother. "I have to try."

His mother shook her head. "No. I forbid it."

The corners of Cons mouth twitched up. "You can't forbid it. It is a decision I have to make."

She stood up. Even though she was tall for a woman, she had to look up into her son's eyes. Her eyes flashed when she did. The skin over her cheekbones turned pink. She walked to him and grabbed his forearm. "You ain't that big, mister. You better jest listen to yer ma."

Con shook his head. "I have thought about him out there—somewhere. I have dreams about him being tortured, forced to work somebody else's farm as a slave. And I know I have to try."

His mother jerked her hand away and turned her head. Con touched her chin with his finger and turned her head back to him. "Ma, I have to try."

Tears formed in the corner of her eyes and she turned her head again. Whether they were tears of pain or tears of anger, Con could not tell.

"You are jest like him. Stubborn."

Con waited. Resig turned back to him, glanced at his eyes again, and sat back in her chair. "What about me and Hiram? How we supposed to take care a' this farm?"

Con walked over and picked up his brother. Hiram squealed and wiggled to get back to his toys. Con put him back on the floor. He turned back to his mother. "I've hired the boy from two farms over. He's a big boy and should be able to do most of the work until harvest. I should be back by then."

Resign shook her head. "No, you won't."

She stared out the window for a second, then turned back. Her shoulders rose and she stood straight. "OK. We'll make do. You go do what you gotta', boy. Jest don' git yerself kilt. I ain't sure I could stand it."

Con smiled and walked to her. Resig stood, awkward for a second, then grabbed her son around his chest and buried her face on his shoulder. Con hugged her gently, feeling the sobs that shook her body from head to toe. The wetness of her tears soaked his tunic.

After several minutes, she lifted her head, snuffed back her runny nose and stepped back. "You'll need somethin' to eat on the way." With that, she walked out of the room and turned toward the kitchen.

The sun rose higher, lighting the whole valley. It would be a long walk to the City. If he moved quickly, he would be there in two days.

There he would find what he was looking for.

There he would find the way to free his father.

Chapter 6

Con stood at the Up Valley gate. The trip had taken longer than expected and Con had spent the night a mile or so from the City, in a wooded area. This morning the evidence of his camp, leaves and grass stalks, still clung to his clothes. His hair flew loose around his head—there had been no stream to wash in or to mirror his face for him to groom himself. A light sprinkling of blond whiskers fuzzed his chin. He scratched at it absently as he stared into the City.

There were guards on both sides of the gate, men in loose fitting armor but without helmets—similar to the ones he had seen that night with his family at the south gate. They carried the same poleaxes that the other guards had carried. These, though, extracted no bribes. In fact, they did not even look at the small groups of people entering the City. They simply stared straight ahead, bored, seemingly ignorant of all that passed before them.

As Con stepped forward, one of the guards looked his way. The poleax dropped to the outward position, blocking the entrance. Con halted, his gut churning. Perhaps his first impression had been wrong. Perhaps a bribe would be needed, even here at the main gate. He thought of the thin pouch at his waist. The leather contained only a few Golds and a handful of Silvers.

The guard looked him up and down. His free hand plucked a leaf from Con's arm and held it up before his face. He examined the leaf for a second then said, "Where are you going?" The question was flat—as if it was a perfunctory question asked a hundred times a day. Still, he held the poleax in position. His eyes shifted from the leaf to Con's face.

Con opened his mouth to answer then shut it gain. He didn't know where he was going. The Government offices—the City Fathers? To the Army? Or was there something or someone else who could help?

The guard frowned. "Look, this doesn't require a lot of thought. I just want to know where you are going in the City."

Con shrugged. "I'm not sure, yet."

The guard nodded. "Farmer after work. Is that it?"

Con shrugged—then nodded. "Yeah, I guess that's it."

The guard pointed over his shoulder. "Keep goin' down this lane. You'll see some big buildings around the main square. That's the City Fathers' place. They got some people there that'll help you."

Con nodded and stepped forward. The guard lifted the poleax. "Look, farmer, I don't really care where you go but you can't wander around lookin' like that. Get yourself cleaned up. If one of the cops see you, he'll think you're a vagrant and run you in."

Con thanked the guard and stepped through the gate, glancing back. The guard resumed his outward stare, ignoring the crowd and Con. Con stepped into the street and entered the milling crowd.

Where was he going?

Generations before, there was only one answer. The Army was the power. They controlled the City government. They controlled the commerce. They controlled even the Dragon and his Raiders.

A couple of generations ago, a group calling themselves The Humans started to rebel against the Army. At first, they only attacked those areas where the Army had abused its power. They claimed only to want to reform the Army's institution. Many in the Army agreed with them and joined them in the "reforms." Many of the regiments held such Human views that it was difficult to tell the difference between them. Subtly and slowly, the Humans attacked. With stealth when they were weak but with rage and fury as they gained strength and support, they assailed not just the institutions but the very command structure of the Army. They questioned the authority of the Commander—at first as an intellectual exercise, claiming that all men need to understand their submission to the Commander, and therefore, needed to truly understand all aspects of that submission; then overtly, claiming that 1.) The Commander did not really exist and 2.) Even if he did exist, he had no authority over, and indeed, wanted no authority over men. They started to question the Army's regulation of the commerce, and of the government, and of the private lives of citizens. Each attack was staged as a legitimate question—a seeking of "Truth" but, in reality, it was a destruction of "The Truth" that the Army held and a substitution of "Truths"—that being whatever the rebels wanted it to be at the time to justify their own actions.

"The Truth", the basis of the Army's control of the Valley, was that the Commander of the Army had created the City and then had defeated the Dragon and all his forces in a battle that had cost the Commander his life but which cast the Dragon into the lower reaches of the Valley. In the Army doctrine, the Commander came back to life and set up the governments of men to bring peace and prosperity. The Army contended that without the Commander in control of the City, all would be lost once again to the Dragon and his forces.

The Humans contended that the Valley had always been there; that the City had been created by men; and that men had the right to rule it as they saw fit. They said that submission to the Commander was slavery—OK, if that's what you wanted but not to be taught or sought by the City Fathers or any of their minions. Further, they taught that the only Dragon was in the minds of men—or, rather, was created in their minds from ignorance of "Truths." Dragon Raiders were mythical and the capture of humans by these beasts that seemed to take place occasionally was really only the natural result of the ignorance of the lower classes. This "Dragon" could be defeated by improving the lot of all humans.

Eventually, the whole Valley split between these two camps. The Army still attracted many—although fewer and fewer as the years went by—and the rebellion accepted the rest by default. Year by year the rebellion gained power in the City until they controlled most things: commerce, government, people.

Only, the Dragon didn't go away. Neither did the Army. As the Commander had predicted, the Dragon came back into the City, almost at will, and raided as he pleased. By some Army accounts, there were more people under control of the Dragon in the Valley at that time then at any time in the past—even before the Commander had defeated him.

Someone bumped Con in the back and pushed him to the side. "Get movin', farmer. This is the City not your bumpkin village."

Con nodded. "Sorry, sir."

He drifted along the street with the crowd.

Con's nose wrinkled and he looked around. An odor, worse than anything on the farm, permeated the air. He was on a narrow, cobblestone street. Running along the side of the road within eighteen inches of the buildings were shallow ditches. Dirty brown water dribbled along in the bottom of the ditch. Out of the building, several open pipes near ground level extended out over the cobblestones for several inches. As he studied the arrangement, a gush of water and its filthy burden burst from one of the pipes. It splattered onto the stones, splashing several in the crowd with spots of malodorous liquid. The rest ran into the little ditch, flooding it for a few seconds. Some of its burden was left on the rocks as the water receded back into the ditch. Those who had been splashed swiped at the spots absentmindedly but continued to walk and talk as if nothing unusual had happened.

Con moved to the side to let the faster paced crowd move around him. As he passed an alley, he noticed the ditches emptied their contents into deeper trenches within the shadows that ran toward the back of the building. The increasing flow of liquid tinkled along the rocks of the trench making much too musical a sound for the burden it carried. Con stepped into one of the alleys, curious about the destination. The stench, though, drove him back to the street. Two women walking along behind Con glanced at each other and giggled.

"Just off the farm," one of them said. The other nodded and giggled again.

Con felt his neck go hot and knew that his cheeks would be glowing. The women, though, paid no more attention to him. Others in the crowd had earned their attention and their wit.

This was not what he had expected from the City. At Market, it was full of farmers who talked like he did, understood the things he understood. It was full of gay colors, festive booths, food vendors, and fun. And it was clean. Con looked again at the filth that surrounded him.

It was then that he realized he had never actually been in any part of the City except the Market Square. His only other contact with the City had been from afar—from gazing at it from his rock on his father's farm half way up the Eastern Barriers. The City had existed for him only as a thought—a dream place created from what he wanted it to be.

The reality was less fascinating. That which had been so engaging from the mountainside lost its appeal here on the street. Those walls that gleamed in the dawn light did not gleam here. They were dull and smoke-stained. Trash and garbage lay on the street, stacked up against the building fronts, damming the ditches at places and causing the sewage to back up onto the walkway. The crowd he was with ignored it all, walking close to the center of the street except when they reached their destination. Then, with mincing steps, they traversed the obstacle course of rubbish and sewage and climbed the steps that led them out of the debris and into their counting office or storefront. Seemingly without noticing the stench, decay, and offal, they would each turn, smile and wave at friends or acquaintances before entering the building.

Dawn starts in the West, thought Con.

The crowd thinned as they pushed further. Soon, the tall buildings and stores disappeared. Squat, drab, multi-windowed buildings with a single entrance took their place. In the street, a group of dirty-faced children played among the refuse, jumping over the sewers to get from one side of the street to the other, yelling at each other and tossing a stick back and forth. A fat, toothless woman in a faded, shapeless dress hung out of one of the windows watching them. She stared at Con as he walked by. Two other women, one skinny and the other just as fat as the first, sat in second floor windows in buildings across from each other. One yelled something to the other. Con could not understand them but glanced to see if they were looking at him. They weren't. The other one yelled something back, then they both laughed loudly.

Con walked on. He approached another squat building. At its entrance, two men sat with their backs against the wall. A small canvas sack stood between them. They stared at Con but said nothing. One of them sucked on a pipe, letting the smoke drift slowly through his nose. He held it out to his friend. His friend shook his head and lifted the sack to his mouth.

Con moved on, walking beyond the apartments. Low shops with dark doorways filled this part of the block. In some doorways the merchant sat in a chair, looking up hopefully as Con walked toward them, then sagging back as they saw his shaggy appearance and dirty clothes.

Where to go?

The Army?

Con shook his head. Although the Army marched and paraded a lot and held drills on the weekends, they didn't seem to accomplish anything. They railed against the Dragon—some of them did, anyway. They railed against the Rebels—again, some of them did. They recruited people to join them. They did not, though, seem to actually fight the Dragon. It was more like they hid from him.

So, then, the City Fathers?

Well, that was the same as saying The Humans. And The Humans didn't even believe that there was a Dragon.

Con stopped walking and looked around the almost deserted street again. He needed knowledge. He needed a weapon. He needed help. All of those seemed to be in short supply.

"Farmer!"

Con looked around. There were shopkeepers sitting on both sides of the street but none of them seemed to be looking at him. He glanced around again.

"You! Out on the street. Come in here."

The voice came from the dark interior of a shop. A bead curtain hung in the doorway. Although there was a large window next to the door, there was no display in it, no sign on it proclaiming the name of the shop or its products. A heavy curtain hung over it on the inside, blocking his view.

"What do you want?" Con called toward empty doorway.

"I want you to come in, Farmer. I want to talk."

"I've no money for your wares, shopkeeper. Don't bother me."

"Posh! You want information? You want help? Well, I've got them."

The voice was of an old man—or a woman. He couldn't tell. It cackled rather than spoke. Con stared hard, trying to figure out if he had been talking out loud a few minutes before.

He stepped toward the beads, trying to get a view of the old man. The interior of the store was black.

"Come on! Come on! I am not going to hurt you."

Con snorted—and smiled. The old man did not sound like he could threaten anyone. He also did not sound as if he was what Con was looking for. Con turned toward the road. The old voice cackled again. "I know where the Dragon is. And I know all about his captives."

At the sound of the words, a cold tightness gripped his belly. He slowly turned and looked again at the store front. "What do you know of this?"

"Come in!" the voice demanded. "I am too old to have a shouting match with you, boy."

Con approached the doorway. With his hand he separated the beads. Light from the street pierced the dark shop and fell on an old man seated on a pillow on the floor. The old man threw up his hand and shielded his eyes. "Drop that curtain, boy. I can't stand that light."

Con quickly stepped through, stopping just inside the curtain.

It was dim in the room but not completely dark. The walls of the shop were bare of decoration, except for an old tapestry hung on the wall to his left. At one time, the back wall had been plastered—perhaps even frescoed if the slight hint of color was really there. Now, though, it was dark and sooty—and the plaster peeled from it like skin from a sunburned back. The wall on his right was of rough stone—the same as the building exterior.

Their was a bitter-sweet smell in the room and smoke hung at the ceiling. Con's head was in the cloud and he coughed. "I can't stay long, old man. I must be about my business."

Next to the old man, on his right, was a smoking pot. The old man held a hose from the pot in his right hand. As Con stood there, he raised it to his lips, drew smoke into his lungs, held it for a time, then let it drift slowly from his nose. The scratchy voice rattled from his throat as he expelled the last of the smoke, "Come in, young one. Don't fear, I'll not keep you long if you don't wish to stay. I have a message from the Masters for you."

Con shook his head. "You said you knew about the Dragon."

"First the message, little farmer. First the message from the Masters?"

"What Masters?"

"In due time, little farmer. In due time." The old man waved his hand in front of him.

The old man sucked on the hose again. He was thin—starved. Con could see his frail body between the folds of his clothes—and could count the ribs plainly. He was clothed in what might have been a white robe—white at one time, anyway. In the dimness, it was grayish white and had dark spots on it. It was not an actual robe but a swath of cloth that the old man had wrapped around him, winding himself up in it. It was slung over one shoulder, wrapped loosely around his chest, more tightly around his waist and across both legs.

The old man sat on a pillow. His legs, so thin that the bones were more discernible than the muscles, were crossed in front of him. His knees were like the knobs on a sapling tree. Bare, reed-like arms thrust out from the cloth of his wrap, ending in wraith-like hands with long, thin, delicate fingers. His skin was thin, almost translucent and the blue veins showed through making his arms look like a parchment map with the roads drawn in deep blue. At first, his head appeared to be completely bald, but as Con stooped to get out of the biting smoke, he saw the sparse white stubble that covered the sides and back.

The old man sucked on the tube again, holding the smoke in. His gaze went blank then he smiled. The smoke exploded from his mouth. With a broader smile, the old man said, "I know what you want and it is from my masters that you shall have it. It is the true Masters to which I listen; it is the message of the Masters that I bring."

The old head bobbed up and down. He raised one hand and waved Con closer.

"Great are they. They have multiple levels of secret gratings. You will have visions, like I am." He sucked on the hose again. His eyes left Con's face and drifted around the room, seeming to see things that weren't there. As the smoke escaped from his lips, he continued, "Yes, they are pretty. The colors are very pretty and they wave around in time to the music. Like the flame of the moth."

He looked at Con again and smiled. "Wisdom. They give so much wisdom."

Con's eyebrows raised and he looked around at the door. "Look, old man. Perhaps you are hungry—or the smoke has dulled you. I don't know how you knew I was looking for the Dragon but I don't think you have what I need."

Con turned to the door and took a step. Something grabbed at his tunic and yanked hard. He looked back and saw the claw-like hand of the old man clamped onto the fabric. The old man's face was screwed up. Hate, instant, intense, burned in his eyes. Hate and fear. Then it was gone. The smile returned and the old man released his grip on Con.

He raised one finger high in the air "Impatience is not a virtue, little farmer. The Masters teach that." The old man sighed and dropped his hand to his lap. "But it certainly is a trait of youth." He waved Con back. "So you must be about your business, heh?"

Con just stared at the old man.

"So, what is your business? Is it not to find the Dragon and set his captive free?"

Con's gut tightened again. He frowned and cocked his head at the old man. "How do you know this?"

"The Masters! You silly little farmer, I keep telling you." The old man cackled then choked. He bent over as a coughing spasm gripped him. His breath rasped in his throat and each attempt to breath brought on another cough. Con finally kneeled down and pounded the old man on the back which seemed help. The man quit coughing, swallowed and sighed. He looked into Con's eyes. "It'll kill me one of these days."

Con raised his eyebrows. The old man nodded toward the pot. "That stuff."

"Then why do you continue to suck it in?"

The old man's eyebrows shot up. "It's worth it, that's why."

Con shook his head, disgusted. His interest, though, was not in this man's foibles but his knowledge. "What do you know of my quest, old man?"

"I know everything. At least, I know what the Masters have told me." He bobbed his head again and pointed at a pillow next to the smoking pot. "Sit down, little farmer. I will talk to you."

Con flopped down on the pillow, finding it uncomfortable but better than squatting on the balls of his feet. And at this level, the smoke was not so thick. In fact, the smell was attractive. His head was beginning to buzz a little bit—but not unpleasantly. It was peaceful—more peaceful than anything he had known since that day at Market.

"The Masters wish only to give." The old man sucked on the hose again. The smoke drifted from between his clenched teeth, which Con noticed were brown and decayed. "They are the benefactors of mankind, wishing only to raise the miserable to a place of peace and joy. They wish to do away with war and conflict. Army! Rebellion! Posh! The Masters want us to love. Everything else is foolishness."

Con waved the back of his hand to clear the smoke from his face. It seemed to be getting thicker again. "That's good, old man. I'm glad to hear this. But I don't need peace and joy. I need power. I need to free my father."

That last slipped out. He had not meant to give this old man any knowledge.

The old head bobbed up and down again. "A noble ambition, little farmer. Noble indeed. A son should honor his father. Noble, I say."

His hand pulled the hose back to his mouth and held it there for a long time. Con wanted to be impatient. He knew he should be impatient. He had to be getting impatient. He just couldn't work it up. Things that a few minutes before had seemed very important were starting to lose their edge. So, he just sat there watching the old man suck on the hose, watching his attention drift further and further away.

They sat quietly for a minute. Then the old man looked at him with glassy eyes. In a second, recognition came back to them. "Yes! Yes. By the way, the Masters call me Fourberie. So you shall also."

Con nodded. It was becoming more and more difficult to react. It was like that time just before sleep when the mind wants to do something but can not get the body to respond—and can't really work up a good interest in it.

"Fourberie. Yes," Con nodded, "Fourberie. And my name is…"

Fourberie held up his skinny hand. "NO! Don't speak that name again. The Masters will give you a new name. Until then, I will call you little farmer."

Con wanted to argue but he had no will for it. If Fourberie wanted to call him something, that was probably all right. He nodded, losing even his desire to speak. Whatever Fourberie wanted was probably all right.

Con was just tired—sleepy. He needed to get out of that shop and find someplace to take a nap.

Con staggered to his feet. Dizziness engulfed him and he tottered to the beaded curtain. When he tried to step through the beads, he got tangled in them and fell back onto the floor. There was a cackling laugh behind him as he strove to get back to his feet.

"Going somewhere, little farmer?" The cackle began again—only now there seemed to be more than one voice. There were many voices cackling at him—all around him. In the air. In the floor. In the ceiling. From the beads. Yes, the beads cackled at him—and laughed as he tried to swipe at them with is foot.

Con rolled onto his belly and tried to rise again but his head swam. He got to hands and knees, braced himself and tried to lift his head to look out the door.

There was a gasp behind him and the sound of the old man struggling to rise.

The beads swayed back and forth revealing, then hiding, then revealing again the street. Across the cobblestones, a man stood. He was tall and covered completely in a white, hooded robe. The hood was pulled over his face so that its shadow hid his face. His arms, covered by the folds of the robe, were crossed in front of his chest. He seemed to stare directly at Con.

Recognition played at the edges of Con's fog-filled mind. He had seen this man somewhere.

"No!" Fourberie screamed. There was a crash behind Con, then the outer wooden door slammed shut, banging loudly against the jam. Fourberie stood next to it. Con rolled into a sitting position and looked up at his host.

There was sweat on the old man's upper lip and his hands shook. Twice he glanced at the door, watching the knob with a fearful stare. When nothing happened, the old man forced a smile. "There, there, farmer. You appear to be tired."

He started back toward his pillow but gasped again. Con rolled onto his hips. Fourberie ran toward the smoke pot that lay on its side. Hot coals lay on the wooden floor in front if it, burning into the planks. Fourberie danced around it, trying to scoop the coals into the pot with his bare hands, swatting at the charcoal then yelling and sticking his fingertips in his mouth.

Con pointed at the hearth behind him. "The scoop, you silly old man." Then he laughed. "Silly old man," he said again and laughed loudly. He wrapped his arms around his stomach and roared. "Silly old man. Yes. Oh, that's funny." He roared again, tears coming to his eyes. "Oh, that's funny!"

Fourberie finished scooping the last of the coals back into the smoke pot. Then he stared at his guest. A smile played at the corners of his mouth as Con rolled on the floor, laughing hysterically. It was not a humorous smile.

"Yes. That is it," he said, as Con's paroxysm subsided. "The Masters have given you a name. In this house and in the realm to which we are going you will be called Benet."

Con shrugged. His head still swam and thoughts did not travel easily inside his skull. The smoke strung sticky webs across his mind, diverting his thoughts, trapping them in flight, and binding them in its will. Benet seemed a silly name but he could not muster the will to argue about it. So, Benet it would be.

What difference does it make, he argued with himself, *what this old man calls me? As long as he really has the power.*

"Benet," Fourberie said in a wheedling tone, "do you have any Golds?"

He reached suddenly for his pouch, which still hung on his rope belt. "A few," he answered warily.

"Then I will make this deal with you. To complete your quest, you must learn of the Dragon and his ways, where to find him, and how to make your way around his lair. Is this not true."

Con nodded. That made sense.

The old man nodded and stared at Con's eyes.

"I have that knowledge. And I have the power of the Masters. All of that, I will teach you.

"For your part, you will stay here. You will pay our expenses and you will buy the dream leaf." The old man nodded at the smoke pot.

"A fair deal," the old man said firmly staring directly into Con's eyes.

The words echoed through the webs of his brain. These avoided the sticky threads and went directly to his understanding. It made sense to him. Perfect sense. It was what he wanted. Con nodded at the old one. "A fair deal."

The old man's sly smile was hidden by his turned head. He rose, threw something onto the coals of the smoke pot, then walked to a drape covered archway in the back wall. "You sit, Benet. I will fix you a meal." He parted the drapes and walked through.

Thick, white smoke drifted out of the pot, filling the room. Con didn't notice. He stared straight ahead, his mind filled with visions of Dragon Raiders and battle. Then he fell over onto his side—asleep.

Chapter 7

Con awoke in a darkened room. The sweet smell of the smoke had faded, replaced by a bitterness in his nose and a bilious taste in the back of his mouth. The wooden door was shut and barred. There was a twilight-like glow in the room from the dim, yellowish light shining from beneath a curtain in the rear of the room. The smoke pot sat next to him. He reached out and cupped his hand around the bowl. It was warm—but just so.

He rose to his feet, swaying a little. His hips were stiff and his side was sore where he had lain on the hard wood floor. His back and arm muscles were stiff, as if he had been working for ten hours instead of sleeping. He limped his way to the curtain, stretching with each step to loosen sore muscles.

He pushed the curtain aside and stepped into a small kitchen. The brightness from the lantern there hurt his eyes and he shut them quickly. He rubbed them with edges of his forefingers, then tried again, barely cracking his eyelids. The smell of soup or porridge, rich and grainy, and wood smoke filled his nose. His stomach grumbled, reminding him of how long it had been since he had filled it.

The kitchen was a small room. Barely five feet by six feet, it contained only one table made up of two planks laid on two old barrels. Two squat, heavy, three-legged wooden stools, barely eighteen inches tall, were pushed under the planks. At the rear of the room was a small basin set on top of another wooded barrel. A pump head reared up on the left, coming out of a hole cut in the floor. A small cook stove was in the right hand corner next to the basin. There was no chimney. The smoke rose from an opening in the rear of the stove and went out a hole in the ceiling. There was a narrow shelf about waist high along the left side. On it were stacked a few dishes and bowls. Two cups with broken handles were stored next to them.

Fourberie stood at the cook stove stirring something in a metal pot. He looked around as Con entered the room. "So, you have awoken. Good. I have a meal for us. While you were asleep I took the liberty of extracting a few coins from your pouch."

Con's right hand grabbed at the pouch on his belt. It still jingled.

Seeing the sudden movement, Fourberie clucked his tongue. "Oh, I took only what I thought I would need, Benet. In fact, your change is there on the table."

Several coppers lay on the planks. Con picked them up and tossed them in his hand, still staring at the man.

"Count them, Benet. I have not cheated you. We made a deal."

Slowly, the conversation in the smoke room came back. Con opened his pouch and looked in. It still contained the five Golds he had started with. He dropped in the coppers and pulled the string to close it.

"Your name is Fourberie?"

The old man nodded. "So, you do remember. Good. Sometimes the dream leaf steals memory."

"And you promised me pow'r? Pow'r to fight the enemy?"

Fourberie frowned. "No, Benet. I promised you knowledge. From that you might obtain power but I have nothing to do with that. I can only give you the true knowledge of the Masters."

Con nodded, remembering bits and pieces of the agreement. "You call me Benet. That's not...." Then he remembered. "Ah. That is the name you say these Masters gave me."

Fourberie laughed and turned away again. "Yes, Benet. That is your name now. Come now and eat. Are you hungry?"

Con nodded and walked to the table, realizing that he was more than just hungry. It was a hunger like he had on the farm after a morning of hard work. He pulled one of the stools, scraping it noisily on the rough planks of the wooden floor. Fourberie set two bowls of gruel on the table and pushed one toward Con.

Con stared at the bowl, then turned his head to watch the old man. Fourberie grinned then dipped his spoon into his bowl. Looking directly at Con, he shoved the gruel into his mouth and began to chew.

Con dipped into his bowl, raised the spoon to his mouth and tasted. It was gruel—without spice, flavorless. But, it was gruel. He ate.

After the meal, which left Con still hungry, Fourberie rose and pushed the curtain aside. "We must return to the smoke room."

He walked through the doorway and into the dimly lit room. Con rose and followed.

Fourberie picked up the smoke pot and walked to the front door. He opened it, stepped out, turned the pot upside down and slapped it, sending clumps of ash and unburned charcoal tumbling to the stones. A cloud of ash drifted down the street on the slight breeze.

His attention, though, was on the street. Several times, he glanced around the street, seeming to search for something. Then he stepped back into the room, pulled the door to, and barred it again.

In the room, he filled the pot with tinder, laid some charcoal on top of it, and struck his steel and flint together. With a little prompting, the flames caught the tinder and soon the charcoal.

Fourberie went to a jar on the mantle of the cold fireplace, loosened the lid, and extracted a few dried leaves. These he dropped into the smoke pot. Immediately, white smoke poured from the top and started to fill the room. That same sweet smell filled Con's nostrils.

Con wrinkled his nose. "Put that out, old man. The smoke dulls me. I have trouble thinkin'."

Fourberie nodded. "Yes. That's right. And that is what it is supposed to do."

Start Spreadin' the News, and SAVE $1.00—or more!

Introduce your friends to Checks Unlimited. Every time you do—if your friend has not ordered from Checks Unlimited before—**you'll get $1.00 off your next order.** Your friends will get our low introductory price for checks. Photocopy the form and tell everybody!

You should:

- Print your name and address clearly in the "Referring Customer" box (see other side).
- Show your friend all of our check designs in the Catalog enclosed with your checks or visit: **www.ChecksUnlimited.com.**
- Receive a Coupon good for $1.00 off your next order as soon as your friend's order is processed.

Your friend should:

- Complete and mail the entire Order Form along with all required documents, including the Referring Customer Coupon.
- Call 1-800-565-8332 with any questions or for instructions about a newly opened checking account.
- Expect regular delivery in 2–3 weeks from the time the order is placed.

CHECKS UNLIMITED™

Checks Unlimited Order Form

100% Satisfaction GUARANTEED

Referring Customer — Please print clearly.

You'll receive a $1.00 coupon for every referral who orders!

NAME _____
E-MAIL _____
ADDRESS _____ APT. ____
CITY _____
STATE _____ ZIP _____

Referral Order Form and Introductory Offer Prices

To order, send....
- Completed Order Form.
- Payment Check made out to Checks Unlimited.
- Reorder Form from your existing check supply OR Voided Check, noting any changes.
- Deposit Slip.

Mail your complete order to:

CHECKS UNLIMITED
PO Box 35560
Colorado Springs, CO
80935-3563
1-800-565-8332

www.ChecksUnlimited.com

OFFER GOOD THROUGH MARCH 15, 2004.

NAME _____
E-MAIL _____ Ex: ourcustomer@yahoo.com
DAYTIME PHONE ( ) _____

DESIGNER COLLECTION CHECKS—SPECIAL FIRST-TIME CUSTOMER PRICING!

Introductory Check Prices ✓ one and enter price below

QTY. 1 BOX	QTY. 2 BOXES	QTY. 4 BOXES
☐ ONE-PART 200 $5.50 *Regular $9.95*	☐ 400 $11.00	☐ 600 $16.50 FREE BOX!
☐ DUPLICATE 150 $6.50 *Regular $12.95*	☐ 300 $13.00	☐ 600 $19.50 FREE BOX!

SPECIAL FIRST-TIME CUSTOMER PRICING! — SPECIAL EDITION

QTY. 1 BOX	QTY. 2 BOXES	QTY. 4 BOXES
☐ ONE-PART 200 $5.50 *Regular $12.95*	☐ 400 $11.00	☐ 600 $16.50 FREE BOX!
☐ DUPLICATE 150 $6.50 *Regular $15.95*	☐ 300 $13.00	☐ 600 $19.50 FREE BOX!

PERSONAL DESK SET CHECKS — ALL QUANTITIES COME IN 1 BOX — INTRO PRICING DOES NOT APPLY

Available in Country Club, Country Scapes, Executive Gray, Pastel Celebrations of Life, Nature's Majesty, and Safety Scenic designs.

☐ ONE-PART 300 $25.00	☐ 600 $43.95	☐ 1200 $78.00
☐ DUPLICATE 300 $34.50	☐ 600 $59.95	☐ 1200 $106.95

Check Design # _____ Check Start # _____

Check price total from the box(es) you marked above $ _____

Custom Lettering — ALWAYS FREE
☐ Arcade   ☐ ARTISAN   ☐ Contempo   OR STANDARD LETTERING   ☐ Calligraphy   ☐ Script   ☐ Blintsor

FREE

Checkbook Cover sent separately $ _____ $2.50

Handling Checks: $1.75 per box Covers: $1.75 each $ _____ FREE

All checks come with one-part deposits.

SUBTOTAL $ _____

Sales tax for delivery to: AL 4%, CO 2.9%

☐ **Faster delivery** ☐ Express Delivery $6.50
Guaranteed 2-Day $9.95 No PO boxes
after printing — checks only
2-day not available on Desk Sets

TOTAL $ _____

Kc: 7960   ob: 1783

INFORMATION REQUEST FOR YOU OR YOUR FRIEND

☐ Send me a FREE Business and Computer Checks catalog. **kc: Y905**

Name _____
E-mail _____ Ex: ourcustomer@yahoo.com
Company _____
Address _____
City _____ State _____ ZIP _____

☐ Send my friend a FREE Personal Checks catalog. **kc: 6CC7**
☐ Send my friend a FREE Business and Computer Checks catalog. **kc: KNQ9**

Name _____
E-mail _____ Ex: ourcustomer@yahoo.com
Company _____
Address _____
City _____ State _____ ZIP _____

Complete and mail to:
Checks Unlimited, PO Box 35630, Colorado Springs, CO 80935-3563
Personal Checks: 1-800-565-8332   **Business Checks: 1-800-667-2439**
($1.00 coupon only applies to actual orders.)

NOW ORDER ONLINE!

It's ✓Safe ✓Easy ✓Convenient

You can also see all of our check designs or request a catalog.

Now Order Accessories Online

www.ChecksUnlimited.com

"Then put it out. I want to git this knowledge you have promised and I cain't do that with my brain so dull."

"Wrong, Benet. The knowledge I have for you can not be gotten until your 'brain', as you say, is dulled. It is your mind that must absorb this knowledge. That physical organ encased in flesh and bone only gets in the way."

Con grimaced. "I don't understand you, old man. How can my mind learn anythin' if ma brain's not workin'? It is like sayin' I should plow the field with a sleepin' horse."

Fourberie cackled. He looked into the smoke pot, examined the smoldering fire there, and dropped in a few more leaves. He watched them for a minute then waved Con to him. "There, see the way they curl up and begin to smoke but do not really burn?"

Con nodded, his head stuck over the pot. He breathed in the white smoke, coughing as he did. Quickly, he leaned back, feeling the buzz starting in his brain again.

"That's how you want the smoke pot. That way you do not burn much dream leaf and get a good effect." Fourberie dropped a loose fitting lid on the pot. "Remember that!"

He picked up the hose and sucked the smoke deep into his chest. With a wheeze, he let the smoke explode out of his mouth toward Con.

"Now. To why we need the dream leaf: you cannot understand, Benet. If you want that power you keep talking about, you have to give up on these silly ideas of what you think is reality. There is another realm. A bigger, grander realm than your brain can ever know. It is the realm of the Masters"

"You means someplace outside the Valley?"

Fourberie shook his head. "No, you silly, little Benet. I am not talking about what you can see. I am talking about....Look, this conversation is ridiculous. You must smoke the dream smoke. Then you will understand."

Con's brain was beginning to slow down. Everything was becoming dreamy. The smoke drifting from the pot wavered and danced on the drafts of the old house. The yellow light from the kitchen turned into golden dust dancing with the smoke, turning and twisting. It was fascinating. A most interesting thing. He stared at it intently, mesmerized by its intricate colors and patterns.

Something shook him. Fourberie's face appeared before him. There was a voice from far away, echoing in his ears. "Here, little Benet. Take this."

The hose appeared before him. Con grabbed at it, missing first because it would not stay still, then grasping it in his fist, as if it was a snake, wriggling and curling around his arm. The echoing voice spoke again, "Suck in the dream smoke, Benet. Then we will travel."

Con stuck the end of the hose in his mouth and breathed deeply. The smoke bit into his throat and he coughed it out, almost retching. He coughed several times, then sat up again. The hose appeared again. Con shook his head and batted at the it with his hand. It moved away but returned immediately. Half-heartedly, he batted at it again. It stayed right in front of him, filling the air around him with white, aromatic smoke. Within a few minutes, he stopped batting at it and once again sucked on the end of the hose.

This time the dream smoke was not so bad. It still bit at his throat but he no longer wanted to cough it out. He took three more breaths, then laid the hose down. His head was light. He seemed to be drifting around the room. Or the room was drifting around him, perhaps. He couldn't decide. Didn't care, either. Fourberie's face drifted in front of him, but there was something wrong with it—it moved around, back and forth. And it was blurry.

Con pointed at him. "You better not suck any more dream smoke, Fourberie. Your face is getting all blurry."

With that, Con fell over on his side again, woozy and slightly nauseated. The room began a slow turn around him and became dimmer and dimmer.

Con stood on the middle of the street. The sun was high and bright but did not seem to warm him. Not that he was cold. He felt—comfortable. But the bright sun should have been burning his head. It was not. Nor was there any warmth from it on his face or hands.

People strolled down the street, talking, stopping to look in the shop booths. None looked Con's way. Though Con could hear them, their conversations were just a jumble of words. Nothing made a lot of sense.

The sound of cartwheels on the cobblestones near him startled him. He glanced over his shoulder at a donkey cart only a few steps away, coming directly at him. Con yelled, "Hey! Watch it," and sidestepped quickly. A man walked beside the cart with a stick in his hand, tapping the donkey on the hips, keeping it moving. He ignored Con completely—as if he did not see him.

Con stepped toward the man to speak to him. Only he didn't step. He moved but there was no feeling of his foot on the pavement. No thrust of his leg. He wanted to move and he moved—but he didn't step. Con looked down to see what kind of pavement caused such a sensation.

There was a pavement—normal cobblestones. In fact, he looked directly at the edge of one of the sewer ditches. Only, there were no feet there.

Nor were there any legs.

Con raised his hands before his face.

There were no hands or arms.

He had no body—no nothing. He stood there—but he wasn't there!

He shook his head and clamped his eyes shut. The scene didn't change. Eyes open. Eyes closed. He still saw the street and the people.

His stomach churned.

Dead!

The thought staggered him. He was dead. He had to be.

He screamed—only there was no scream, no sound at all.

That startled him more than anything else: that terrifying, soundless scream that existed only in his panicked mind; that emotion in his intellect that could not express itself.

He screamed again.

"Benet!"

Something gripped his shoulder. Darkness rushed from the edges of his vision to cover the whole scene. The smell of dream smoke filled his nose again. He grasped at his shoulder, gripping the thin, frail hand he found there so tightly that Fourberie squealed. Con's eyes flew open.

He stared wide-eyed. The old man cocked an eye at him, nursing his hand to his chest. "You left?"

Con stuttered for a moment. "I somethin'ed. Fourberie, I...." Con shook his head to clear it, only partially succeeding. "I was on the street. People were all around me. But I wasn't there. I looked." Con yelled at the old man, "I wasn't there!"

Fourberie nodded. "My, such a good student. You are quick, Benet. You seem to have a talent. The Masters are pleased. They do not let many travel so soon."

Con stared at the old man. For a moment there was a gleam in his eye and the smile seemed to convey something other than pleasure. Then he turned and walked to a table in the corner. He picked up book and returned to his pillow, plopping down with a grunt and a sigh.

"It is time to start your studies, little Benet. You have much to learn." With that he opened the book.

It was an old book. The patterns on the fabric cover were worn and faded but Con could see that they were squares and triangles and five pointed stars. The pages were yellowed with age. Fourberie carefully turned each one. "Be careful with this, boy. The wisdom of the Masters is here. You may read it. In fact, you must read it. But do not abuse it. It is irreplaceable."

Fourberie placed the book in Con's lap. Con stared at it for a moment then looked up. "Where...?"

"At the beginning, boy!" Fourberie snapped, then smiled and patted Con's knee. "At the beginning, Benet.

Con turned to the first page and began to read. A moment later, he looked back at the old man. "This makes no sense to me."

Fourberie held out the hose to the smoke pot. "Suck on this. In a few minutes, try again. Then you will begin to understand."

Con did as he was told, then returned to the book. He read the opening paragraph again. This time, the paragraph made sense. At least, it seemed that way. Con read the second paragraph—and the third, pulling on the hose now and again when things again seemed to be confusing.

He was unsure when he fell asleep again.

He awoke with that same ravaging hunger. The kitchen curtain was pulled back. Fourberie stood at the stove, pouring meal into the metal pot. Con stood and walked into the kitchen.

The sessions in the smoke room grew longer. Meals were skipped. Con's body became thinner. His muscles sagged. His once strong back became stooped and his stomach began to pooch out. When Con mentioned it, intent on getting out of the shop and getting some exercise, Fourberie shook his head.

"What is useless wastes away. What is important grows. Continue your studies. Strengthen your mind, Benet. Let the flesh go the way of flesh. It is unimportant."

Con wanted to argue but the draw of the dream smoke became stronger every day. The thrill when he left the confines of his physical body was greater each time. The time he stayed out of his body grew longer; the distances traveled greater and greater. His return to the confines of the physical were starting to become times of disappointment. He wanted to stay in the other realm.

As Fourberie had said, he was gaining knowledge. With that knowledge, though, he knew power was coming. Soon, as his mind grew stronger and the wisdom of the Masters pervaded his being, he would have the power he needed. Soon, he would travel to the Citadel, find his father, and free him. Soon.

Con had been in Fourberie's house for three weeks. True to the bargain, Fourberie had taken from the pouch only what was needed for the dream leaf and for food. Still, the contents of the leather purse dwindled. Con checked it periodically but for the most part he left it sitting on the rough plank table in the kitchen for Fourberie to use as he saw fit.

On the morning of the first day of the fourth week, Con walked into the kitchen to find Fourberie leaning over the table. On the table sat the pouch, crumpled. Several silvers and coppers sat on the tabletop. Fourberie stirred them with his finger.

"No Golds," he mumbled, his face showing disappointment. Quickly, he scooped the coins off the table and dropped it back into the pouch. He flicked it at Con. Con caught it and stared at it, unsure of what the problem was.

Fourberie waved at the pouch. "Put it away, Benet. You won't need it where we are going."

"Where is that?"

Fourberie smiled. "Where you have wanted to go all along. To the Citadel."

Con smiled also. "Yes. I thought I was ready. Now, I will have my revenge."

Fourberie cackled. "Really, little Benet? Have you learned nothing from the Masters."

Con frowned. "I have learned much," he declared, his pride puffing out his weakened chest.

"Then what did the Masters say about Reality?"

Con thought for a moment, then quoted, "Reality is a mist that gives up its secrets in bits and pieces. Knowledge is always woven with threads of truth and threads of prejudice: threads of truth supplied by the Masters; threads of prejudice supplied by our own minds."

"And what lesson did you learn from this?"

"One must never presuppose reality. Our perception of reality depends too much on our prejudices. The only way one may know reality is to have the Masters reveal it."

Fourberie laughed again. "Then don't presuppose what you will find. Wait for the Masters to reveal it to you."

Fourberie spun on his heel and entered the smoke room. Con, confused by Foiurberie's lesson, followed him.

Chapter 8

With only a few puffs of dream smoke, Con was able to set his mind free. He and Fourberie drifted out of the shop and rose high above the City. The wood, stones, and humanity drifted below, going about the business of the City, unaware of the observation from above.

Higher, he thought. With that, the City receded further until he could see from wall to wall.

Con did not look for Fourberie. He could not be seen. Nor was Con visible to Fourberie. He knew Fourberie was there because he could feel his tugging. Perhaps feel was the wrong concept. He simply knew that Fourberie wanted to go in a certain direction because he felt his will. He assumed Fourberie knew his desires the same way. Here, in the realm of the dream smoke, there was no other conversation—no other communication.

There was a tug toward the south and the City began to slip away under him. There was no sense of movement—no wind blowing in his "face", no vibration or inertia. Indeed, it often seemed that he was staying in one place and everything else was moving around him. The ground rushing past attested to their great speed, greater than the swiftest horse could muster for the shortest of races, greater than the kestrels as they dove at their prey.

Elation danced in Con's mind. A sense of power—unlimited power—filled him. If he wanted to move—he willed it and it happened. If he wanted to travel through walls and rocks and buildings—it was no difficulty. His will was supreme. His will controlled everything.

The land known to Con soon fell behind. Below, the canopy of a virgin forest spread out before him into the misty distance. Dull red, burnt umber, orange and green mingled and blended into a crazy quilt spread over the whole land.

Lower, Con thought. He started to drop down but the force that was Fourberie resisted, holding Con at the same level.

Lower! Con demanded but the altitude stayed the same. The Fourberie force kept pulling him along.

Never had that happened before. His movements had always responded to his will. The Fourberie force had never been able to hold him.

Or never tried to.

The thought shocked Con, and he rejected it quickly. For three weeks he had been with the old man. They had traveled throughout the whole city together. Never once had Con gotten an inkling that he was not in control of his own "being."

There had to be a reason. A good reason, he was sure. He quit trying to descend and followed Fourberie.

The edge of the forest came. South of it was a glade—miles and miles of grass, green in the early summer sun but showing signs of turning brown. Then it too passed and the forest reclaimed the land.

Hours passed. There were no men in the land below. No furrow disturbed the grasslands. No ax had cleared the forest. No beasts of burden walked beneath a pack, nor did a cow graze on the richness of the fields. It was deserted of men and man's ways.

They still traveled below the level of the barriers. During one of his first travels, Con had tried to rise above the Barriers to see what was on the other side. He could not. There was a ceiling. Invisible and untouchable, it limited his mind, even his vision, to the Valley. This day, even though they were very high, they were well below the tops of the mountains.

So the Citadel was inside the Valley.

Not that the solidity of the mountains would matter if there was not the barrier there. Solid material was no obstruction. Con had played that game early in his lessons. He could travel through walls. He could enter buildings at any point and travel from room to room to room without doors or windows.

The mind, though, was still the mind. Without Con directly willing himself to go through a wall, he found his mind looking for a door or a window, or trying to rise above the structure. Some things the mind simply did not accept.

There was a tug, a strong pull downward. With the speed of a diving eagle, they plunged toward the ground. Con's chest tightened. It was the high point of all of his travels, this sudden decent toward the solid Earth. No matter how much his rationality told his mind that there was no danger, his mind reacted with near panic, producing a rush that was unlike anything he had known, even the rush produced by that first lung-full of dream smoke. He wanted to scream out his joy—but there was no voice with which to do it.

Just above the ground level they stopped. Two men stood in the midst of a field of wheat. The older one was talking to the younger one as he fingered the head of one of the stalks. They were well dressed for farmers and they seemed well fed. The farm was neat and obviously prosperous. Con's eye could see that the yield from that field was going to be of record proportions if the weather held.

The Fourberie force tugged at him again—up this time. He rose rapidly and hovered above the scene, watching the two men turn onto a dirt lane and stroll back toward the farmhouse. It was a large one, painted bright white, with a large, neat, red barn to its rear. Specks of chickens and ducks dotted the farmyard. Four cows were penned in a pasture behind the barn.

This, Con thought, *is exactly what a farm should be.*

The Fourberie force tugged again and they started to move south. Shortly, they passed over a village of round, thatched huts. Fourberie tugged down again.

There was a festival going on in the village. People filled the little square, dressed in bright colors. They laughed and chatted with each other. Produce filled the booths and the butcher shop was filled with red meat. Everyone seemed happy and satisfied.

Con tried to drift lower but the Fourberie force pulled him back up. Soon, he was traveling again at high speed. They seemed to aim directly at where the East and West Barriers joined, forming the lower end of the Valley. A gray-white wall circled out from the mountains. As they got closer, he saw that there was a complete city behind the wall, rising up the slope of the mountains.

The Fourberie force tugged harder and sped toward the wall. At a tremendous speed, they approached the top of the wall, then stopped abruptly. The wall was thick—perhaps twenty feet. The top of the wall was flat—like the surface of road. Parapets were staggered down its length on both the inside and the outside. In each, stood a black uniformed archer along with a small drum of arrows wrapped in rags. Next to the drum was a barrel filled with something dark and oily. A lamp sat on a stand on the opposite side of the archer.

A defense, thought Con. *But who would attack this place?*

"The Army."

The words seemed to come audibly, but the sound was only in his mind. Con looked around. None of the archers looked up or paid any attention to them.

"It is I, Fourberie. Here, in the city of the Citadel, our minds are more in tune. We may talk to one another directly."

"You don't sound like Fourberie. You sound like a young man."

There was a cackling laugh—certainly Fourberie's.

"Yes, Benet. I tried to tell you about the physical and how much of a lie it is. There, in the City, I am trapped in an old body. Here—Here, I am young forever."

"Where is here?'

"Why, the Dragon's realm."

The Dragon! This was where the captives were kept. This is where the Dragon oppressed his slaves.

Con looked around again. The cobblestone streets were swept clean. No sewage ran in them. No trash contaminated them. The buildings appeared new, and sparkled in the brilliance of a bright sun. The whole square upon which he gazed appeared warm and homey.

Homey. Con thought that a strange word to describe the scene. He could see no homes but that was the feeling the whole scene inspired in him. It was homey. This was a home-place.

Fourberie's voice came again. "Yes, Benet. Your enemy. The oppressor of men. Right?"

Fourberie tugged at him again and they drifted over the city. Below them, people walked, shopped, did business. They entered and exited the clean bright buildings. They smiled at each other and called out friendly greetings. It was a copy of the scene in the village.

Four children suddenly ran from the building directly below him. They squealed in delight as a being in a black robe chased them, threatening to tickle them. The being, what appeared to be a Dragon Raider, smiled and laughed as he ran bent over. Finally, he caught the littlest one and lifted him high over his head. Then he pulled him close to his chest and tickled the child until he squealed out his surrender. The child threw his hands about the beast's neck and hugged him.

"I told you not to presuppose reality until the Masters had shown it to you."

Con hovered there, confused. This was not what he had expected. This was not what he had come to fight.

"If this is the Citadel, why does the Dragon raid the City to capture people to bring here? Why doesn't he let them come on their own?"

Fourberie's voice cackled again. "Yes, Benet. You are getting right to the heart of the issue. Perhaps, Benet, there is some opposition, some force, some organization in the Valley that does not allow people to come on their own."

It was clear what Fourberie was leading to. There was only one organization that opposed the Dragon and tried to keep people from going to him: the Army.

Con nodded. At least, if he had had a head, he would have nodded. Perhaps the Dragon was not the villain. Perhaps it was the Army—always had been the Army, or the Commander—who was the real oppressor of the people.

Con looked again at the smiling, well fed faces around him. There was no poverty here. There seemed to be no want here. People seemed truly happy.

"And they do not have to cow-tow to anyone, Benet. Here, they are truly free."

Freedom. True freedom. Con's virtual chest swelled. Yes, true freedom from rules and regulations and commitments to Commanders and to parents and to the land. Yes. That was what he saw here. Freedom.

That was it. That was what he had been looking for, dreaming about. It was so simple, yet so hard to grasp. He had wanted freedom. The City, with its rules of Market only meant to oppress the farmer; the Army with their insistence on discipline and blind obedience; even his father with his constant work and the rules of farming—plant at the full moon, harvest by the quarter moon, don't plant grain next to the tobacco. That was captivity. That was what had ground Con's spirit down. That was why he had to escape to his rock and gaze out over the valley.

Freedom!

And here, in the Citadel, he could find it.

Con shook his virtual head. That was not what he had come to the Citadel for. He was here to get his father and take him home.

"NO!" a portion of his mind screamed at him. "No. You can have what you have been searching for."

He shook his head again, his resolve starting to waver. As he did, he caught a glimpse of a familiar figure. Almost directly below him, a man walked along with a Raider at his side. Con dropped quickly to the pavement.

"Father!"

Incor continued to walk away. He was in a deep conversation with the Raider but it seemed pleasant enough. In fact, he laughed and slapped the Raider on his back.

"He can't hear you," Fourberie said. "But you see how well he is. You see how pleasant his surroundings are. Does he look as if he needs rescuing, Benet?"

Con wanted to shake his head. He was confused. He had spent two months planning what he would do when he found his father. Now, all those plans were a waste. Nothing was as he expected it to be. Nothing fit the pattern that he had developed in his mind. Now that he was in the Citadel, there was nothing he could do—and nothing he wanted to do.

So, it was all a lie. All that his mother and grandmothers had told him about the Dragon; all that the Army had been spouting in their speeches; all that the old women of the Valley told on dark, cold nights to keep the little ones in bed—all of it was a lie.

Something flashed into his mind: Market day, cobblestones. Then it was gone. He tried to think but the memory struggled back, detaching itself from the smoky mists. A broken table. His mother lying in the filth, crying.

The memory burst open, like a puss-filled boil, spewing the pain and sickness throughout his being again. He saw the bodies of his sisters lying in their own blood. He saw the sneer of the Raider as it tried to decapitate him. He saw the cowardice and supplication of the men and women of the City as the Raiders ran their horses through the crowd.

Gall rose within him. He screamed. Then he yelled as loud as his virtual voice would let him. "No-o-o! This is the lie. THIS is the lie."

There was a loud snap. Con fell to the pavement, landing hard on the stones. The Fourberie force was gone. Con willed to rise. Nothing happened. He still lay on the cobblestones. They he realized that he literally was on them. He could feel the slime with his hands. He could smell the damp moldy odor of them.

He looked out. The scene melted, replaced with another. The neat housing turned into hovels, damp and cold with green mold growing everywhere. The bright sky dimmed. Smoke hovered just over the tops of the buildings almost blanking the sun.

The people no longer were dressed neatly but were covered with filthy rags. Each one carried what looked like a large leather sack on their shoulders. They were stooped over with the weight of them. Dragon Raiders ran alongside of them, whipping them to move faster.

One man fell. A nearby Raider stabbed him with a sharpened wooden stick. The man screamed. Another Raider brought a whip down hard, creasing the man's back. He arched and screamed at the pain. Blood spurted from the long, red wound. The Raider raised the whip again, growling at the man.

He struggled to his knees and stopped gasping for breath and writhing as his burden swung across of the open sore. The whip came down again, this time on his buttocks. It almost knocked the man to the street again, but he lurched to feet then began to stagger off. The Raiders pointed and laughed, then looked around for any other slackers in the crowd.

Con turned toward where he had last seen his father. He was about half a block away. Con rose to follow but Incor was shoved into an alley by the beast along side of him. In the few seconds he was in view, Con saw that he was dressed in rags. The red welts across his bare back attested to the same treatment as the man on the street. There was a leather sack on Incor's shoulders, but smaller than the others Con had seen.

Con started toward the alley.

A screech from behind him raised the hair on his neck and he spun, involuntarily, toward the awful sound.

Fifty feet from him, a woman lay on the ground. She was young, perhaps Con's age. Though skinny, she was well formed. Under the streaks of filth, her face was unlined and might be pleasant to look at if it was not screwed up in terror or pain. Through the thin, ragged dress, Con could see she had a pleasing shape.

A beast, half wolf, half man, stood over her. Suddenly, it dropped to its knees, straddling the woman. Its man-like arms gripped her shoulders, pulling her off the ground. Its wolf-like muzzle reached toward her bare neck.

The woman wriggled under the beast but could not get free. She managed to break her arms free, though, and grabbed at the tufts of fur on the sides of the beast's neck. With stiff arms, she stopped the beast's fangs only inches from the tender skin covering the life flowing in her veins.

The beast laughed, seeming to enjoy the struggle. It whispered something to the woman, but she shook her head and screamed again. The beast laughed again.

Under the constant pressure, she began to weaken. Her elbows bent slowly, letting the beast's fangs almost touch her. Her mouth opened wide but nothing came out. The beast's tongue slurped around its lips. Its saliva fell onto her bare chest.

This was the enemy. This was power and hatred and death. With no doubt now, he knew. This was the evil in the Valley—all of the evil.

Con screamed, "Stop! You can not do this!" He began to walk toward the beast.

The wolf-man looked around at his call, a look of puzzlement on its canine face. Then it shrugged and returned its stare at the woman.

Con yelled again. "If you want to fight something, dog-man, fight me."

The wolf-head turned again in his direction. Its eyes were wide, then they narrowed. Its head turned first to one side, then to the other, cocking an ear toward Con.

It can't see me, Con thought. It can hear me, but it can't see me.

Con stopped a few feet from the beast, unsure of what to do. The woman was weakening fast. Her elbows bent with each thrust of the wolf's snout. The fangs scraped the skin, leaving little red scratches. The woman was gasping for breath, mewling with the effort and the panic.

"Let her go, dog-man!"

Con stood spread-legged only four feet from the beast. It was large—over six feet from feet to the tops of its pointed ears. Its body was perfectly human, but at the neck, short, thick hair sprouted. Above the neck, it was a wolf, or dog.

The beast's head snapped around toward Con. It looked back and forth, puzzled, then its eyes, green, evil eyes, rested on him. "Ah, there you are." The dog man laughed—only the laughter was in Con's brain, not in the air around him.

Con's gut tightened and fear flurried in his stomach.

The beast rose off the woman and waved her away. "Go away, my pretty. I will get back to you."

The woman scooted backwards on her elbows, bloodying them, then rolled over and lunged to her feet running before she had balance. She stumbled, hit hard on one knee, then lunged ahead again limping heavily.

The beast laughed, staring at the retreating figure.

Con began to retreat, realizing he was no longer separate from the realm—no longer invincible. The beast stepped toward him. "So, you've come for your father, have you? What a kind son. Did you think he would be lonely?" The words formed in his brain—or in the air, he was unsure.

The beast's pink tongue slurped around its jaws again. "Why, we may even throw you in the same hovel." The beast laughed again, throwing its head back and ending with a loud howl.

Con looked both ways, then backed quickly toward the tall wall behind him. Beasts of every description came at the wolf's howling alert: slithering things, shelled beasts with dagger-like claws, giant cats with human heads—all manner of odd shapes and sizes—all with large, growing, gaping mouths filled with yellow fangs and pointed teeth. Blackness, deep, complete, filled their throats.

Con willed himself to rise. He did not. He willed himself to go through the wall. It resisted. His will no longer moved him.

"It never did, you foolish, little Benet." The voice was that of Fourberie. "I captured you. I towed you. You are my captive—you stupid, little farmer."

A hideous laugh split the air. Or, his mind. He could no longer tell.

One of the cat-men swiped at him with its claw. Con blocked it with arm. The claws passed through his outstretched arm. There was a slight resistance but not pain. Con looked at his arm, expecting to see blood dripping. There was nothing. The claws had passed through him without damage.

He was slowly becoming part of this realm—but he was not entirely of the realm yet. He pressed hard against the wall, trying to force his way through. It did not yield.

The beasts around him closed in. Con turned from side to side, pressing so hard into the stone wall that he scraped his back as he turned. They lunged at him, knocking him from side to side, but not able to actually grab him. Each hit, though, was a little harder. Each swipe dragged him further and further toward their power. Now, he could feel their hot breath and smell the foulness of their bodies.

"Someone," he yelled. "Someone! If I am to die at their hands, let me fight them. Give me a weapon."

Fourberie laughed. "Quiet, Benet. Soon, you will be totally in our power. No one who cares for your cries can hear them in this place."

A nursery rhyme from his youth popped into his head. His mother had recited it to him as he sat on her knee. He had not heard or thought of it in years. He did not even believe it. But it was there in his brain—with strength that could not be denied. He recited it to himself.

"Remember this, my little dear
When you cry out from where you ran
Who can, once more, bring you here?
Cry to the Commander. Only he can."

"The Commander can," Con yelled.

Screeches of pain poured from the beings around him. Their faces showed panic and they backed away. The Fourberie voice started to scream but it was cut off by an "Oof!" as if he had been punched in the stomach.

There was an explosion behind Con. He was knocked forward, towards the gaping jaws. Bright light flooded around him, casting his shadow on their figures. The faces in the light began to distort, to run, as if they were melting. Con spun on his heel to face the new threat.

The light was so bright that he had to throw up his arm to shield his eyes. A fresh wind blasted his face, driving out the smoke and the smell of the musty rocks. Con sucked it in, filled his lungs with the luscious smell of freshness. Again, he breathed deep, driving out the smoke. His brain came alive. His senses awakened. The vigor returned to his arms and legs. He spun back toward the beasts.

They were gone. The mold-covered rocks of the hovels, the slimy cobblestone street, the smoke, the smell of mildew were all gone. In their place was little room with a tapestry hung from the ceiling, peeling plaster walls, and a rough plank floor. There was a bald, skinny little man dressed in a loincloth lying across a pillow, with a reed-like arm flung across his eyes. He whimpered.

Con turned. The beads of the curtain were scattered at his feet. The wooden bar on the door was split in two. The doorframe was broken at the latch. The door hung askew on one hinge.

Sun burst through the door warming Con's face and scouring the room of the darkness that had once owned it.

Without hesitating, Con burst through the door and onto the street. Joy filled him. He sucked in the fresh air. The City smelled delicious, like a newly mown pasture, like a spring morning. He turned and ran down the street, away from the shop of horror, away from that gate to the Citadel. He ran harder. Not because he was afraid, but because he was not afraid.

He ran for two blocks, then stopped, staggered to the wall of a building and leaned one hand against it. He bent over gasping for breath. Pain filled his lungs as he ripped the air in and out of them. It was good pain, though.

He was alive!

He had entered the Dragon's Citadel and he had lived through it. True, he had not defeated them but they had not defeated him either. He could do it! He could free his father.

His breath slowed and his brain calmed. Reality tempered the joy he had felt at his escape. He could free his father if he could find him again. And, if he could find the right weapon. And, if he could find the right resources.

As his breath returned to normal, Con stared around. The street was almost empty. A few shopkeepers sat in the doorway of their shops, staring at him but otherwise there were no people about—except directly across the street from Con.

There a figure in a white hooded robe stood. Con could not see his face because it was deep within the hood. It was a tall person—and one with broad shoulders and chest. Con felt like he should know this man but his mind would not place him. The figure seemed to stare at Con, although Con couldn't actually see his eyes. It just felt like the figure was staring at him.

Then the hood nodded. The man turned and moved down the street. He turned into an alley and was gone.

Con remembered.

Chapter 9

Con ran across the street and into the alley. As he entered the darkness, his left calf cramped up. He stopped and grabbed the lumpy muscle with his left hand.

The hooded figure, though, was gone. The alley was a full block long, running out to another main street. No one could have traversed the distance that quickly.

The cramp let up. Con limped along the alley, stretching the muscle as he walked, looking for openings into which the man could have ducked.

The walls of the alley were solid. There was one door on each side but garbage was stacked all around them. It did not appear that anyone had entered them for a while. Con stopped and stared back at the street from which he had come then forward to the next street. If the hooded figure had not entered one of those doors then he was extremely swift—perhaps as swift as Con had been as he scooted down the Valley with Fourberie.

He continued to the next street—a market street. People wandered around in seemingly random patterns from booth to booth. Con searched the crowd for a white robed figure but there was none—there was not even anyone of his size.

Disappointed, he looked up and down the street. He had no idea where he was. The walls of the city were not in sight. The street he was on was not wide enough to be the main thoroughfare and he had no idea how to find that road.

He moved to the building front next to him and leaned against it.

"I've got to plan," he mumbled. A woman passing him glanced his, then quickly looked away. Con lifted his hand to his face to scratch, and realized he had a scruffy beard—three weeks old. He could not remember the last time he had bathed and his hair had to look as bad as the crumpled tunic he wore.

The words of the guard at the Upward Gate came back to him. He could not wander around the city looking like that or the cops (whoever they were) would haul him in (in to what he was not sure.)

Con pushed off the building and began to walk toward the afternoon sun. He needed to find a public bath and a place to get some clean clothing. He also needed to think.

He passed several booths with pots and pans and cooking utensils, then came upon an ironmonger's tent. Under the blue roof of the tent, a wooden table was laid out with knives, swords, plow points, eating utensils, iron pots, chains—all manner of iron and steel.

In the center of the table, a short sword was propped up, handle raised, point stuck in the wood. Con stared at it. He needed a weapon. His adventure in the Citadel had proven that. The Dragon was capable of massive deception, but he also had massive power. To face him again without a weapon would be foolish.

The sword was about two inches wide. Its double-edges glinted in the sunlight. No more than thirty inches long, it appeared strong and deadly. Wooden grips filled the area behind the hand guard. He grabbed the weapon and lifted it, feeling its balance. The ironmonger stepped out of the shade of his booth and stood at the table.

He was a short, broad man. His arms and chest were thick, and stained with the soot of the forge. He had a wide face with a prominent, beak-like nose. A scar ran across the bridge of the nose and down across his left cheek.

Reality started to temper Con's enthusiasm, like the temper on the broad heavy blade. He had little money for such a weapon and he was a farm boy, unschooled in warfare. He shook his head and started to put the weapon back on its support.

"It's a good weapon, farmer. One that has the skill built in."

"What do you mean—skill?"

"Ah, yer not a swordsman. That is not a problem. Look at the handle."

Con opened his fingers.

"See the grooves? Now place your fingers so they grip the weapon in those grooves."

Con did so and the edges of the blade aligned with the bones in his forearm.

"You see, that is the most important part of sword fightin'—gettin' the grip correct. Any swordsman will tell you that."

Con looked up at him again and the man nodded. "Once you have that grip c'rect, the rest of sword fightin' is instinct. Anyone can do it."

"Anyone?" Con scoffed.

The ironmonger held out is hand, palm up. Con handed him the sword. The ironmonger jiggled it a few times, changing his grip, then clasped his fingers around it. As he tightened his grip, the muscles and tendons of his forearm bulged.

The man looked around in the booth, his gaze coming to rest on a one-inch thick wooden plank. He set one end of the plank on the table and the other on the back of a chair, moving the chair so that there were only a few inches of span. He stared at it a few seconds with the sword held straight out in front of him. Slowly, he raised his hands till they were directly over his head, then with a grunt and he slammed the edge into the board. The sword rang with the impact but the board split into two pieces. These tumbled into the air and landed with a clatter on the stone pavement.

The ironmonger picked up one of them and set it back on the supports. "Come 'round here, farmer. I'll show you that with this sword, anyone can be a soldier."

Con walked around the table and took the offered sword. The ironmonger set him before the suspended board.

"Get yer distance there, farmer."

Con put the sword out at arms length and set it over the board.

"Good. Now, spread yer feet. No. No." The ironmonger grabbed Con's ankles and placed his feet where he wanted them. "I said spread yer feet, farmer, not manure."

A few city people had gathered outside the booth, watching the display. A chuckle arose from the group. Con's face reddened but the ironmonger patted him on the back. He whispered. "Don't you worry none, farmer. Yer gonna shut 'em up here in a few seconds."

Stepping back, the iron monger said, "Now, you move that hilt around in your right hand 'til them grooves line up with those big fingers a' yer'n. With them muscles in yer arms you won't have no trouble grippin' that sword."

Some one in the crowd yelled, "Just like a plow, farmer."

Another jibed, "Grip it like your gettin' hold of one of them cow teets, boy."

The crowd laughed again, getting worked up now at the spectacle, expecting this farm boy to make a fool of himself, all for their pleasure and entertainment.

The ironmonger winked at him and nodded. "Now, wrap your other hand around that one and lift that sword like I did. You hold it 'til I say now. Then you bring that edge down on that board with everything you got."

Con lifted the sword and held it. The crowd grew quiet. Con wanted to look to see if they were staring but he couldn't take his eyes off the board. That short span held him fascinated.

"Now!"

Con chopped with the sword, bringing it down as if it were an ax aimed at a log. With hardly a tremor in the sword, it bit into the wood. The blade rang and wood pieces rose straight up into the air, spinning. One tumbled onto the table, raising a clatter as iron utensils bounced all over the surface.

A murmur started in the crowd, then a smattering of applause. The crowd drifted away, head's nodding, lips shot out in appreciation of the show.

The ironmonger took the sword from Con's hand. He went back into his tent to a grinding wheel. The blade sang as the wheel cleaned up the edge.

Over the high pitched song of the honing steel, the iron monger called, "What do you say, farmer?" He stopped grinding and touched his tongue to the edge. Shaking his head, he put the blade to the grindstone again. It sang its squeal again, whether of joy or pain, no one could tell.

"I don't have a lot of money."

The man walked back out of the tent. Con returned to the street side of the table. The man put the sword back on its stand in the center of the table. He began straightening up the mess the wood block had made. Con stared at the gleaming edges of the sword, remembering the feel of the blade as it bit through the wooden plank.

"It won't be a sword fashioned by blacksmiths that will be your weapon."

Con looked up. The shopkeeper stared at him.

Con said, "What did you say?"

The man raised his eyebrows and shook his head, thrusting out his lips as men do when they want to indicate they know nothing of what you say.

"I heard someone speak."

The man shook his head again. "No one spoke that I heard, farmer."

Con looked behind him but no one was close. Nor to the side.

"Maybe somebody on the street said somethin' and you thought they was talkin' to you."

Con looked all around him again. Then he nodded. "Perhaps you're right."

The ironmonger leaned on the table. "You look like a lad on a quest. My thought is that you need a weapon like this." The man stood straight, folded one arm across his chest and rested the elbow of the other on it. His free hand grasped his chin and pinched it between thumb and the edge of his forefinger. "Tell you what. No bargaining. I'll give you this sword for two silvers and five coppers."

Con grabbed at his waist. His much depleted money sack hung there. He pulled it off and loosened the drawstring. There were many coppers and a few silvers—perhaps five or six. He looked back at the sword.

He needed a weapon.

"It won't be a sword fashioned by blacksmiths that will be your weapon."

Con looked at the man again. "What does that mean?"

The ironmonger's eyebrows bunched and he shook his head. "What does what mean?"

"That a blacksmith won't make my weapon."

The man raised one eyebrow. "He won't? Who will?"

Con frowned. "You didn't just say that?"

Both of the man's eyebrows rose into his forehead. "What are you talkin' about, farmer? I made that sword and all the other things on this table. Who else would have made them?"

Con frowned again. He reached into his sack and pulled out the coins. The ironmonger smiled, wrapped the sword in an oilcloth and handed it over. "You won't regret it, farmer. That sword will make a fighter out of you. The Dragon himself wouldn't attack a man with a sword like that."

Con's hand stopped in mid-grasp, surprised at the man's statement. Then he realized it was just a figure of speech and grabbed the sword. He began to unwrap it when the ironmonger spoke again. "Son, don't open that thing on the street. The way you look, the cops will be sure to haul you off. You wait 'till you get out of the City before unwrapping it."

Con looked around, still unsure what a cop was but sure that he did not want to meet one, since they always were hauling people off or in. Then he nodded at the ironmonger, thanked him and walked off.

Toward evening, Con quit walking. He was in a residential part of town. Two story buildings filled both sides of the street. The windows of each apartment were raised trying to cool the interiors before the night fell and working people had to climb onto their straw ticks and try to sleep till the morning. Pots and pans rattled out a syncopated tattoo to the dirty, tired men marching home with their empty lunch sacks folded under their arms. The smell of cabbage and grease hung in the air like a fetid fog at each ground floor windows. The men turned by ones and twos into the tenements. Screeches of joy from some apartments, of anger from others, added to the din of the street.

Con continued to walk, despair growing rapidly. A weapon he had. Help he did not. Even with a weapon as formidable as his sword, he would need much help to attack the Dragon. Was it the Army? He rejected that, finding that one revelation in the Citadel had been true. He wanted nothing of that discipline. He wanted nothing of that mind-robbing, mind-dulling obedience for which the Army Regiments were famous.

Still, according to his Gramma, the Army at one time had been a grand one. They had fought the Dragon over and over and defeated him. Of course, Gramma had never mentioned exactly what the weapons were and did not exactly know where the battles had been fought, but she read from a big history book about these mythical heroes who had fought the Dragon to a standstill all over the Valley.

Con sighed. Too bad they were just stories. He could use that kind of power against the enemy.

He walked a bit further, then growing tired, he leaned his back against one of the buildings and slowly sank onto the pavement. Little money. No clothes other than what was on his back. No food. No place to sleep. And it would be dark in another hour. Con laid the sword next to him and pulled his knees up to his chest. This was not how he had pictured this battle.

There was a loud metallic clang out of the alley next to him. Con ignored it, his legs tired from the day's walk. A human voice yelled, then another clang—like steel striking stone—reverberated out of the alley. Con leaned over and peered into the opening.

It was a dark alley leading back perhaps one hundred feet into what appeared to be an enclosed square or cul-de-sac. The square was brighter than the alley, indicating that it was large enough to still catch some of the rays of the waning sun. A running figure appeared, silhouetted against the light of the square. He rushed headlong, his arms flailing about. Con rolled back out of the way as the man sped onto the street. The running man tried to turn but skidded on the wet stones and landed hard on his side, sliding for several feet. He scrambled back to his feet, looked back into the alley, and then limped off as fast as he could.

Con climbed to his feet, alarm rising in his chest. The look on the man's had been terror—wide-eyed, blanched-skin, drooling-mouth terror.

There was another loud clang from the alley—as if a battle was occurring in that little square. Steel rang on steel. People yelled. Rough, growling yells punctuated the din regularly. Con picked up his wrapped sword and stepped into the alley.

Another man burst from the square. He screeched—his face screwed up like the last one. Con threw himself against the wall, barely escaping entanglement as the panicked man flew by.

Con's belly grew cold and his knees weakened. These had not been small men running from the alley. Certainly not warriors, they still had been men with strong arms and strong backs. Whatever was in the square had to be powerful.

He stared down the alley. His heart melted in his chest. Something more than the sound of battle was at work here. He unwrapped his sword and hefted it in his right hand. The feel of the heavy metal calmed him. He remembered how the blade had torn through the plank, remembered the small jolt he'd felt with the blade bit into the wood, remembered the surprise and satisfaction he'd felt as the pieces spun into the air. He swung the blade a few times in front of him, happy at the buzzing whistle that came from it. What was in the square might be formidable but with this sword in his hand, he was a match for anything.

He stepped forward but stopped again. His soul still resisted. The whole scene was too much like the Citadel—dark, dank, smelling of mold and mildew and imbued with a sense of doom, of capture and oppression. Con looked back at the street.

He shook his head and raised the sword. He slashed at the air a few more times clumsily then dropped the blade back to his side. "This is not the Citadel," he scolded himself. "And one can not sense doom or capture or oppression."

He forced himself on for another two steps. More of the square was visible. A man and two women ran across the opening, looking back over their shoulders. Following them, a large being flashed across the opening.

Con's breath caught in his throat and he felt his stomach churn. The being had been very large. It was dressed in a black robe and wore a helmet of some type. Its footsteps, sounding like a steel-shod horse on the stones of the pavement, echoed in the alley.

Con took a step backward, raising the sword tip. Another black-robed figure flashed by the opening. It carried a long pole with some sort of blade on the end.

There was no doubt. Raiders. They were here. They were capturing humans again.

Con turned and walked quickly toward the street. He didn't want to fight. He wanted away. He needed away. He quickened his step—his eye on the street at the end of the alley.

A high-pitched scream, full of fear and despair, stopped him. Chills ran from his spine to his neck, pulling the muscles there as tight as fiddle strings. He gasped at the air but could only manage short quick breaths—his ears demanding to hear above the sound of the air roaring through his throat. Things began to go white all around him. He spun around. In the square, a lump lay on the paving stones—a ragged lump of something.

It was the bodies of his sisters. Con stepped forward, shaking his head, his heart pounding against his ribs. No. They were buried. They were gone.

Con stepped again. The lump changed. The rags turned into a brown dress. His mother's head rose from the damp stones, her mouth open in a wail of agony but there was no sound coming from it. Con rushed toward her—not understanding how she could be there. His terror turned to anger and he pounded down the alley.

His mother's face disappeared. The lump turned into the woman of the Citadel crying out with the wolf-man slurping the blood from her bleeding neck.

It was them. It was the enemy. It was the Dragon. They were here. They and all they stood for were in that square.

Con screamed. He raised the sword over his head and ran into the stone paved quadrangle. He skidded to a halt; the sword still raised high.

A group of twelve Raiders in long black robes surrounded a group of fifteen or so humans—men and women. The Raiders were all similar. Each stood over six feet. Their arms were massive. Large, round heads sat directly on their broad shoulders with only the hint of a neck. Even their loose robes could not hide the bulge of the middles—stomachs and rears that pooched out the fabric. Each head was covered with a leathery helmet with a nose guard that extended to the end of a large, bulbous nose. The skin of their faces was covered with pimples or large warts or possibly moles.

The Raiders herded the humans with their long poles, slashing at them when they refused to move. They drove them toward a large sled sitting in one corner of the square. The vehicle—if that was what it was—was made of massive wooden beams a foot thick with two-inch thick planks as a deck. Four-inch square posts rose from the deck several feet and wooden rails, set every foot, tied them together. It was at least 40 square feet—large enough to carry all the humans in the crowd.

It had no wheels. It rested on immense wooden runners, squared off at the rear but curving up to a point in the front. There were no beasts of burden in harness. In fact, there was no harness, or tree in place.

The humans were all poorly dressed. Some of them were bleeding from the slashes of the Raider's spears. They huddled together, trying to move behind one another to get away from the Raider's half-moon shaped spearheads.

The woman screamed again. Con spun toward the sound. A Raider stood over a man who lay bleeding on the stones. The man's woman knelt next to him, her hands up by her face and her mouth open in a soundless shriek. The Raider had the edge of his spear pressed into the man's side, the metal grating on the man's ribs. The beast thrust with the pole, moving the man a few feet along the stones toward the cart. The man, who should have been dead, jerked and twitched with each thrust.

Con ran at the beast, his sword held high. With a scream, he swung the blade with everything he had in him. As the blade came around, he planted his feet only to feel the smooth sole of right sandal slip on the wet pavement. He fell hard onto the flagstones, losing his grip on the blade. It tumbled through the air toward the Raider's head.

Thud! The blade struck the Raider's helmet. There was the sound of breaking glass and the sword shattered, rattling onto the stones in a thousand pieces.

The Raider looked at Con, then snorted. He returned his attention to the man on the ground and thrust the blade into him again.

Con rose from the wet pavement. "You are a beast," he screamed. He grasped the Raider's arm and pulled him. The Raiders snorted again, then shrugged. Con flew off his feet and landed in a heap on the stones again.

He rose more slowly, unsure of what to do next. The woman screamed again as her man jiggled under the pressure of the blade.

Con charged.

The beast turned its head toward him, green eyes with red, glowing pupils, like those of the dog-man, staring with unconcealed hatred and contempt. Con skidded to a stop. The fear from the battle of the Citadel rose like gore in his throat, choking him. He gasped and back-pedaled.

The beast returned to the man on the ground.

Once the eyes turned away from him, Con's courage revived. He dove at the beast, determined to at least knock him away so the woman could drag her man to safety. Something slammed into his back, driving him into the pavement. White-hot pain exploded throughout his body and the breath rushed from him. He croaked, trying to breath but getting nothing for his efforts. The square became dark, the sounds waning until they seemed far away. He lay face down, his nose in a crack between the bricks.

When his chest began to fill again with air, he rolled onto his back. Standing over him was another Raider. This one had on a silver colored helmet and there was a silver band around one arm. He leaned over and fixed his green eyes on Con's.

"Don't get involved, Ataxia. I have no orders to capture you but that doesn't mean I won't bring you along as my own slave. Now get out of this place and don't bother Raiders again when they are about the Dragon's business."

A bugle call echoed in the square. The Raider looked quickly at the sound, then backed up barking orders to the others in a strange, guttural language. The Raiders ignored their captives and formed up in a line, spears or poleaxes thrust out defensively.

Con pushed up to his feet.

Just entering from the alley were five people. They each carried a large double edged, broad sword vertically in front of them They were dressed in armor—pretty plain stuff: a breast plate, a helmet, and a broad, leather buckler. They each carried a shield on their left arms. Thick-soled sandals gripped the wet rocks of the pavement. Their movements were precise, practiced as they spread out into a line and moved forward.

Soldiers, Con thought. Not like he had seen in the past, but obviously trained soldiers.

The soldiers lined up, much like the Raiders had done. Then they stood, staring at the enemy. Con was about to join them when a robed figure came from the Alley.

Although he could not see his face, it had to be the same man he had seen at the south gate and the one who had been outside Fourberie's shop. The figure did not speak but as soon as he entered the Raiders backed up one step. Only the growl of their commander stopped them.

The soldiers stepped forward again and spread out, hemming the Raiders into the corner with their sled. One Raider on the far right of the squad slipped sideways, toward the wall. Con saw the hooded man look that way but none of the soldiers responded. The whole squad stepped forward again.

The Raider on the flank smiled and lowered his spearhead. With only the sound of his hooves on the brick, he rushed at the soldier on that flank. Just before the spear struck, the soldier spun toward the movement. The blade of broadsword blurred in the air then leapt at the spear, striking it with a loud thunk just behind the head.

The edge bit into the wood, almost severing the shaft. The beast screamed and dropped its weapon. It shook its four fingered hands and blew on them as if they were burnt.

The soldier wiggled the sword and the spear dropped off, clattering at his feet. He faced the beast, sword out, its blade horizontal, its tip only a step away from the broad, black robed being.

The Raider hissed at him, sharpened fangs gleaming in the failing light. It raised its stubby hand and splayed all four of its fingers. Claws sprang from the fingers like curved, sparkling daggers drawn from hidden sheaths. It slashed the air in front of it and snarled.

The soldier set his feet on the paving, twisting the hobs on his sandals until they gripped the edges of the cobblestones. He lowered the sword point until it was at chest height to the Raider. Then he stood still, waiting.

The Raider snarled again, and laughed. His green eyes glowed with scorn for the smallness of his opponent. He stepped toward him, his chest thrust out.

The soldier thrust. The tip of the sword leaped out, seeming to stretch the metal as it sought the flesh of the Raider. It cut through the robe and, hissing like a hot poker in water, it pierced the beast's chest. The soldier twisted the blade. With a flick of what appeared to Con to be very small wrists, he lifted the edge of blade. The sword cut through the beast, peeling it open from breastbone to chin. The soldier withdrew the sword and assumed a ready posture again.

It was not pain that registered on the fat face, but surprise. Slowly, the beast sank to its knees, green fluid pouring from the terrible wound. Then it fell over with a loud thunk.

The soldier stepped back in line and faced the rest of the beasts again.

The Raider with the silver armband shook his head, grimacing. "Lord Cleato, these are rebels. You have no right to interfere here. They are legal for my Lord."

Con looked around to see who he addressed. No one answered but the Raider seemed to be looking at the hooded man. If so, he got no answer that Con could tell.

The Raider, though, flinched and grimaced again. "Then may I carry my wounded with me?"

Again, he seemed to address the hooded man. Again, there didn't seem to be an answer, but two Raiders left their line and grabbed at the feet of the fallen one. They reached from arms length, watching the soldier all the time, insuring they did not come within range of that sword. One on each leg, they dragged the body with them to the sled, letting its head bounce on the cobblestones.

Without their captives, the Raiders climbed on the sled. The two dropped the body of their comrade onto the deck without ceremony. All stood in the middle of sled, watching the big hooded man. His hand rose in a sign of dismissal. Without warning or noise, the sled rose fifteen feet into the air, then with a slight pop, disappeared.

The squad of soldiers sheathed their swords and headed for the captives. The soldier who had pierced the Raider, knelt beside the man Con had tried to help. Con walked over and kneeled down beside him. The soldier examined the wound with his hands then clucked his tongue.

His hands were thin with long fingers. There was no jewelry but it looked like there should have been. The nails were not clipped short but were allowed to grow out beyond the tips of the flesh—more like a woman would wear nails than a man. Con frowned.

The soldier removed the helmet, letting long, straight brown hair tumble down across the back and shoulders of the tunic.

"A woman!"

Con's exclamation turned her head. Soft brown eyes looked at him. A deep tan, as if she spent much time outdoors, colored the skin of her face and her hands. Her nose was long and thin, as was her jaw line. Her cheek bones were high and prominent and her cheeks were flat. The red rouge of natural health colored them.

"Yes. I am a woman. Who are you?"

Her voice was not deep but it was not the tinkling, high-pitched sound that so many women try to produce. Not exactly husky, it was a confident voice that did not back down from what she knew she was. And she was a soldier—a sword-wielding, armor-bearing soldier.

From the looks of her deft probing of the wound, she was also an excellent nurse.

"I am Con Ataxia. I was here fighting the Raiders before you arrived."

She had returned her attention to the wounded man but turned back to Con at that. "Are you a soldier?"

Con wanted to answer but got caught up in the brown pools that stared at him. He stammered.

She looked at him in the eye for a full five seconds, then said, "No, I can see that now." She returned to the wound.

He tapped her shoulder. "Hey, I'm no soldier, but I want to help. What can I do?"

She gazed at him with a slight frown and slightly pursed lips, then shook her head. Con's heart flipped once under her stare. "You better talk to our squad leader," she said, nodding toward one of the other solders: a tall, thin man dressed in the same brown tunic and dark trousers.

Con snorted. "It's that hooded man I want to talk to." He looked around the square but there was no hooded figure in the sight.

The man was gone. Only the soldiers and the Raiders' victims were left. The girl frowned. "Who?"

"The man in the white robe with the deep hood. I've seen him several times. During the battle, he seemed to be the one in charge."

The girl's mouth formed an "O", and then smiled. "Lord Cleato. Yes, he appears that way to some."

"I don't see him anymore."

She looked around, and smiled again. "Oh, he's still around. If we need him, he'll be here."

Con looked around the square again, then at the alley. Perhaps the big man had gone out that way, or was still there in the darkness.

The soldier at whom the girl had nodded rose from talking to one of the captives. He looked at Con, frowned, then walked toward him. He was a tall, thin man with straight black hair. Con was surprised to see streaks of gray along the sides of his head. His face was tanned, as was his rough hands—the hands of a laborer. The skin around his eyes was crinkled. The lines at the ends of his lips were etched deeply in his cheeks. A thin, salt and pepper beard covered his jaw line. He appeared to be in his thirties, perhaps slightly younger than Con's mother.

"Who are you?" he said as he approached. Before Con could answer, he grabbed his shoulder and ushered him away from the girl. "Sarah's busy. Let's not disturb her or her patient."

Ten feet away, the man stopped. Con turned to face him. "I came to the aid of these people before you arrived. I came here to fight."

The man's face was somehow familiar. The set of the jaw. The shape of the eyes. Even the way he held is lips just before he was about to speak was familiar.

The man stared at Con for several seconds. "Are you ready to join the Army?"

"No!" The vehemence even surprised Con. It was, though, the truth. He wanted nothing to do with the ineffectiveness of the Army—with their rules and drills and traditions. What he wanted was to fight the Dragon.

"I don't need to join the Army. I have already fought the Dragon. Twice. And I did not see any soldiers there in the battle. What I want is for the Army to join me."

The man looked into his eyes. Con wanted to flinch away from the stare but he forced himself to return the gaze.

The man shook his head. "Son, you didn't fight the Dragon. You were defeated before you ever got to fight him. In the Citadel, you barely escaped. Here, the Raiders destroyed your only weapon and ignored you."

Con stepped back. "How did you know...?"

The man smiled slightly, a kind, almost sad smile. A memory flashed through Con's brain—the same smile, the same sad eyes, the same set of the jaw in his mother's face, each time his rebellion hurt her. The memory relieved the fear that was rising in his gut. Con did not know how this man knew what he did but he was confident that he had not gotten it from the Dragon. There was just something so familiar about him, so comforting that Con knew he was not of that realm.

Con shook off the memory. Anger replaced the fear and he stepped forward again. "I fought," he declared. "I was here when they needed me. And I have been to the Citadel and returned. Have you done that, soldier?"

The man shook his head—whether in answer to the question or dismissal of the assertion, Con could not tell. "Son, you need to be changed. You may continue to fight the Dragon. I hope you do. But you will never defeat him—or even slow him down—until you are changed and submit to the Commander."

Con spun on his heel and started away from the group. "That is the one thing I don't need," he barked over his shoulder. He stalked toward the alley

The sound of marching feet stopped him. Con spun around. "Raiders," he yelled. "They've come back."

The soldier smiled and pointed over Con's shoulder, the smile becoming a grimace. Out of the alley marched a squad of soldiers. They were all in full dress uniforms of blue jacket and trousers striped with red bunting. Red scarves encompassed their necks, fluffed out to fill the area between the lapels of the jackets. They wore blue berets on their heads. Their feet were shod with shiny, black shoes with pointed toes. They carried a white banner with a large, red lion's head in the center of it, almost filling it. They marched in step to the cadence being called by a young officer marching at their side.

The lieutenant in charge yelled, "Halt!" The squad halted in a snappy movement and came to parade rest. The lieutenant walked out in front of them and stared at the group.

"We are of the John Wiley Lion's Head Regiment. In the name of the District Committee for the Preservation of Lion's Head Tradition and Benevolence, what is going on in this place?"

The captives groaned, and moved toward the back of the square. The militiamen continued to work on the more seriously wounded.

"Hey, I asked a question. I'll have all you militia persons know that I have a degree from one of the most prestigious military colleges in the City. Now, answer me."

The soldier who had talked to Con spoke up. "The Dragon Raiders were attacking these people. We ran him off. Now we are binding up the woun...."

"Oh. It's you." The regimental officer stepped forward and stuck out his hand. The militiaman smiled and stepped forward. He grasped the lieutenant's hand and shook it heartily.

"Hello, Relig. It has been a few years."

The Lieutenant nodded. "Yes, it has. I didn't know you were back in this district."

The soldier smiled again. "We go where we have to."

"Have to," the lieutenant snorted. "So, what's going on?"

"I told you. The Drag...."

"Oh, come on," the lieutenant interrupted. "Every time this riff-raff gets in trouble, you militiamen claim a big fight with Dragon—which you always win, I might add. So, where's the bodies?"

The soldier smiled that sad smile again, the one that reminded Con of his mother. Then he grabbed the lieutenant's shoulder and turned him toward the alley. "I think my squad can handle things now. Let's you and me go talk about old times." He looked back at the rest of the squad and pointed at a few individuals still on the ground. One of the other militiamen nodded and moved toward them.

The Lion's Head squad snapped to attention, performed a perfect about face, and marched back into the alley. The lieutenant and the militiaman walked behind them. As they disappeared into the alley, the lieutenant said, "Pistis, you could be running the district by now, if you hadn't ticked off all the big-shots with this Dragon-fighting stuff. So, are you still slinging hash at that greasy, little restaurant for a living?" Then the two of them disappeared into the Alley.

Con looked for the girl but she was busy with another captive. The one she had been working on sat up on the stones. His woman cradled him in her arms, crying softly. Con tried to catch the eye of one of the others but they ignored him, concentrating on the work.

Con turned to the alley, rejection burning in him. There was no help here—at least, there would be no help if he wanted to maintain his manhood, his independence. He walked into the alley just as the regulars were exiting it on the other end. The sound of marching feet quickly faded. Con walked toward the street.

Something clicked in his brain. The final words of the lieutenant rang in his ears. "That officer called that militiaman Pistis."

The eyes. The jaw. The smile. The name.

Con ran down the alley, pounding onto the street. He looked up and down but there were no soldiers there. There was no pounding of marching feet in the air. There was no lieutenant or squad. Nor was there the sight of his mother's brother.

Chapter 10

Con stood on the pavement as darkness covered the City. Few people walked the street. The windows of the apartments glowed dimly as what little light the burning tallow provided escaped into the darkness. Candles would soon extinguish and the men and women of the City would lay upon their straw ticks to rest for another day of labor.

His only weapon was gone, busted into a thousand pieces by the impact with the Raider's head. He had found the Army—the fighting part of it, anyway—only to find they would not join him in his quest. No, they wanted him to join them—to quit being a rebel and to accept their silly ideas. He shuddered.

After a month in the City, he was almost out of money, had been defeated by the Dragon twice, and had found nothing and no one that could tell him how to free his father. Despair began to fill his throat like phlegm. Con spat on the ground.

After twenty minutes, he entered a shop district. The lane on which he wandered was less dark and more people passed him, some staggering as they did. Each doorway in this block had a sign over it announcing the name of business.

Bulls and chickens. Kings and lions. Hares and hounds. Each sign was brightly painted, though the colors were lost in the yellow light pouring from the open doors. Con approached one with a sign that had a bulldog and rooster sparring in the middle of it. The lettering around the figures announced that it was the Bull And Cock Tavern.

His stomach growled suddenly, having been reminded that there was food around. Con entered. The sharp, heady smell of ale saturated the air of the room. It was a small room; perhaps ten feet by fifteen feet between the rough log and white plaster walls. On one end was a large hearth—dark in the heat of summer. Lanterns were hung in each corner of the room, casting dim amber light and deep shadows throughout the room. The floor was stone.

Along the back wall was a counter of two rough planks supported by two large barrels. A large, fat man in an apron stood there talking with three other men. The three men, dressed in the rough leather clothes of workingmen, held onto the handles of tankards sitting on the planks. They all looked with mild curiosity as Con entered. One of the men said, "Farmer," then turned back to his tankard.

Crowded onto the stone floor to his left were four rectangular wooden tables. Long benches on each side provided places for patrons to sit as they ate or drank.

Con walked to one of these, pulled the bench out and sat heavily upon it. He was tired—and hungry. He rested his elbows on the table and held his head in his hands, looking down at his lap.

And dirty, Con thought.

Shuffling steps roused him. The man in the apron approached the table. Con said, "Ale."

The man didn't move. Con looked up at him. "I said, Ale."

"You'll get ale, farmer, when I see some money."

The innkeeper tapped his right palm with a short club he carried in his left. Con dropped his head, wagging it back and forth. He wanted to get up and hit the fat face of the innkeeper. He wanted to hit him, then move on to the other three city men who smirked at him from the counter. He wanted to hit them all in the face, then start smashing up this rough, cheap furniture. He was sick of this city. He was sick of the people of it. He was sick of the Army and Dragon and everything else about this inane quest.

He wanted to go home.

He pushed the stool back suddenly. The innkeeper jumped back and raised the stick. Con smiled, reached into his sack and pulled out two coppers. He held them toward the innkeeper then dropped them on the table.

The innkeeper frowned, but he picked up the coppers and returned to the counter. He returned quickly with a mug. "Warm is all we got." He plunked the mug onto the tabletop. The contents sloshed, spilling amber liquid onto the wooden planks. They soaked it up, like they had a thousand others.

The innkeeper returned to the bar. He pointed over his shoulder and said something to the three men. They all laughed. Con picked up the mug and ignored them.

The ale was good—and he was thirsty. He drained the mug. After a loud belch, he slammed the mug down and yelled, "Another, landlord."

He pulled two more coppers from his pouch and laid them on the table. The innkeeper swept them up with one hand and the mug up with the other. A minute later, a full mug plopped down in front of Con.

Con sat up straight, the first ale starting to improve his mood. He sipped at the second. The taste was just as good as the first mug, and within a few minutes, the tankard was empty. Con raised it up in the air and wiggled it. The landlord retrieved it from his hand and brought back a full one. Con dug out two more coppers, noticing that there weren't many more in there. Nor were there many silvers.

The landlord retreated and Con gulped at the aromatic liquid. The tightness in his stomach was gone. The anger was gone, also. He breathed deep and rested his cheek on one hand. He looked around the room, which seemed to be wavering slightly.

The Army wouldn't join him. Well, so what. Who wanted to be with a bunch of stuff-shirts anyway? They probably couldn't really help him. Or wouldn't even if they could.

The memory of the Raiders scrambling onto their sled and away from the soldiers intruded. He shook his head. The Militia had defeated them. In fact, they had run them off without a fight.

Con shrugged. But, at what price? Was he to cow-tow to some officer just so he could go do something they wanted him to do instead of what he wanted? All he needed was one of those swords like the Militia had.

The words of the Militiaman who might be his uncle came back to him. "Son, you need to be changed....You will never defeat him...."

Con shuddered again. That was the real message of the Army. You had no control of your own destiny. You couldn't even change. You had to *be* changed.

His foot jerked spasmodically at the humiliation. It struck the leg of the table, rattling it, jamming his bare toe on the wood.

The innkeeper and his patrons looked around. Con grabbed his sore toe and rubbed it. "Foot's asleep," he mumbled.

The three turned back to their conversation.

The Citadel rose into his memory. The look in the eye of the dog-man and the fear that had melted his heart jolted him.

"No!" he yelled, forcing the memory out of his mind.

The innkeeper picked up his stick and started toward Con. Con shook his leg and rubbed his foot again. "Can't git it to wake up."

The innkeeper stared at him. Con quickly picked up the mug and took a big swallow. "Good ale," he said, lifting the mug toward the innkeeper.

The innkeeper grunted and returned to his place at the counter.

Con returned his head to his hands and stared down at the table. The raised and stained grain of the wood formed shapes—like the shapes in the drifting clouds of a warm summer afternoon. And like the clouds, if one looked, one could see meaning in the random shapes—a famous face, a dog chasing a rabbit, something conjured more by the vagaries of the mind than by the vapor in the air or the random lines of tree growth. This picture, though, jumped out of the grain with no effort. There were flagstones laid in rows, like the Market square. What looked like rags lay there on the stone. Con jerked at the sight, spilling his ale. The liquid flowed across the scene, somehow giving it color.

Red-stained calico formed on the tabletop. The faces of his sisters formed over the whole scene, rising from the wood. They seemed to call, for their mouths were working, forming words that Con couldn't hear. There was desperation in their eyes. Tears streamed down their cheeks. They looked directly at Con, calling to him.

The faces dissolved and he stared at the bloodied neck of the girl in the Citadel. Con turned his head, looking around the room, fear and pain mounting in him. Determined not to look back, determined not see the apparitions in the wood, still he turned back to the table, unable to resist.

It was no longer the Citadel but the square he had just left. A woman sat next to her bloodied man and screamed a silent scream into the air of the tavern, her hands held stiffly at the sides of her head.

Con jumped to his feet, pushing the stool. It turned over, crashing to the stone floor. The boom reverberated off the close walls like a cannon shot.

The vision popped at the sound. Con stood, grabbing his head to keep it from flying off. The innkeeper advanced on him, the stick again in his left hand.

"You! Get outta my shop. I don't need no loonies in here."

"No. You don't understand. The Dragon!" Con yelled. His tongue refused to wrap around the words properly. His mind refused to form them. He wanted to tell the four men of their danger but he couldn't get the thoughts to come out of his lips.

"Ain't no dragon in here, you crazy farmer." The innkeeper took another step toward Con, raising the stick to waist height.

One of the men at the counter yelled, "Throw him out, landlord. We didn't want to no filthy, drunken farmers in here no how." The others murmured their agreement.

The innkeeper raised the club and started toward Con. Con staggered toward the door, trying to avoid the man. The upset bench jumped in front of him, bashing his shin and tangling his feet. He tumbled over it, landing hard on the stone floor. He kicked it away, screaming now in unreasoning fear. His nails scraped along the stones of the floor as he fought to rise. Half way to his feet, he lunged toward the door. It hopped to one side. His head hit the door jam and he corkscrewed into the door, hitting it with his shoulder. It bounced open with a crash, dropping him onto his face in the street.

The innkeeper kicked at his feet to get them off the sill, then slammed the door closed. Con climbed unsteadily to his hands and knees. His head hurt where he had hit it and his shinbone ached from rapping it on the bench. He rose to his feet and stood for a few minutes, trying to get control. Finally, he staggered off.

He wanted to get away, to find the gate of the City, to make the long climb back to his farm. He moved to the side of building and leaned on it. Where was he? He looked up and down the street. Which way was the gate? Con pushed off the wall and staggered on.

Someone laughed. Con spun toward the noise but there was only blackness. The laughter came again—mean, spiteful laughter. Con spun around, the hair on his neck rising up. All around him in the night, faces floated in the air—the faces of those the Raiders had taken prisoner regardless of how much he had tried to stop them. They laughed at him. They laughed so loudly that Con could hear nothing else; think of nothing else.

He ran from them but they followed. The face of a Dragon Raider appeared directly in front of him, sneering at him. Con dodged right, saw an opening and ran into an alley, careening off the wall. He slipped to the filth, slid and then lay still—sick, weak, unable to rise again. Everything spun around him then went black.

Something poked him in the side. "Get up, drunk."

Con rolled onto his back. Pain shot through his head and he retched. He rolled back over onto his hands and knees. The last of the ale in his tortured stomach gushed out in a long, noisy spasm. He retched twice more, then rolled into a sitting position.

Something rapped him on the shoulder. "I said, get up."

There was a big man in a blue suit standing over him. The suit had shiny buttons on it, like those the regiments wore, but this didn't appear to be a soldier. He carried a long, black, thin club with which he tapped the side of his leg. Con stared for a minute, then his mind supplied the answer. "Cop," he said.

The big man nodded, then rapped Con on the top of the head with his stick. "Drunk!"

He put the end of the stick under Con's chin and lifted his head. "Now that the introductions are done, GET UP!"

Con wanted to explain that he wasn't a drunk. He knew he had to speak plainly, to convince the cop that he should not haul him off or run him in—which ever cops did to farmers. He opened his mouth. "Join the Army! Bah! That's for weaklings."

That was not what he had wanted to say. He opened his mouth again but his time the words got hung up in his thick tongue and just a long belch came out. The cop frowned and slapped the side of his pants with the stick, making a loud pop.

Con raised one hand, actually wanting to rise but knowing that he would just fall down again if he tried. He shook his head. "Wait. You see, the Army can't even protect two little girls playing on the streets of this stinking and filthy city. It's the Dragon that's strong."

The cop's mouth screwed up in consternation. He looked off to the side, as if trying to decide something. Then he cracked Con on the shoulder again. "I ain't gonna tell you again, drunk. Get up!"

Con's head dropped back to his chest, not paying any attention. "But those militiamen did fight the Raiders. And they beat 'em, too. "

Anger flared through him. He looked back at the cop and yelled, "How come they were out there protectin' a bunch a' whores and loafers? If they're so powerful, how come they couldn't protect my ol' man and my little sisters? How come they was protectin' a bunch a' filth?"

The cop's eyebrows shot up and he laughed. He lifted part of Con's muck covered tunic with his stick. "And who are you to be callin' other people filth, you drunk farmer?"

Anger blazed in Con's chest. His foot lashed out, catching the cop in the shin.

The cop cursed and jumped back. He grabbed at his leg with his left hand and rubbed the spot twice. "You stupid farm…" The black stick flicked out, slamming into the side of Con's head. Bright lights exploded all around him, then blackness rolled over him, almost absorbing him. He felt himself tumble over onto the stones but he could muster no resistance to the movement. He lay there, breathing in his own foulness.

The cop grabbed a fistful of Con's hair and dragged him toward the street. The pain broke through the dullness but Con could not generate any struggle. He was dragged limply along the alley. The cop dropped him back to the stones when they entered the street. He put the stick on Con's chest and pinned him to the stones, leaning over to look into his eyes. "Stay there, farmer."

Con quit struggling.

The cop looked up and down the street, then sighed. "Woodinchew know. Ain't never a wagon around when you need one."

He turned back to Con. "Look, you stupid, drunk farmer." The cop rubbed his shin again. "And I do mean stupid. If it weren't so much trouble, I'd run you in."

Con's mind was working again. He knew he had to explain to this cop why he was here. "But the Dragon killed my little sisters and ran off with my father. He ran them down. Crushed 'em right here in Market not a month ago. I got to find my father and free him."

The cop stared down at him, his brow knit. After a few minutes, he rolled his eyes toward the sky. "Why is it always me?"

He knelt down along side of Con, who had sat up. "Dragon got your sisters, huh?"

"No," Con shook his head. "The Dragon got my father. He killed my sisters."

The cop nodded his head. "Ah, I see. An' how old were they?"

"Ten."

"That, farmer, is tough. I think I see you got special problems. Maybe you ought to go downtown to the Wellbeing office. Say, where you stayin' here in the City?"

Con thought for a minute, then shrugged. The cop nodded again. "Thought so. Been livin' on the streets. And out of a tankard, from the smell of it."

Con shook his head. "No. This is the first time I've ever been drunk. 'cept on some applejack my daddy used to make."

"Yeah, an' I bet you was good at drinkin' that. Knowed a lot a' people that got started the same way."

Con started to protest but the cop waved the stick at him. "Tell you what, farmer. You got any money?"

Con nodded, thinking of the few coppers and silvers left in his pouch. The cop's eyebrows shot up. "You do? Good. Then I'm gonna run you in to the station. That way, you get a free ride downtown and we can git you hooked up with them Wellbeing folks."

"And they can help me fight the Dragon?"

The cop smirked. "Son, they'll rid you of all your dragons."

With that, he rose and walked away. Over his shoulder he called, "You stay there. I'll find us a wagon."

It was daylight by the time they arrived at the station, a large white building made of huge blocks of stone. Stone steps rose from the street level by several flights to mammoth double doors set back from the face of the building. Although the doors themselves were lost in the shadows of that entrance, glints from the polished iron and copper hardware twinkled in the morning light.

On the street, in front of the steps, a group of soldiers paraded in gaudy uniforms. Red pants, blue tops and orange braiding set them off against the stream of workers in conservative blues and grays just beginning to pour into the square from the surrounding streets.

Con looked at them with a wary eye. "You're not turnin' me over to them, are you? Are these the Wellbeing people?"

The cop sniggered. "Naw, boy. They on'y get the rejects."

They started up the long steps. The few people entering the building stared at Con's filthy clothes and dirt streaked hair, then moved far away from him. The cop kept the long stick in the middle of his back, poking him occasionally when Con slowed down to look at something.

The cop sniggered again. "Are they Wellbeing.? Boy, you really are from the farm.

"Wellbeing and these old soldiers are about as compatible as fat and fire." The cop beamed. "Yeah, fat and fire. That's good. You put 'em together and they start to sizzle and spit. On'y, I ain't sure which is which." Then he guffawed.

"Wait," Con said. "Isn't Wellbeing part of the Army?"

"No, no," the cop said, laughing. "Old Wellbeing is a part of the Rebel Government. You won't find them referring you to the Army. The only ones these," he pointed at the soldiers marching in the street, "ever get is the real strange birds, the ones nobody else wants anyway,"

Con craned his neck to look at the top of the building in front of him. "This is a heck of a station you got here."

"You're kidding me, ain't you?" the cop asked.

Con's face remained blank. The cop shook his head and muttered, "Farmers."

After a few seconds he said, "This here is the seat of the Rebel Government. It used to be the seat of the other Government but they been turned out now."

"It must have been a terrible fight to get them out," Con said, awed at the size and beauty of the building.

"Naw," the cop said, waving his hand. "Weren't no fight at all. The Army just give up the place. They started walking out as soon as the Rebels walked in. As a matter of fact, it seems to me that some of 'em kinda' wanted the rebels in. Said they were better able to deal with the problems of government than the Army was."

Con's jaw dropped. "Now you're kidding me. They just gave it up?"

The cop nodded and Con ran his eyes over the exterior of the building. "Was it quick? They just sort of give up?"

The nightstick tapped Con on the back and the cop pointed up the steps. "Just move along there. I got to book you before I can give you over to the Wellbeing people and that has to look good."

The cop continued, "It wasn't real quick. When it first happened you couldn't tell the difference between the Rebels and the Army. Shoot, it still is hard to tell sometimes. They all talked the same and they all said the same things. They all took lunch together and they even worked in the same offices. Pretty soon, though, the hard-liners on both sides got involved. The Army kept backing off and the Rebels just moved in to fill the vacuum.

"There was a lot of talk each time a particular office changed hands and the Army screamed about it every time. Well, maybe not every time and never the whole Army. Some of the Regiments always seemed to think it better if the Rebels had a particular office than one of the other Regiments. There was always more problems between the Regiments than between the Army and the Rebels.

"Well, pretty soon the whole government was in the hands of the rebels and the Army was out completely. That's when the Rebels started passing laws to keep the Army out. Boy, these guys ain't wishy-washy. They got control and they're gonna keep it."

"Which are you, then, Rebel or Army?"

"I just work here, boy." He pulled open the big double doors and tapped Con on the back. "Move along, there." He pointed his stick down the hall.

The hall was wide, with floors of white marble waxed to a brilliant shine. Every four feet a lamp made of black, strap iron with a large single candle in it hung from a cable attached to the ceiling. Reflecting from the polished stones and bright white walls, the lamplight illuminated the long straight hallway almost as brightly as if it was outside.

The walls were white plaster broken only by the dark alcoves that contained the brown, wooden doors. The openings stood like soldiers in formation, one after another, on and on down the long hall.

They trudged past each office door; their footsteps echoing and reechoing like the syncopated roll of an imperfect drummer in the empty hall. Con stared into each door alcove as they passed, noticing the signs above each that proclaimed its purpose.

"Hold up there, farmer. This is our stop."

The cop held his hand on the doorknob of one of the brown doors. Con glanced at the sign above the door: "Justice."

The cop pushed the door open and held it for Con, sweeping his stick forward in an invitation.

As Con stepped past him, the cop stuck out his foot and shoved Con's back. He stumbled into the room. Strong hands grabbed his arms and kept him from striking the ground. As the cop lifted him back to his feet, he whispered, "Sorry, kid. I gotta reputation to uphold. You jest do what I say and we'll git you outa' here quick."

The room was about twenty feet square. Con stood in an aisle between rows of chairs set out four to a side. Five rows extended in front of him to a wooden rail. There was a gate in the rail. The cop shoved Con toward it.

Beyond the gate was an open area. Two tables with two chairs each, one on one side of the room and one on the other, were the only furniture. Along the far wall was a tall desk made of dark wood. Seated behind this desk, reading something, was a man with long white hair combed straight back from his forehead. It curled slightly at the back and hung over his collar. He had on small round spectacles with thin, wire frames. His face was wrinkled and his nose was large, with blue veins tracing intricate patterns over its surface. His wrinkled hands had brown splotches scattered over the skin randomly. No one else was in the room.

Con stopped at the gate but the cop shoved him again. The gate swung open at his touch and he stepped forward. He and the cop stood before the desk of the white-haired man.

"What's that?" the man said, still staring at the papers on his desk.

"Drunk farmer, Judge," the cop stated.

Con stared at the man. He had never seen a judge nor a courtroom.

"Why's he staring around like a fool?" The Judge finally looked up from his papers. He pulled the wires of the spectacles off his ears and carefully folded them across the lenses. Holding them in one hand, he used them like a pointer.

The cop shrugged. "He's a drunk and he's a farmer. Either one's a pretty good reason."

"He stinks, too."

"Yeah, well. He's a drunk and a far…" A stern look from the Judge cut him off. The cop said, "Well, I found him lyin' on the street, your Honor. The cop leaned forward and tapped his temple with one finger. "I think he's a little…"

The Judge returned the spectacles to his face and began reading again. "Thirty days."

"What?" Con asked.

The Judge looked up at him again, pulling the spectacles down on his nose so he could see over them. His eyes drifted to the soiled clothes and he wrinkled his nose. "Good grief, O'Rourke, can't you clean 'em up before you bring 'em in." Turning his eyes to Con again, he said, "That's your sentence, farmer."

"My sentence? You haven't even heard my side."

The cop chuckled. "You ain't got a side, kid. You was guilty when I pushed you through the door. Now, with a little persuasion, I'm sure the Judge could see his way to a suspended sentence."

Con twitched his head and raised one eyebrow.

The cop screwed up his mouth. He looked toward the desk. "'Scuse me, yer Honor. I got to talk to him a little."

The Judge nodded and waved his hand in dismissal. The cop pulled Con toward the railing again. "Now is the time you pull out that money sack of yours, farmer."

Con glanced back the man at the desk. "A bribe? The Judge wants a bribe?"

The cop shook his head, grimacing. "You farmers are sure dense, but it gets through after a while. Sure, he wants a bribe. That's what makes the rivers of justice flow, kid."

Con reached for his money sack. There was nothing there. He slapped around his belt, looking for the leather.

Finally, he looked at the cop and raised his shoulders and hands. "It was there when I left the tavern."

"You had your money in a sack on your belt?"

Con nodded.

"And you thought it would be there after you fell asleep in a City alley? Man, you farmers really are dense."

The cop looked him over once, sighed, then turned to the Judge. "He ain't got nothin' worth nothin', Judge."

The Judge scribbled something on a piece of paper and waived it at the cop. He didn't even look up.

The cop walked over to the desk, read the paper, then walked back to Con. "OK, kid, I got to take you to jail."

"Jail? I didn't to anything."

"Don't matter. You look like you done somethin'. You ain't got no grease. So, you go to jail."

Con backed away from the cop. "Wait a minute. You told me we were going to Wellbeing. That they would help me find my father."

The cop laughed. "I don't think that bunch will help you find your pappy—but what I promised, I'll do. I just gotta do it differ'nt than I thought.

"Now, let's go. I gotta take you to jail."

They walked back into the hallway. The cop pushed him to the left. Almost immediately, he pushed him left again, into a branch hallway.

This one was not as bright—nor was it polished. Only a few candles lit the way. Dust covered the floor in swirls on its way to the corners and cracks.

Con sniffed. "It stinks in here."

The cop laughed. "How can you tell?" Then his face screwed up. "You know, your right, kid. It is kinda' rank in here. Glad I ain't gotta stay."

The cop pointed at a doorway. Con stepped through it.

The room was much smaller than the courtroom, more like a large closet. The floor was bare wood. Dust piles were built up in the corners and dust bunnies drifted across the floor on the occasional waft of air from the open window high in the back wall. The walls were partially covered in a peeling paper print. Faded gray horses pulled faded gray chariots on a faded blue field. There was one lamp, hung from the ceiling in the center of the room. It was directly over a narrow desk scattered with papers. On the top of the untidy stack was a plate of fatty meat. The papers all around and under the plate had grease stains here and there on them.

A fat man in a blue uniform, similar to O'Rourke's, sat at the desk, picking apart the meat with his fingers, sporadically plopping a choice piece between his greasy lips. He looked up at the interruption.

"What you got there, O'Rourke?"

"A new baby for your care, Sean. A farmer what can't hold his likker. Judge says put him away for thirty days."

Sean raised his eyebrows hopefully. O'Rourke shook his head. "Not even a copper, old son."

Sean grimaced and ran his greasy hands through his thin white hair, leaving trails on his scalp. O'Rourke tapped Con on the shoulder with his nightstick. "Sean, here will take good care of you." He turned and walked out the door.

Con yelled after him. "What about Wellbeing?"

Sean pointed at a tall stool in the corner. "Sit there, farmer. When I'm done my lunch, we'll process you."

"What about Wellbeing? The cop said I would be going to Wellbeing."

Sean smirked. "Wellbeing, is it?"

He pointed at the stool with a greasy finger and nodded. "There's your well-being for the time-being." He chuckled at his joke. Con went over and sat down.

Con wanted to be angry. He tried to work up a good outburst but it just wouldn't come. The best he could do was bewilderment.

The fat clerk ate his meal. When all the meat was gone, the man stood, looked around holding his hands out in front of him, finally shrugged and wiped the grease onto his pant legs. From the dark stains there, it was not the first time.

"Now, for you."

The man sorted through some of the papers on his desk, mumbling. Finding one of interest, he looked back at Con. "You gotta name?"

"Con Ataxia."

The man shook his head and tossed the paper back on the stack. He rummaged through some more then noticed a folded paper in his breast pocket. "Oh!"

He pulled the paper out, read it and mumbled, "Uh-huh."

He flipped it over and read the back, nodding again. "Uh-huh!"

"Well, you little drunk, crazy farmer, we gotta place for you."

He reached for a quill lying on the side of the desk, dipped it into an ink well and made a mark on the paper. With that, he tossed it onto the stack.

"What's your name?"

Con frowned. "Same as it was a couple a' minutes ago."

Sean's face reddened. "A wiseacre, are we? OK, smart guy, you better learn this and learn it quick. Your name ain't whatever you said a few minutes ago."

Con started to tell him but the man held up his hand. "I just tol' you, wise guy. That ain't your name. Your name is 201406295."

Con shrugged. "I was born Con Ataxia."

"What you was born ain't got nothin' to do with it, boy. We got you now."

Con shook his head. Sean's shoulders slumped. "Look, boy. O'Rourke left me a note that says you got mental problems so I am making allowances. Let me explain.

"That name your parents give you was OK in the old days. But we got to change. We got to get more efficient. If we are going to take care of you, improve you, make you into a model citizen what can vote an' all, then we got to start by gettin' rid of all that ol' nonsense about you bein' a individual with your own name an' all.

"This here name I am givin' you is efficient. We can right it down quick on all our forms, you see. An' we can keep records. An', really, this name is more like a individual than them old words your family give you. See, nobody got the same number as you got."

Con shook his head again. "But, it ain't a new name that I need. I need a weapon—a way to fight the Dragon."

"Don't be talkin' about weapons, wise guy. You don't need no weapons—ain't allowed to have none, anyway. We will give you all the protection you need. An' this here new name will git you that, too."

Con was more bewildered. "Look, Mister, I appreciate what your sayin'. But I'm only goin' to be here for a few weeks. Why don't we just…"

Sean looked down at his clipboard. "A few weeks? No. No. You're a part of us now. We will keep you until you become a good productive citizen what knows his place."

Con stood up and raised his hand, palms out, to slow the man down. "Now, wait. The Judge said thirty days."

Sean stepped forward. His hands whipped out toward Con. In a flash, a set of metal bracelets with a chain between them was clasped onto Con's wrists. Con pulled back and tried to separate his wrists but he was held fast.

"There, 201406295. Now we can start."

Sean grabbed the chain and pulled. Con pulled back but pain shot through his wrists and he was forced to step forward.

"Come on, 201406295. It does no good to resist. It is much better to go along."

Sean opened a door in the back the room and entered a narrow, dark corridor, dragging Con behind him. "To get along, we go along. That's our motto here."

Chapter 11

The corridor ended at a set of wooden steps that descended into darkness. Sean grabbed a lantern from where it hung on the wall and stepped onto the dark steps. Con jerked back involuntarily at the top of the steps but the pain in his wrists moved him forward again.

At the bottom of the steps, Sean pushed open a thick wooden door. Bright light poured into the stairwell. They entered a long, stone hall way. Here the stones were not polished but rough cut and poorly fitted. Rows of doors extended down both sides of the hallway. Each door had a small, barred window in it. The doors were hinged to swing outward and had large latches on them with a keyhole that was at least an inch tall. Faces appeared at the windows, the eyes alive with curiosity. Before Con got past each cell, the inhabitants turned away, interest in the new prisoner lost as quickly as it had flared.

Con's spirit went cold within him.

Jail. Prison.

This was not what he had expected from the government.

This was not what he had expected from this quest.

Jail! Prison!

It was like a burden on his shoulders growing heavier with each step.

Sean stopped in front of a cell, grabbed the keys dangling at his waist, and selected a large iron one. He inserted it into the keyhole and twisted. There was a metallic snick. He withdrew the key and pulled the door open.

"This is…" He hesitated, looking at Con's expression. "Hey, don't worry about it, kid. It ain't as bad as you think. Just remember what I said. We go along to get along."

He waved his hand toward the cell. When Con didn't move, Sean looked over Con's shoulder and nodded. Two guards, whom Con had not heard approach, grabbed his arms and propelled him into the cell. They spun him around and shoved him up against the wall, holding him there. Sean came into the cell and removed the metal bracelets. The three of them exited. As the door slammed shut, Sean said, "Somebody'll be with you soon."

The cell was unlit but not dark. Light filtered in from the hallway and from a thin, horizontal slit, no more than four inches wide, just below the ceiling on the outside wall. It was a small room, perhaps five feet wide and seven feet deep. The ceiling was about eight feet off the floor. The bed was a wooden frame sticking out of the solid rock of the left sidewall. Rope was strung across the frame, secured through holes in the wood by a large knot. Rolled up on one end was a straw tick.

There was a hole in the floor in one corner. The stains on the stone around it and the smell of human waste made its purpose plain.

He walked back to the door and looked out the barred window. Nothing but a few feet of hallway on either side was visible. "Hey!" he yelled, hearing the echo come back to him quickly.

"Hey!" he yelled louder. "Hey! What's going on?"

No one answered. "Hey! I got to get out a' here. I've got to get back to my farm."

A face appeared in the window of the opposite door. It was an older man—toothless, with thin gray hair standing out all over his head.

"Shut up, farmer. I'm trying to rest over here."

"Hey, maybe you can tell me. How do I get out of here?"

"Out?" The old face looked puzzled. "Why would you want to? Got three squares. They don't bother you much, 'cept tryin' ta make you a good sidsen. An' all they mean by that is you got ta vote for them when they take the poll."

"But I have a farm to take care of. An' I have my father to get back from the Dragon."

The old man's face screwed up like he had bit on something sour. "Oooh! Don't be sayin' that in here. That is the one thing that'll set 'em off. They don't like ta hear nothin' about no Dragon. Or the Commander, neither. They get real testy if you start that stuff."

"They don't want to hear? That's why I'm here. That's why the cop brought me in—to get me help to fight the Dragon."

"You tol' a cop you was about fightin' the Dragon?"

Con nodded. The old man's head bobbed up and down. "That **is** why you's here, boy. But it ain't ta he'p you fight nobody. They got you here to get them silly ideas outa' yer head. They're gonna re-edicate you.

"Now, jest you hesh about that stuff. I'll give you some advice. Don' be sayin' nothin' about Commanders and Dragons and the like. It'll go easier on ya'. Remember, we go along to get along in here. Now, shesh. I got to take a nap."

The old man's face disappeared. His words, though, didn't. The people in the jail were going to re-educate him. That sounded an awful lot like changing him. Con shook his head. Another trick. It was just the Army line dressed up in another uniform.

Con backed up to the wall, walked his feet out, and slid his back down the wall till he was on his buttocks. He stared at the closed door. "Oh, Commander!" he mumbled the common oath but with more real meaning than he had ever put in it before.

There was a scraping noise in the hallway. A face appeared in his window. "Number?"

Con stared for a minute. "What?"

"C'mon, you nut. Your number. I need your number." The man must have been tall for he leaned over slightly to look in the window. His face was fleshy and he had the shadow of a slight beard, although it was still very early. His brown hair was cut short and brushed back from his high forehead. He held up a clipboard and waved it, revealing his long sleeve white shirt, like the ones the two guards had worn.

Con thought for a minute then repeated, "201406295"

The man at the door stared at the clipboard and nodded slightly with each number, with a final bounce of his head on the last digit. "Good. That is excellent. You ain't as dumb as they all said you were."

The man unlocked the door and stepped inside carrying a bundle of cloth. He looked from side to side in the cell, mock fear on his face. "Ain't no dragons in here, are there?" Then he laughed and dropped the bundle on the bunk. "Bedding," he said and retreated from the cell.

Con undid the bundle and found two sheets and a blanket. He quickly made up the bunk, realizing just how tired he was. Then he looked down the length of him. His tunic was stiff with dried muck and his trousers were caked with filth. His skin felt as dirty as his clothing. He could not lay on those clean sheets.

The door opened again. The same guard stood there with a large tub of steaming water on a pushcart and what appeared to be clean clothes in one hand.

"That's right, farmer. It's a bath and a clean uniform."

Con stepped toward him but the guard held up one hand. "Hold on. I got to have your number." He picked up the clipboard and stared at it, waiting.

Con, still looking down at the tub of water, raised his eyebrows and stared at the man. "I just gave you my number not ten minutes ago."

"Don't matter. Got to hear it again. That's the rules. There's a bunch a' you jer...uh, cidzens in this place and there ain't no way for me to keep you all straight 'cept I hear your numbers each time."

Con shrugged and repeated the number. The guard pushed the tub into the room and laid Con's new clothes on the bed. "You get cleaned up and I'll be back with some food."

The door slammed shut. Con pulled off his filthy clothes and jumped into the tub. At first, he lay still in the hot water, letting the strain in his back and shoulders soak away. Then, he grabbed the soap and scrub brush. The water turned milky white with the soap, then brown and finally almost black as the caked dirt loosened and dissolved away. When he was done, he dried off and put on the fresh clothes.

Fresh, dressed in clean clothes, and with a reasonably comfortable bunk inviting him to sleep, things didn't look as bad. The old man was right. This wouldn't be too bad for a while. In fact, of all the things that had happened to him in the City, this was turning out to be the best. He sat on the bunk, then stretched out and was asleep in minutes.

"Hey! Wake up!" The same guard stood in the open door holding a tray of steaming food. Con sat up groggily but his stomach rumbled when the smell of the meal hit his nose.

"201406295." Con yelled and grabbed for the tray.

The guard pulled it back out of reach. "And I thought you were learning."

"What's wrong? Ain't that my number?"

"How would I know? I ain't got my clip board yet. And I ain't ast you for no number."

"But you always ask for my…"

The guard harrumphed and put the tray on a wagon outside the door. His fists found his hips and he stared at Con. One hand came out and he wagged a finger in Con's face. "Now, don't you be tellin' me what I always do. It ain't up to you to tell me. I tell you. When I want your number, I ask for it. You don't be given me numbers 'til I ask for 'em. Got it?"

There was a chuckle from across the hallway. The old man said, "You tell 'im, Hardy. That boy got ta l'arn."

Con sat back on the bunk and stared at the irate man, embarrassment turning to anger. Then his eyes drifted toward the cart in the hallway and his stomach growled loudly again. He nodded. There would be a meal of crow before any of that bread passed his lips.

The guard stared for a long time. Con stared back. Finally, he said, "All right. Now we can move along."

The guard picked up the clipboard. "What's your number?"

Con rattled it off. The guard checked off something on the sheet then handed Con the meal tray. When Con took it, the guard stepped quickly out the door and slammed it shut.

No one else bothered him that day, except for the delivery of another meal that evening. Con spent the rest of the day sleeping or pacing the floor.

The next morning breakfast arrived at dawn. A different guard brought it but the routine was same. Wait. Respond. Get fed.

As the guard closed the door, Con asked, "Say, when do we start to get re-educated? When is something going to happen?"

The guard smiled and said, "Sooner than you think, buddy. Sooner than you think." He turned and walked off, his boots clicking on the stone floor.

Nothing happened the rest of that day, except a guard came by with some books. Con looked them over but they were pretty boring—politics and social responsibility. He set them under his bunk.

For three days, he was fed and allowed to bathe himself but that was all. Out of sheer boredom, he picked up the books and began to read. They were still boring but less so than staring at the walls.

After an hour or so, he put the books down and lay back on his bunk. They were all very astute and were written with the vocabulary of scholars but they made little sense to Con. What he could glean from the first one was that no individual could care for himself as well as the whole could care for him. It was important then for each individual to submit himself to the whole, working as hard as he could for the good of the whole and receiving what he needed from the whole—including the proper way to think about things. Since the whole was made up of many people, it had to have more wisdom and intelligence that any one of the individuals that made it up. The whole is greater than the parts, is what the books said over and over. So, the individual no longer should try to figure out the proper way to do things because the whole was so much smarter and better than the individual that no thought the individual could have could possibly match the wisdom of the whole.

A week passed. The routine didn't change. Con's only contact with other humans was with the guards and the occasional word from the old man across the hallway. He ate. He slept. He cleaned himself.

He read the books.

After he had gone through most of the stack, the concept was starting to make sense. The whole is greater than the parts. That certainly made sense.

The wisdom of the group was greater than any individual's wisdom. Ok. That made some sense, too.

Individuals shouldn't try to out think the group but rather should go along with what the group thinks—that has to be the right way. Yeah, if you accepted the first parts then this part made sense.

"Then, who wrote the books?"

The voice shocked Con and he looked around. The door was shut and there was no one at the window. He rose from his bunk and went to the door. No one was there.

Con glanced up at the small window at the ceiling. If anyone was there, they couldn't see what he was doing—they certainly couldn't tell what he had been thinking. He pounded the side of his head with the heel of his hand a few times. "Must be dreamin'."

Only the voice didn't seem like a dream. It seemed real. Like the voice at the ironmonger's tent that day.

He sat back on his bunk, puzzling. Then, after glancing around the room one more time, he went back to thinking about the texts.

People should try to do the most they can for the whole so that everyone was better off. That made some sense, too. If everyone was doing the best they could then things would have to get better.

"Then, why aren't they getting better?"

Con jumped and ran to the window. No one was there.

"Hey, ol' man."

There was a scraping noise in the other cell, then the sound of bare feet padding on the stone. The old, grizzled face appeared in the door, his eyebrows raised at Con.

"Did you hear somebody in the hall?"

"When?"

"Just now—within the last few minutes."

The old man puzzled for a minute, then shook his head. "Nooo. Can't say I did. 'Course I wasn't payin' no attention, ya' know. I was nappin'."

Con nodded and turned back to his bunk.

No more voices came.

During the second week, Con picked up the final book. On its cover was a stylized picture of the Commander in full battle gear. The sword in his hand was aimed at a goat that walked on its hind legs and had the face of a man. The title was, *Destroying the Myths that Keep Men in Bondage.*

Yes, thought Con. Now, I am going to start getting something that will help.

He flipped to the first page chapter, titled, **Commanders and Dragons.**

"The greatest myth perpetrated by the Army is that of a powerful enemy from which humans need protecting. For centuries, the leaders of the Regiments have used the figures of the good Commander and the evil Dragon to scare ignorant people into giving their time and earnings for the benefit of those same leaders. If one did not obey the Regimental leaders, Dragon Raiders would come and steal one's children taking them to the Citadel, they reasoned. If they did obey and give a portion of their crops to the Regiments, then the Commander would send his all-powerful general, Cleato, to protect them from these mythical beasts.

In the last century, the Rebellion has done all it can to debunk these myths. These selfless protectors of the downtrodden have proven beyond a shadow of a doubt with logical, wise thought that there is no Dragon, no Dragon Raiders, no Cleato, and, finally, no Commander. They have proven that there is no Army camp in the upper valley and the only thing in the lower valley is a series of geological marvels that spew steam and smoke almost constantly."

Con dropped the book to his lap. "Huh?"

He read the paragraph again. "There is no Dragon. There are no Raiders."

He looked at the other books, then back at this one. He picked it up and read again.

"The only evils in the Valley are caused by humans. Greed, hate, avarice are all caused by individuals who want individual gain as opposed to improving the lot of the Whole. Only those who cannot remember that the Whole is greater than the parts can truly be called evil. And that evil can be redirected, changed, corrected and made good. For no one is evil—and no one is good. They are all just minor, sometimes insignificant, parts of the Whole needing positive reinforcement to continue to support the Whole."

The same message as the other books. Only this book started with an error. Con knew there was a Dragon and there were Dragon Raiders. And, if those militiamen were not crazy, there was a Cleato—though Con didn't know much about him.

The door swung open and Sean stood there, hands on his hips. His face lit up as he saw the book in Con's hand. "Ah, 201406295, good timing. You finished the best book and it is time for your next phase. Follow me."

With that he waddled away from the door. Con followed him.

They walked down the long corridor and out another big wooden door. They entered a large room with a low ceiling. Desk after desk were set in rows, filling the open area. Behind each desk a clerk sat filling out forms. In front of about half the desks, sat people dressed in the same gray uniform. The clerks asked questions. The uniformed people answered. It all combined to make a deafening din after the quiet of the cell.

Sean led Con to a desk, pulled a bunch of papers off the clipboard and laid them on the desk. The clerk, who could have been Sean's twin, looked up. "Another one?"

Sean nodded. "Finished all his books, he did."

The clerk raised his eyebrows. "One that can read. Oh good." There didn't seem to be any pleasure in the exclamation.

The clerk pointed at the seat in front of the desk. Con sat. The clerk's eyes dropped to the papers that Sean had dropped on the desk.

Finally, the plump man looked up at Con. A tired set of eyes, dead to the duties, greeted Con. Then, as he watched, the eyes took on life. A smile spread across the man's face and he stuck out his hand. "Well, well, well. I'm your counselor. I'm here to make your stay as easy as possible and to make your re-education to a new life in the Whole as smooth as possible. Now please give me your number so we can continue."

Con stared at the thrust out hand. "What am I doin' here? Where, for that matter, is here?"

The plump clerk dropped his hand and frowned. He yelled at the door where Sean had disappeared. "I thought you said this one was trained."

He looked back at Con, large ridges creasing his forehead. He stood, his hands on his hips, and clucked his tongue. "Now, you've made me lose my place. Where was I?"

He thought hard, his eyebrows almost touching. He pinched his chin between his thumb and forefinger, then shook his head. "I'll just have to start over."

"Well, well, well. I'm your counselor. I'm here to make your stay as easy as possible and to make your re-education to a new life in the Whole as smooth as possible. Now please give me your number so we can continue."

Con stared at the man again. His interruption had been just that: an interruption. Con didn't really exist to this man outside the script laying on his desk. He said, "How come your book says there ain't no Dragon or Dragon Raiders?"

The exasperated clerk snorted. "Look, you trashy criminal. I ain't got time for this. Answer my questions or I'm gonna have to call somebody on you."

Con scratched his cheek and looked askance at the clerk. "Answer my questions and we can get on with what ever it is you have to do."

"That's it," the clerk yelled standing up again. "It's bad enough that I got to sit here and be nice to a bunch of drunks and scum. I don't have to put up with your mouth. You're outta' here, big boy."

The man tapped a bell on his desk. Two large men in white uniforms standing along the wall looked at the clerk. He pointed at Con then jerked his thumb over his shoulder.

The two guards walked up behind Con. Con looked over his shoulder at one of them. "Look, I ain't causin' trouble. I just want some answers. I am trying to free my father from the Dragon and I need help."

Gasps came from the people all around him. One of them leaned to another and said, "He said dragon." The other covered his mouth and sat back.

His clerk stepped back. "An individual. I knew it when I looked at him."

One of the guards slapped the back of his head. "Watch the way you talk in here, jerk!"

Con grabbed the back of his head and stood up. "What? I just said the Drag…"

The guard placed his hand over Con's mouth. "I told you, you ignorant jerk. Don't use that kind of language. It's taken us years to free some of these people from that kind of thinking. They don't need to hear garbage."

"Garbage? That ain't garbage. I've seen the Dragon Raiders. I've been to the Citadel. And I've seen that Cleato you people say don't exist."

The punch came straight up from the guard's side. Con didn't even see it until it contacted his jaw. He flipped backward over the desk and the two guards pounced on him, flipping him onto his back, and binding his arms. They pulled him roughly to his feet. One of them punched him in the kidneys. Con fell again, slamming his face into the side of the clerk's desk.

"Filth!" the clerk yelled. "Nothing but filth. How can anyone use such awful language?"

All around him people nodded. One of the guards grabbed his shoulders. The other got his feet and they hauled him toward the side of the room. Several people spit at him as he was carried by. One man kicked him in the ribs. "Filthy individual. I got kids in this place. They don't need to hear that garbage you spout out." He kicked again but the guard brushed him aside.

The guards moved along the wall to a hallway. There they dropped Con's feet to the floor and pushed him into the passageway. Ten feet along the passage, a door blocked the way. One guard pulled a key from his belt, twisted it into the lock, and pushed the door open.

Bright sunlight poured in, hurting Con's eyes. He squinted hard. One of the guards loosed the ropes on his arms. Something slammed into his back, shoving him out the door. He sprawled onto flagstones and skidded to a halt. He heard the door behind him slam.

Chapter 12

Con pushed himself off the rocks, his head still light and aching from the punch. When he straightened, he gasped and reached around to massage the soreness in his left side, over his kidney. He flopped back down into a sitting position, waiting for the dizziness to pass.

The door opened and one of the guard leaned out. He tossed something at Con. Con threw up an arm to protect himself but the objects rattled harmlessly onto the stones in front of him. A Gold and two Silvers lay on the pavement. "Here, pervert. It ain't my idea but the rules say you git a Gold and two silvers when you leave."

The door started to close, then opened again. The fat clerk stood there with a brown envelope in his hand. He sailed it at Con. "You take that. It says you can leave here. And don't be spoutin' any more of your perversion to anybody—else we'll get you back and really educate you."

Con picked up the package and climbed to his feet. Still woozy, he swayed slightly then got control of himself. The clerk watched from the doorway—a glint of pleasure in his eyes at Con's obvious discomfort. Con looked up at him and yelled, "Commander. Commander. Commander."

The clerk's face went bright red and he slammed the door shut.

He was in a square, like the one where he had met the militiamen. Across from him, there was an alley. Con walked to it. It led to the street.

On the street, he stopped to think. He was in the City. He was close to the seat of the Rebel government. So, he had to be close to Wellbeing. His jail time had been shorter than the judge had indicated but it had been long enough that summer was waning. It had to be August and time was wasting for Con to get on with this quest. Within a few weeks, he would have to go back to the farm for harvest. Then there would be no time until after the planting to try again.

The cop had told him that Wellbeing could help him. The cop had said that Wellbeing had the power and the resources to get rid of all the dragons, whatever that meant. Even after such a long delay, it was to Wellbeing that he had to go.

He was on a narrow side street. Tall buildings encased him on both sides. A slight hill lifted the road all the way to the corner of the buildings at least 300 feet away. Traffic was heavier there. People crossed almost continuously.

So, where was the Wellbeing place? His eye caught sight of a blue uniform across the street and about halfway to the top of the hill. He trudged toward him.

The cop watched Con approach. His stick began to thump along his pant leg. Con painted a big smile on his face and looked the cop in the eye. "Hi. I'm lookin' for the Wellbeing office. Can you tell me how to get there?"

The cop looked over Con's shoulder, then back at him. "Didn't you just come out of that alley?" He pointed with his stick.

Con twisted and looked. He turned back to the cop. "Oh, yes sir. But they let me go. Served my time, I did." He held up the envelope the clerk had tossed at him.

The cop pushed the brim of his hat back with his stick. "You just got throwed out of Wellbeing's back door and you want to go back in the front?"

Wellbeing! Con spun around and looked at the alley, seeing for the first time the sign on the building proclaiming the main offices of the organization that was supposed to help him.

That mindless, mind-dulling routine, those days filled with intelligence sapping books had been Wellbeing. That was what was supposed to help him free his father. Con's knees went weak with disappointment and he wobbled a little.

The cop's hand on his shoulder steadied him. "You OK?"

"Just a little light headed from that place."

The cop nodded at him. "I would be, too. Why don't you just get along? Find some work or somethin' before you end up back in there."

"Go along to get along." The phrase jumped out before Con could stop it.

The cop grimaced and turned Con's face to look at the bruise starting to spread on his jaw. "Yeah, I can see." He tapped Con's back with the stick. "Go on. And get some new clothes. That uniform will give you away every time."

At the top of the hill, Con sat on a white stone bench. He leaned forward, resting his face in his hands. Wellbeing had been his hope—a false hope, as it turned out. Wellbeing was just another Rebel lie. No better than the Army.

No. That was wrong. At least there was some part of the Army that recognized that there was a fight going on, that there was an enemy that needed fighting. Wellbeing—the Rebels, in general—couldn't even understand that. And without understanding that, they could not possibly be part of the solution.

Home.

Perhaps that was it. It was just time to go home.

Con wagged his head in his hands.

Footsteps approached and stopped in front of him. Con opened his eyes. A small man in red pants, blue jacket and orange braiding stood there. He was an older man, with thin, light brown hair. He had a look of softness in his eyes, but of genuine concern. He smiled gently at Con.

"Are you all right?"

Con sat up straight and looked at him. "Yes," he snapped. "Now, go away."

The man recoiled. Then he leaned forward again. "Well, OK. If you are all right. I just wanted to make sure you didn't need anything."

Con waved his hand at the man. "The only thing I need is a way out of the City."

"Oh!" the man exclaimed. "Oh, my. That is a long way. I'm not even sure that I know exactly. Oh!" He glanced around in several directions.

The little man walked over to group of similarly dressed individuals. One of them glanced at Con, then walked to him. "You need a way out of the City?"

Con nodded. This one was taller—with dark hair under his stiff, squared off uniform cap. He had an agreeable face, a longish, thin nose and an angular jaw. A slight smile played at the corner of his lips as if he had found something he liked, something that made him very happy. He was calm. His hands remained folded in front of him while he talked. A picture of inner peace with just the right amount of compassion mixed in.

There was something, though, in his eyes—something that caused Con to shiver inside and want to get away as quickly as he could. It was the look of a hunter—a predator sizing up its prey. Or a horse trader who had found a gullible customer.

The man spoke in a gentle voice—as if speaking to a child. "It is very complicated but here are the directions." He directed Con toward a main thoroughfare across the square then began turning and twisting his hands this way and that, explain another road and another turn with each gesture. Half the street names he could not remember and the other half he could only guess at. Con listened politely and nodded each time the man looked at him. The only thing he could remember, though, was the first street. He stood and edged away.

"Thanks for the directions. I got to be going now."

The man stepped after him. "Wait. I want to tell you about the Commander. I can see that you have problems. The Commander can fix them for you. He can...."

Con waved at him. "Yes. Yes, I am sure he can. Thank you."

He turned and walked swiftly toward the road the man had originally pointed to. The uniformed men walked a few steps after him, then stopped. Con glanced back. The look on the darker man's face was no longer of peace and compassion. Anger simmered in the flash of his eyes and the tight set of his lips. Con increased his pace.

It was a wide road filled with shops. On this street, carriages pulled by prancing horses competed for space with pedestrians and ox carts. No open sewers polluted the air but slabs of close fitting stone covered drainages that carried the animal and human waste away.

Neat, colorful shops with open fronts lined the road. Well-dressed people bustled up and down, jostling others who ambled from shop window to shop window. Gleaming merchandise, handsome clothing, colorful fabrics, and spindly wooden furniture filled the front of the shops, attracting the well-deserved stares of the crowds. Shopkeepers in jackets and shopkeepers in aprons stood in open doorways, calling to shoppers, holding up merchandise for sale.

Con drifted, staring at the sights. This was so different from what he had previously seen in the City. This was more like he had dreamed the City would be when he stood on his rock and stared out into the distance at the gleaming pearl. Forgetting his quest—forgetting his problems, he wandered down the street, watching people and staring at the goods that were beyond anything he could afford.

"Disgusting. Why do they let them wander around like that?"

Con turned toward the voice. Two women stood about fifteen feet away, staring at him. Puzzled at first, he followed their stares to his gray uniform. He spun on his heel and walked quickly away, his cheeks filling with heat.

Seeing a clothing shop, he ducked in the door. A short, dark man with a long tape around his neck grabbed his arm and pulled him through the shop. "Not here. You come with me. I got just what you need."

Con jerked his arm from the other's grip and planted his feet. The man looked back at him. He shook his head. "No attitudes, here. You need clothes. I got 'em for just the right price. A lot of you people come here first."

The man turned and walked toward a curtained opening in the back of the shop. Con followed.

He entered a room lit by two windows on either side of a door. From the view through the dirty glass panes, it opened onto an alley. There were two tables loaded with folded garments—trousers on one, blouses on the other. The shopkeeper turned and looked him over.

"Hmmm. You're pretty big—least you look like you will be when you get over that slop they fed you in there." The man riffled through the clothing, seeming to touch everything yet the stacks were left undisturbed. Finally, he pulled a set of trousers and a blouse from the tables. The trousers were brown. The blouse was a dark blue.

"Here, try these on." He handed them to Con and pointed toward a door in the back of the room. Con stepped through it into an empty closet. He quickly changed out of the gray uniform. The trousers were loose around the waist but not uncomfortable. They hung to his sandals. The blouse was loose fitting with the front open to the middle of his chest. A leather string wove back and forth across the opening and could draw the collar closed if desired. The baggy sleeves stopped halfway down his forearms, ending in a cuff with a drawstring that could hold them there.

"One Gold and your old uniform."

Con looked up at the man. "You know how much they gave me?"

"I know, boy, but I ain't cheatin' you. I made these clothes so that I could sell them to you people when you got out at a price I knew you could afford. It's a public service, like."

Not having much choice, Con handed the man his old clothes and the coin. The two silvers he jingled in his pocket and stepped toward the door of the shop. The shopkeeper grabbed his arm. "Go out the back, son. That way nobody knows you came from here and they won't know that you just got fresh out of that place."

Con frowned, thinking that it was more likely the shop keeper didn't want his more affluent customers to know he sold goods to people like Con. He stepped out of the shop into the alley.

At the street, he entered the traffic and walked in the direction the soldier had said was the gate. Nothing looked familiar and he could not see the wall of the City. The sun was far in the west. It would not be this day that he found the way out.

Con's stomach growled. Breakfast had been a long time before. The jingle of the silvers in his pocket started him looking around for an inn. A large, colorful sign hung from a black iron rail stuck into the stones of one of the building fronts caught his eye. Even from half a block away, Con could see that it proclaimed the "Grand Inn."

He walked to the front door and pushed it open.

Inside the thick oak door, Con found himself in a large, low-ceiling room. Bulky whitewashed wooden columns rose every ten feet or so to support black timber beams that stretched across the room. Rough white plaster filled the spaces between the beams. The walls were dark wood from the stone floor to a height of four feet. Above that, they were the same rough plaster as the ceiling. Round tables of wood filled the floor space. Heavy wooden chairs surrounded them. On the four faces of every column about five feet off the floor, black iron lamp holders were attached to the wood. About half the lamps were lit. The lenses were all clean and polished and the flames lit the room with a soft, flickering radiance.

The door closed with a click behind him. The sound of the street ceased, replaced by the soft murmur of the conversation in the room. Con stepped forward, aiming toward one of the tables along the back wall.

He pulled out a chair next to the wall, wanting his back to something and his face to the crowd. Before he was completely seated, a man in a stiff, white apron approached. He held a slate in one hand and chalk in the other. Con adjusted his chair and said, "What do ya' got?"

The waiter pointed with the chalk at a large slate hung over the mantel. The menu of the day was printed there with prices. Con ran his eyes down the list, realizing there was little there he could get for two Silvers. But, toward the bottom, there was one thing.

"Stew and bread."

The waiter nodded and waited, chalk poised over the slate. Con looked away. The waiter shrugged, then walked toward the kitchen.

Con glanced around at the almost empty room. Conversations were quiet, with only an occasional word discernible. Someone across the room laughed out loud but peace returned quickly. Even the bustle of the wait staff seemed as background to the overall ambiance of quiet gentility.

A large group of well-dressed men entered the building. There was brief laughter and calling between them and others in the room. Then they, too, seemed to adapt and walked quickly to a large table by the hearth. Although they still laughed and talked, the noise melded with the buzz of the other conversations and became a buzz itself.

Several couples came in and quickly found seats in the dining room.

The noise level increased with each addition but the prevailing buzz soon absorbed it, grew to accommodate it, and then settled into familiarity again. As the buzz grew, tension drained from Con. He sat back and smiled. This was what he had been looking for, thinking about, dreaming of during those quiet hours on his rock. This was what he had wanted—to be among people who could talk, relax, and live well. This was what he had wanted—without knowing it—until the Dragon had taken his father and killed his sisters.

Maybe this was still what he wanted.

The waiter returned with a flask in his hand. He set a glass before Con and started to pour red liquid into it. Con held up his hand. "No. I don't...."

The waiter cocked his head to one side. "You sure? It's free. About the only thing the skinflint gives away. He thinks it makes people eat more."

Con shrugged. "Fine. If it's free, I'll take it."

Con sipped from the glass. It was good—like the tart wine that his father made from the fall apples. He drank more, letting the gentle warmth radiate out from his belly to his limbs. He sat back and stroked his chin, starting at the shot of pain as he rubbed the bruise.

A tall man in a luxurious cape entered the room. He removed the cape with a flourish and held it out for the smiling attendant. He wore dark trousers and a navy blue jacket. His blouse was ruffled between the lapels of the jacket. Con expected to see white hair and a lined face to go along with the obvious affluence of the man. When the wide brimmed hat was swept toward the attendant, though, it revealed a young man—not much older than Con. He had a laughing face and eyes that sparkled with energy.

The man stood at the doorway for a few minutes, sweeping the room with his eyes, as if looking for someone he knew. His eyes swept past Con, then quickly reversed, coming to rest on his face. With deliberate paces, the man walked across the flagstone floor to Con's table.

"Excuse me. You have an extra chair. May I join you?"

The man had straight black hair, combed straight back. It was neatly trimmed at the collar and around the ears. There was a pin stuck in the front of his shirt with some sort of shiny stone mounted on it. His smooth face was tanned deeply—as if he was an outdoors person, not what Con would have expected from his current dress. His right hand, which held the head of a walking stick, was also tanned but soft—not the hand of a working man. A paradox, Con thought, the word dredged from some long ago vocabulary lesson in a one room school in a village so far from the City as to be in another Valley.

Con realized he was staring and had not answered the man. He nodded and pointed at the chair.

The man laughed and sat down. "Don't let the dress fool you. I am not a popinjay or a fop. I dress this way in the City because it is what they expect of me. Where I do my real work, I dress more reasonably."

Con smiled. "And what would that real work be?"

The man held a hand out over the table and twisted it back and forth. His head swayed back and forth with it. "Ah, a little of this. And, a little of that. And all of it full of money."

He laughed again, then stuck out his hand. "I'm Decev Croesus."

Con took the hand and shook it. The man had a firm grip. "Con Ataxia."

The pair fell silent, not having anything of common to start a conversation. The tension, though, soon became unbearable and Con blurted, "You better flag one of them waiters. They seem to be ignoring you."

Decev shook his head. "No. I eat here quite often. They know what I want. I'm sure it will be out shortly."

Decev looked him up and down. "So. You are a farmer and you recently had a bout with Wellbeing or with the Rebel jail. Why in the Valley would a farmer be in the City at this time of year and what could you have possibly done to deserve that fate?"

Con's jaw dropped and pushed himself back from the table. "Mister. Perhaps you better explain yourself. The only people who know that kind of stuff is the Dragon or the Army—and I ain't interested in either right now."

Decev held up a hand and laughed again. "Con, you are right. I apologize. I am too impetuous. I am always too impetuous. But I am not spiritual and I have nothing to do with the Dragon. Each of those bits of knowledge I got simply from observation."

Con looked down the front of him, not seeing anything that would have given away any of that. He looked back at the man—still keeping his distance from the table.

Decev smiled. "You don't know? OK. Look at your shoulders and your arms. City people aren't built like that. I deal with both farmers and City people all the time. Farmers have a special musculature that City people never develop because they don't need it. But I can see that you have deteriorated somewhat. So, you aren't just off the farm."

Con glanced at his hands, softer now than they had ever been. He nodded. "OK. So how did you know the rest? Did they brand my forehead, or something?"

"Well, that was somewhat of a guess. You wear the clothes of an ex-prisoner but your eyes aren't dull like most of them. I figured they must have thrown you out before they could complete their work on you."

Con looked at his new clothes. There didn't seem to be any identifying features there. "What do you mean, ex-prisoner clothes? I just bought these."

"From a shop about three blocks from here, right?"

Con nodded.

Decev nodded back. "And you paid five silvers. And you were taken to the back room and shown a table full of these."

Con shook his head. "Paid a Gold for them."

Decev barked a short laugh. "The old crook has raised his prices again. Con, that man sells the same type of clothes to everybody that gets out of there. You came out in a gray uniform. You paid a Gold for another uniform—this one of brown trousers and blue shirt. Everyone who sees you knows you just got out of Wellbeing."

Con glanced around nervously. Decev waved at him. "Don't worry about it. Just get rid of them as soon as you get a job."

Decev looked over the dining room again, then turned back to Con.

"So, why are you in town?"

Con shrugged. This was not the time to tell a stranger about Dragons and sisters and lost fathers. In fact, he wasn't sure he wanted to tell anyone ever again about those things. "I had business after Market."

Decev snorted. "Must've been important business to keep a farmer from his summer fields."

Con nodded but did not speak. Decev shrugged and turned toward the kitchen door. "Where is that meal?"

A waiter approached with a steaming bowl and a plate of dark bread. He set it before Con and retreated. Decev waved a hand at him. "Please, go ahead and eat. I am sure that my meal will be here soon."

Con nodded and reached for the bread, the rich, spicy smell of the stew drawing out growls of complaint from his stomach. He dipped the bread into the thick, pungent liquor and stuffed it in his mouth. The strong, rich taste filled his nose and throat. He quickly dipped his spoon into the bowl and started to eat with earnest.

A chuckle from the far side of the table stopped him. He looked up to find an amused Decev watching him. Decev waved his hand again. "Go ahead, Con. I know what that first meal after that pap that Wellbeing serves must be like."

Con returned to his bowl, unconcerned about what Decev or anyone else thought. The small bowl was soon empty except for a trace of gravy. Con mopped it up with the last of his black bread.

"Ah, finally."

Con looked up. A man weaved his way through the tables carrying a large tray over his head. He stopped at Decev's side, lowered the tray for his inspection and held it. Decev looked over the contents. A ham, sliced then put back together, anchored the display at the center. The roasted carcass of a small bird, like a chicken only much smaller, was in one corner. A long, fleshy fish, head and tail still attached, was in the opposite corner. Stacks of dark, sliced meat filled another, and a rack of ribs, roasted and covered with some aromatic sauce completed the tray. Between the meats there were steaming plates of vegetables—carrots, peas, asparagus, sliced beets, mashed turnips, roasted potatoes.

Con stuttered. His whole family could not eat a meal like that—in a week. He stared first at the tray, then at Decev, who nodded at the landlord. The tray was lowered gingerly to the tabletop.

Decev waved it off. "Oh, I just get all this so that I know there will be something I like."

Con swallowed the bread in his mouth and looked back at his place setting. The empty stew bowl was a mimic of his still empty stomach. His eyes returned to the tray.

Decev pointed at the tray with his fork, swallowing hard. "You want some of this?"

Con looked away quickly. "No, the stew was fine. It's very good."

Decev nodded, stuffing a fork full of carrots into his mouth. Around the vegetables, he said, "You're sure. I always have much more than I can eat. And I know the landlord will take it back in the kitchen when I am finished and sell it all again."

Con swallowed hard, his eyes riveted to the plate of food. Finally, his desire overcame his pride. "Well, if it would be a help to you."

He dipped his fork into the tray, taking first some ham, then some of the ribs. Vegetables were next. He filled his bread plate, then the stew bowl.

Decev reached over with a knife and cut a piece of the fish. "Here," he said, lifting the delicate white meat on the side of the knife. "You have try this. It is a specialty of the old crook."

They ate. And ate some more. When Con thought that he could not get any more into his stomach, Decev snapped his fingers. A waiter nodded from across the room.

Decev waved the landlord over to take away what remained of the tray of food. Con pushed back from the table, full—no, stuffed for the first time since he left the farm. He rested his hands on his belly. A loud belch drew the stares of some patrons close by but Con didn't care. He was happy.

Decev smiled. "Well, Con. It is apparent to me that you are not going back to the farm. What are you going to do?"

Con's eyes narrowed. Again, this man was reading his mind, for he had just said to himself that perhaps he would not go back to the farm this fall. Perhaps, he would continue his quest—or a similar one: to find the resources he needed to fix the things that were wrong.

Two waiters arrived carrying small trays. They set them on the table, one before Con and one before Decev. In the center of the tray was a small, delicate china bowl with slices of a white fruit in it. The slices were covered in a brown sauce.

Unsure what to do with this, Con looked up as Decev winked. "Watch."

One of the waiters lit a straw off of a nearby lantern and held it over Con's dish. There was a weak "pop" and a blue flame jumped up several inches above the bowl. Con scooted back from the table quickly. Appreciative murmurs sounded from the nearby tables.

The flames quickly subsided. Decev, smiling, picked up a spoon and held it over the bowl. He looked at Con and nodded. A waiter handed Con a metal spoon. Con looked at the bowl, then followed Decev's lead. He lifted one of the wafers of fruit to his mouth. Sweetness, as if he was eating honey from the comb, flooded his mouth—along with a bite in the back of his throat. All in all it was very tasty.

Decev sat back. "Con, it may appear so, but I'm not really trying to poke into your business. I spied you when I came through the door and realized you were just the type of person I wanted: smart, experienced," he pointed at Con's clothes. "I know you have been around enough now to know what's what."

"And you are a farmer. Con, I can't tell you how much that can mean to my business. A man who knows the City and the Farm. Just what I need."

Con stared—still wondering what the man had up his sleeve. When he didn't react, Decev's shoulders slumped. "And suspicious, to boot. Well, that's an advantage too."

He pushed back his chair and stood. "Let's go someplace more private to discuss this." Decev strode out of the dining room toward the sleeping section of the inn.

Con pushed back his chair unsure he wanted to follow. The aftermath of the meal he had just finished, though, was not just a stuffed feeling but a sense of obligation also—something that Decev had counted on, Con was sure. He rose and followed the man

Decev approached a low counter and gestured to the man standing there. The man lifted a key off a rack on the wall behind him and handed it to Decev. "All ready, Mr. Croesus."

Decev took the key and turned toward Con. "Where are you staying the night, Con?"

Con started to answer, then realized that he had no place to stay. His only accommodations since leaving the farm had been with Fourberie and in Wellbeing. He certainly could not go back to either place. "An inn down the road," he lied.

"Marvelous! But say, why don't you move up to this one? I do want to talk to you and it may be very late by the time we have concluded."

Without waiting for an answer, he turned to the man behind the desk. "Would you have another room for my friend?'

The clerk looked Con up and down, then sniffed. "For a friend of yours, we can arrange it, Mr. Croesus."

"Good, it's settled. Give him a key and we will be on our way."

The clerk laid a key on the counter. "That will be two Golds."

Con's belly tightened. He had no Golds. He now had no Silvers. He looked toward the doorway, intent on making some excuse and exiting. Decev, though, intervened.

"None of that, now George. Mr. Ataxia will pay as I do, when he leaves."

The clerk bowed slightly. "As you say, Mr. Croesus."

Decev took the key from the counter and headed up the steps. Con hesitated, unsure of what to do. He could follow—and put himself into a debt he could not pay—or he could run. His feet wanted to walk out. His hands strained to reach toward the door. His heart, though, wanted to follow—to get one night in an inn like this one, even if it meant working in the stables or the kitchen for the next month to pay it off.

He headed up the steps. Decev looked over his shoulder and nodded. A smile spread across his face as he turned back to the steps.

The room they entered was large—twice or three times as large as his bedroom on the farm. The floor was covered with a thick carpet the color of golden fleece. The walls were hung with tapestries—the progressive stages of a wolf pack bringing down a stag. On the wall on his right, the wolves brought down the noble stag, not with out significant loss of their own to the pointed antlers and sharp hooves.

A small fireplace was centered on the rear, outside wall. It was empty of flame on this warm night. Two lamps, mounted on either side of the room, lit the scene. There was a door way in the wall to the left. Since there was no bed in this room, Con assumed it led to the bedchamber.

"Sit down, Con." Decev pointed at a large, winged, overstuffed chair. "You look like that dinner has weighed you down."

The chair was soft. Con sunk into it and it seemed to wrap him in cotton arms as his head sunk into the pillow between the two wide wings. Decev sat opposite him in a similar chair. He removed his shoes, scooted a small fabric covered stool in front of him and put his feet upon it. He waved at Con. "That's what they're there for."

Con loosened his sandals and slid them to the floor. Then he did the same with the small stool near his chair.

"Well, Con, is this the life?"

Con stammered a little. "Decev, I can't….I can't a…"

"You can't afford it?"

Con nodded.

Decev waved his hand in front of him. "I didn't think you could. Not too many farmers can. Don't worry about it. I've arranged to have it all on my bill."

Con frowned. "Why?"

"Because I needed to talk to you. And I needed to talk to you in private. I want you to accept my offer—and I wanted you to see the rewards you would get for doing so."

Decev stood up and walked to the mantle of the fireplace. On it was a tray with a glass decanter and two goblets. He poured an amber fluid from the decanter into each, gave one to Con, and resumed his seat.

He sipped the liquid then set the goblet on a table next to his chair. "Con, you said you are a farmer. My guess is that you are, then, also a Rebel?"

Con shrugged. "Rebel. Army. All seems to be the same to me. They all talk. They don't do nothin'."

Memories of the Militia's battle came back but he thrust them away. Absently, he lifted the goblet and sniffed. The smell was pungent but very pleasant. He gulped the liquid.

"Gak!" His throat closed off. Tears sprang from his eyes and he gasped for breath. Finally, he wheezed out a breath. "What was that?"

Decev roared. "Brandy, lad. Haven't you ever had it?"

Con shook his head, still unable to breath freely. Decev roared again. He leaned forward and patted Con's knee. "It'll get better, Con." Then he laughed again.

Con set the goblet on the table. "Maybe I'll get back to that later."

Decev nodded and chuckled. "I did the same thing with my first gulp. It does, though, get better with practice." Decev lifted his goblet. "And, if you sip it instead of guzzling it." He sipped gently.

"I was a Rebel when I first came to the City. Now, though, I lean toward the Army. Oh, not those fanatics that have to talk about the Commander all the time but there are some very sensible Regiments out there."

"Like the Militia?" Con asked.

"The Militia? Commander, no!" Decev grinned and cocked his head. "Now, that was a stupid oath wasn't it, considering the topic of conversation."

Con smiled. His father had used that oath all the time: calling on the Commander when he actually never expected him to show up—or wanted him to, for that matter.

"Con, the Militia is the worst of all the Army. Not only will they talk your ear off about the Commander but keep talkin' about Cleato—that old time Army general—as if he was alive today. No. Stay away from that Militia.

"I'm talking about the Lion's Head Regiment or the Living Brook Regiment—sensible groups like that. They make more sense to me than the militants on either side—Rebel or Army."

Decev leaned forward in his chair. He rested his elbows on his knees and peered over the goblet in his hands. "You see, Con, none of these men who are making policy for the Army or the Rebellion take into account what you and I both know—that life has to go on and the best way for that to happen is for the business of life to continue. Regardless of what Army they are in—or if they are not in any—after their weekends they have to come back to the real life of the City and make a few Golds or Silvers."

He sat back and lifted the goblet in a salute. "I realized that shortly into my search for truth and that truth has yielded me many returns." He sipped from his drink.

Con rested back in his chair. The wine, the food, and the brandy, which he again tried, all worked to put him to sleep. He wasn't doing all that much to fight it. Con realized that Decev had quit talking.

"I can see your point." was all he could finally get out, nodding knowingly as he said it.

"Are you tired?" Decev asked.

Con straightened. "Oh, no, no." Then he laughed. "I'm afraid that the food and the drink have taken their toll. But I ain't so disabled as to not listen to you. Please continue."

He stood and walked around the room to shake off the grogginess that had set in.

Decev watched him and smiled. He waited for Con to sit back down before he continued.

"Con, you are an honest man. I think perhaps I have a job for you. Would you like that?"

His quest flashed before him. Pictures of the beast in the citadel and his sister's bodies intruded on the pleasures. Con shook them off. "That, of course, depends on what you want me to do. If you are going to tie me into a boring, useless, repetitive job like farming where I have no chance of finding what I'm looking for, then I can't say that I want a job."

"I can appreciate that," Decev said. "I felt the same way when I started. Let me assure you. What I have for you will be the enabling of your search not the impediment."

Con glanced sideways, narrowing his eyes. "Decev, I'm just a farm boy. What could I do for you that would be worth your pay?"

Decev slapped his thigh. "Good question—good mind. Look, Con, I need a man who likes adventure and wants to move up into a life style where some of this is available to him." He waved his hand around his head.

Con looked around and acknowledged Decev Croesus's business acumen with a nod. It was an excellent tactic. Still, his main reason for being in the City was to find his father, not to go into business. Con stared at the ceiling and tried to think straight.

His sisters were dead. Nothing he could do now would help them. His father was in captivity and Con had no way of freeing him. He needed resources—resources that had thus far eluded him, except for that ridiculous offer by the Militia. A business venture may prove to be just the sort of thing he needed. If he had the cash, the ability to pay the militia—perhaps then he could get one of those swords and some help. Everyone responded to the offer of a little cash.

Con stood and stuck out his hand. "I'll take it."

"Good. Good!" Decev jumped up and pumped his hand.

"Why don't we both retire then? Join me for breakfast in the great room." He led Con to the door. "At six then?"

They shook hands and Con walked unsteadily out of the room. The hallway seemed to shift under his feet and he bumped the walls gently a few times before he found the gold numbers that marked his room. He tried to insert the key into the lock but the keyhole kept moving around. He speared it with quick jabs, but it eluded him each time. By grasping the door handle with one hand and the key with the other he was able to limit its oscillations enough to hit a bull's eye. He turned the key and pushed the door silently open.

The Great Room was not crowded at six. Most of the City would not move for another hour. Early rising was second nature to Con and he had been up for two hours, bathing and shaving, to make himself as presentable to his new employer as possible.

Decev was also an early riser and waited at a table heaped with food. Con smiled and walked to the table.

They ate and indulged in the small talk of men in the morning whose main concern is filling their bellies and not starting the business of the day. When he was satisfied, though, Con broached the subject. "Well, Decev, I am your employee. Just what is it that I am employed at?"

Decev pulled a thin cigar from his vest pocket and nipped the end off with his teeth. Using it as a pointer, he said, "I'm glad to see that you are eager, Con. I knew you would be so I brought these." His free hand dipped below the table and retrieved a roll of parchment from a case at his feet.

"And what is this?" Con grasped it and spread it on his lap.

Decev pulled the small candle from the table and lit his cigar. He waved at the thick smoke. "They are a proposition for you, a partnership agreement in a venture of mine. It will yield big dividends for me. For you, it will be the start of a new life and, if handled well, could lead to your financial security."

Con dropped the parchment quickly onto the table. "I'm sorry if I've somehow misled you, Decev. I do not have any money for investment."

Decev cut him off with a wave of his hand. "I'm not asking for any. What I need from you are your wits and your time, of which this project will require much. For that investment, with my backing, you'll get twenty-five percent of the profits. Any losses will be absorbed by me and all capital will be provided by me."

"But what can I possibly do for you that would be worth that risk?"

"Give it time, Con. You'll see."

With that they rose and left the inn. They walked slowly at Decev's direction. The early street was deserted and the upper parts of the building glowed in the bright, yellow light of the rising sun.

"Look, Con, each year at Harvest, I travel the farm country and purchase crops. Although most of the crops are sold at Market, there are always a few farmers who have not sold all of their crops or who have a crop much larger than anticipated."

Con grimaced. "You're a bootlegger."

Decev drew himself up in mock indignation. "An entrepreneur, Con. An Entrepreneur. I go to these with cash in hand, a closed mouth, and a wagon. The rules of Market do the rest.

"I admit that, since the farmers have already made the best deal they can for each field, they have tentatively committed all their produce to the original buyer, the one who gave them the down payment at Market. But that contract has a minimum delivery clause in it and that is what the price buys. The merchants consider the extra the field might bring in as profit for their early investment. To these farmers, it's a big loss of capital."

Con glanced sideways at him. Decev nodded. "It's a bad deal for the farmers and nothing but gain for the merchants."

Con nodded also. "But it is the normal way for business and it is the law,"

Decev shook his head. "Not really. The merchants want you to believe that but the only legally binding part of the contract is the minimum delivery clause, on which payment was based. The farmers feel cheated when they grow extra crops for which they can't get paid. My business becomes simple.

"I buy up the extra crops of those farmers which have them at a drastically low price. And I also buy any unsold crops at an even lower price. Then I resell them to farmers whose fields have not yielded the agreed upon amounts and who would end up paying a penalty to the merchants. So I provide a service to Market which keeps it all in balance."

Con smiled and shook his head. "You're a bootlegger."

Decev laughed and pounded Con on the back.

"Well, I admit that I do normally end up with a wagon load of produce which I have purchased for ridiculously low prices. And there is no sense in letting good food go to waste. I bring it into the City and sell it to some needy vendor who hasn't gotten all he'd hoped for from the Merchants."

"And you normally make a good profit from this charity work?"

Decev half closed his eyes and smiled broadly. "I can normally pay for the trip, I guess."

"Doesn't the Government stop you?"

Decev smirked. "Actually, since it results in lower food costs for the majority, and only the fat-cat merchants pay for it, bootleggers are respected as good businessmen. The Rebel Government officially looks down on the practice but in reality ignores it".

Con had seen these men in the fields. The farmers, including Con's father, all dealt with them at one time or another for all of them found themselves in one of the two conditions necessary for the plan to work at one time or another. Some farmers, who would never sell their excess crops to the bootlegger because of their integrity, would not hesitate to buy excess crops from him to make up a deficit in their own contracts. And there were always enough farmers with excess who would sell to make the system work. The farmers didn't really like the bootleggers, nor did they respect them, but they did find them a necessity for survival.

"It sounds as if you have done well, Decev. For what purpose would you need me?"

Decev leaned close. "You are right, my friend, I have done well but I could be doing better. I could be covering much more territory and therefore end up with much more produce if it weren't for the necessity of hauling the surplus back to the City then spending days selling it. I need someone in town arranging for sales so that the wagon can spend more time out in the farms."

Con held up one hand. "But I can't sell and I don't know the prices to charge."

Decev nodded. "That is what I will do. I want you to go to the farms and buy for me. If you can get word to me prior to coming back to the City or if we can purchase a warehouse in the City you will be able to spend all your time buying and I selling. I figure that you can spend at least fifty per cent more time buying than I could and that means even greater profits."

Con thought it over for a minute. It certainly made sense. A good season and frugal living would put him into a position of having the resources to continue the pursuit of his father's captor. Several seasons would make him a very rich man, able to hire the militia or whatever necessary to make his attack successful. And a few years of good living wouldn't hurt anyone.

"But I do not have the buying and selling experience that you have. I'm not sure I could get as good a deal for us as is needed for the big profits you expect."

"Don't worry about that. The farmers who won't sell will tell you quickly and the ones who will are desperate enough to give you the crops without any long-winded bargaining sessions. But to be sure, I'll go out with you for the first week. I seldom have enough surplus to bring back in for a week anyway."

That settled it. For a short time—a few years at most—he would team up with Decev. "I'll join you as a partner, Decev Croesus," Con said. Decev smiled and put his arm around Con's shoulder as they walked into his office building.

Chapter 13

Con slapped the reins on the rump of the lead horse. A month had passed. Fall touched the trees, bringing amber and gold to replace the pervasive green of summer. Ridge after ridge spread out in front of the lumbering, half full wagon. Wave on wave of color advanced across the valley—trees, wheat, barley—crop and forest all responding to the cool nights and lowering sun. Con Ataxia noticed none of it. His hands held the reins lightly and his mind dwelled on the calculations of profit. All four horses, trained to pull, used to pulling, living only to pull that wagon, walked lightly in the traces, moving the wagon slowly over the low hills.

The figures staggered him. As a farm boy he never knew abundance. That day, thousands of Golds were in his grasp. It was intoxicating, even more intoxicating than the brandy that had swelled his head five weeks before.

The harvest had run its course. Filling the wagon one last time would do it. Within two days, he would be back in the City. He had visited every major farm in his region and had also stopped at many of the smaller ones, an innovation he had brought to the business.

The smaller farmers of the valley had to band together as one to attract the attention of the Merchants. This didn't often work out because they were fiercely independent—to the point of all failing instead of cooperating. Often, they came back from Market with no buyer.

Although never sure of his reception at a large farm, he never doubted the feelings of the small ones. Since he understood and sympathized with their plight, he often gave them much better prices than his partner had in the past (if he stopped at all) and better than he was giving to the large farmer. Word had gotten around to these farms and Con was welcomed. Crops became easier to acquire and there was more than enough to meet the demand at the farms who had oversold their yield. His load was in need of shedding more often than Decev's had been.

He had returned to the City, not once per week, but once every three to five days. His partner was ecstatic and praised him exuberantly for the abundance. Con wondered how ecstatic he'd be when he saw that the profits were going to be lower on a per pound basis due to the higher price Con paid the small farmer.

Soon he would know.

A small lane ran off from the main road through a stand of trees. It was not really a lane, just a rutted trail leading back between two broken down fences. Behind the trees, Con saw chimney smoke. If there was a farm then there would be crops. If crops then perhaps excess. He turned the horses and started back, being careful of the deep ruts.

"Hey, you! Don't be goin' in there."

Con spun on the wooden seat. A farmer, head covered with short gray hair that stood straight up and smoking a long, corn cob pipe sat upon his own wagon, waving Con to him with a big right hand.

Con set the brake, climbed down, and walked out to the road. "Morning to you. Is there somethin' I can do for you?"

The man was dressed in a one-piece blue coverall. He had brown boots instead of the normal sandals. A dirty, white undergarment covered his chest and arms.

"Nay, but there's something I'll do for you, bootlegger. Don't be goin' back that way. It's evil. That place has been under a curse all year. There'll be trouble awaiting you just as it's awaited every other soul who's ventured back there."

Con's eyebrows rose. "What kind of trouble?"

"Tis a widow, newly made, who lives on that farm. They run afoul of the Dragon and he's been seen there, attacking and devouring—him or his followers."

"A new widow?" Pangs of guilt shot through Con's chest—a vision of his own mother trying to get in a harvest that was too much for her. He forced it back down, justifying his absence quickly with the wagon of profit behind him. "Hasn't anyone tried to help her?"

"Aye, lad. At first, just after her husband died, many a one of us went over to lend a hand. But like I said, the place is under a curse and for all our help it just fell apart. Besides, whenever we'd help her, the Dragon would send foul happenings our way. Soon we gave up and no one's been back there in months."

The old farmer lit up the pipe stuck in the corner of his mouth. He puffed vigorously filling the air around his head with white smoke. "You won't be gettin' no crops from them, bootlegger."

"How d'you know it's the Dragon doin' things to this farm?"

"Can't be nothing but. Things happen that couldn't be done by no one else. Besides, it was common knowledge that Col Porteur was saying things and doing things that was going to bring down the wrath of the Dragon."

"What kind of things?"

"Why, shoot, boy, old Col had joined the Army. At his age, no less." The old man shook his head and laughed. "Had a wife and two kids and still he joined the Army. Should have known better, if you ask me. Anyway, he was out preachin' the Army line to all the farmers in this region. Looked like he might make a few recruits, too.

"But that surely ended. The Dragon just slipped up on him one day and slit him open. Or maybe it was one of his cronies. But anyway, it was done and there has been attacks on that place, reg'lar, ever since."

Con turned and looked up the road again. The old man dropped his voice and glanced from side to side. "I'll give her this. She ain't give up."

Strange emotions rose up in Con. Fear. Anger. Hope. Guilt. Some combination of all of them played in his mind. He had to go back to that house to talk to the woman who was standing up to whatever the Dragon could do—including killing her husband.

"Still fightin', huh? I guess I have to see someone like that." Con shook the old man's hand and turned toward his wagon.

The old farmer slapped the reins and drove off, shaking his head.

Con picked up the reins but didn't snap them. The lead horse, who expected the command, looked back along its flank at the man who was not following routine.

The desire to see the woman and to know what she did to battle the Dragon was strong but fear was stronger. He remembered his ineffectual battle with the Dragon's army and the terror he felt when he looked into the eyes of that Raider.

A woman's voice came out of nowhere. "Are you going to visit me or are you, too, going to run?"

Con lurched around, startled by the sound. When his eyes found the voice's source his agitation turned to embarrassment. The threat was just a middle aged, thin woman standing on the other side of the broken down fence. In her hand was a staff and around her a few sheep grazed.

She had straight black hair, streaked with gray, drawn back into a tight bun. Her dress was long, going all the way to her ankles. It was a shapeless, drab gray.

Something in her face, or in her eyes, intrigued Con. Normally, resignation ruled the mood of the small subsistence farmer. This woman's eyes danced. There was life in her look and in her voice.

"You're the owner of this property?"

"I am that, ever since my husband passed on."

"May I light then and talk a little business to you?"

"Would not be good to talk business out here. Drive on to the farmhouse." She pointed at the tree line. "Yonder. I'll have you to a meal and we'll talk then."

"I'll not cause you trouble or expense to do business. What I need won't take all that long."

"From the looks of your wagon I know your business and from the looks of you, you've not had a decent meal in a while. You'll be neither trouble nor expense. Food we have aplenty and a meal has to be made anyway. Join us."

She turned and walked toward the tree line, cutting across the still green pasture.

As he wound his way back on the rutted path Con considered the farm and the situation. The old farmer's story didn't mesh with the image he now had. The woman he'd met was not a defeated widow. Her statement about food aplenty certainly did not indicate a farm in complete ruin.

Just beyond the trees was the barnyard. A large, two-story, clapboard house stood off to one side. Across the whole front was a porch with a shake roof like the main structure supported on thick knurled posts. Splotches of bare wood showed through the thin white paint on the sides of the house. The barn stood on the opposite end of the yard, directly across from the trees. It was large and unpainted and had a few boards missing on the sides. Other boards had been nailed onto it over ragged edged holes and across wide gaps in the siding. It was a poor farm—but not one that was falling apart.

The damage to the barn drew his attention again. Some of the damage was obviously caused by strong winds. Boards on the side were missing, broken off top and bottom in jagged rips. It was the large holes in the roof, three feet in diameter that puzzled him. They looked as if large stones had made them.

In Con's mind, the picture of a Dragon Raider lifting a huge rock formed. Con quickly got down from the wagon, involuntarily glancing toward the sky.

"I see you've seen the holes in my roof." The woman stood on the porch, grinning. "Don't fear, I've taken care of that line of attack."

Con looked at his hostess. "Excuse me?"

The woman turned and walked toward the house. He followed.

Two young boys met him just inside the door. They both studied him with cold stares. The woman laughed. "Boys. You'll scare off our visitor with your menacing looks. Now greet him in love."

The oldest, about fourteen and as tall as his mother, stepped forward and stuck out his jaw. He had pitch-black hair, straight and wild. He wore homespun britches with patches over both knees. His feet were bare. His shirt was also homespun and showed wear at the elbows and cuffs. The boy was deeply tanned. He was thin—but the thinness that comes from hard work, not from lack of food. The muscles of his arms, shoulders, and chest were just starting to form into adulthood. "I'm Albert. Whadda ya' want here?"

His mother boxed his ear gently. "Albert, enough." She turned to Con. "Sir, I am Priscilla Porteur. And these two scalawags are my sons, Albert and Charles."

Charles was four or five, with both front teeth missing. He was dressed in a miniature version of Albert's clothes. His feet were also bare. When Con stuck his hand out, the lad scooted behind his mother's skirts. Con stood erect again and bowed slightly at the waist. "I am Con Ataxia."

They were in a large kitchen. It was connected to the rest of the house by two large arches. Through one was a dark parlor with a spindly legged, upholstered couch and a matching chair. They stood neatly in front of a small fireplace. A thin, dark red and purple rug, worn thread bare in a path from the fireplace to the kitchen, covered the floor. The walls were painted dark blue. Against the far wall, next to a curtained window, was a bookcase filled with thick volumes.

A pot on the stove started banging its lid. Another stood next to it, also steaming. The kitchen was filled with the smells of bread baking, potatoes cooking, and some sort of spiced meat roasting in the glowing oven. His mouth began to fill with saliva as he looked around the light and airy kitchen.

"Mr. Ataxia, we have potatoes, corn, turnip greens, several breads, and a roast almost ready. If you care to wash up, I'll put the meal on."

"Albert." She turned to the young man who now stood at the door, eyeing Con with more curiosity than enmity. "Take Mr. Ataxia out to the pump."

Con sat to a meal with the family and stuffed himself. Mrs. Porteur was a good cook and she had not lied; food was plentiful. After the meal was over, Mrs. Porteur set the boys to cleaning up and led Con to the parlor.

"So you are a bootlegger, Mr. Ataxia," she said, the hint of a smile stealing across her face.

"An entrepreneur in an unrecognized trade, Madam. Bootlegger is the term given us by them that compete with us—a jealous lot, for sure. We are traders, aimin' ta fill a needed hole in the Market."

Mrs. Porteur laughed. "And you've a silver tongue, too, young man. But can you drive a bargain fit for an entrepreneur?"

"If you've excess crops, I'll buy 'em. My partner and I have a market for what I can get. There's room on my wagon for one more load and I've time to return to the City and still get a fair price for my work. I won't pay market price, 'cause I have to haul 'em, sort 'em, and find a buyer. But I won't cheat you, neither."

"Well, that will be a novelty. But, in truth, my whole crop is excess. And it is much too large for your one wagon to carry. It would take you at least two trips to haul it all."

It was too late in the year to dump anything at one of the nearby farms. They would have all left for market with their last loads, either having bought what they needed from another or taking their beating on the contract. Anything he picked up would have to be hauled all the way back to the city.

"Mrs. Porteur, I said I won't cheat you. And I won't. But you got to realize that I'll have no place to dump any of this. I got to haul everything back to the City. Ain't time for several trips."

She nodded. Then, raising one finger and winking, she said, "Maybe we can work something out."

The haggling began and soon ended with a deal favorable to both. Con paid her cash for the crop and she agreed to allow him the use of her wagon and one son to drive it to the City. The deal depleted the last of his cash. He had to sell the crops to realize any profit from the trip.

The afternoon was spent loading the wagons with the crops and covering them with the big tarp. Near four o'clock, they returned to the house for a cold drink and some rest. Con's curiosity was still piqued, though he was sure that the old man had lied.

"Madam," he said as he sipped on his glass of cool cider, "I'm glad that the rumors I heard weren't true. It's a pleasure to find you in such good fortune and health."

Mrs. Porteur cocked her head and frowned. "And what rumors are they, Mr. Ataxia?"

"Foolishness, really. An old farmer I met at the turn hailed me and said that your farm was cursed, that you were ruined, and that the Dragon had attacked and ruined you. I can see from that you had a rough year but you ain't devastated."

"Oh, but I was, Mr. Ataxia. The Dragon did everything he could to ruin me. My husband was slain by one of his soldiers and my barn ruined by giant hailstones. Every time the men of the area mended it the wind came and opened it up again. My crops were trampled in the fields by unseen feet. My livestock was run off time and time again."

Con leaned forward and studied her face. "That still goin' on? Don't seem like it. You've a good crop, although unsold until I came, and your sheep looked contented enough."

She nodded, returning his stare. "Occasionally an attack still comes, but for the most part, it has ceased."

No one in Con's experience had ever defeated the Dragon except the Militia. Mrs. Porteur did not seem to be a member of that group—at least, not on the surface. "The old farmer who told me about the curse also told me that your husband had joined the Army and was doing recruitin.'"

Mrs. Porteur winced. Her voice quivered a little as she started to answer, then firmed. "My husband and I both joined the Army. To answer your real question, yes that was when the attacks started. Before we were soldiers there was no reason for the Dragon to fear us. After we joined, he knew we held the power to defeat him and he feared for his authority in this area. When my husband started to recruit others—and doing it well—the Dragon attacked us."

Her jawbone set hard and her eyes glared as she spoke. Con admired her, and was a little awed.

She continued. "Just after my husband joined the Army, a group of Dragon Raiders visited the farm. There were four of them. They blustered and threatened and busted up a few things, but my husband and I stood our ground and threatened to call the Commander for reinforcements.

"They acted very surprised that we stood up to them. For Col and I it was a real triumph. We had only the week before finished our training and our ability to handle the sword was barely acceptable. In most regiments we would not be allowed to use the sword at all. But in the Militia, of which we had become members, the use of the sword in battle is encouraged. And with what little skill we had we were able to drive off the Enemy force. It was very heady. Pride crept in and we started thinking that we had already all the training we needed."

She stopped her story as a frown came over her and that pained look returned. Con, not knowing what to say or do, waited until she decided to continue. He sipped at the drink in his hand.

Mrs. Porteur sighed at some private thought. "Forgive me, Mr. Ataxia. I slipped into some memories."

Con stumbled for some words but had nothing really to say. Mrs. Porteur smiled.

"We thought that we were fully capable of fighting the Enemy. Instead of waiting on instructions from the Commander, we went off on our own plan of attack. I see now that the Dragon has much better tactical skills than we had credited him with. Those four didn't withdraw from the farm that day because we scared them. They withdrew because they wanted us to fall into the their trap, to draw us out before we had the experience and humility to be effective in battle.

"And they succeeded. They gave us a few more victories' and then they attacked. If we had stuck with the Commander and his plan, listening to his messengers, we would never have been drawn out where we were vulnerable. Our pride made us presumptuous, Mr. Ataxia, and we ended up out by ourselves, in an unprotected position.

"The Dragon's forces caught us out trying to recruit on a farm that had sold out to the Dragon. We knew they were there but our pride made us think we were invincible. The Raiders ran before us until we were well inside their perimeter. Then they turned on us and surrounded us. I can remember—the fear ate at me suddenly. The sight of twenty or so Raiders surrounding us, jeering at us, frightened me so badly that I screamed and started to run. Col ran with me. In our panic we forgot our swords. They dragged behind us, bumping the ground. That is what happens to young warriors.

"The Dragon's forces grabbed at me as we went through their lines. Col picked up his sword and slashed at them, cutting several of them in frightful wounds. He was not using it with skill, but the sword is so powerful that even ineffectually used, it will damage what it's aimed at. I've found since that it will even damage other soldiers when used in the wrong fashion.

"With Col's sudden attack, I was forgotten. He swung wildly and yelled for me to run. They all turned on him and I ran from the field, my sword still dragging uselessly behind me.

"My husband did not come off the field. Although several of them were down when I looked back, he was overcome finally by fatigue and shear numbers."

A sob welled up from deep inside her and she covered her eyes with her hands and shook violently. Con leaned over and touched her arm lightly to comfort her. She grasped at his hand and held it tightly.

"We never even called for reinforcements," she cried. "We panicked and forgot all our training."

She sobbed a few times more then choked it back. With shaking hands, she lifted her apron and dabbed at her eyes. "Forgive me, Mr. Ataxia. I didn't mean to burden you."

"There is nothing to forgive, Madam. You had quite an experience. Many wouldn'ta' stood it as well as you have."

Con waited for her to compose herself. His interest was not in her defeat. He was familiar with defeat. What he wanted to know was how she overcame the Dragon, how she had defeated him at his own game.

Mrs. Porteur rose and walked around the room, looking out the windows and picking up various knickknacks, staring at them, then putting them down. Finally she went to the bookshelf and pulled down a book. Without opening it she returned to the couch.

Con spoke, "But Madam, that was how you were defeated. How have you then turned that into victory?"

"It wasn't easy, Mr. Ataxia. The Dragon sent his forces against us daily. Our fields were trampled, our livestock spooked and run off, the barn was almost destroyed. The worst blow though was when our neighbors gave up trying to help. It wasn't that we were being defeated, as the old Man told you. But—let me continue in order. Then you'll understand."

She laid the book on the table and patted it with the tips of her fingers. The book was old and worn, with the binding coming loose. The title, which once was embossed on the cover, was all but unreadable. In the dim light of the parlor Con could not make it out. He sat back, knowing she would get to it when she was ready.

"When I returned to the farm, the Dragon's forces were already at work. I could see the damage as I ran through the fields. But my main concern was for the boys. I did nothing to combat what I saw, still dragging the sword behind me. I ran quickly until I reached the house. The boys were here, cowered in the parlor, and I gathered them up in my arms and hid back in a corner. We heard the sounds of destruction but did nothing.

"We cowered, but they never came. That was when I realized that the Dragon was afraid to attack anything truly given to the Commander for fear of the reprisal. It was then that we started to fight back. I went and got this book."

She lifted the old book from the table, still unopened. "It is our instruction manual. Each soldier gets one when he joins the Army. But it is more than just an instruction manual."

She had a strange smile on her face and her hands were poised to open the book when she seemed to decide against it and put the book back down on the table.

"In the manual it tells how to contact the Commander through—I really don't know what its through. If you call out in the right way, the Commander seems to know it. I'm not real sure how it works.

"I learned a lot in the next few weeks. The attacks continued but I was able to meet them with the knowledge in the book," again she patted the book on the table, "and, at times, with reinforcements. Some more damage was done but nothing very serious. The neighbors pitched in to help and we were overcoming all the obstacles when suddenly people quit coming around.

"When I asked what was wrong they evaded the question and my eyes. I heard the rumors that the farm was cursed and also of rumors that the farms of those who helped me were also cursed. Although we were defeating the Dragon at every turn, the rest of the people in the valley acted as if we were totally defeated. I didn't understand it until the Commander revealed to me through one of his messengers that the enemy had spread the lie among them and they chose to believe it."

"But didn't you battle that also?" Con asked, caught up in the story.

"Oh yes, we started to but were warned by the Commander not to do battle over that issue. So we backed off and the boys and I have cared for the farm and the animals ever since."

"But you didn't go to Market?"

"I couldn't leave the farm. The Enemy would have destroyed us."

"Then what good was the overcomin' if there would be no sale of your crops? It was a worthless victory, if you ask me."

"But I have sold my crop, Mr. Ataxia," she said, smiling.

Con guffawed. "Yes, but on'y because I happened along here and decided to buy one more load before goin' back to the City."

"Oh, you didn't just happen along, Mr. Ataxia. I'm sure the Commander directed your path. You see, he promised to sell the crop for me. You're just his agent, fulfilling his promise."

Anger leaped up into his throat. Why did all the Army types think it was a virtue to be under somebody else's control?

"Madam, I don't mean to be rude. No one but myself directs my path. It was good luck for you that I stopped here, but it was my decision not some order from the Army. I ain't a soldier, and I don't want to be." He stood suddenly.

Mrs. Porteur opened her mouth but no sound came out. Her eyes sent a message of hurt. Quickly, that was replaced with a resigned smile. "You are much like my Col, young man. I hope it does not take you as long to find the truth."

Her statement struck him like a fist but he kept his mouth shut. Slowly, he bowed low. "I'm sorry to end this peaceful time but I got to be headin' back to the City. I'm two full days journey by the best route and I got to get there before all the farmers do to get back some of the extraordinary price you got from me. Would it be possible for your son to leave with me now?"

Mrs. Porteur looked as if she would say something else. Her eyes rested on the book and she started to reach for it. She stopped, her hand almost touching it. Then she straightened and rose to face him. "Certainly, Mr. Ataxia. And I thank you for your compliment but I'm sure, at the price you paid, a fair return will be made."

They started to walk to the door when she once again looked at the book and started to speak. Once again she stopped herself in mid-word and said, "No, never mind. I'm sure you're not interested."

Con turned to look at the book, "What is it about that manual, Mrs. Porteur? You've wanted to show me somethin' for a while."

"It is—well, it is many things. It's the source of our strength." She stopped and shook her head. "No, that's not true. The Commander is the source. Cleato has often made that lesson plain to me."

"Cleato." Con's eyebrows rose. "You know him?"

"Why, of course. All members of the Militia know him and many of the Regular Regiments know him also. He is a leader among us. He is most often the messenger from the Commander and more than that, he directs the battles." Her eyes dropped away from Con's and she mumbled, "When the participants allow him."

Not wanting to get into that again Con continued, "I've seen him."

"You've met him? But I thought you said you weren't a soldier."

"Yeah, I've seen him," Con said, happy to be able to surprise her with some knowledge of his own. "Big man. Wears a hooded robe all the time."

A smile spread across her face and then her mouth formed into a tight "Oh!" like the girl in the square. She nodded. "Yes, he does appear that way to some. But, Mr. Ataxia, he normally only appears that way to one is he recruiting."

Con snorted. "Well, he ain't done that. And he might as well not ever try."

She spun toward the table so suddenly Con shied. "That does it. Mr. Ataxia, you've wanted to know about my victory ever since you came in here. I sense that you have a desire to fight the Dragon but don't know how. I don't want to snoop and if you don't want to tell me what your trouble with the Dragon is, that is your business, but I have the power you're looking for. More precisely, I am a user of that power and you can be also."

She waited expectantly.

Con shook his head. "You're right. I have trouble with the Dragon. But it's my trouble and I don't need to be burdening you with it. I'll find the way to fight 'im. And, I'll find the way to beat 'im."

Mrs. Porteur reached out and touched his arm. "You are a lot like my Col. Don't you know that the only way to defeat the enemy is through the Army? You don't have the ability."

Anger flared again. "Why is it that you soldiers always project your weakness on everyone else? I don't need the Army. I need a weapon. OK, I could use some help—but that's what I want. Help. All the rest of that stuff is not for me."

"You need more than help, Mr. Ataxia. You need the Commander."

Breath exploded from his lips. "Not the Commander. That sword you were using. I saw the other Militia with those swords also. That's what I need. With that sword I can at least fight."

Mrs. Porteur looked at Con without speaking. Con grew uncomfortable under the gaze and was about to spin around and leave when she turned and grabbed the manual on the table.

She lifted it up over her head and stared at Con, smiling. Con shrugged and shook his head.

The book began to glow. The glow grew into the air around it, bathing the whole room in a rose colored light. The intensity increased. Fire crackled in the air. Con reached for Mrs. Porteur to pull her from the flames but he was beaten back by the brightness. He tripped over the low table and landed hard on his back.

He bounced to his feet, getting turned around in the process. When he turned back, the fire was gone and Mrs. Porteur stood with a her hands raised over her head. A golden, two-edged sword reached from her raised hands toward the ceiling. It was thick, obviously heavy, yet the small, thin woman handled it with ease.

Con's mouth dropped open.

Mrs. Porteur lowered the sword and let the tip rest on the floor. She stood strong and solid, the image of a soldier prepared for battle. "This is the sword, Mr. Ataxia. It is available to all soldiers of the Commander's Army, though many have never taken up the training and some refuse to even acknowledge its existence.

"Con, there are many different soldiers out there with the sword available to them. Some parade with it, some abuse it, deliberately dulling its sharp edge or removing the blade completely, some carry it in its fullness yet never draw it against the enemy, and still others carry it and use it but only on each other. The common denominator between all of them is that the sword is always available, in its full strength and power, if they will only use it.

"You could have it. And I sense that you could learn to use it effectively, if you'd only give up your rebellion."

There it was—the sales pitch. Hidden, disguised cleverly, and with a new twist, just right to meet his current weakness, it was still the old "give up your independence and cow-tow to the Commander" routine. But she had made a mistake. It was not the Commander he needed. It was that sword. That was the one weapon that he knew the Dragon feared.

"Mrs. Porteur, I have a few Golds left. What will you take for that sword? I will not bargain with you. I will pay you whatever you desire. If I don't have enough now, I'll return with the difference. But I must have that sword."

Mrs. Porteur's eyes danced with amusement. "Con, I told you. If you want this sword, you can have it by joining the Army. You can't purchase it."

She laughed again. "Watch!"

She laid the sword down on the table. A flash and a loud pop shook the room. The sword disappeared. Where it had lain, the old, dog-eared book appeared.

Con was unable to react. Mrs. Porteur stood quietly, waiting for him. He looked at her, then at the book, mute. Finally, he managed to squeak out, "How?"

"The book is the sword, Con. It is transformed in the hands of a soldier into the fighting tool needed."

"But, how? You handled the book before and it did not transform. How did you do it then?"

"Con, that will all be in your training, if you'll give in and join."

Con snorted and turned away. He wanted to yell at that dense woman. It wasn't the Commander or the Army that he needed. He only needed that book. He spun on his heel and marched to the door. "We'll be off, now. If you will release your son to me?"

Mrs. Porteur's shoulders drooped. She stared with sad eyes for a few seconds, then shrugged. "Yes, of course. Let me fetch him. I'll only be a minute."

She left the room. Con walked to the table and lifted the book in his hands. It was a thick volume but identical in appearance to any book which has been used often. He tossed it in the air and shook it next to his ear. Nothing seemed out of the ordinary. He opened it, expecting to find it hollow with the sword somehow compressed within its limits. The book contained just paper, leaf after leaf. Each page was printed upon, like any other book.

"The power in here is the power I need." Con mumbled. "If I could have this, I could defeat the dragon."

He heard the scrape of feet along the hall and, before he could think about it, he dropped the book in his pack and buttoned the flaps over it. He lifted the pack and walked quickly to the door.

Albert appeared with his mother. He was not large but had been a worker for a few years already and therefore was solid. He carried his pack over his shoulder. They left the house together and he walked straight to the rear wagon.

Con threw his pack up on the lead wagon's seat and climbed after it. Guilt rose up to choke him but he controlled it and grabbed up the reins.

"Well, Mrs. Porteur, we'll be off. I'll send your son and your wagon back to you as soon as I can." He tapped the lead horse with the reins and the big wagon eased forward as the steeds leaned into the leather.

She looked up at him with sadness in her eyes, as if some secret thought suddenly distressed her. "Yes, please do send all my property back to me quickly, Mr. Ataxia."

Con glanced sharply at her, afraid that she knew of his theft, but more afraid of having to give the weapon back. There was no accusation in the stare only disappointment. Con quickly averted his eyes.

She knows, he thought. But even as the wagons left the barnyard she said nothing. She stared after them, her hand raised in an unspoken farewell, her face hopeful, expectant. Con continued, ignoring his screaming conscience.

Chapter 14

Con stood on top of the bouncing wagon. They had not covered more than a third of the distance and the sun was already low. Dark woods of oak and ash, the leaves blazing in the setting sun, surrounded them.

The single, rutted lane wound tortuously through the trees, following the natural twists of the land and skirting the large trunks. There was no place to pull two wagons off the lane. Con dropped back onto his seat and waved at Albert. The big wagons lumbered forward.

Within a quarter mile the land flattened, running straight between two high ridges as far as he could see in the dim light. On the left, under the branches of an old oak, there was a clear area. The tree's massive cover approached the lane's edge and extended full circle around the trunk for a hundred feet. The lowest branches were over fifteen feet from the ground and were so thick that the worst storm could not break them. The blackened remains of previous fires dotted the area like polka dots.

Con signaled the boy to pull off the lane with him. They lined the wagons side by side, then unhitched the stock and led them to the trunk of the tree. Little grass grew under the massive giant so Con fed the horses from the larder of the wagons. The boy started a fire and prepared some grain cakes for Con and himself'.

Night fell heavily on the forest as they prepared their food on an open fire. The dancing flames played on the bole of the tree and the lower limbs making them seem to dance and sway to the same crackling tune. Giant winged apparitions appeared on overhead branches as moths, drawn by the light, circled the flames. A tense silence settled over the area, abnormal because of the crackling fire and the man creatures who did not belong.

The snap of a branch or the sizzle of a too-wet piece of wood only made the silence heavier. Con and Albert stared into the flames, lost to their own thoughts, chewing on the grain cakes prepared by the boy. Pungent smoke and the smell of moldy leaves spiced the bland meal.

"No moon," Albert said.

Con jumped, startled at the sudden speech. He raised his eyebrows and looked over at Albert.

Albert pointed up and said, "New moon. Wouldn't get down here, though, even if there was."

Con nodded.

They both fell back into silence. The creatures around them decided the intruders were harmless. The quietness of the forest gave way to the din of living. Con ears pricked at the sudden noise, then he relaxed. The night creatures were better than a watchdog.

The two sat silently after eating, tired from bouncing and jerking on top of the wagons. Eventually, Con pulled his pack over to the fire and removed two blankets. He laid them out in a bed, the pack itself being his pillow.

As he lay down the book in the pack jabbed him in the head. The feel of it there brought a pang of guilt and he looked quickly at the boy to see if he noticed the sharp outline stretching the cloth. Albert threw out his own blankets and paid no attention to Con or his pack. Con breathed out a sigh of relief, then rested back on the pack, patting the hardness of the book.

Albert rose suddenly to his knees, glancing around the clearing, searching into the shadows as if he could see through the inky blackness. His mouth hung open and his brow knit. He bent low, then crawled to the fire, gathering dirt to smother it. As it went completely dark, Con jumped up to his knees and whispered, "What is it? What did you see?"

"I saw nothing."

"Then what did you hear?"

"Nothing," the boy said, waving at Con to be quiet.

Con stood and walked over to the fire. "Then why'd you kill a perfectly good fire and start actin' like you'd seen a ghost?"

"Don't start it again," the boy said. "The Dragon's forces are near."

"The Dragon? How do you know? Did you see 'im or smell 'im or somethin'?"

"I don't need to," Albert whispered. "I just know when he or his forces are about. I can tell without seeing or hearing or smelling them. I don't know what it is. Mama says it is a gift. She says when I get sent into battle it will be a big help. For now, I just use it on the farm to warn Mama, so she can get her sword out."

The mention of the sword pained Con again. The guilt started to rise like gall in his belly but he shoved it back down and put it out of his mind. If the boy was right, he would need that sword right there before the night was out.

Con rested on one knee and hushed his own heavy breathing. He listened closely. A grouse or chipmunk scratched for food in the underbrush. A small animal of prey moved through the brush, crushing the dry leaves rhythmically. It was normal. There was nothing to fear in the forest.

He listened for a while more then stood up, stamping the foot that had gone to sleep. "There is nothing there. The forest is alive. It is only your nerves and the darkness of this wood."

"No, Con. They are there. When I know, I just know and I'm not wrong. Before the night is out they will come searching for us. And they will probably find us."

The boy flopped down on his blanket and turned his back to Con, wrapping the blanket around him. Con returned to his own blanket and sat upon it. His confidence wilted before the sureness of the boy's predictions and the darkness of the wood. He watched the forest, listening with all his senses to those sounds, the absence of which would signal the intrusion of someone or something into their realm.

At some point he dozed—at least he couldn't remember the passage of time when next something caught his attention. He was suddenly alert but he could not figure out what it was that had alerted him. Albert was still wrapped in his blanket. The fire was just a few glowing coals. The forest was dead still.

The realization hit him with a force. The whole forest was dead still. He raised his head and listened.

Nothing.

He crawled over to the fire and threw on a few sticks. They smoked lazily, then burst into flame. He shook the boy awake, holding his finger to his mouth. "Someone's here."

Albert sat up immediately and appeared to be listening. He shuddered and whispered, "They're here. Very close."

They both stood and peered into the blackness. A tight ball of fear grew in Con's gut. The night was thick—the humidity of the forest, clinging—the fear making his skin crawl. No sound disturbed the silence of the forest except for the spasms of air rushing through his half open mouth as imagined movements were seen in the blackness.

A light breeze sprang up and the dry leaves overhead rustled. Con's pant legs began to make the same noise as his knees shook uncontrollably.

A shriek! An unearthly, ungodly shriek! It was like the sounds of two tom cats, their tails tied together and thrown over a branch—no, it was worse—there were no earthly similes to that terrible grating sound.

Con and Albert froze at the sound, unable to scream, run, or fall. The fear paralyzed every muscle. When he could, Albert dropped to his knees. Con peered around, trying to see the source of the noise.

"It is a beast, wounded by a hunter. Or a...a...a night animal, capturing its prey through fear," Con blurted.

"You are right on the last, Con," Albert said looking up from his busy-ness. "It is an animal of the darkness. But I don't think they are after one of the forest creatures. It is the Dragon's forces and it is us they are going to try to take tonight."

Con started to dispute the boy but a voice from the blackness interrupted him. "You have stepped in where you have no business, Ataxia."

Like when fingernails grate on slate, chills climbed Con's backbone, freezing him again.

The silence exploded in screams and taunts. All around them, outside the small ring of light cast by the low fire, noises erupted in the forest. Con twisted and turned trying to see the sources but the darkness remained solid. The boy remained on his knees repeating some chant.

"Show yourself, cowards," Con called into the darkness. "Show yourselves for the robbers you are and stop tryin' to scare a man. I ain't afeared of you. I got the pow'r to destroy you."

Con reached down and grabbed his pack. He thrust it at arm's length over his head.

The cries and squawks ceased. Strange voices, like the sound of birds of prey rather than men, murmured just beyond the light. Silence ensued, broken only by the sound of Albert's mumbling.

The voice that had called him before spoke again. "You have nothing."

The challenge brought confidence. He called out brashly, "If you don't think so then come in here and test me."

The boy at his feet gasped, "No, Con!"

Too late. With fearful shrieks and maniacal laughter the beings surrounding them swooped in from all directions. They flew over the heads of the humans on leathery wings, swiping at them with dagger-like talons on the end of impossibly thin legs. Con batted at them with his pack as they went by but the boy returned to his mumbling.

Con kicked him. "Get up, boy. Don't just give up and die under their feet. Get up! We'll go down fightin' any way."

The boy shook Con off with a desperate look and returned to his mumbling.

The ferocity of the attack diminished. The beings flew higher and higher, screaming in rage at the two humans but ceasing to lunge at them. They all dropped to the ground within sight, landing lightly and bouncing, like buzzards approaching a carcass.

They were bird-like at first glance—but upon study the image was more of a bat than a bird. They had long, leathery wings that did not fold well along their bodies. They stuck out, drooping slightly as they bounced back and forth. Their bodies were covered with a light fur. Arms and legs terminated in long claws instead of hands and feet. Their faces consisted of large, round eyes and a huge curved beak—like a bird of prey.

The leader stepped forward. His beak opened, then twisted to shape his words. "You are disturbing things not of your concern. You bought that slut's crops, Ataxia, and for that you must pay."

Albert looked up and yelled, "My Mama ain't what you called her!" His anger flared through his eyes at the bird-thing. The whole flock of them laughed out loud and stepped forward.

The leader snorted at him. "She sold herself to the Commander. A female slave who sells herself is a slut, boy."

Suddenly, Albert dropped his head back to the ground and started mumbling again.

Con started to answer this time but the boy grabbed his ankle and muttered lowly, "Don't answer them. They almost tricked me. If they get movin' again, I'm not sure I could stop them."

Shrieks split the air again. All the beings stumbled backward.

Con's eyes flew wide open. "You? You think you held them? You haven't even stood up since the battle was joined. How are you doing anything?"

"I don't have time to explain. Nor can I break my concentration for that long. I am not an expert at this. I have very little experience."

The creatures stepped forward again, pressing into an unseen force. Albert glanced at them and dropped his head.

His mumbling began again. The beasts screamed and retreated. Confusion reigned in Con's mind, but he held his peace.

The chief beast advanced again. A grimace formed on its distorted face, as if it were in pain. "How long can you hide behind the boy, Ataxia? He can't last too much longer. When he collapses, then we will have the two of you."

"We will fight you to the death, beast." Con broke the command of the boy and received a rap on the ankle for it.

"Your death, Ataxia, not ours." The being sneered.

Con held his peace. For all the lies this thing was full of, it spoke the truth when it said the boy could not last long. Al sweated profusely and the mumbling was a moan at times.

The beasts seemed agitated. The leader retreated and spoke to them harshly in a language Con did not recognize. They quieted down but continued to mill about, looking around nervously.

"My men want your flesh, Ataxia. They long for it like a man longs for a woman. But look! The boy grows weak and soon we will be satisfied!"

Al swayed and barely caught himself. His voice continued the chant strong and sure. For all his gameness, the lad would soon collapse. Con needed to do something or else lose everything.

His thoughts went to the sword that the woman had held and the book he had in his pack. He had used the pack as a club earlier, swinging at the flying talons, trying to keep them off of him and the boy. Now it lay at his feet, shredded. Through the rips he saw a corner of the book.

He kneeled slowly, starting to smile. With one hand, he eased the book out of a rip in the pack then stood. When the beasts advanced another step, he thrust the book up in plain sight. "So you like to fight young boys and old women? See how you like the taste of steel handled by a man."

At the sight of the book the beasts retreated. They stopped when their leader growled a command.

The beasts cowered, caught between their leader and the book. Con thrust the book high into the air and yelled, "Now to have my revenge."

No fire issued from the book. Con glanced up, then grabbed it with two hands as Mrs. Porteur had done.

Still nothing happened. No flames burst forth; no glow lit up the darkness.

A low growl started in the midst of the beasts and grew to a piercing screech. The laughter started again and they advanced. The boy groaned. His words became louder. He kept repeating a name over and over. The beasts pressed in, the front members being shoved by the ones behind.

Albert looked up at Con, shaking his head. The shake stopped when he saw the book. "My mother's manual!" he shouted.

Shame and fear washed over Con in equal portions. The beings, seeming to sense it, screamed in victory and surged forward. Albert started repeating the name again and the bird-things in the lead stopped suddenly. The ones behind ran into them. Several fights broke out behind them.

Con dropped his hand to his side, his face glowing with the shame of the discovered theft. He turned away from the boy, choosing rather to face the enemy than look into Albert's eyes.

The boy tugged at the book. Con let it go. Better it be in his hand at the end. Perhaps it would be a comfort to him. He lowered his head for a minute, working up within himself a scream to equal the worst shrieks he had heard that night.

The beasts advanced, wary but gaining confidence. Con picked up a log laying near his feet and turned to face the nearest one. Suddenly, there was a bright light behind him, so bright that the reflection of it off the surrounding woods hurt his eyes. The beast closest to him threw up its arms to shut it out. The shrieks of victory turned to screams of pain. Talons slashed at leathery wings and fuzzy bodies as the beasts tried desperately to get out of range of the gleaming light.

Albert stepped forward with a gleaming two-edged sword held in both hands. The sword burned with a bright and solid flame of fire—so bright that to look at it was to be blinded. Con shaded his eyes and grabbed for the boy.

"NO!" Albert yelled, "Do not touch me or the sword. I don't yet know how to handle this thing but I do know that you can't even touch it. Back out with me. We'll leave everything to them."

Con nodded and they retreated toward the woods. The ring of beasts broke to both sides as they approached then reformed after them, forming a line across the glade. They moved slowly backward, Con in the lead, Albert protecting the rear. The beasts swiped at them from a distance, shrieking and taunting in their bird-like screams. They never tempted the sword, staying quite out of its reach.

At the edge of the woods the beast leader barked a command and all but two of the beasts broke off the pursuit and ran for the wagons. Albert turned then and yelled, "Run, quickly, run!"

Con ran. A small path opened up between two closely spaced trees. Beyond the trees, the path widened but twisted in ankle punishing turns around smaller trees and bushes.

The light of the sword illuminated the dark path for a few feet, enough to keep them on it.

Branches tore at his face and hands. Ankle height roots grabbed at his feet. Brambles and briars gripped his clothes and ripped his skin. Con was oblivious to it. He knew only running. Fear pumped his legs. Horror squeezed the breath into and out of his lungs. Panic guided his steps and picked him up when he fell. Lungs burned and gasped. Legs knotted in pain.

Finally, Con stopped and wrapped his arms around a tree. He grabbed Albert as he ran by and gasped out, "Enough, Al. Let's fight now. If we run anymore we will collapse and be overtaken anyway, with no hope of fighting."

Albert, gasping for breath, said nothing but nodded his head and turned to face the path from which they had just come. He tried to lift the sword but dropped its point again onto the ground. Con picked up a three feet long dead branch and stood alongside of him.

Nothing happened. No beings rushed at them, no spears pointed at their lives, no pursuit tore limbs from the trees. They looked at one another, amazed. Then Albert pointed at their back trail. Still gasping, he cried, "Look! At the sky!"

A red glow filtered through the tree branches. High above them, a tongue of flame was visible.

"They are burning the wagons," Con said. "I'm sorry."

"You're sorry?" Albert said. "We've lost a wagon, but you've lost a wagon and all your crops. Be sorry for yourself."

They stood for several minutes watching the glow in the sky. Suddenly, Al turned down the path and said, "I must return this book to the farm before the Enemy has a chance to get there."

Albert hefted the sword up and, with a pop, it changed again to the book. How the sword was evoked and how it was again returned to the book was a mystery. The boy had accomplished it with just a touch but what touch Con could not tell. He kept his peace, embarrassed to ask, afraid to bring the topic up for fear of the question as to how the book came to be in his possession—afraid he would have to say out loud that he'd stolen it.

The boy walked off. "We will return to the road soon," he called back over his shoulder. "This travel is much too slow and the road doubles back toward us within the mile."

Con trudged behind in silence, contemplating his explanations when at last they reached the farm and the woman. He was tempted to simply veer off and leave the boy, returning to the City by the most expeditious route. His manhood—the same pride and sense of responsibility that drove him to fight the Dragon—forced him to go on. He would face the people he had wronged and make it right—if he could.

As the East started to turn gray, they saw the broken down fence of the front pastures. Before the sun was full up they stood at the back door of the farmhouse. Albert pushed on the door but it was latched from the inside. He knocked on it and called for his mother. Con stood back, dreading the confrontation to come.

There was a stirring in the house and the latch lifted. Con stepped forward and grabbed the book in the boy's hand. "I need to hand this back myself, Al."

The boy stared at him, showing no emotion, then released the book.

A crack appeared slowly around the door. Then it swung wide and Mrs. Porteur rushed through it, lifting the boy up in her arms, smothering him with her affection and crying loudly. Con stood back, uncomfortable at the show of emotion and remembering the sobbing of his own mother at the death of his sisters. He stood in the dissipating shadows of the building trying not to disturb the scene.

Mrs. Porteur released the boy, pushing him away to look at him as if she realized for the first time that he might be injured. She looked him over and, seeing the scratches on his face, ran her hand over them gently. "Do you hurt, Albert?"

"No, Mama," he answered. "I'm just tired."

His mother hugged him to herself again and began sobbing once again. "Thanks to the Commander. Thanks to the Commander."

Looking up from her embrace she saw Con standing back. His eyes dropped from hers. She pushed the boy off to the side, still hugging him with one arm.

"And you, Con. Are you safe? Did they harm you?" Her tone was not accusing. The concern for his well-being was real.

Con's eyes dropped from the contact again. He stared for a while at the rough planks of the porch, then snapped his head up, lifting the book from his side.

A large, strong hand grabbed his wrist. There, not a foot away from him, stood a large man robed in white with a hood covering his head. Even this close, with the morning sun shining over his shoulder, the hood hid the features of the man. Only the gleam of his bright eyes was discernible.

Con wilted under the stare. Summoning all his courage, he squared his shoulders and looked at Mrs. Porteur, who had moved off to the side with her two sons. He would not crawl. That was what this Cleato had always wanted. He had committed a crime. He would admit his guilt and he would accept his punishment but it would be as a man, not a sniveling coward.

"I wronged you, Mrs. Porteur. Ain't no excuses for it. I thought your book would enable me to fight the Dragon and I stole it."

He turned to the big man. "I was wrong, on both counts, and I ask her forgiveness. I'll make any restitution you may say."

The meaning was obvious. The woman would forgive him. She had her son and apparently, by some communication, knew of their danger and fight during the night. She would forgive anything. But this man—this hooded, hidden, horrible herald—who had come to comfort the woman and protect her, would not be placated so easily.

Mrs. Porteur moved along side of Cleato. "Forgive you? Why, of course. If the book hadn't been there then perhaps you wouldn't be here to apologize to me. There is no restitution, Mr. Ataxia. You've brought…"

"No, Priscilla," Cleato interrupted. His voice was deep, resonating Con's chest. Although he was sure he heard with his ears the sounds, he was as sure that he heard them also with his mind, and his heart. The sound in his ears seemed redundant—a split second after his understanding—a continuous deja vu. "You may forgive him. Indeed, you must. But I will determine the restitution that Mr. Ataxia will pay. He stole your book, but he stole our weapon."

The hooded face never turned from Con. Although only the hint of his eyes, eyebrows and cheeks could be seen, Con knew that this man stared him in the eye. Each word he spoke with stern gentleness hammered Con. "You took the second most powerful weapon that is in this Valley and held it up to ridicule before the Dragon. The sword of the Army will never be effective in the hands of thieves, robbers and liars—

though they will ever try to use it to their own purposes. No, Con Ataxia, your debt for that action is not forgiven. You will make restitution."

The flow of words from Cleato's mouth was like hot oil pouring over his soul and he struggled to hold back tears. He shook his head. He had not cried since he was fifteen when the horse had kicked him in the stomach. His face burned with the fires of shame. What this man said spoke to his heart and he knew that he had been called correctly what he would never, could never call himself: a thief and a liar.

His soul was exposed. Things about himself that he had hidden from himself leaped into his mind, each one digging at him with claws of remorse. He shuddered, realizing for the first time the futility of his quest. He was not fighting the Dragon—he could not fight the Dragon. He had been captured by the Dragon years before—in fact, all the Rebels had. They were just waiting to be drug off like the Raiders had done to his father. Con wanted to hang his head, to slink away from the stern presence that raised so many unwanted thoughts.

Outwardly, though, he stood fast. "How do you want be to repaid? How can I make it up?"

The eyes in the hood gleamed and Con could see the hint of a smile in the crinkling of the skin around them. "Go back to the City. I will visit you there and exact my payment."

Con bowed and backed away, preparing to leave.

"You'll not leave without a meal," Mrs. Porteur said. "Come inside."

The hood nodded at Con. Then one hand waved Con past him and into the house.

Hunger grumbled in his belly and the thought of her cooking overcame Con's desire to be away from the hooded man. Con walked gingerly around the man, careful not to bump him or touch his robe. The hood turned as he passed, the eyes still staring at him.

Con hunched his shoulders and walked on. When he got the table and Mrs. Porteur pointed at a chair at the back of the kitchen table with the spout of a teapot, Con turned back to the doorway, expecting to see the big man following him, staring at him.

The doorway was empty. Bright sunlight streamed in.

"He's gone," Con said.

Mrs. Porteur stopped pouring the tea into his cup and looked. She smiled. Con had not noticed it before but there was something about her that reminded him of the girl soldier in the square. Not physically, because they were not anything alike. It was a quality—something in her rather than on her. Her next words rocked Con—for they were just what that girl had said. "Oh, he's still around. If we need him, he'll be here."

Chapter 15

The sight of the massive walls through the glare of the setting sun was pleasing to Con's travel weary mind. He picked up his pace, ignoring the pangs in his stomach and the pains in his feet. The City gates would close at dark. He had to be there before that happened.

The gates of the City were still open when Con arrived. He rushed through and turned down the small street that led to Decev's office.

The day of Reckoning. It excited him. He would not be rich. He had lost a lot with the loss of the wagon and crops. Still, he had a nice sum on account with his partner. With winter almost upon the City, he had nothing to do except return to the farm—provide for his mother and brother. Next year, after planting, he could come back and look again for a way to free his father—maybe even look into the Army. Maybe they did have the way. Maybe they were the way.

Con turned off the small road into an alley. The winding way took on a new look in the dim light of a smoky dusk. He kept a watch on the numbers, trying to remember exactly where Decev's office was.

Yellow light spilled from a window half a block away splashing across the darkened cobblestones. The white stone stoop and dark door were familiar. He stepped up to the door. The small brass plaque read, "D. Croesus". Con lifted the big knocker and let it fall with a loud thunk.

The door flew inward and Decev thrust his face out, a snarl on his lips. At the sight of Con, the snarl spread into a broad grin. "There you are. I was worried about you. Thought perhaps you'd gotten lost."

"No, not lost—but I did have my troubles."

"Yes, we've all had them." Decev spun around and marched to the center of the small room. "Speaking of troubles, you don't know how hard I've worked to set up buys for this last load."

Con stepped in and shoved the door closed. Decev spun around with a frown on his face and marched back to the door. He yanked it open and stuck his head out again. "Where's the wagon? Did you take it to the warehouse already?"

"Decev, I want to tell you about that but I am famished. Is there any food?"

"No, I ate while waiting for you. You should have been in this morning, you know."

"Yes, and I would have been, but I ran into difficulties on the road the night before last and was delayed."

Decev marched to his desk. "Yes, yes, you told me. Trouble. But you're here now. That's what counts. Yes, sir. The last load of the season always thrills me."

There was no thrill in his eyes—or his voice. There was a detachment—a preoccupation. He kept glancing at the door. He paced back and forth, mumbling. Twice he went to his desk and jotted something on some parchment. Finally, he smiled and grabbed his cloak. "Come on, Con. Let's get the goods and sell them off. Believe me, a lot of people are going to be glad to see those crops."

Con stood still in the middle of the floor, holding his hat in his hand. "Decev, there are no crops."

"Let's get down to the warehouse and pick them up," Decev said, apparently not hearing Con.

"Decev, *there are no crops*," Con repeated.

Decev stopped at the door and looked back. His brow knit then brightened. "Do you mean you sold them *all* in the fields? How in the world did you do that?"

"I didn't sell them. They were burned along with the wagon."

Decev stared. His jaw began to work soundlessly up and down.

Con shrugged, then lifted his hands to his side. "The Dragon attacked me on the road two nights ago. He burned the wagons and the crops on them. We barely escaped with our lives."

"We? Who else was there?"

Con told him the story of his visit to the Porteur farm and the subsequent deal for all her crops. The story of the attack came more slowly for Con wanted to be sure to explain fully.

Decev glowered through the whole story, then spat at the fire. "Do you expect me to believe that nonsense?"

"Nonsense? I risked my life that night. There is no nonsense in it."

"Try it again, Ataxia. Money has been missing since you started. The margin is way down. Unless you have a whole pocket full of Golds to give me, the only explanation is that you've been skimming."

It was Con's turn. Twice he started to speak but could find no words. Decev yelled again. "Can't come up with a better one? I can. You're a stinking thief!" He kicked a spindly chair up against the wall, shattering it.

The sound broke Con's stupor. Fire started to rise in his chest, heating his cheeks to cherry red. "Look, I didn't skim any money and I didn't steal anything from you. There was less margin because I went to a lot of small farmers who needed more money for their crop than you normally gave the big ones. I gave them a higher price than normal."

Decev's face grew red, then violet, then purple. "Gave? Gave? You expect me to believe that you gave anything to anybody. You're a liar, Ataxia. What's worse, you're a lousy liar.

"You have stolen my money, my goods and my wagon. I want them back. They will do no good for you. I have the contracts tied up. That food will rot in the wagon unless we make a deal."

"I can't make a deal for food that doesn't exist. The food has been burned up as well as the wagon."

Decev face turned red again. His eyebrows rammed each other and bounced there. His hand came up and a stiff finger began to wag in front of Con. Then he stopped, put his hands in front of him in a placating manner and forced a smile. "Look, Con. I know what you're trying. And I'll admit, it must be pretty tempting. But, don't you see, that's how I got started in this business. I found a way to skim enough off the guy who gave me my start to get my own wagon. I got to admit that it wasn't as audacious as your plan but it worked. I put him out of business the next year—knowing all his customers and all his suppliers. Don't you think that I would protect myself. Can't you see that is why I kept you in the field and away from the customers? I have them locked up. They won't buy from you. So, why don't we just make a deal. What do you want, another 10%? Done. Now let's get the wagon."

Con shook his head. "Decev, I don't have any wagon. I don't have any crops. And I don't care who your customers are. The Dragon burned it all."

Decev turned toward the fire and spat once more. "Have it your way. But, you mark my words. You'll never sell an ounce of that produce. Not an ounce. I have people all over the market who will let me know as soon as you walk through the door."

Con threw up his hands and spun away from his mentor. He turned back, thrust his chin out and yelled, "I don't have any crops or wagon or anything else. The Dragon burned them."

"Dragon! You keep yelling about this Dragon. That's a fairy tale, Ataxia. Do you think I'd fa…." He spun around and walked off, his hands flailing the air. He spun back. "Stupid farmer," he screamed at Con. He thrust out his hand, "Now, give me your purse. I, at least, have that."

"I have no purse. I used the last of the money to buy out Mrs. Porteur's crops."

Decev exploded. "You thief! You and this Porteur woman. You're in league with all the Merchants, aren't you?"

His hands flew straight out to his sides. His fists clenched and unclenched over and over. "I gave you a chance. I taught you how to become rich. And this is how I am repaid? You have ruined me!"

He stared around the room wildly, his eyes coming to rest on the poker next to the fireplace. With a quick lunge, he snatched it up. "Out! Out of my office!"

Con raised his hands, palms out. "Decev, I haven't stolen anything. And I have worked a full season for you. There is supposed to be money on account. Now, you can take the cost of the wagon out and you can deduct the capital you gave me for this last trip, but I want the rest. I've earned the rest."

Con ducked as the poker whistled past his ear. Decev ranted, "The rest? You idiot. I've been trying to tell you. There isn't any 'rest.' We needed the profit from this run just to break even."

Con straightened his back. "Hold on. I've kept a ledger. There should be almost a thousand Golds in my account—ten thousand in the whole business."

"I've had expenses," Decev shrieked, then he turned away and almost mumbled, "and a few setbacks."

Con frowned, the reality starting to penetrate his understanding. There was no money. There never had been any money. "That's not my concern, Decev. You promised me a percentage." Con stepped forward, anger clouding his judgment.

Decev looked around the room again, his ears glowing purple. "You idiot. You blind, stupid, farmer, idiot." His eyes came to rest on something and he lunged again toward the fireplace. His hand came away with the cast iron ash shovel. He raised it over his head and charged Con.

Con backed quickly to the door and ducked through. Decev's heavy steps drove him off the stoop and out into the alley. He stopped and turned back. Decev stood on the stoop, the shovel still raised.

"You are a thief and a scoundrel, Con Ataxia. You have stolen my very livelihood. Run now or I'll have you thrown back in prison where you belong!"

Anger leaped into Con's throat. "My money, Croesus. I want my money." He stepped forward.

Decev swung the shovel in a wide arc, missing Con by several feet but getting his point across. Con backed up a step.

"The only money you'll have is that which you stole from me, Ataxia. You better read that parchment you signed. According to it, you owe me seven thousand Golds."

A cold chill swept over Con. He remembered the parchment that morning in the inn but he had never read it. He had signed it and handed it back to the man who had just bought him the most expensive night he had ever spent, trusting in his goodwill.

Decev hopped down and grabbed up a rock. "Get out, little farmer. Get out while you can. If I have to call the cops, you'll go to the prison—and it won't be as pleasant as the last time." He laughed wickedly, then hurled the stone toward Con. Con ducked around the corner and ran. The missile rattled off the wall and shattered on the pavement.

He ran for half a block then slowed to a walk. Anger ate at his belly—anger and frustration. He wanted to go back, to demand his share from Decev. Decev's threat, though, was not idle. He could handle the cops, and the judges—he had the 'persuasion' the judge wanted. Con had none.

"Bah!" He kicked at a loose rock, sending it flying through the air. He had put all his hope in that money. The farm. His quest. The payment to Cleato for stealing the book. Without that profit, there was nothing.

He slapped his pouch and was answered with a jingle. Slowly, he reached in and pulled out two Silvers and a Gold—enough to feed himself and obtain shelter for the night.

He chuckled. Then he laughed out loud. There he was, standing on a street of the City with a storm gathering. He was dusty, unshaven and unkempt. Fourberie. Wellbeing. And now, Decev Croesus. He laughed again. After months of his quest—he had two silvers and a Gold.

Con cupped his mouth and began to shout. "A month ago I had just enough for a meal in my pocket. I was a poor lad from the farms. But now, I have the experience of being an entrepreneur, of having been in business and tasted of success and riches."

He spun around. "I built myself up from a nobody with barely the price of a meal to an ex-bootlegger who has not just the price of a meal but enough for a room for one night also."

Shutters creaked all along the street. Dark eyes stared out at him from darker windows.

To each, Con turned and bowed. Each slammed the shutters as he did, leaving him speaking again to an empty street.

"I am a successful businessman, you see," he called out. "I was gonna fight the Dragon. I was gonna get all I needed for my war with the profits from my business."

A slow, cold drizzle began. Con dropped his head. As the cold rain cooled his anger, truth penetrated his brain—screaming at him—mocking him. He had entered the most blatant example of the rebellion there was to be had in the City: bootlegging—which was rebellion against the rebels—and tried to obtain the means to destroy the Dragon. He had taken on the ways of the Dragon to try to defeat him.

He laughed again, and with a disgusted wave of his hand, shuffled down the street, head hung low and feet scraping the wet and slippery stones. A cold drizzle ran down his collar. Con lifted the collar and stooped over farther.

Defeat was what he'd purchased and that is what he'd gotten.

Chapter 16

Rain splattered on the small rectangular panes of the window and seeped through the long diagonal crack. The gusts of wind that lashed at the old building sprayed the leaking water into a mist, which floated like a silvery haze gently to the floor, soaking the threadbare rug in a rough semi-circle below the rotting sill. The black mold on the wall testified that this was not the first time this window had leaked in the centuries since it was installed.

Gray clouds scudded over the nearby roofs, seeming to scrape on the spires and corners. Rain fell in sheets, running in gushing rivulets across the courtyard below.

Once that courtyard may have been the playground of royalty but, for Con, it was just the back yard of a cheap inn. Its cobblestones, which had been laid in military precision, were tossed and buckled like waves on a stormy sea. Garbage lay in dark, shapeless clumps on the stone. Lighter debris, lifted by the wind, pressed itself into corners and hung on the brick walls.

Con shivered, left the window, and paced the drab room. He stirred the coals of a fire. It did not help. The cold dampness that plagued him could not be dispelled by the glow of charcoal. It was too deep within to respond to simple fire.

In the three weeks since he'd left Croesus' office he had found no friends, no place to go except the small room, and no prospects for accomplishing his mission. His job, cleaning a stable, enabled him to feed himself and sleep in this dilapidated inn. The Dragon still raided. His father was still a captive. His mother and brother were alone on a hillside farm. Con returned to the dreary window, standing just outside the wetness.

Footsteps shuffled in the hall. A light knock sounded on his door. Rap. Rap. Rap.

Con ignored it. He wanted no visitors—needed no one to try to cheer him or discourage him.

He snorted. "It'll be more likely discouragement. That seems to be the only thing available in this City."

Rap. Rap. Rap. It was no louder, no quicker.

"Who's there?" Con called.

The caller remained silent.

"I'm not interested in whatever it is. Leave me alone."

The knock came again, slow, deliberate, imperative, but no quicker, no louder than the first: three strokes, equal cadence, equal force.

Con shrugged and turned back to the window.

Rap. Rap. Rap.

Con went to the door and stood before it. At least by answering he could stop the noise. On the other hand, he would have to converse with someone—an idiot, no doubt, who knew nothing of his plight, nothing of his desires, nothing of his quest. It was the old lady from just below him that wanted a cuppa'. Con had figured her out pretty quickly. At mealtime, she would borrow a cuppa'—of whatever it was she thought Con had that she could get from him for her own meal.

He yelled. "I have nothing. I have not been to market."

Rap. Rap. Rap.

Disgusted, Con skewed up his face and snatched the door open. "What do you wa...."

The large hooded man stood there, his shoulders hunched and his hood ducked to keep from hitting the low, dingy ceiling.

Con backed up into the room, his eyes wide. Cleato stepped into the door jam, his head ducked even further. The hood almost faced the floor.

"Will you invite me in, Con? I'll not enter if you wish not." The deep voice reverberated in his chest again. There was the same feeling as at the Porteur farm: each word was like deja vu for he received it in his soul before he heard it with his ears.

"Yes, of course. Forgive me." Con motioned with his hand to enter.

The hooded figure entered and stood upright, the top of his hood almost brushing the ceiling. Con grabbed a chair and set it before him. "May I offer you a small meal? I have little but what I have I would gladly share."

"Is this payment for the meal at the Porteur's."

Con thought for a moment, then shook his head. "No, it's because you are my guest."

The hood nodded up and down. "I will eat a meal with you, Con. Go ahead and prepare it. What I have to speak about can wait."

Con turned to the small, curtained alcove that he used as a kitchen. There he kept tea, flour, and some potatoes. He could offer nothing grand to this man of the Army but he would offer what he had.

He mixed up biscuit dough and put on some potatoes for boiling. He returned to the room. "Have you come for your payment?"

The hood and robe jiggled, as if the big man it laughed. "Payment is probably the wrong term, Con. I think I told you I would want restitution."

Con nodded. "That is what you said. I assumed that meant I had to pay you something."

The hood shook. A bright flash of lightning lit the room and Con glimpsed bright, lively eyes deep within the hood. The eyes were narrowed, but not in anger. The crinkles at the corners and the lift of the cheeks told him the man was smiling—smiling a broad smile.

The tone of the voice was light when it came again. "Con, restitution means that you must restore something. Money can not restore what you took."

Con walked back to look at the boiling pot, more for a chance to think than to complete the meal. He stuck a fork in the floating pieces of potato, decided they were not yet done. He pulled open the door on the small oven on the side of the cook stove. The biscuits were just turning brown. "A few more minutes," he said. Instead of returning to the room, though, he stood and stared at the pot.

What could he restore that he had not already returned?

Cleato laughed. "Why, our reputation before those rebels."

Con spun around. "How did you know what I was thinking?"

Cleato held up one big hand. "That you will learn soon. For now, let me explain your restitution. You held up our weapon to ridicule before the rebels. That must never be allowed to stand. That is what you must restore."

Con shook his head. "Look, Mr. Cleato…"

Cleato held up his hand again. "You may call me Lord Cleato or just Cleato. But do not call me Mister. A mister is one who is part of the City or the middle Valley. My place is much larger than that."

"Uh…fine. I think. Cleato, I didn't hold up your weapon to the Rebels. I was fighting Dragon Raiders."

The gleam returned to the eyes in the hood. "Those are the real rebels, son. They are the original rebels. This thing that humans do is just a copy—a poor copy—of the Dragon's true rebellion."

Con raised his finger to say something when he heard a sniff. The hood rose as if the big man was testing the air with his nose. "Seems I smell biscuits."

Con spun around and pulled open the oven door. The biscuits were big and fluffy, better than he had ever made them for himself and they had just turned a golden brown. Con pulled the tray from the oven and placed it on the small wooden table. He pulled the pot of potatoes off the stove, poured them through a strainer, and set the strainer full of potato chunks on the table also.

The big man rose, pulled his chair to the table and sat before one of the cracked plates that Con dealt there.

There was a moment of silence, then the big man lifted the strainer and served himself a load of potatoes. A teapot whistled. Con grabbed it and poured tea into the two chipped cups he had. Then he sat himself on a stool next to the table.

The big man said, "Con, tell me of your adventures since we last met."

Con chuckled. "Now, that would be boring dinner conversation. I've done nothing except fail."

"Hmmm," came from the hood.

Con grinned broadly, surprised at how good it felt to have the big man in the room with him. "I didn't get the fortune I wanted. It seems my partner did not believe my story about the Dragon's attack and felt that I'd stolen the money from him."

"Most people never do believe that the Dragon does the things he does, Con, until the Dragon attacks them. Normally, that is too late. Think of yourself before the Dragon killed your sisters and enslaved your father. Would you not act as your former partner did if given that excuse?"

Con's fork stopped in mid-flight to his mouth. He put it back on the plate. "How...?"

The hood shook. "Con, just accept the fact that I know. How, we will get to when you can understand it. Now, do you think you would have believed that the Dragon is real if you had not experienced his attack?"

Con nodded, "Probably not. But, I don't think that had anything to do with it. Seems he was plannin' on cheatin' me from the start. Had somethin' in the contract that I signed."

The hood bounced up and down again. "I know."

"You do?" Con waited for an explanation but the big man just continued to eat.

Con shrugged, able to accept the mystery of this man without the suspicion that had accompanied all his other experiences in this City. Then he realized. The feeling of desperation was gone. The foulness of his mood was lifted. In the presence of this man, sitting here breaking bread with him, he was comfortable—as comfortable as he had been in his own home, years before.

There was no sense to that. He had done nothing but avoid the man and his Army since they first met back at market. He stole a sword that somehow belonged to Cleato and insulted him in the "battle". And yet, each time he got into trouble, or near trouble, the big hooded stranger had been near, waiting for him. Con began to feel regret.

The Army! He criticized, accused, and fought the Army. He tried every other avenue to fight the Dragon when it was obvious that the only ones who were successful at that were the Army troops, or more precisely, the militiamen that he'd observed in the square that day. And for them he had nothing but insult.

It seems like he'd searched for years for the answer and rejected it or substituted everything else for it whenever it was presented to him.

He looked up at Cleato. The big man sat back from his meal. It seemed like Con could see more of his face, as if the whole room was brighter and reflecting light into that hood. Con glanced toward the outside. The storm was breaking up. He rose and walked to the dim and dank portal. Though late in the day, light was streaming in from the west, making the window panes glisten where the drops still clung to the glass. The wind had dropped to a gentle breeze. Con thought he heard a robin singing—but knew that could not be true. Spring was still months away.

"Tell me about the Commander," Con said suddenly, still staring through the panes at the sky that was rapidly turning blue as the clouds scudded away. He turned back and flopped down on the stool again, his elbows finding the table and his hands finding his chin, his plate of potatoes and bread ignored.

Cleato leaned forward and stretched his massive arm across the table to rest his hand on Con's arm. With a flick of the other hand, the hood flipped off his head, bunching on his shoulder. A broad, clear beaming visage faced Con with a smile that threatened to leave his cheeks and capture his big ears. His eyes were dark pools. Con read compassion, strength, stern discipline and pure love—all at the same time. The man wore a full beard, perfectly black and several inches long. His pure black hair was curly and hung down his neck in ringlets. The only blemish to that perfect face was at the hairline. A series of scars showed where he had suffered some injury in the past.

The man spoke—this time, it was all in Con's head—or his heart. Although he heard with his ears, the real hearing was deep within him. Cleato explained the Commander, who he was, where he was, and what he wanted. His explanation lasted late into the evening. It was never complicated, yet, in every way it was complete.

Chapter 17

"I want to join, Cleato."

The big man cocked an eye at Con.

"I'm sure," Con answered. "I have heard all these things before but I never understood them. Your explanation was…" Con shrugged. "It was right."

Con stood and walked toward the darkened window. Halfway there, he turned. "I still want to fight the Dragon."

"And you shall. But there is a stipulation."

"And that is?"

"The only way to fight the Dragon is in the service of the Commander. That you've discovered. Additionally, the only way to fight the Dragon is in submission to the Commander."

Pangs of rebellion stung Con's heart. The Commander demanded submission, something Con had never been willing to give. Con turned back toward the window and stared into the darkness. His independence was something that he cherished. His freedom was something that was in-born—something that was his birthright. To give it up felt wrong, as if he was violating his parents.

A large hand fell onto his shoulder and rested there. "Con. Do you really believe that rebellion, freedom as you see it in your mind right now, is a birthright? Do you really think that you have had this desire since you were a child?"

Con turned and looked up at the dark eyes. "Yes, Cleato. It's a part of me. It's who I am. Now, I ain't sayin' I won't give it up. But it ain't easy."

Cleato walked back to the table and sat down. He pointed at Con's plate. "You going to eat that biscuit?" Con shook his head. Cleato smiled and reached for the bread.

"I have a special liking for bread of any kind. It represents life, doesn't it?"

Con shook his head. "I thought we were talkin' about my freedom."

Cleato plopped the last morsel into his mouth, then waved his hand at Con, swallowing the bread down. "Son, think for a minute. Have you always had this strong desire for your 'freedom'?"

Con's head shook up and down vigorously. "Of course." But something tickled his memory. Something there didn't ring true. The Citadel. Happy, smiling faces all around him and Fourberie's voice in his mind speaking of freedom. "And they do not have to cow-tow to anyone, Benet. Here, they are truly free."

It was a lie. It was a part of the whole lie of the Citadel. It had entered his brain, his soul, his mind and like a prickly burr had stuck there, gotten entwined into his being until he thought it was a part of him. But it was not. It was a LIE like all the rest of the things that the Dragon had shown him.

Freedom was not doing what one wanted to do regardless of consequences. True freedom was knowing truth—the present truth, the past truth, and the future truth—so that decisions made could be based on reality instead of fantasy. True freedom was true knowledge. It had nothing to do with disobedience, external discipline, or lack of rules. It had everything to do with will.

He looked up into Cleato's eyes again. "Oh, Commander. I've been deceived. And deceived really good."

Cleato smiled. "Con, in the past that phrase has been a vain curse. In the future, you will find that it is a true call to action. Use it very carefully."

Con was puzzled for a moment then realized what he had said. His face flushed but Cleato clapped him on the back. "You will learn, son."

Con turned away from the big man and stared again at the window, settling his emotions, trying to make a rational decision. Finally, satisfied, he turned back.

"I am ready to give up the rebellion. I want to join—not in spite of the Commanders authority but because of it."

Cleato's face exploded in joy. He jumped to his feet and danced around the room. Con expected the floor to tremble under the weight of the big man's quick steps but there was barely a shake in the old building. Cleato sang a song in a language unknown to Con. Words and beautiful tones poured from his mouth.

A rap sounded on the door—not the slow, patient sound of Cleato but a rapid, insistent sound. Con backed up to it, still watching the big man twirl and jump in his flowing robes..

The knock came again. Con spun around and yanked the door open.

A girl stood there. She was about five feet three, about seventeen years old. Her long brown hair flowed down her back to a point halfway between her shoulders. She had brown eyes that glowed and crinkled at the edges as she smiled. Her face was thin and angular.

"Hi." She raised one hand and wiggled her fingers at him.

He didn't answer, trying to place her familiar face. She frowned and peeked around him. The big man stood in the center of the room, stooped by the low ceiling, his hands raised up so that the tips of his fingers were touching the dingy plaster.

The girl smiled again. Her head cocked to one side, making her long brown hair bend on one shoulder. "Are you going to ask me in?"

Con moved out of the doorway. She glided into the small room, laughing at the sight of Cleato. She ran to him and clasped him around the chest in a hug.

"He joined?" she squeaked with excitement.

Cleato nodded. The girl squealed again. "I knew he would. I knew you'd convince him."

Con stood in the middle of the room, watching the two of them, bewildered. Cleato grabbed his arm. "Join us, Con. The Commander and the whole of headquarters are celebrating your decision."

"The whole of... How would they know?"

"I've told them, of course."

Con cocked an eye at him. Cleato laughed. "You've much to learn of our communication network, Con. And of the power of the Commander."

Cleato looped his arm around Con's shoulder and the other around the girl. The girl, in turn, grabbed Con with her free arm and they danced around the room in a circle. Con moved with awkward steps, unsure of how to respond. He had never seen so much emotion let loose at once, except at a funeral.

They ended the twirl with a hug, each pulling the other in. Con resisted the embrace, embarrassed by the closeness of other people. The strength of the big man, though, was not to be resisted.

Con pulled back and glanced first at one then at the other. They plopped down on the floor and stared back at him.

Con stared at the girl, recognition playing at the corners of his mind. "I know why Cleato came, but I can't figure out why you are here."

The girl laughed. Cleato answered, "She is one of the reasons I am here. She has asked me about you daily since you first met. She has pressed both myself and the Commander to not let you be. I guess you might say she is your benefactor."

Con looked at her again. A face standing on a dirty, slum street, looking up at him after a battle flashed through his mind.

"Of course!" Con exclaimed. "You're the soldier."

She nodded.

Con was puzzled. "You kept askin' about me? Why?"

"Because you needed me to, Con. I could see your desire to be a part of us—and your need, but I could also see you were headstrong. I just kept asking the Commander to save you from that and keep the opportunity to join in front of you."

"And the Commander was willin' to do that just 'cause you asked?"

Cleato spoke again. "No, Con. he was willing to do that because that is his desire. I told you that months ago. The Commander knows you, much better than you know yourself. Sarah's pleas simply lined up with what the Commander was already going to do.

"Of course, that does not take away from the affect that Sarah's pleas had. The Commander is very fond of her—as he is of all of his soldiers—and her constant attention to your need was gratifying."

Con stared at the girl in appreciation. Her beauty, not so much outward—although that was nice, too—but her inward glow attracted him. She stared back, seeming to examine him just as thoroughly. Cleato watched the two of them for a few minutes. Finally he said, "There will be time enough for THAT later. Now is the time for training."

Sarah jumped, then laughed. Her excitement took over again, "May I train him, Cleato?"

"No, Sarah. You know that would not be good practice. You may help, though. When the training is complete, I think we can insure that he is assigned to your company. That is, if you both still desire it."

"Oh, I think we will," Sarah said with assurance.

Cleato answered with a brief smile. He stood up. "Yes, that may very well be true. For now, it is late. Con, tomorrow, we will start your training. Tonight, sleep well and prepare yourself."

"Where shall I go in the morning? Is there a trainin' ground or a camp someplace?"

Cleato laid his massive hand on Con's shoulder. "You will report to work, as usual. You will be trained in the evenings, during your lunch hour, on your days off, whenever you will free yourself up to do it. Training will be as quick as you desire it to be. The only limit will be your willingness to submit yourself to its rigors."

The large hand grasped Con's and lifted him to his feet. Cleato's huge, craggy face was only inches away. "We will teach you the communication system, the tactics, the drill and ceremony, the basic skills of warfare. We will give you your manual and the sword that comes with it. We will teach you to use it and we will drill you in it daily. As you become able, and we have need, we will send you on missions."

He had been chosen. A little thrill inflated his chest. HE had been chosen by the Commander.

Cleato frowned. "During it all you will work everyday to earn your wages, live right here or wherever else you and the Commander may decide. You will shop in the market, walk in the streets, clean, cook, sleep, bathe, and live right here in the City. Indeed, you will find that the biggest battle ground you will ever encounter is in the very place where you live and work."

One of Con's desires had been to get out of the surroundings, out of the menial job he had and into something more satisfying, more enlightening—less humble. It was pride.

"Do ya' always know what I'm thinkin'?"

"Anytime you try to let that pride—which you have in abundance—creep up and absorb you again, I will remind you. But that is not why I am going to train you this way."

Con looked up at him again, expecting to see the stern face of a disciplinarian. Cleato smiled, his hand on Con's shoulder. "I'm going to train you this way because it is the best way. It will train you better for the mission I have for you than sending you away to a secluded camp."

Sarah and Cleato went to the door. Cleato turned back. "Tomorrow."

Con nodded and they disappeared into the hallway. He ran to the door and waved to them as they turned into the stairwell.

Returning to the room, he flopped down in his one soft chair and blew out a sigh. How all that had come about he was not sure. So many decisions had been made; so much had been opened to him that evening.

The next day, training started. The thrill came back. Just get hold of Cleato in the morning and…?

He went cold. How was he to get hold of Cleato? He got up from the chair and rushed to the door, flinging it open. They were gone.

A voice, still and small, sounded in the back of his mind. "I will never leave you anymore. If you need me just call out."

It surprised and scared him. He shut it off, then realized that he had been introduced to the communication system he had heard about so often. For the first time, he knew what Albert had been doing in the forest and what Mrs. Porteur had been talking about in her description of the battles with the Dragon Raiders. Con chuckled. He had it. He really had it. He really was a part of the Army.

He was still chuckling as he turned down the lamp and went to sleep.

The next morning dawned bright. Con arrived at the stable early, sure Cleato would be there to take him away. It was a large building with three rows of stalls and large aisles between them. Fifty horses could be kept there at once, but it was seldom full. There was a loft above that held all the hay for the beasts. The aisles were crowded with stable hands and horses as they lead the inhabitants of the stalls out two by two into the corral behind the building.

He stopped at the entrance and looked around. No one other than the usual characters was there.

He went to the little room off the tackle room where the owner kept a desk. No one was there either. The street and the nearby doorways revealed no hint of flowing hair or broad shoulders. Finally, as starting time approached, he went into the stables, his shoulders drooping.

He pulled the leather apron off the hook on the wall and flung it up over his head. At the first stall, he grabbed the pitchfork and began throwing straw and manure into the barrow in the aisle. It was not a pleasant job and far below what Con had thought of himself just a few months prior. It was steady work, though, and no one challenged him for it.

It was not new work for Con. On the farm, he had done it often. Animals kept inside had to be cleaned after. Because of that, he was able to throw himself into the work right away. This made him popular with his employer but unpopular with the other laborers in the stable.

A scratchy, voice called from behind him. "You pitchin' into that dung first thing again?"

It was Rusty, another laborer. Rusty normally started his work at the same time Con did. Other than that similarity, he and Con had never found anything in common. These were the first words Rusty had spoken to him since the first day on the job when Con had told him to get lost. He stood against the front post of the opposite stall.

"Might as well, Rusty," Con said. "They don't pay me to sit here."

"That's true, Con. And we gotta try ta please our bosses. If we do a good job, it'll reflect well on the Army. If we do bad, then ever'body talks badly 'bout the whole Army, not jest us."

Con glanced around nervously to see if anyone else had heard the conversation then he turned toward the little man. He looked him up and down, frowning deeply.

"How'd you find out?" He spoke just above a whisper.

"I had to know, Con. I'm yer trainer."

Con stared. "Naw! How could you…?"

Rusty was five feet five and plump. His face was round. He was dressed in a worn leather shirt and cheap, coarse trousers that were too large for him. He used rope as suspenders and tied it through button loops on the pants. He looked no more like a soldier than—than—than Con did!

No one liked him. All of the laborers and hands scoffed or sniggered when his name was mentioned. To Con's recollection, Rusty had always been open and friendly to the others, not even taking offense at their crude jokes and rough snubs.

Rusty was a plump, little man with coarse, black, curly hair covering his head and smothering his neck and ears. His voice was scratchy and hard to listen to for any length of time—like a rusty hinge, which gave him his nickname. He was not what Con figured a soldier would be.

"I ain't what you 'spected?" Rusty pursed his lips and lifted his eyebrows.

Con planted his hands on his hips and stared at the man. "No, you're not! I expected someone like Cleato, or maybe my uncle."

Rusty cocked his head. "Your uncle?"

Con nodded. "He's in the militia, somewhere. Name's Pistis. You know him?'

Rusty shook his head.

Con shrugged and turned back to the manure, half hoping the little man would go away. Rusty was the butt of every joke, the topic of all the gossip, and the least likely person for Con to associate with in the whole workforce. He wasn't sure he wanted to join the little man's social status.

Rusty continued. "Wall, Con. I'm the one the C'mmander has sent to train you. You can work with me, or not. You make up yer mind."

Con stopped and looked back at him. He wasn't very articulate—a tradesman's or farmer's education, at best. He was unpopular. He was plump and unathletic. And he worked in a manure pile!

Rusty's eyes fell away from Con's and he returned to his work. "Well, if we wait any longer there'll be talk. Now that you've joined up, Con, they'll be watchin' you. If'n you do anythin' out of the ord'nary or anythin' wrong they'll take it as a opportunity ta attack the C'mmander. It al'as happens."

"Who're they?" Con asked, looking around for anyone new in the vicinity.

Rusty laughed a little and said, "You'll find out."

He returned to his work and Con did the same, looking up now and again for whoever it was that would attack them.

Chapter 18

At lunch, Con retreated to the stump at the back of the property. Few ever ventured there and that was just the way Con wanted it. He sat down on the wide, sloped surface and leaned forward, resting his chin on his fist. A few minutes later, Rusty came out of the stable and walked toward him.

A group of laborers stood in the stable door whispering back and forth. They watched intently, nudging each other. When Rusty stopped and began teaching Con, it would be obvious he had joined—had placed himself at the same level, in their eyes, as the plump little man. Con swung himself around on the stump, turning his back on the scene.

Rusty's shuffling step grew louder, then ceased. "You'd better count the cost of what you've done and make sure you are willin' ta pay it." His gravely voice was stern.

He stooped next to Con and plucked a blade of grass. "I know the first day can be hard, Con. But it's better faced."

Con swung his head to look at Rusty, embarrassed that he had guessed at his feelings so quickly. He remained silent.

Rusty put the grass between his teeth and stared off toward the roofs of the surrounding houses. 'You're gonna find that nobody wants you 'round now, Con. You ain't a rebel no more and that makes 'em uneasy. They'll bad mouth ya', stab ya' in the back, make life more miserable than it has been and'll ridicule everythin' you say or do, if it concerns the Army, the C'mmander or the Dragon. The on'y way they'll stop the criticism is if you can change them from rebels to so'diers."

Con stared off at the same distant point. "I could always rejoin them."

"Nope." Rusty shook his head once. The thick hair followed slightly out of phase. "They'd call you a hypocrite and reject you anyway. If you want to rejoin them after bein' in the Army, it would mean bein' their slave, not their equal."

Con scooped up some dirt and flung it across the lot. The dust floated gently back to the ground.

"Con, you got one more chance. If you've changed yer mind, or if the price is too high, tell me and I'll walk away from you. They'll think that I was jest bothering you as I do them from time to time. They'll even pat you on the back fer rejectin' me."

He paused. "It's up to you."

Con stared at the short man. Slowly his mind grasped the truth. There was no control and despotism, as Con had imagined. The obedience was voluntary. What had apparently been lording-over by the Commander was actually the willingness of the soldier to serve. Nothing in the Army was forced. All obedience, all authority, all control, was voluntary.

Rusty smiled a little. "I can see you're mullin' the whole thing over in yer mind, Con. Good. I'll tell you," he took the blade of grass from his mouth and shook it at Con. "Yer never done decidin'—never done choosin'. Almos' daily you'll hafta make yer choice to be a member of the Army. Daily, you'll hafta say to the C'mmander, 'I'll do it.' It ain't a one-time decision that is good for the rest of your service. It gotta happen time and time ag'in."

Rusty fell back onto his rump and crossed his legs "You can go back right now and there won't be hardly no cost to you, but there won't be no benefit, neither. The decision is your'n. The C'mmander won't have nobody in the service who ain't a volunteer. 'N you gotta know what the cost is up front."

Rusty picked up another blade of grass and chewed on the end. Sniggers rose from the group behind them. A crude laugh broke out, followed by more murmurs.

Con debated. Rusty couldn't be right. There had to be a better way. There had to be a way that wouldn't turn the whole City against him.

A voice sounded in the back of his mind, still and small, "Not the whole City, Con. Not everyone. Just the Rebels. I will be there—always."

Con jerked erect at the voice. Rusty raised his eyebrows in question, then nodded and laughed. He returned to his contemplative position.

The voice was right. Con turned and looked at the group in the barn door: unkempt, crude, sheep without a shepherd. He looked back at Rusty. It was then he realized what it was that made Rusty a soldier. Courage. Courage to submit. Courage to stand. Courage to go against the standards. Con bounced to his feet.

Rusty struggled to rise from his cross-legged position. Con reached out his hand to the smaller man. Rusty glanced at the hand, then up at Con's face. His brow still questioned. When their eyes met, Rusty smiled and reached for the help.

Con put his hand on Rusty's shoulder and boomed, "Of course I've joined, Rusty. I am a soldier, loyal to the Commander, and I want to learn from him and Cleato and from you. Teach me."

Rusty laughed out loud and clapped Con on the back. The workers in the doorway muttered and turned back into the stable. One of them stopped, stared a moment, then threw up his hands and turned back to the darkness of barn.

Con laughed and clasped Rusty in a bear hug. "I've paid the price, Rusty."

Rusty pulled away from Con. He cocked his head to one side and scratched at his scalp. "Wall, you paid the first one, anyway."

"Three months, Con," Rusty said. "Minimum. I don't think we could go faster."

"I'll be in training the rest of winter and into the spring. I wanted it to be faster."

They had left the City after work and walked a short distance north, then turned west toward a clearing. Con found that the way out of the City had actually been short and easy—if one knew the right streets.

Rusty continued in this squeaky voice. "If you can get through all the trainin' in that time, I'll be surprised." He looked ahead and said, "Ah, here it is. And my helper is already here."

Con's heart quickened at the glance. Long, flowing, brown hair blew in the slight breeze. Brown eyes gazed in his direction.

She was dressed in a warm, quilted jacket and the trousers he had seen her wear in the battle. Her feet were shod with sandals but she had stockings on also—for the weather was chilly and the breeze bit into unprotected skin. Con realized his own hands were stuffed into the pockets of his horse hair coat—something picked up at a second hand shop with what little excess his pay provided.

Sarah walked toward them. She went to Rusty and hugged him then turned to Con. "So, Mr. Ataxia, you are ready to learn?"

Con shrugged, still excited to find her here but slightly embarrassed, realizing that he really didn't know her. Suddenly, she stepped forward and threw her arms around him, hugging him close. Then it was over. She stepped back and turned toward Rusty.

Con's face glowed. Never had a girl done that to him before—except his mother and sisters. Rusty laughed out loud. "It's OK, Con. We all get hugged like that."

Chuckling, he turned back to Sarah. "So, is it ready?"

Sarah nodded, turned, and marched off toward a little shack next to a line of trees. Con knew there was a stream there from the way the trees grew.

At the shack, Sarah handed Con a satchel. "In there is some clothes. I'm goin' in the shack and change. You and Rusty can go into the trees and do the same."

Con held the package of clothing up and stared at Rusty. "Change? Is this part of the training?"

Rusty nodded. "It is the first step, Con. It has to be the first step. Let's go get changed and I'll tell ya 'bout it."

They walked back into the woods. Con heard the door of the shack slam shut. They continued to the side of a small stream, in an area with underbrush between them and the road. Rusty dropped his pack and began taking off his jacket.

"Con, yer dirty."

Con looked up and down his trousers. "Did I leave some muck on me?"

Rusty laughed. "Not there and not that kinda' dirt. You got deep stains that can't be gotten out with normal soap and water. You cain't see 'em. I cain't see 'em. The C'mmander does. What's more, the Dragon 'n his Raiders can see 'em—and they know exactly how to get you 'cause of 'em. You cain't go inta battle with them stains still there."

Con had stripped to his shorts and was starting to shake from the cool air. He reached into the bag and pulled out a long woolen garment. It was a single piece of cloth with a hole in the center. Rusty had one in his hand also. He flipped it up and over his head, letting his head stick through the hole. Then his arms came through two sleeves that Con had not noticed before. He nodded at Con. "Put that on. Don't put on any shoes."

Con slipped on the robe. It was a thick, warm garment.

"Rusty, I was just about as bare as I care to get in front of anybody and I didn't see no stains. I'm not sure what this is all about."

Rusty nodded. "I understand what you say, but I ain't sure we're supposed to understand. Let me say that the C'mmander can wash them stains away—completely. He does it when we are obedient to do what we are about to do."

"And what's that?"

Sarah's voice caused them to turn. "You boys decent?"

Rusty said, "Yes. Hold up and we'll join ya.'"

He pushed through the brush and onto a narrow trail. It led to the bank of a stream. The bank dropped gently a few feet to the shallow brook where the clear, sparkling water babbled incoherently among the rocks of its bed. Tangles of roots lined the banks, thrust out of their natural state and into the air by multitudes of spring rains that had eroded their concealment.

They walked along the top of the bank for about fifty feet. There, the stream widened and deepened into a pool, dammed by an energetic beaver to a depth of several feet. The water trickled noisily over the top of the aquatic engineer's construction, escaping the stillness of the pond to resume its noisy travels toward the main river. It's vociferous travel made it seem as if many people gathered there and talked—no, sang; sang a song that Con did not—could not—know.

Rusty and Sarah walked into the water until they were thigh deep. Rusty measured Con's height with is eyes, then stepped deeper into the pond. He was shivering.

"C'mon, Con. I don't wanna stand here all day, son. It is cold."

"You want me in there?"

Sarah nodded. "C'mon, Con. It's cold." She hugged herself and shivered.

"So, why…?"

Rusty shook his head and walked back toward Con. He held out is hand. "C'mon, big guy. This is what's got to be done."

Con stepped off the bank. The water was several inches deep. It was frigid. Con wanted to pull back but Rusty had a strong grip on his hand. It was move forward or get pulled over. Con stepped in, gasping. "Wh…What are we gonna do?"

"Come over here and find out."

When they were deep enough, Rusty got on one side of Con and Sarah on the other. "Con," Rusty said, "we are going to dunk you in the water—completely. Gonna lay you down on your back until you are covered. Then we're gonna pull ya back up. Then we are gonna get out of this water and these wet clothes. Got it?"

""But, why?"

Sarah looked up at him, shivering. "Con, the Commander will do the work while you are below the water to remove those stains. It's sorta' like dyin'. After your dead, what you did when you were alive don't matter anymore. What we're gonna do is bury you—then we're gonna raise you back up. That's what happens here. In that other realm—the one you visited back aways?"

Con nodded, starting to shiver also.

"Well, in that realm, it is like you died with the Commander when he was killed in the big battle. And when we pull you up, its like you were raised with the Commander when he come back to life and defeated the Dragon centuries ago. That's what the Dragon sees. He can't see what you did before. Or, if he can, he can't use it anymore to defeat you."

Con shook his head. "I ain't sure I understand everything you say, but I'm too cold to argue. Let's do it."

Rusty smiled, put Con's hands in front of him and put a hand on his back. Sarah did the same. They thrust him backward. Con let himself sink into the water.

The water rushed up over his face. Then he was back up. He stumbled backward, getting his balance, spraying water out in front of him as he exhaled. Rusty laughed. "Let's get outa' here."

"Caw!"

They all stopped and turned toward the sound. On a branch stuck out over the pool sat a raven. It's feathers were blue-black and its beak shone like the polished black leather harness of a show horse. It opened its beak again. "Caw!"

Rusty turned away and said, "Let's get out of here. Crow or no crow. I'm freezin'. Yer clean, now. We can get warm."

"Un-clean!" The crow spoke the word.

"What?" Con looked up at the bird. It laughed—almost like a human.

Sarah started to walk out of water, splashing water up the front of her as she went. "Let's go. Someone has taught the bird a few words. That's all."

"Unclean! Unclean!" The bird started its shrill speech again. It danced from foot to foot and cackled out its laughter. It's cocked head cast a gleaming little eye at Con, then slowly swung it toward Sarah.

Con's gaze followed the bird's. For the first time, he noticed that Sarah's gown clung to her, revealing very plainly that she was a woman—a beautiful woman. His eyes searched out hers. She was staring at Con's chest. He looked down and realized that his robe clung to him, outlining the muscles of his chest and shoulders.

The bird laughed again, then jumped into the air. Its big wings pounded the air as it lifted itself up and away. At the top of the trees, it circled and screamed, "Unclean! Unclean! Unclean!" Then it cackled again—driving chills up Con's already frigid spine.

The spell was broken. Blood rushed to Sarah's cheeks as she struggled from the water. On the path, she started to run but reached back to pull the robe away from her. "I'm freezin'. I'll see you boys later," she called over her shoulder. Con could not tell if the tremble from her voice was from the cold or from something else.

Con and Rusty ran after her, then ducked through the brush where they had left their clothes. A quick strip and brush down with the rough towels Rusty had brought and they were soon fully dressed again, ready to meet the world.

Con stopped Rusty as they walked back toward the clearing. "Rusty, nothing happened. I don't feel any different. In fact, I feel worse. That crow 'n all."

"Con, it ain't about feelin'. Some people come up outa' the water all floozy and excited. Some come up jest like they went down. It don't matter. What matters is that you did what the C'mmander said. Even when it was so cold I thought I was gonna freeze my toes off."

Con rubbed his thighs with both hands through the heavy trousers, trying to put some warmth back in them. "It was that."

"I know, 'cause it happened to me, too—happens to all the so'diers or they cain't really be so'diers—that you are now cleaned of all the things what the enemy put on you and what you put on yerse'f. All that is gone. You jest gotta believe that, son. You'll find out it's true when you need to."

They met Sarah in the clearing. She had a fire going and sat on a log next to it. There was a pack lying on the ground and she had several things laid out on the log next to her.

She smiled as they approached. Rusty went right to the fire and put out his hands. "Now, that feels good."

Con joined him, afraid to look at Sarah, afraid of the embarrassment that was sure to follow. She leaned forward and flipped her damp hair up over her head, letting it hang in front of the flames. With a stiff bristled brush, she combed it several times, then flipped it back. "That'll have to do until I can get home." There was a bright smile on her face, and she stared happily at Con. The embarrassment in the pond was either gone or pushed out of the way.

The hair lay flat again framing her face. Her eyes danced in the firelight and her teeth glowed white where her broad smile revealed them. Con stared—too hard and too long. Rusty harrumphed, bringing him back.

He jerked his head around, expecting a frown from Rusty. Instead he stared into the bearded face of Cleato. The big man stared at him then at Sarah. His eyes showed expectation. "You two have something to tell me?"

Even though his cheeks flushed with heat, Con shook his head. "No. Can't think of anything."

Rusty grimaced and shook his head. Cleato looked at Sarah.

She stood and nodded. "Yes, Cleato. In the pool, when the crow spoke, I looked toward Con for support but, instead of a fellow soldier, I saw a man. And I wanted him as a man instead of as a brother in arms."

Con's mouth dropped open, then snapped shut. He wasn't sure whether he was more shocked that she confessed or at what she confessed.

Cleato looked at Con again. "Now, Con. Do you have something to tell me?"

Con spread his hands. "Well, I guess you know already. I was just…"

"Yes, Con I do know already. That is not the point. If you are going to be a soldier and be effective, if you are going to do battle with the Dragon, you must always be honest with me. Trying to hide will only make you vulnerable."

Con swallowed, the rebuke burning his cheeks. "I looked at Sarah as a woman—a very desirable woman. I never meant to. It wasn't in my mind. It just happened."

"You two come here." Cleato held out his hands. Sarah moved forward. Con reluctantly stepped in front of the man, half expecting a rap on the side of the head, like his father used to do when he had erred.

Instead, Cleato laid his hands on both of their heads. Con felt something in his brain—no, deeper than that. In his heart—no, it was deeper than that. It was in a part of him he did not even know he had. It was like something raking through his being—like fingers through water. It stirred him but it did not hurt or bother him.

Then it was gone. Cleato lifted both their chins until they were looking at him. "There. That is taken care of." He turned toward Rusty. "And you?"

Rusty nodded. "Yes, Cleato, there was a pang of desire there. I put it away quickly, but it was there."

Cleato nodded. He approached the man, lifted his hands, as if to lay them on his head. His fingers penetrated Rusty's head, delved into his skull. They raked forward coming out his forehead. Darkness came out with them, just a small patch of darkness. It had no form or substance. It was just darkness. This Cleato flung away. It flew out a few feet then disappeared.

Sarah spoke first. "Was it the crow, Cleato? Did he do this?"

Cleato shook his head. "The crow is a deceiver and he tricked you into it but he did not put the desire within you. Children, the crow is ephemeral."

"Yes," Cleato nodded and held up one hand as they started to object, "you heard him and saw him. Listen to me. He is a deceiver. In fact, the crow image is a deception in itself. It is no more than a feather in the wind. Resist him next time, and he will flee."

Con hung his head. "Guess we were the source of the problem, then."

Cleato smiled. "No. The Commander put that desire in you. It is always in you—strongly at your age. But it is never to be satisfied until the Commander sanctifies it.

"The Commander gave you that desire for his purposes. You must control it. The crow simply knows the things to do to ignite the desire and make it burn. "

Cleato set them down on the log and sat across the fire from them. "Look, my soldiers, the crow is clever and a liar. But that is all the power he has. He can enflame your passions but he can't make you fall into them. That is up to you. But what he will do is condemn you, even when you do not fall. He will condemn you, accuse you, and make you feel guilt when there is no guilt. That is what he did today. And it was the guilt that I took care of.

"That attack will come again and again. You must learn to call on me. If you resist, I will put out those flames quickly."

Con shook his head, thinking back on the situation. "But, Cleato, I didn't want to resist. I didn't want to call on you."

Cleato smiled. "Ah, the soldier learns his first lesson. When you least want to call on me is when you most need to.

"Enough time on a silly, powerless bird. We have things to do."

Cleato was dressed in armor. He had on a bright, steel breastplate. He carried a long sword attached to a leather buckler. On his head was a bright brass helmet that covered his ears and protected his forehead. He was shod with thick, leather sandals—well used but not worn.

He walked to the items laid out on the log and picked up a pair of sandals. "These are for you to wear—always. A soldier has to have these on all the time. It takes too long to don them to wait until the enemy is in front of you."

He handed them to Con. Con sat on a rock and set his old sandals aside. The new ones had thick soles and were hobbed. The straps were of wide, thick leather. The front strap covered his toes. The rear strap grabbed his heel. A long wide strip of leather wound around his lower leg and ankle, holding the sandals securely to the bottom of his feet.

"The rest of this you must have with you at all times but you may not always be wearing it." He handed Con a large length of broad leather. "This buckler you must put on before you put on the rest of the armor—it anchors everything else. It is uncomfortable some times and you'll think you would be more versatile without it. Don't attempt it. You will die in battle quickly without this thick protection for your bowels."

Con put it around his waist to see how it fit, then laid it aside.

Cleato picked up a helmet. "This you will always have. Put it on before you enter battle. You must protect your mind from the spears of the enemy. The only thing that can do that is this helmet."

Con took it and looked it over. It was not at all fancy—just a plain, brass-colored helmet with earflaps and a visor that could be dropped over the eyes. The inside, though, was lined with fleece, to make it comfortable for long periods wear. Being a farm boy, Con recognized that it was the soft, downy fleece of a lamb—not the thicker hair of a full-grown sheep. He sat it on the buckler.

Cleato picked up the breastplate—a golden contraption that had not just frontal protection but thick leather and chain mail across the back. It was thrown over the head and attached front and back with leather straps to the buckler—anchoring it against all blows that would attempt to shove it aside.

Cleato said, "Although you will always have this, and it will protect you, you must insure that you put it on before battle. It does no good sitting on a shelf in your house. It is heavy. It is sometimes a burden. It will become a source of irritation, even during heavy battles. Without it, though, the enemy's spears will pierce your heart with the first thrust. With it on, no weapon that the enemy can use will get through to your heart and breath. You will be safe—as long as you never take it off during battle. Like all the armor, you must keep it with you all the time. You must be ready to put it on at my command and stand in the line with the rest of your fellows."

Con looked at the pile of equipment then back at Cleato. "All of this is to protect me, Cleato. Where is my weapon?"

Cleato picked up the last of the items on the log. Sarah stood. Rusty walked over toward them.

It was a book with a black, leather cover. Cleato handed it to Con. "This is the only weapon you have—the only weapon you are allowed—the only weapon that works."

Sarah lifted her hand. In it was similar book, though it was smaller of size and light brown in color. Rusty raised his hand. He, also, had a book. It had a tan cover and was about the same size as the one Con held.

They both stepped back, lifted the book over their heads, and swung it in an arc in front of them. As it traveled, the books blurred, shimmered, took on a golden hue, then with loud pops, became fiery swords. The flames roared as the blades cut the air. Rusty and Sarah thrust the sword points in front of them, then lifted them straight up. The flames extinguished and the soldiers dropped to one knee, holding the swords toward Cleato.

Cleato nodded and the two stood, dropped the point of the sword to the earth and leaned on the hilt, legs spread.

"That is the drill, Con. Can you do it?"

Con raised the book, swung it in front of him. Nothing happened. The book was still a book.

He looked at Cleato. "I think this one is defective."

Cleato roared in laughter. "Well, something is defective but it is not my sword, young man."

Con looked puzzled. He flipped the book open. It was just a book, like Mrs. Porteur's: filled with pages and printing. He clapped it shut again and looked back to Cleato.

"Then, I guess I don't know what I'm doin.'"

Cleato stepped forward and pounded him on the back. "Now, that is the right answer."

He turned to Rusty and Sarah. "Train him."

He turned back to Con. Con heard two loud pops and looked at the two soldiers. They stood with books in their hands again.

"Con, no one can use the book as a sword until they know what the book says. These two are going to study it with you. Listen to them. And listen to me. I will be there to answer any question—to clarify any instruction.

"Listen to me well. In a few weeks, you will be able to evoke the sword. In a few months, you will be able to wield it with power." Cleato frowned, a deep frown. He stared into Con's eyes. With his finger, he tapped Con's chest, emphasizing each word. "If." Tap. "You." Tap. "Study." Tap, tap tap.

With that he turned and walked toward the road. "Enough for the first day. Get some rest."

Chapter 19

Cleato walked toward the road. Sarah pulled a folded up piece of canvas from her pack and tossed it to Con. "Here is your pack. Start packing up your stuff. We need to get back to the City."

They all began to put things away. Con glanced up to see how far ahead Cleato was but he was nowhere in sight. He stood, then looked around. The big man wasn't there. He shrugged and went back to packing.

"Caw!"

The three soldiers looked up. The big, black bird was perched above them in the tree. It dropped to the ground and began to wobble forward, hopping from foot to foot. Sarah reached into her pack and pulled out her manual. The crow looked at her, then scooted far out of range.

"Oooh! Real soldiers," the crow said. Then it cackled again. It stepped around the fire, its eyes on Con. Rusty stepped between them. He held out his book and cocked his head toward the bird.

The bird jumped up and fluttered away about fifteen feet. "Caw! I just want to talk to him. I have a message from…"

Rusty pursed his lips and blew. The bird tumbled over backwards as if a strong wind had struck it. It rose, ruffling his feathers. "No need to do that, soldier."

Sarah stepped in front of Con, alongside of Rusty. The crow jumped and flapped its wings, rising to a branch. It looked down over their heads at Con. "Whats'a matter? Ain't you got one of them swords, boy?" Then it cackled again.

"'Course not. They wouldn't trust a new slave with a weapon."

Rusty pursed his lips again. The bird shrieked and jumped to a higher branch. "Listen to me, Ataxia. Don't believe all these lies. I still see you."

Rusty blew hard and the bird tumbled from its perch. It spread its wings and climbed into the sky. At treetop level, the bird circled once and yelled. Its voice was barely audible. "I can still see you, Ataxia. You ain't been hidden. I will come for you whenever I want you."

Rusty blew again, vibrating his lips. The crow tumbled over in the air, screeching at the insult. Then it winged toward the City. It became a speck of black, then disappeared into the growing darkness.

"What was that all about?" Con stared after the bird, searching the sky.

"Lies, Con," Rusty said. "Remember what Cleato said. Lies."

"But how did you blow it? I don't understand."

Rusty smiled. "Remember, Cleato said that this thing wasn't really a bird—just a fake image. I just heard Cleato saying, blow at it. That's all it took."

The rest of the training was done in the City. Rusty drilled him in the use of the manual during lunchtimes. Every evening, Sarah and Rusty taught him new drill. By the end of the first week, Con's head was spinning but he knew the major topics of the manual. Details were yet to come but the overall theme of various chapters he understood.

What had always been held up to him by his parents, his teachers, and his friends as Army nonsense became perfect sense. There was a richness in the manual that none of those who had criticized the Army could have guessed at. The "contradictions" they all laughed about disappeared as the book was revealed to him. The fables became history. The rules and regulations became formulae for success. The oppression by the Commander became the caring of a loving leader for wayward and rebellious, and truth-be-told, a slightly mentally deficient people.

"Con stand up."

Rusty entered the training room through the side door. The room they used was just a large, bare one with a high ceiling in a wooden building. There was a vacant lot on the side that was used for drill. The floor was bare wood. The walls were unfinished. The only furniture was a dilapidated bookcase shoved up against one wall. Several cushions were spread across the floor. Con, who had been sitting on one of these reading the manual, stood. He held the manual in his right hand.

"Grab that manual in both yer hands an' lift it over your head."

Con did so, gripping the manual hard. The one he had was thick with a soft cover and was hard to support like that.

"Con, I want you to think of somethin' in the manual—the part that says about our armor, how you put it on and how you use it. D'ya remember that one?"

Con nodded. "Yeah. It says we should put on the full armor."

Rusty smiled. "Good. And why the full armor?"

"Because anything less leaves some part of us open. All the armor works t'gether to keep us safe in battle."

Rusty smiled and nodded again. "Good. Now, in that part, what's the last instruction? What is it that we take up after we get dressed?"

"The Sword."

"Swing the book, Con. Swing it an' believe that it's that Sword."

Con swung the book out in front of him, slightly embarrassed at the action. It wasn't a sword—it was the book he had been studying for a week every free moment.

Con completed the swing. The book was still a book.

Con looked at Rusty. "So?"

Rusty stood still, staring at Con. A slight smile stretched the corners of his mouth. "Con, when you believe that it's a sword, when you see it as a sword, then it…"

"Aaaugh!"

Con spun around to find the source of the scream. Sarah ran at him, a gleaming sword in her hand, poised to chop at him. Con smiled at her but she did not smile back. There was a look of determination on her face and the edge of the sword gleamed in the lamplight. At the last minute, she planted both feet on the floor and brought the sword down with all her might.

Con yelled and swung the manual at the descending blade. There was an explosion of light. Flames danced all around him and roared through the air. A steel blade shot from the book. The cover transmogrified in his hands, becoming the hilt of a heavy sword. At the last minute, his blade stuck Sarah's. They clanged with an ear-splitting noise. Both stopped dead in the air.

Sarah stepped back and dropped the point of her sword to the floor. She stood as she and Rusty had that day in the field, tip of the sword resting on the floor, her hands resting on the hilt, her feet spread.

Con lowered the sword, holding it in his right hand. He screamed at Sarah, "What was that all about? You almost killed me!"

"That, Mr. Ataxia, was to get you to evoke the sword. And it worked." She winked at Rusty and smiled.

Con slowly shook his head, his cheeks still glowing with anger, the adrenaline still draining from his limbs. "You idjit. You scared me half to death."

Rusty patted Con's shoulder. "Sometimes, that's the on'y way people will evoke the sword—when they think their life depends on it. Now that you've done it once, I think you'll be able to draw it out with less reason."

Rusty nodded at Sarah. She raised the point of the sword until she held it vertically. Her hands were straight out in front of her. She nodded at Con.

Con shrugged, still trying to calm his shaking nerves. "What?"

Rusty clapped him on the back. "Do like Sarah does. She is gonna show you how ta' put it away. You want ta carry that sword around all the time?"

Con raised the sword and held it in front of him. There was a pop and Sarah's sword became a book in her hands. She lowered the book to her side.

Con's sword remained a sword. Sarah laughed. "Quit thinking of it as a sword, Con. Think of it as a book, again."

Con stared at the sword, concentrating. It remained a sword. Sarah laughed again. "Con, its not how hard you squint that makes it happen or how funny your face is screwed up."

Con looked up at her, exasperated. "Sar—ah," he complained.

There was a pop and Con's manual appeared in his hands again.

Con's head jerked back and he stared at the book. "How 'bout that?"

Rusty and Sarah laughed. Rusty wrapped his arm around his shoulder and hugged him. "Con, we're not laughing at you. We all did the same things when we were learning. But it is funny to watch a new recruit the first time."

Rusty walked toward the door. "I think you get the idea. When you want the sword, think of a sword. When you want the manual, quit thinkin' of it as a sword. It's really pretty simple."

Rusty walked to the door. "They should be here by now."

He opened the door and stuck his head out. Then he gestured outside the door with one hand.

Two people entered the room. They were dressed in street clothes but Con noticed immediately that they wore the thick-soled sandals of the Militia. Both carried a manual.

One was a girl—late teens or early twenties. She was plump and wore thick glasses. She had light brown hair, which was cut short and curled at the ends. Her cheeks were ruddy and she had friendly, green eyes that glowed with excitement as she looked around the room. Her smile was bright and open, revealing lustrous white, perfectly straight teeth. There was a bubbly joy in her whole countenance. Con immediately liked her.

The other was a man—or a boy. It was hard to tell. Perhaps nineteen or twenty, he still had the look of a boy about him. Probably, Con decided, it was the eyes. They danced around the room, barely resting on anything—looking for something new all the time. He had flaming red hair and large, dark freckles all over his face and on the back of his hands. He was as tall as Con but not as heavy. He had long, thin arms and a thin chest. His eyes were bright blue and held a hint of mischief whenever he let them rest on anyone or anything. Whereas the girl stood quietly, this one jittered all the time. Something on him was always moving. As he stood there, his manual pounded his leg over and over, making a popping sound.

Rusty waved them toward Con and Sarah. "Two more recruits. They've each just learned to evoke the sword."

The red head put his hand on the back of the girl, as if he was directing—or claiming ownership through the touch. The girl, though, wriggled at his touch and shot him a hard glance. He dropped the hand, then stepped in front of her. Con stepped forward and stuck out his hand toward the red head. "Con," he said smiling.

"Dugan," the young man said, not offering his hand. Con let his fall to his side. Dugan did not smile but looked Con up and down, as if sizing up a rival. Con stepped over to the girl. "Con Ataxia."

The girl beamed at him. She was short—a least a foot shorter than Con but she reached up, wrapped her arms around his neck and pulled him down into a bear hug. When she had let him go, she stuck out her hand and said, "Hi. I'm Beatrice."

Con stepped back, a little warm in his face. Beatrice dropped her hand said, "Oh, my. I thought…."

Rusty wrapped his arm around her shoulder and laughed. "You thought right. Con just ain't been exposed to that.

"Look, Con. A lot a' the militia units greet each other with a hug. It's sorta' traditional but it also has a meanin'. It means we care for each other and we're close to each other. It also means we can make ourse'ves open to one another. You ain't gotta do it, mind ya'. Ain't no rule. But, I think you'll get to enjoy it."

Dugan walked up to him and wrapped his bony arms around him and hugged him also. Con did not respond. He just stepped back when Dugan let go and looked them all up and down.

Sarah laughed. "Con, I've never seen you act like that when I hugged you."

Con's face flared again and the whole group laughed.

Dugan looked at him, then at Sarah. A big grin covered his face and he nodded. "Oh, OK."

Rusty, still chuckling, said, "OK, I think we've bated Con enough for one day. Let's get down to work."

He motioned toward the cushions on the floor. Each member plopped down on one. Rusty stood in front of them. "We are now a squad. We're gonna train together. We're gonna work together. We're gonna support one another. We are gonna become a team. And when were done with trainin', we're gonna go into battle together."

Rusty let that sink in. "Yep. We're goin' inta battle. That's the whole purpose of trainin' you.

"For now, Sarah and I will be yer trainers." Sarah raised her hand and nodded at everyone. "We've already been in a fightin' unit and have been in battle. So, listen to us. We know a little bit of what you need. Soon, Cleato'll assign a new leader to this squad—one who has been through a good deal of fightin'. 'Cause this squad has got some fightin' ta do."

The questioning looks from the squad got only a raised palm from Rusty in response. "I don't know what it is. I jest got a feelin' that it ain't gonna be yer routine patrol."

Dugan raised his hand. "Rusty, how come you put me with this group? I already've been through the manual twice."

"Dugan, when did'ya evoke the sword for the first time?"

"Last week. But that's because you were explainin' wrong. Once you explained it right, I got it out quick."

Rusty stared at him for few seconds, then shook his head. "OK. Whatever you think the reason was—you still ain't used the sword. You ain't even sparred with it, have you?"

Dugan shook his head. "But that ain't my fault. You haven't set nothin' up for me."

Rusty raised his hand toward Dugan. "Dugan, I don't want to fight about it. You ast for more trainin'—more intense trainin'. That's what yer here for."

"How am I gonna git intense trainin' with a bunch a' trainees? Kinda unfair for them, ain't it? I mean, they don't know the manual like I do. How much practice are they gonna be for me? I need partners that can teach me somethin'." Dugan's nose was up in the air as he looked around the squad.

Rusty dropped his head and shook it. He shrugged.

"OK, Dugan. Let's see how much you can teach these two others." He turned to Con. "When d'you evoke the sword the first time?"

Con shrugged. "Half hour ago?"

"Stand up there in the sparrin' box. Dugan, you face him. The rest of you, git back."

"Evoke yer swords."

Dugan lifted his book overhead and swung it out. There was a whistle in the air, a few crackles of light, and the shape of the sword shimmered in front of him. Rusty shook his head. "Concentrate, Dugan."

Dugan nodded. There was a pop and the sword formed in his hand.

Con thought hard about the sword. He concentrated on the phrase in the manual: "take up the sword." He swung the manual. There was a blast of light and flames roared through the air. Before he had swung his hands half way in front of him, the sword gleamed strong and sure in his hands.

"Present swords!"

Dugan immediately stood straight and raised the tip of the sword until it was vertical. He held it out in front of him. Con just looked at Rusty, unsure of the command. Dugan snickered. "Oh, this ought to be fun."

Rusty's hands guided Con's sword into position. Con held the heavy sword awkwardly, the tip wavering in a tight little circle. Rusty went to a sack laying on the floor and withdrew two, long, thin leather pouches. He approached Dugan and nodded his head. Dugan lowered the blade tip and Rusty slipped one of the pouches over the blade, covering the edge all the way to the hilt. He turned toward Con and nodded. Con lowered his sword as Dugan had done. Rusty slipped the other pouch on his blade..

"The sword is pow'rful. Even in sparrin' with each other, you can get hurt by it. So we put these on to protect you. Don't never spar without that coverin' on the blades."

Both of the men in the sparring box, a square painted on the floor, nodded.

"When I say go, I want you two to try to touch each other's chest with the tip of yer sword. Don't try ta hurt. Control yer blade so that you jest touch the other guy. Got it?"

Both men nodded, staring at each other.

"An', a' course, you also got to stop the other guy from touchin' you."

Again the two nodded but did not take their eyes off their opponent.

A hundred things ran through Con's mind. Partial phrases from the manual flitted across his consciousness. None of it made sense. He tried to think out his first move but nothing came. He just did not know what to do.

A little anger started to rise within his chest. He knew he was going to get a licking—and he wasn't sure he liked it. This was an unfair contest. He was about to drop his sword point and protest when Rusty yelled, "Go!"

Dugan yelled and lunged forward, thrusting with the sword. It's tip leaped at Con's chest. Con twisted sideways and stepped away from the blade. It skimmed past him, dragging Dugan with it. Dugan stumbled forward, almost leaving the box. Con backed up to the other side of the box, still holding his sword in the ready position.

Dugan recovered and spun toward his opponent. His face was bright red. Twice his eyes sought out someone on the sidelines. He looked back at Con. "You did that on purpose."

Con nodded. "Yeah, I did. Wasn't I supposed to?"

Dugan didn't answer. He raised the hilt over his head until the blade pointed down his back. "I'll show you," he screamed and charged forward.

Rusty yelled, "Dugan!"

Phrases from the manual of arms leapt into Con's mind. With each phrase the blade tip moved, the edge of the sword realigned. Dugan planted his feet and yelled with all his might. The blade screamed through the air. Con's sword tip jumped at the hilt in Dugan's hand. There was a twist, a flick of the wrist, and Dugan's sword spun up into the air. Con twisted his wrists again, and the sword point dropped to Dugan's chest—resting lightly on the third button of his blouse. Dugan's sword clattered onto the floor, outside the box.

Dugan's eyes went wide at the sight of the blade over his heart. He threw himself backward, landing hard on his rump. Elbows and heels starting scraping at the wood floor, trying to drive himself back out of Con's reach. Seeing that Con was not pursuing him, he stopped and collapsed onto his back.

"Oh, man." He scrunched his eyes up and slapped the floor next to him.

The rest of the squad applauded. Con dropped the sword tip down, holding it again in just his right hand.

Rusty walked over, smiling. He guided Con's sword to the rest position: tip on the floor, hands on the hilt. Then he spread Con's feet to the proper separation.

"There, soldier. That is the proper rest position."

He patted Con on the back and walked over to Dugan. He stuck out his hand.

Dugan took it and was pulled to his feet. He looked at Rusty sheepishly. "Maybe I do need some practice."

Dugan picked up his manual. Con lifted the sword and thought of it as a manual again. It popped back into the shape of a book.

The leather pouch fell to the ground and Con retrieved it. He pitched it at the sack just outside the square. Then he walked over to where Dugan had left his pouch laying on the ground. He flicked it with his toe toward the sack.

Dugan's eyes met Con's. After a few seconds, he walked over and stuck out his hand. "That was good sparrin'. Maybe you can show me how you did that last move sometime."

Con shook his hand and smiled. "If I knew, I'd be glad to show you."

Dugan frowned and heat rose into his cheeks but he turned away and sat down with the rest of the squad.

Rusty stood and pulled out the manual. "Turn to page 400. We have a lot to learn."

At the end of the evening, Con grabbed his cloak and headed out the door. Outside, in the shadows, two people stood—Dugan and Beatrice. They didn't see Con. It was obvious they were having a private conversation. Dugan's voice came out of the darkness but Con couldn't understand the words. There was a whining quality to it, though. Beatrice shook her head. "But I do like you, Dugan. But, right now, that's all. I just like you. You are a fellow soldier."

Dugan mumbled something else.

Beatrice replied, "Well, who knows what the future will bring. We certainly will be together for a while, it seems."

Dugan mumbled again. Beatrice said, "Oh, Dugan. It has nothing do to with the way you handled that fight." She reached up and patted his cheek. "I...Look, let's just wait and see. But we can't let this interfere with our training."

Con backed into the building, embarrassed to have heard that much. He waited for ten minutes, then went out again. There was no one there, this time.

They trained. Each day. Cleato was at every practice—questioning, drilling, correcting, perfecting. No incorrect movement missed his eye. No dropped guard, no let down of effort escaped him. He drilled them unceasingly for weeks.

Close order drill—patrol tactics—patrol procedures—enemy recognition—proper communication—week after week the subjects grew.

For hours each day they sparred or practiced the manual of arms with the sword. Every free hour was dedicated to it. Each became proficient in his or her own way. Each found unique moves—thrusts, parries or blocks.

Throughout the training, Con' proficiency with the sword grew. The sword fit him. Its weight. Its balance. The drill. The commands. The manual of arms. They were in him. And he was in them. He quickly outstripped his fellow students, then Sarah, then Rusty. He began sparring with three, then with all four.

He wasn't the only one who increased in ability. Each one had come to the squad with a strength. To each one, Cleato added more, along with abilities they never had. Con's slight ability to recognize the presence of the enemy was increased, but nothing like that of Dugan. Dugan knew when the enemy was about before there was any indication of them—before they even had thought of it themselves.

Dugan also like to help when someone was hurt, or needed care He seldom got the chance. Sarah constantly prowled among them during the rest periods, soothing and massaging sore limbs. Just her touch was enough to heal most of their ills.

Sarah, in turn, wanted to extend her ministering to cooking and carrying. She seldom got the chance, either. Beatrice always seemed to be ahead of them. She was able to anticipate the needs and make provisions for meeting them well in advance of anyone else in the squad.

Rusty was the administrator. He always had everything arranged and scheduled. Everyone knew his or her place and duties. Rusty insured that.

So, the squad fed one another. What was strong in one was a part of all. What was lacking in one was made up for by the ability and strength of another. As individuals, they were normal. As a team—they were becoming a fighting force.

On a Saturday, early in spring, Rusty called them into the training building. They entered the building to find a tall, thin man standing there. He had a thin face and hair streaked with gray. Con had seen him. He knew him.

Sarah waved at the man. "Hello, Pistis. What are you doing here?'

Pistis! His uncle—maybe.

Con stepped forward, then feeling awkward, stepped back again.

Pistis waved at Sarah, then hugged her. Rusty grinned from ear to ear. The rest of the squad glanced at one another.

Rusty hugged the thin man, then turned to the squad. "This is Pistis. He is our new squad leader."

The three trainees glanced at each other. Dugan mumbled something under his breath. Con looked at him. There was fire in his eyes, as he stared at the new man. "Another one. Man, I am never going to get promoted," he mumbled. He glanced at Con, realizing he may have been heard. Seeing the knowledge in Con's eyes, he quickly turned away. Rusty shook his head. "They ain't real disciplined, Pistis."

Pistis grinned. "Militiamen normally aren't. That's why I like 'em so much."

He stepped forward and grabbed Dugan's hand. "You're Dugan, I suppose."

Dugan eyebrows rose, but he nodded. Pistis said, "I've heard a lot about you, son. Great scout, is what I'm told."

Dugan swelled a few inches and he smiled for the first time in a couple of days. "Well, I can smell 'em out for ya."

Pistis stepped over to Beatrice. "And you have to be Beatrice. I want to tell you, young lady, that no squad is complete without one like you. I am told that you are the backbone of this whole group."

Beatrice's face flushed but her eyes said that Pistis had just captured a heart.

Then Pistis's eyes saw Con in the back. He stepped between Dugan and Beatrice. "You are Con, our swordsman."

Con nodded. Pistis glanced at the manual. "You really good with that?"

Con shrugged his shoulders. "I don't know if I'm good. *It's* good. I suspect its much more the sword than it is me."

Pistis laughed and slapped him on the shoulder, knocking his sideways a little. "Right, Boy! And the reason you are so good with that thing is because you recognize that. That is what I wanted to hear!"

He turned to walk away. Con said, softly, "Uncle."

Pistis turned back, "What?"

"You are Pistis Trueblood? Your sister is Resig Ataxia?"

Pistis frowned and cocked his head. "How did…"

A light came into his eyes. "Con. You're Con Ataxia, my sister's baby."

Pistis grabbed him by the shoulders. "My sister's little boy. Only you ain't so little any more. It's been twelve…no, more than fifteen years since I saw you. How did you get here?"

Con started to tell him, but Cleato appeared at the door of the small room at the rear. "Come here, soldiers. We need to talk."

The whole squad turned and marched off.

Pistis grabbed Con around the shoulder and walked with him. "You look like your Daddy. How is the old coot, anyway?"

Con briefly told him the story of Market.

Pistis's eyes became moist. "She had twin girls, too."

Con nodded, "Melissa and Jennifer."

"And the Dragon killed them?"

"Good as. His Raiders ran their steeds right over them, crushing them."

Con felt the hurt pierce his heart again—hurt and anger. The old hate rose in his chest. He struggled to put it back in its place.

"And my sister?"

"She's on the farm—taken care of for now."

Pistis nodded. "We need to talk more, nephew, but now is not the time. Let's go see what Cleato has for us."

They entered a small room. The squad was seated in a line of straight back chairs. Two were empty on the right end. Con and Pistis moved to them. Across the front of the room, six small packs and one large pack were lined up. On the black slate board above the packs was drawn a map of the valley.

"The time has come."

The big man stared at them, his face chiseled in stone. No one spoke.

"The time has come for this squad to go on a mission. It is not an ordinary one."

Still the squad maintained its silence. Cleato nodded and turned to the board. "We are located here." He pointed at the City. "Here," he tapped the very southern end of the valley, "is the Citadel of the Dragon. That's where we're going."

Dugan whistled lightly through his teeth. One of the girls gasped.

Cleato nodded again. "It is well you should be surprised. It is not every squad that we send into the Citadel. In fact, very few ever get the chance."

Dugan rose to his feet, still staring at the map. "Why us, Cleato? Are we that good?"

Cleato pursed his lips then smiled. "Let us say, you've learned the skills necessary to do it at just the time for it to be done. And you have a member who has desired it even before he was a soldier."

Sarah and Rusty glanced at Con. Con's face burned with pleasure. A promise, from what seemed liked long ago by Cleato, was to be fulfilled.

Dugan turned toward Pistis, accusation in his stare. "Who is that blamed fool, as if I didn't know?"

Con raised his hand. Dugan's head snapped toward him, his eyebrows rising in question. "Whatever for?"

Cleato coughed. "That, Dugan, is for Con to tell you on his own. For now, the mission is important. Are you ready? Do you want to go?"

Dugan dropped into his chair and stared back up at the wall. He shrugged. "Yeah, I mean, I've trained all this time. Ain't the mission I would choose but it'll do."

A slight shake of Cleato's head signaled his disturbance with Dugan. He returned to his briefing. "We will be taking the South road for some of the trip. Then we will leave it and enter the lower valley through a devious route. Up to that point of deviation, it will be a routine patrol. I want all of you to go that far." He stared at Dugan. Dugan did not respond. "After that, the trip will become very hazardous. Only volunteers will be taken beyond that point."

Quiet fell over the group again. Cleato tapped the packs. "I want you all to get your armor on and....Yes, Dugan, full gear." Dugan's face screwed up in disgust. "When you are dressed, grab the pack with your name on it. We leave in fifteen minutes. Form up out front."

Chapter 20

They left the City through the Down Valley gate. The road was a wide dirt lane. Two wagons could travel on it at the same time. Along each edge was a footpath, beaten as hard as rock by the treading of untold feet over the centuries. The surface of the road, which should have been full of ruts, was smooth—as if someone or something routinely graded it to eliminate anything that might slow the traveler. Fine dust covered the surface, rising in little clouds into the still morning air with each step.

They tramped south. The dust hung in the air around them, marking their passage. A large, warm, yellow sun hung high above the mountains, turning the sky a brilliant blue, bringing warmth to the chill air. Sweat began to form on Con's forehead and under his armor. "Man, this is going to be uncomfortable before this day is out," he mumbled to himself.

Cleato appeared at his side. "And that is exactly the thought the enemy would like you to have this early in the mission."

The big man walked faster and caught up with Sarah, directly in front of Con. Con's face glowed, but he had to smile. Whenever he started to drift, Cleato was always right there to help.

About two miles from the City, Cleato called a halt. He led them off the right side of the lane to a grove of trees. Inside the tree line, there was a shaded glade. There, he signaled them to sit. The squad pulled off their packs and plopped down onto the ground.

Cleato remained standing. "Soldiers."

The squad looked up. In the middle of the clearing was a stack of…something. Con was sure it had not been there when they entered. He looked around. No one but the squad and Cleato was present.

Cleato spoke again, "We will be entering the Dragon's realm soon. I have for you a new piece of armor—your shield."

He nodded at Pistis. Pistis went to the stack and lifted the top shield. His left arm wriggled into something on the inside of the shield, then the shield came up in front of him as if he was entering battle. He drew his sword from its scabbard (for the militia always had their swords evoked when on patrol) and held it at the ready in his right hand. The shield was a large thing, covering him from the ground to his head. Only his helmet and his eyes were above it. Only his sword showed to the side of it. Nothing of his feet showed below it. Yet, he appeared to wield it as if it was paper.

The whole squad stood and approached the stack. Pistis smiled. He sat the shield on the ground and wriggled his left arm. The shield stood there as Pistis walked away.

"Each of you, come here. Cleato is going to give you your shield. Never—again, I say never—go into battle without it. And never drop this shield while in the presence of your enemy."

The squad fell into line and Cleato lifted a shield off the stack. He turned it over and looked at the name printed on the inside. "Dugan."

Dugan stepped forward. Cleato handed it to him. Dugan returned to the line.

Each in turn was called. All went smoothly until Beatrice received hers. She looked at it strangely, trying to fit her arm into it. She struggled for a few minutes, then walked over to Pistis. Con could not hear the conversation but Pistis moved behind her, put his arms around her, and lifted the shield into position. The Beatrice's arm slid easily into the straps. She turned around to him and nodded.

Cleato watched the exchange expressionless. Then, as Beatrice returned to the squad, he turned back to the stack. A small smile stole across his features.

Most of the squad had ignored the incident. Dugan, though, was staring hard at Pistis. The tips of his ears had turned pink.

The shield was made of thick, rough leather stretched like a drum head over a wood and bone frame. Inside there were two straps at the balance point, just right to fit with his forearm through one and the other resting in the palm of his hand. The shield moved easily with every move of his wrist and arm.

Cleato stood. "These seem fragile, but they are not. There is not a weapon the enemy possesses that can penetrate them—even the fire arrows they are so fond of raining down on us whenever we approach their walls. That does not mean that they cannot get around the shield. If you are sloppy with its use, if you fail to keep it in front of you, between you and the enemy, then you will be open to his attacks. Listen to Pistis. He has been in those battles. He has succeeded and he has failed."

Pistis stood and nodded. "Thank you, Lord Cleato." He turned toward the squad. "I have succeeded when I have listened to Cleato. I have failed when I became sloppy in my use of the armor, the sword, or the shield. You will have the same experiences, for no soldier is any better than this armor, his instructions, and his obedience."

Dugan's leg jerked, kicking a stone. He sat on the ground, his shield laying next to him. His eyes were down and there was a dark look on his face.

Pistis walked over to him. "What's the matter, Dugan?"

Dugan looked up and sneered. "This is when you tell us that it's you we have to obey, right?"

Pistis cocked his head to one side and scratched at it with one finger. "Well, Dugan, Cleato has made me the squad leader here. So, yes. You should be obeying me. But that is only because Cleato is giving me his orders and instructions, and I've learned how to obey and follow them."

Dugan looked over at Cleato. "Look, I can hear Cleato myself. Why should I listen to you? It's inefficient. I don't think we need any leader—except Cleato, of course."

Pistis squatted down in front of Dugan. "Son, I have been in many battles. I have fought with many squads. I have seen many soldiers ruined and killed on the battlefield. The squads that have been successful and who have all come back alive from the missions were the squads who had caring leaders who were attuned to Cleato's commands. The squads that have failed and been killed are those who had a leader who was not listening to Cleato, or who had no leader—allowing every member to do what they thought Cleato was saying. That is the route to confusion and failure. Take it from me. I've been there."

"Bah! If we all hear Cleato, why do we need you?"

Pistis frowned deeply. "We do all need to hear Cleato. That isn't the point. In your individual fight with a Raider or one of his guards, you better be listening. It is in the overall strategy and tactics of the battle that Cleato will use me—and that, my friend, is more 'efficient' than him trying to explain all of that to each of you every time."

Cleato stood quietly during this exchange. When Dugan opened his mouth to answer again, Cleato spoke. "Enough, Dugan. Listen to Pistis. He speaks wisdom."

Dugan's mouth snapped shut. He nodded at Cleato, then dropped his eyes back to the ground.

Pistis stood. "Dugan?"

Dugan's head remained down but he answered, "I'm listenin'."

The squad lined up on the road. Cleato set them in order. "Rusty, take the point. Pistis next. Dugan, you in the center. Beatrice, left flank. Sarah, right flank. Con, you take the rear. Sing out if any one comes toward us from that quarter. I will be roaming up and down the squad."

Pistis raised his hand, then waved it forward. The squad fell into position, took up the proper interval and started a route march down the dusty road. Con waited until they were fifty feet in front of him, then took up the same pace, as he had been taught. Cleato walked in among them, talking first to one, then another.

The sun rose high in the cloudless sky. Dust rose to join it, making its own yellowish, gray cloud that hung over the squad. They passed out of the populated areas of the valley, moving toward the purple bulk in their front that was the intersection of the East and West Barriers.

More dust puffed up, billowing from each step. It was a hazy cloud between Con and the squad. Then it moved back and sifted down on the trailing soldier.

The squad approached a set of low hills that cut across the valley from east to west. Whenever the dust cleared, they were there, growing larger with each viewing. They were only a few hundred feet high and they were rounded and smoothed by eons of storms, wind, ice and snow. Never the less, they rose quickly from the plain, looking like a wall set across their route.

Pistis stepped out the line of march and stood still, signaling the squad to keep moving. As each passed, he pointed toward the hills and said something. When he got to Con, he fell in beside him.

"That's the border, nephew," he said, pointing at the low hills. "Beyond those hills, we will be in land that the Dragon claims is his own. Keep an eye out. I am sure we will see some of his scouts as we get closer."

Con nodded. Pistis clapped him on the shoulder and started to jog back up the line.

The morning passed into afternoon. The hills grew higher. The hot sun beat down through the dust. Con's feet and ankles began to ache. The dust was caked on his face and clumped on his upper lip under his nostrils. He wanted to call a halt, to get a drink, to wash off and wash down the gritty grayness that had settled into every crack.

Con turned to look at the back trail, to check for activity. There, far in the distance, was the wall of the City, its twenty-mile width still stretching the imagination and blocking the view of the rest of the valley. Stretched out beyond were the roofs of the buildings. Con could not yet see the far wall but would be able to soon. They had risen several hundred feet above the Valley floor.

The land sloped gently up all around them except to the rear. The road climbed the side of the hills in front of them, turning, disappearing and reappearing further on. In the distance, perhaps five miles, it topped the hill and disappeared behind the crest.

Pistis turned and raised his hand. The squad stopped. Sarah lifted one leg and rubbed at her ankle. Beatrice bounced from one foot to the other. Each one showed signs of fatigue. Pistis waved his hand to both sides and the squad slipped to the grass, first one to the right, the next to the left. When they were all in position, hidden in the tall, green stalks, he walked back to each one and whispered something.

When he reached Con, he slipped to the ground.

"Shortly, we will turn east and walk along the northern edge of the hills. Cleato wants this to look as if it were a normal patrol so we will head directly across the valley, not descending any farther. Keep your eyes open and if you see anything, bring it up the squad. I want no fighting until I say."

"If we are attacked?" Con asked.

"I don't think we will be. I think they would prefer to just know where we are right now. Seldom is a squad attacked on this side of the hills." Pistis stared into space for a while, then said, "Even if we are attacked. Don't fight except to protect yourself. Cleato does not want the word to go back to the Dragon that there is a trained team entering his lands. It will only slow us and allow him more time for subterfuge and harassment."

Pistis sat down next to Con. He picked up a blade of grass and put it between his lips. "Your father, Incor. What was he doing that got the attention of the Dragon? I mean, Incor was ever a rebel but there are plenty of those around."

Con shrugged, a little embarrassed. Pistis remained quiet.

Finally, Con shrugged again. "He became a line jumper."

Pistis grimaced. "Ah! So, he finally fell to that temptation. I thought he would sooner or later. That lure of a big farm on the Valley floor was always a hook for him."

Con glanced at him with a question but Pistis continued to stare off into space. They were silent for a few minutes. Then Pistis spoke again. "Doin' it long?"

Con looked up. "Huh?"

"Had he been jumpin' line long?"

Con looked back at the ground, examining the growing grass under his legs. He shook his head. "First year."

"And the Dragon took him? Man, that is rough—but when you decide to follow the Dragon's ways, you give him the right to call in the debt at any time. Even if its before you reap any benefit."

Con nodded again and looked off into the distance at the Eastern Barriers. "Yeah, I know."

Pistis leaned back on the grass and stretched. Then he sat back up. "So, what are you gonna do when we get him?"

"Are we gonna git him?"

Pistis nodded. "Oh, yeah. We'll get him. That don't mean he'll want to be gotten."

"Why? Why wouldn't anyone want to be rescued from the Dragon?"

Pistis pulled the grass from his mouth and threw it away. "Hmmm. Good question."

They sat quietly for another five minutes.

"When we turn off the road the terrain will be rougher," Pistis said, suddenly. "Close up the formation and stay within ten feet of Dugan. I'll send Rusty out a little further to make sure nothing is ahead of us and I am pulling the flanks in a little."

Con nodded and Pistis said, "I'll start us now. Wait until I get to the head of the column. Then get quickly up on the road and follow my lead. We will travel no more than a few hundred rods more on this road. When we move onto the side path, close up quickly. Stay under noise discipline until we are well clear of the road. I will let you know when we can talk again."

Con nodded again and rolled onto his belly as his uncle walked back down the road. Cleato stood in the center of the road and Pistis walked right to him. He nodded or talked to each one of the squad as he passed. When he reached Cleato, he saluted and stood at attention. Cleato nodded at him, then walked to the head of the column. His right arm came up, palm up. Con jumped up and centered on the road, seeing each of the others do the same. They started off at a trot, the dust quickly rising as high as it had been when they quit.

Cleato moved straight down the middle of the road for two hundred yards. The pace was double-time. The dust was extremely thick. Con was wheezing. Looking up, He saw Dugan struggling to breath, also. Suddenly, Cleato stopped. Pistis raised his right hand, palm forward. The squad halted. Pistis waved his hand in a circle then swept it toward the ground, palm down. Con did not recognize the signal and stood still, waiting to see what the others did.

Rusty and Sarah dropped to the dusty road, Sarah lying flat, Rusty kneeling. They both appeared to be breathing very hard. Beatrice ran toward Cleato, drawing her sword. When she saw what Sarah had done, she stopped, sword half out, confused. Dugan ran forward, then back toward Con and finally just stood looking around.

Cleato turned with a dark look on his face. Pistis turned on the squad, spread his legs and placed his one free hand on his hips. He hung his head.

Sarah stood up and wiped off her front. Rusty rose. They all looked at one another, confused.

A shrill scream sounded above them. Four beasts flew there, over a hundred feet up. Long, brown, leathery wings stretched out against the blue sky, buoyed by the spring breezes. Small, furry bodies hung between the wings. Thin legs trailed out behind each and long, spindly arms pointed down at the squad. They seemed to float effortlessly, high above the squad, hanging directly over them. The beasts chattered to one another in cackling, grating, squeaks and squawks.

The small squad drew their swords quickly, but in disarray. Dugan had trouble getting his out, his eyes glued to the beasts in the air. No one followed the drill. None of them fell into battle formation.

The screeching sound from above came again, shrill and piercing. Con realized quickly that it was not a scream of rage, or of fear, or of terror. It was laughter.

The leathery wings beat the air and the beasts sped off toward the south mountains, still screeching.

"Come here, all of you!"

Pistis stood in the center of the road and gestured the squad to him. Cleato walked to stand next to Pistis. He was smiling. Con sheathed his sword and walked forward, head down.

The whole squad gathered around Cleato. He reached out and touched each one on the shoulder. "You all did well. I think we won that round handily."

Heads snapped up all around the circle. Confused exclamations accompanied the puzzled expressions. Rusty spoke first. "You think we did well?"

"Yes, you did very well. You looked like an undisciplined squad of trainees."

Dugan blustered. "Trainees. Of course we did. Where in blue blazes did you get that stupid hand signal, Pistis? I never saw that in two years of training."

"It was not in blue-blazes that I got that command, Dugan. I do not get things from blue-blazes." Pistis frowned at Dugan, his jaw thrust forward.

Dugan retreated. His face flushed wildly, losing its freckles in the overall redness. He looked at Cleato, "I'm sorry, Cleato. I let my mouth speak before my brain thought."

"You're forgiven."

That was all he said. He smiled again.

"But, Cleato," Beatrice asked, "how did we do well if we looked like a bunch of trainees?"

Pistis spoke up then. "Because that's how Cleato wanted us to look. And if he had told us to act that way, it would not have been very convincing."

Cleato beamed. "Yes, that's correct."

Sarah still seemed confused and asked, "Why? What's this all about?"

"Sarah, I knew that the enemy was above us, spying to see who we were and whether we would be a threat. I do not yet wish to encounter any enemy troops and certainly don't want a battle with them. This mission will go much smoother if the enemy does not find out how strong we are until we are well inside his territory, preferably very close to our goal. Those spies had to be convinced that you are just trainees taking your first assignment at patrolling the border. If I had told you about it, you would have been trying to act like trainees."

Con laughed. "Now they think we've failed our first patrol and will be returning to the City."

Cleato nodded. "Now we may turn off on the path ahead and the spies will not question. That will put us in position to enter the Dragon's domain undetected.

"Form up. We move out immediately."

Chapter 21

On the left, a footpath led east, winding along the base of the hills. Waist high grass and brambles bordered it on both sides. A small stand of trees stood off about a quarter of a mile. The path seemed to lead directly to them.

Cleato stood at the entrance to the path. Pistis turned down the path and the squad followed. The path was only two feet wide—truly a just a foot path—but it was hard packed and smooth. Cleato called to the squad as they walked by, "We have been patrolling this path for years. There probably won't be any surprises here, but keep your eyes open."

Pistis raised one clenched fist and pumped it up and down several times. He began to double time. The squad followed.

The fields on either side were filled with flowers; red, blue and hues of gold painted petal after petal in a variety that astounded even Con, a farm boy. Tall flowers, short flowers—every height, thickness and size from pinheads to platters. Sarah and Beatrice, city girls, stared around, open mouthed, at the piebald meadow. Dugan stared straight ahead, not seeming to notice the sundry tints and hues clamoring for his glance. Insects shot from flower to flower, buzzing past the ears of the jogging soldiers, ignoring the plain, unsweet things in favor of the outlandishly attired flowers that beckoned them. Birds chirped and sang, claiming their territory for the spring mating. They burst into the air as the squad ran past but quickly settled again, grabbing the stalk of the tallest plant and bouncing it in time to their declarations. The air smelled of dust and pollen. Except for the tattoo of the soldiers' feet pounding the hard earth—everything spoke of renewal and growth.

Within five minutes they entered the woods. It was all birch—second growth stuff—still young, perhaps as young as twenty years. This land had been cleared at one time. Thin, white trunks, like hundreds of painted, peeling columns, burst up through the leaf litter. Sunlight filtered through the bright new leaves, dappling everything under them. The tangle of vines and brambles fought with the thin trunks for their portion of the sunlight, filling every narrow gap with greenery.

The path wiggled between the trunks. Pistis called an unintended cadence with the rasp of his breath. The squad fell to the rhythm, feet falling with his, lungs sucking air at the same meter. Cleato sang gently from the rear, urging them on into the dense forest.

"*On, Soldiers.*
On, Soldiers.
Don't let the enemy see.
Oh, soldiers of mine.
We'll soon cross the line
And into his realm we will be.
On, Soldiers
On, Soldiers
My soldiers, warriors and more.
His legions you'll best.
There is no time to rest
For I call you to action and war."

The trail turned right suddenly and broadened into a long, thin clearing, about twenty feet wide. Pistis raised his hand and made a circling gesture. The squad wound down its run, then slumped onto the forest floor. Pistis dropped down with them, struggling to control his breathing. Cleato entered the clearing, glanced briefly at each soldier, then walked to the far side.

The path climbed the side of the hill for fifty yards, then seemed to end in a stand of trees. Con guessed that it turned again at that point to run along the face of the rising land.

Cleato glanced back at Pistis, then walked over. Con heard the conversation. "Rest for a while. We will eat a meal here and then push on for a few miles more before sunset. I do not want to camp in the woods tonight but in the hills yonder."

The valley was narrower and the upward thrust of the East Barriers was only ten miles from them. Cleato pointed over the tops of the hills they were climbing at a ridge of high hills which jutted out from the larger mountains. It appeared to be another five miles or so.

Without another word, he walked back to the exit of the clearing. Con took up his position at the entrance to the clearing and watched their back trail. The whole woods buzzed with life: birds, insects, and small animals scraping and rustling the underbrush. The sound of Beatrice preparing a meal was the only unnatural sound Con could hear.

Beatrice slammed and banged inside Cleato's pack, pushing cooking utensils around and heaving things to the side that she did not want. Finally, she withdrew her manual, set it out on the ground, and began reading. As she read, she reached back into the pack and pulled out a slab of fresh, red meat—perhaps a pound or less. With her eyes still on the book, she pulled a knife from the pack and prepared to slice the meat into separate portions. Con wondered at its sparseness.

The knife cut into it. Two pieces lay on the block, but each was the same size as the original. She cut again, and again obtained two pieces as big as the first. When she had cut five pieces, a sixth was left which was equal in size to the others.

Rusty stood. He walked around the clearing picking up sticks. When he had an arm load, he moved next to Beatrice and started a fire. Beatrice smiled at him in thanks and withdrew a large, black, iron pan from Cleato's pack and set it over the flames. Rusty plopped down next to her.

Slab by slab, she threw the meat into the sizzling pan. The smell of frying meat seasoned with the tang of the wood smoke filled the air of the clearing. The smoke rose, then spread out over them, as if it had hit some invisible barrier. Con's mouth watered and his stomach growled loudly.

There was an answering growl near him. Sarah, who lay on the grass a few feet away, sat up and looked at him, then began to laugh. Con grinned. The rest of the squad stared at them. "You two moonin' over each other, again?" Rusty called.

Sarah laughed again. "I don't think that's what you'd call it." Con laughed also, and waved his hand. "It's nothin'. Go on back to the cookin', Rusty."

Pistis sat up and looked, surprise in his face. "Oh!" he said. Then he lay back down, grinning from ear to ear. "I had missed that."

After a few minutes, Rusty reached into the pan with tongs and took a slice of meat for each of the six plates lying on the ground. He took the manual from Beatrice and flipped to a different page. Seeming satisfied with what he read, he removed five cups from the pack and a small beaker. With that, he slammed the book closed, picked up one plate, a cup, and the beaker, and walked toward Con.

"Wine," Rusty said as he handed Con the cup. "It'll refresh you and restore your vigor."

"And rob my senses, Rusty. No thanks, we're in a dangerous place and I need my wits about me. I'll drink water, if there is any."

"You don't need ta worry about this wine robbin' you of anythin', Con. This wine is from him." Rusty nodded toward Cleato, who still stared down the trail. "He gives it to us anytime we are out like this and become tired. Drink up, Con. You will need it before today is out."

Rusty returned to the fire and picked up another plate. Beatrice grabbed the plate and a wine goblet. She said something and Rusty shrugged. He picked up another and started toward Sarah.

Beatrice took two plates in one hand and the stems of two goblets in the other. Wobbling and balancing, she walked across the clearing to Pistis. She handed one of each to him, then plopped down alongside of him.

Con cut into the meat. It was an inch thick and cooked rare. Juices oozed from it as he stuck in his fork. Its aroma filled Con's nostrils and his stomach growled again. In his mouth, the taste exploded, rising to fill his nose and sinuses. What meat it was, he couldn't identify. Certainly not pork. Nor was it exactly like beef—or lamb—or venison. He had no experience of it. The desire for more overcame him and he quickly cut and plopped the next piece in his mouth. The same exquisite flavor filled him. He cut the rest, eating it piece by piece.

Within minutes it was gone. He stared disappointed at the empty plate. With an eager tongue, he licked the juices off of it. When he finished, he looked over at the fire, hoping to see more available. There was nothing left over—and, he realized, nothing more was needed. His hunger was satisfied.

He placed the plate on the ground next to him and lifted the cup. The goblet was cool to his touch. Small beads of water trickled down the outside.

He sipped it. The taste was like fresh grapes—sweet and yet still tart enough to quench the worst thirst. The sip warmed his stomach, then his whole abdomen. It radiated out to his legs and up his back to his neck.

Fatigue dissolved. Knotted muscles relaxed. Con sipped again, then gulped it.

His strength returned rapidly. More than strength, his alertness increased. Energy flowed through him so that he could not sit still. He bounced up and stretched, elated. "Now, that's wine," he remarked. The others looked at him, then at their own goblet.

Sarah sipped it, then turned and smiled at Con. "Wow!"

Rusty finished serving the rest of the meals and picked up his own plate. He walked over to where Con stood and flopped down on the ground, propping his back on a tree stump.

"Well, Mr. Ataxia, it don't look like you been robbed."

Con grinned at him, still feeling the vigor that the wine had instilled in him. 'No, not robbed, certainly. What was that, Rusty?"

"That wine you on'y get from Cleato. It's special. On'y his so'diers can taste of it." Rusty looked pensive for a minute then continued, "I b'lieve that on'y his so'diers really want it. Others who take it, even so'diers from the regiments, seem to reject it. Some actually get drunk on it and waste its power. On'y the militia knows what's it's really for, or so it seems."

"Rusty, what're the regular soldiers like? What do they do?"

Rusty stared at his plate for a minute, then looked up with his fork stuck into his mouth. He shook his head. "Don't know, Con. I ain't never been a part of the reg'lar Army. I was recruited like you, straight from being a rebel. I've heard stories, but they'd just be stories and no way for me to know the truth of 'em."

He ate for a few minutes more, then said, "I guess they got their jobs and we got ours. I figure, they wouldn't be any good at this'n and we wouldn't be any good at their'n. Else, I can't figure any reason for the two differ'nt groups."

Rusty finished his meal and picked up his cup and plate to go pack. Cleato crossed the glade.

"Con, I heard your question," he said as he approached close. Con looked over at the far side of the glade and then back at Cleato. It was fifty feet and he and Rusty had been talking very low. Cleato smiled and said, "I hear most of what goes on between my soldiers. But as for you, don't question the usefulness, or actions of others. They answer to the Commander for what they do or do not do. Your concern must be with your own response to what I and Pistis tell you."

It was not said with anger or malice. There was no rebuke in it, simply instruction. He stood again and walked back to the other side of the glade.

Sarah sprawled on the ground and appeared to be napping. Beatrice lay next to her reading her manual and occasionally throwing a twig at a nearby tree. Dugan stood next to the forest and examined the trees or something on the ground. Rusty finished up the packing, tying the pack straps back in place.

Cleato retrieved the pack and walked toward the trail. Pistis stood, put on his pack and said, "Saddle up, folks. Time to go."

The squad rose as one and formed into marching order. Con dropped back onto the path from which they'd come to check around the blind corner. It was empty. He stepped back and signaled. Pistis motioned with his arm and they marched out of the clearing.

Con was right. At where the trail seemed to dead end into the trees and brush, it actually turned sharp to the east. Con could see that the brush only extended for a few feet and stopped at the face of a low cliff.

Cleato stopped there and nodded at Pistis. Pistis raised his hand. Cleato raised his finger to his lips and shook his head. Then he pointed at the ground and waved for the squad to follow. He dropped down on his hands and knees and crawled into the apparently solid underbrush.

They all got down on their bellies and looked. There was a tunnel there through the brambles and bushes. Cleato's big feet disappeared into the darkness of it out of sight. Pistis held his finger to his lips, then pointed at Beatrice. She looked around, then shrugged, dropped to her hands and knees and crawled into the hole. The rest followed. Con stood his ground watching for any sign of the enemy until Rusty's feet disappeared. Pistis pulled him close and whispered, "You go. I'll take the rear."

Con dropped down and crawled into the brown and green, tangled mass.

Before he had stretched out to his full length, he saw the entrance to the tunnel. Rusty's feet were just disappearing into it. Con pushed forward, stopping at the entrance to the darkness.

Rusty's feet, pushing and digging into the loose grit a few yards in front of him, were the only part of the squad he could see. The grunts and scraping up ahead of him, though, assured him the rest were there too.

The cave height was lower than the hole in the brush. As Con tried to push into it, his pack caught on the roof. He dropped onto his chest and began to low crawl. This was a technique they had been taught during training. From the rest position, you pushed up slightly until your breastplate cleared the ground. Then you pushed yourself forward with pumping legs, balancing your torso alternately on your bent arms, walking your hands forward.

It was effective for moving in tight places but it was extremely tiring. Your arms had to support all the weight of your pack, armor, and upper torso.

Minutes passed. Con's arms ached. Ten minutes went by. Dust tickled his nose and made his mouth gritty. Fifteen minutes. His thighs tightened in exertion and his shoulders and biceps screamed.

Suddenly, Rusty's feet shot forward. Light bounded in. Con struggled forward another five feet and hands reached in for him. He grasped at them and was dragged from the cavern.

He stood and brushed off his clothes. The others did the same. They were in a sunken area. To their backs was the hill they had just crawled through. All around them was a ledge of dirt and rock about five feet off the floor of the sinkhole. Cleato stood tall, towering over the ledge, looking all around the area. His hand continued to wave them down.

Pistis's head appeared at the hole and Rusty leaned down to extract him. Con reached back and helped.

Cleato turned to them and smiled. He raised his finger to his lips. Then he climbed up onto the level ground. He waved the squad forward, then lifted his finger to his lips again, raising his eyebrows. Each one nodded and began to crawl out of the hole.

They were in a clearing, much like the one in which they'd rested. This part of the forest was not second growth. It was like the forest where he had lost his wagon to the Dragon Raiders. There was no underbrush at all and hardwood giants soared all around them. The boles of the trees looked like houses and the limbs like gigantic beams holding up the heavily laden ceiling.

"Quietly!" Cleato warned in a whisper. "We will talk when we camp."

They formed up and moved off, Cleato at the point and Pistis watching their rear. Cleato quickly started to double time. The squad picked up the pace and followed.

Cleato headed up hill. A mile passed. The trees thinned, grew smaller, then ended. The dogtrot continued. Con started to breath heavily. Ahead of him, the girls and Dugan seemed to be holding up all right. Rusty appeared to be struggling. He could hear the heavy, steady breathing of Pistis just behind him.

The pace continued. Con started to feel the strain. Rusty, his sides heaving in and out, started to stagger off to the side. Con ran along side of him and grabbed his pack.

"Take it off," he said between breaths. "I can carry it."

Rusty gasped, but nodded. He slipped one arm out of the pack, then the other. Con flung it up over his shoulder.

"Can you go on?"

Rusty nodded and picked up the pace again.

They ran for another fifteen minutes, then Cleato signaled a halt. Con thankfully stopped and bent over, gathering his wind again. He dropped Rusty's pack to the grass, and dropped to his knees. Slowly, his breath came back.

There were on a long, gentle upward slope. A sweep of low, green grass carpeted the side of the hill. Scattered thinly throughout the green were scratches of brown where the blackberry and raspberry staked a claim. Large, brown boulders, some tens of feet high, others barely breaking the soil, thrust up from the side of the hill here and there, even to the distant ridge. Honeysuckle vines struggled up the closest ones making them look like stubby, tan fingers poking through a tattered glove.

The sun dipped behind the western mountains. Long shadows crossed the hill faces and darkened the valleys and gullies. The tips of the boulders on the ridge flared into brilliance in the pale, dusky light.

It was like a dream scene. Con stared at it, drinking in the beauty. Warfare seemed far away.

"Enjoy it. It will not last long," Cleato's voice interrupted his reverie. "This is the last beauty we will see for a while."

Cleato led the group to the edge of a deep gully. He stepped off and slid down the eight-foot bank. The squad followed, stumbling and tripping. At the bottom, he grabbed each one and set them back in marching order. "Quietly, now. We must move with a minimum of sound."

The bottom of the gully was strewn with small jagged rocks. In the very lowest portion, a small brook gurgled. The wet, moldy smell of moss and lichens filled the air. Cleato moved forward, almost trotting. The squad stumbled after him. "Cleato," Sarah called, "I can't keep this up."

Cleato stopped, raised his finger to his lips, then started off again. His pace was only slightly slower.

The sides of the gully were steep, almost vertical. The bottom area was narrow. It twisted and turned, never going in a straight line for more than a few feet. It was impossible to see what was ahead. Still, Cleato pressed hard.

At first, ground level was well over their heads. After the first half-mile, though, the walls were low enough that Cleato had to walk in a crouch to stay under the lip. Within a half hour, they all crouched to stay below the diminishing rim.

The sky turned blue, then black. Pale stars winked through a light haze. The darkness engulfed everything. Con could no longer see the path. There were a few, "Oofs" and more descriptive exclamations from in front of him.

"Ow!" Dugan's voice broke the silence. The squad kept moving. Con came around a bend and found Dugan sitting on the ground, holding his ankle. He looked up at Con. "This is stupid. I didn't come out here to get myself hurt."

He rubbed his ankle again, then said, "It's all your uncle's fault, you know."

With that, he stood and stepped gingerly on his foot. Satisfied, he limped off toward the rest of the squad.

Con heard breathing behind him. Pistis stood there, shaking his head. He motioned for Con to move on.

Cleato stopped and turned to the squad. As they all drew close, he waved Pistis forward. "We will stay in the gully for a short time more. When we exit it we will be close to our first camp. Take them up the hill and make camp at the top. Set the squad in a defensive position, arrange for a watch, then rest. For the rest of this day, take the lead. I will be scouting for us in the darkness. I will leave you the light for the path."

Cleato moved off again. Pistis turned to Con. "You have the rear. Don't let any of them lag." He looked at Dugan as he said it.

The squad struggled back into close order formation. Darkness had become complete. They milled around, slipping off the rock faces and into the water, splashing and scraping along. Dugan cursed. "How in the Citadel are we supposed to do this? It's impossible." Beatrice mumbled her agreement.

Pistis hushed them. "Sometimes you do act like trainees. Look down, the way is lit."

Con looked at his feet. A circular splotch of light illuminated the rocks and the path. He looked at the others. There was no light there. He shook his head. How was this going to help?

Sarah called in a breathy whisper, "Pistis, I can see my path!"

Dugan laughed. "Hold on. I can plainly see a light at my feet but there isn't any at yours. Nor can I see any others."

Pistis appeared out of the blackness. "Be quiet! The enemy is trying to locate us. He knows we've entered although he hasn't determined how or where. We must make him expend precious energy and time trying to discover those things while we wend our way to his citadel."

"But our feet, Pistis!" Sarah exclaimed.

"Yes, soldiers. Cleato told you he would light your paths. Why are you so surprised? Come, now. And for all our sakes, be quiet!"

They marched on for another half mile. The gully walls became waist high ledges and then just gentle slopes a foot high. Pistis veered to the left up a small hill. The squad followed.

At the top of the hill they stopped. Pistis looked around, then turned left and walked down a steep grade alongside a ten foot high stone. He rounded the stone, stopped, then pointed under the overhang. The squad gratefully flopped onto the ground.

The site was covered with a mossy-like growth that was dry and springy. Rusty slid the pack from his shoulder and groaned. The girls stripped their packs off and laid back. Sarah rolled her head back and forth and said, "I ain't gonna' leave again."

"Prepare the evening fare, Beatrice," Pistis said, then climbed to the top of the outcropping.

Beatrice groaned and struggled back up. She worked hard, with Rusty joining her again.

The meal went as it had earlier, the meat satisfying and the wine refreshing. Pistis remained on the top of the rock, watching until all of them had eaten. Then he slid to the ground and accepted a plate.

"Dugan, take the first watch."

Dugan looked up at him. Con thought he was going to refuse, but he finally rose and climbed up the rock.

Within a few minutes, they heard a grating noise. Dugan plopped back onto the ground. "Cleato's up there. Said to get some rest."

Pistis looked up from his plate for a second. Then he nodded and pointed with his fork at the ground. "Good idea for all of us."

The squad settled down. Con walked out of the overhang and looked up at Cleato, more because he wanted to see him than to be sure Dugan was telling the truth. He was there. His massive frame blocked out enough of the stars to be plain.

Something moved in the sky behind him. Con stared, trying to catch a glimpse of it again, not wanting to alert a tired squad because of a wandering owl or hunting eagle. For several minutes he saw nothing. Then, a star cluster in one of the big constellations went blank and came back.

Successively, along a straight path, the stars blinked out and back on. Con called in a whisper, "Cleato, above you. Something flies."

"I see it, Con. Don't be concerned."

Cleato seemed to stare off at the horizon. Con glanced that way. Nothing moved. "No, Cleato, over top of you."

"I've seen them, Con," Cleato said patiently. "I'm not looking at them, but I see them."

"Them?" Con saw only movement. He certainly could not tell if there was one or two or a hundred. "How do you know?"

"There is much about this realm that you must learn. When we came through the tunnel we crossed more than ground."

He said no more but jumped down to the squad's level. He landed lightly (much lighter than Con could have at that drop) and moved back into the cover of the overhang.

"They will not see us tonight. I have covered us."

Con stared up. A mist. Clouds. Twinkling, weak stars. No cover. Puzzled, he walked back under the overhang. Something moved in the darkness at the far end. Con walked over and plopped down next to the movement, figuring it was Pistis.

Pistis reached out and patted his leg. "So, nephew. How is your first patrol?"

Con chuckled. "I am tired. I am sore. I am scraped. I am scratched. I am frightened. Need more?"

Pistis chuckled in return. "Me, too."

Con tried to see his face but it was too dark. He asked, "You're frightened?"

Pistis's hand hit him again. "Better believe it. Anyone who is not frightened shouldn't be here. Now, I don't mean I'm paralyzed with fear—or that I am afraid that Cleato can't handle anything that comes up. But, I am concerned. Concerned for you and your friends, there. And for me. The Dragon will retaliate for this. He will not be pleased."

There was a silence for a while. "Well, we just have to keep our guards up."

Con nodded, knowing that Pistis couldn't see him.

"Con, you have feelings for that girl?"

Con felt his face redden and was glad it was pitch dark. "I guess."

"You guess, or you do? In this Kingdom, son, you don't guess about things like that."

Con listened to the sounds of steady breathing and the slight snores coming from the squad. It sounded like he could talk freely. "I mean, I ain't talked to her about it. Guess I couldn't say for sure."

"Well, that don't make sense, Con. You mean you have to talk to her to know what you feel?"

Con shook his head. "Naw. That ain't what I mean—but I…"

He stopped. Pistis was right. The question was what he felt, not what Sarah felt. "Yeah. I got feelin's for her."

Pistis's hand slapped his leg again. "Good. You got that out, any way. Look, Con, Sarah's a soldier."

"She sure is. And a good one."

Pistis stirred in the darkness, squirming a little to resettle his weight more comfortably. "An' we're on a mission. Normally, those sort of feelin's and soldierin' don't go together."

Con waited, unsure of where this was going.

Pistis cleared his throat. "I'm just trying to tell you to be careful. Try to put this on hold till we get back to the City. Then, I guess it'll be OK."

"You guess. Don't that have to be more concrete in this kingdom?"

Pistis chuckled. "Got me. Yeah, it'll be OK if that is the way you two want it."

They were silent for a while. Con laid back on his pack. He thought Pistis had done the same. Out of the darkness, though, Pistis' voice came again. "Soldierin' is tough. Sometimes, it just don't go with gettin' a wife." There was a wistfulness to his voice, a tinge of regret.

Con heard the creak of Pistis's armor as he lay down.

Chapter 22

Something nudged him in the side. Sarah stood over him. "You gonna sleep 'til noon?" Her speech was thick. The dim light revealed her puffy eyes. Sleep had not long left her, either.

Con smiled and rolled over onto his back.

It was still dark under the overhang of the rock. Dew lay on him, and the air was as moist as a sponge. The smell of rotting leaves around and under him filled his nose. The dawn sounds of the forest, though, had already begun. Birds chirped and a few insects clicked and clacked out their own mating messages. Small rodents rustled in the leaf litter, scratching and burrowing for worms and bugs, sounding like the footsteps of a staggering man or an injured animal.

Con stood. Out from under the rock, the blackness was not solid. Gray light spread across the sky in the East.

Pistis nodded at Beatrice. She went to each soldier and handed him or her a small cake. "Breakfast," she said as she handed it to Con. "It's all we'll get."

Con nibbled at it. It was crumbly and somewhat dry but it tasted good. There was a hint of sweetness to it—like honey but not as blatant. When he finished it, he felt satisfied.

The sky grew lighter. Con looked west but there were no glistening mountain tops there. All he could see was grayness.

"Overcast," he said to Rusty.

Rusty shook his head. "Smoke." He went on packing. When Con didn't respond, he raised his nose in the air and sniffed. "Smell it?"

Con sniffed. It was there. A slight smell of burning sulfur. He looked the sky over again, with a new interest.

Pistis called. "Let's saddle up, folks. And gather 'round. Cleato wants to say something."

"Not here," Cleato said. "Follow me."

The squad rushed to grab their packs. Slinging them over their shoulders and struggling to get arms through the proper loops, they trudged out of the camp, back up the trail they had taken the previous night until they were again at the crest of the hill. Cleato raised his hand, then waved them all to him.

"Look around. To the north is the City, the place of men."

The squad turned and looked. They were standing on a high ridge. To the north, the land dropped away to the plain of the City. Only the bump of the hills they had approached the day before broke the descent. Far in the distance, the line of night was just reaching the walls of the City.

Con was amazed at the distance. He had never seen the City looking so small. "Cleato, the distance is too far. We just didn't walk that far yesterday."

Pistis nodded. "Con, Cleato told you last night that when we crawled through that tunnel we crawled through more than just ground. You are further from the realm of men than you have ever been. It is almost as far as you can get."

Cleato slapped his leg. Everyone looked back to him. "But, you will get further still before this mission is out. Look south."

The squad turned and looked. The land dropped away in that direction, also. The distance, though., was lost in the thick smoke. Nothing in it was visible.

"That is were the Citadel is. That is where we are going. If you want to."

Dugan snorted. "I can't see nothin' but smoke. What's so different about that place than the City?"

"It's a dangerous place, Dugan. It is far more dangerous than any of you have experienced, except for Pistis. He has been there several times."

Everyone turned and looked at the older man. Even Dugan showed some new respect in his gaze.

"The way to that place is full of traps and snares. It is guarded by some of the best troops the Dragon has. A few of the most famous soldiers of history have fallen before they could even get close.

The battles you will fight to get there will be worse than anything you have imagined. The battle you will fight in there is beyond your imagining. The Enemy will get desperate the closer you get to his gates. His savagery will be unlimited. There is the possibility that some of you will not make it."

Cleato stared into the eyes of each one. The fear fluttered in Con's chest but he clamped his mind down on it. This was what he had signed on for. This was what he wanted.

"You have to depend on me," Cleato continued. "You will find your own will tested over and over—and it will fail you. You must put your trust in me. And you must trust those I have assigned to lead you." His eyes swept the whole squad but rested on Dugan longer than on the others.

Cleato stood up tall and looked out over the valley. "This is the decision point. If you continue, I will fight with you and I will fight for you. I will protect you as much as you will allow me to do. I will never leave you defenseless nor will I desert you."

The squad remained quiet, staring at the smoky reaches of the Valley. Cleato slapped his leg again. "If you want to go back, I will go with you. If you want to go forward, I will go with you. Which will it be?"

Rusty stared out as if he was seeing something that the others were not. Then he shuddered. Sarah moved next to Con. Her hand sought his and he squeezed it. She smiled slightly. Dugan moved toward Beatrice but she stepped forward to stand next to Pistis. Dugan stepped back, looking around to see if anyone had seen.

Con raised his hand. "I'm going forward."

Rusty turned to look at Con, a sadness around his eyes. There was a message there, but Con could not read it. Rusty stared like that for a few seconds, then he nodded. "Me, too. I al'as wanted to see that place."

Sarah hesitated. She looked at Cleato. "I'm scared, Cleato. In the City, warfare was always over in a few minutes. This looks like days or weeks of it. I don't know if I can do it like that."

Cleato smiled at her. "Good, Sarah. You always bring reality to the decision. Don't worry about your strength. Only depend on me. So long as you do, you will have the endurance."

She nodded again. "OK. Then I want to go, also."

Beatrice looked at Cleato, then at Pistis. "I'm goin'."

Dugan stood alone looking out at the smoke. Finally, he said, "Yeah. I'm goin'. That's why I walked all this way, ain't it?"

Con walked up behind Dugan and clapped him on the back. Dugan looked back in surprise, then he smiled. Suddenly, he broke forth in a song, a rousing song of battle. Beatrice joined him, then Pistis. Finally, Con and Sarah joined in.

They interlocked their arms and sang as loud as they could. Verse after verse about the victory of the Commander over the Dragon centuries before. Their voices echoed back from the rocks and trees. The air shook at the volume of the song. There was power in the words and the tune. There was power in their voices. There was power in their unity. Con looked back, expecting to see Cleato smiling at them. Instead, he found the big man singing with them, shouting out the victory on that famous day. The whole Earth shook at the sound of his rich baritone as he emphasized, "And I crushed the Dragon's head as he sought to bruise my heel."

Con quit singing and stared hard—for the song did not go that way. It was not a "first-person song." The soldiers all sang that, "He crushed the Dragon's head as he sought to bruise his heel." Cleato sang it as if it was about him—as if he had personally been there, participated.

Cleato saw Con staring and laughed. The rest quit singing and turned toward the big man. When they grew quiet, he laughed again. "Ah, the soldier learns his second lesson."

Pistis turned. "Saddle up. We have a long march in front of us."

Cleato led them off the ridge and down into the canyon at their feet. A stream ran down there. Briars and brambles grew all along its banks. The stream meandered back and forth making the path twice as long. Roots, limbs, stickers and vines reached for their legs, their arms, and their faces as they pushed through, trying to keep up with the hurrying Cleato.

After an hour of struggle, Beatrice yelled, "Aargh!!" and stopped in her tracks. "I can't take this anymore." She dabbed at the scratches on her face.

The squad stopped, breaths coming short and quick. They just stared, too tired to go back and see what was wrong. Pistis, who had the point, came back. "What's the matter?"

Beatrice lifted her face. "What's the matter? You askin' me, what's the matter?" She pointed to the scratches on her face and arms, at the red mark across her cheek where a branch had whipped her in retaliation for being disturbed by the passing humans. "You see all this and ask, 'What's the matter?'"

Her eyes swelled suddenly with tears and one trickled down her cheek. Con stepped forward to comfort her, but Sarah grabbed his arm. She shook her head slowly back and forth, pulling on his arm. "Boy, do you have a lot to learn. She ain't hurt. She's mad. Huggin' her is the last thing you want to try right now."

Pistis wagged his head. "Are you just a bunch of trainees?"

That's when Con noticed that Pistis had no scratches or scrapes. All the other squad members were bruised and bleeding in a few places. Pistis spun around, lifted his shield in front of him, ducked his head until just his eyes were showing, then trudged off. The underbrush scraped on the shield then moved aside. He stopped and looked back.

"Got it?'

Beatrice looked a little sheepish. The tears where gone replaced by a reddish tint in the cheeks. "Oops,' she said.

They moved off again, this time with their shields in place.

They marched for twelve hours through the brush, never seeing more than a few feet. As the last glow of the setting sun turned purple, Pistis raised his hand. The stream they had been following had spread into a bog. Cleato stood on some dry ground between it and the canyon wall. "Make camp."

Dugan looked around. "C'mon, Cleato. Let's go up to the top of the hill and camp."

Cleato shook his head. "No more hill top camps. We must stay hidden as much as possible."

Dugan frowned. He set his shield down, then folded his arms across his breastplate and leaned up against a tree.

Dugan displayed it but the rest of the squad felt it. Each sulked about the hard march in his or her own way. Cleato circulated among them, rubbing a sore muscle here, applying salve to a scratch there. When he got to Sarah, she said, "Cleato, can we walk on the hill tops tomorrow. This canyon is too rough."

Cleato's head shook again. "No, we must stay in the canyon for a while. It's not the most pleasant place but it actually is the better route to where we are going."

Her face fell and she slumped forward, picking up and tossing some twigs at her feet. Cleato's face softened. Gently, he said, "On the way out, we will stick to the road. For now, it must be this way."

Dugan turned back toward the group and snapped, "This is better? You gotta be kiddin' me. We wore ourselves out, today. Tomorrow will be worse. When, or rather, if we find the Dragon, we'll be dead."

Cleato frowned at Dugan. "On the bare hill tops," Cleato said, "you would be picked off one by one by the enemy sharpshooters. Here, you are protected from them. Indeed, you aren't even noticed by the enemy forces who are looking all over the heights for you.

"On the hilltops, the travel would be easier—so easy that you would begin to trust in yourselves again, instead of looking to me and your armor. Then you would be easy pickings for the enemy. He would have his victory without ever fighting a battle.

"Dugan, don't question my motives. If you allow that little seed of doubt to sprout now, how will you survive the battle to come?"

Dugan dropped his head and stared at the ground. When he looked up again, his face was crimson, all the way to his ears. Con could not tell if it was from embarrassment or anger.

Cleato met his stare. Dugan finally looked down again. Cleato's brow creased and he stared down the canyon.

"For a few days we will be in this canyon. Then we will start into some new lands—and some new and very present dangers. Get some sleep. It will be better in the morning."

For four days they marched through the canyon. Cleato was right about the enemy. There was no sign of him, nor of any scouts. The squad seemed to have evaded all of the Dragon's defenses and were pushing deep into his realm.

On the fifth morning, they marched out of the canyon and onto a broad plain. A grassy park spread out before them, ending within a mile in a stand of trees. Beyond that, the giants grew, their tops visible over the smaller, newer growth. Behind them were the barriers, thrusting suddenly from the valley floor, reaching into the smoke. The mountains wore the forest like a green cloak high into the smoky haze.

Cleato gathered them. "Hurry across the opening. We will rest in the trees." He took off at a lope, leading the tired soldiers. Pistis followed up.

Inside the tree line, Cleato slowed and signaled the squad to stop. They all staggered and flopped onto the ground, panting hard. When they had calmed down, Cleato nodded at Pistis. Pistis stood and waved them to him.

"This is the Forest of Kleinmensch. I've only been here once, so I am not an expert but I do know a few things. We will be in this forest for days. It is a long way to the sides of the mountain, even though it appears very close.

"We are going to skirt the outer defenses of the Dragon by going up the mountains. When we come back to the plain, we will be almost at the Dragon's door.

"As to this forest. There are dangers here, folks. Real dangers. I don't think anyone gets through this place without a fight. It might be today—it might be just before we leave. But it will come. Check your weapons. Check your armor. And be alert. We do not want to be ambushed.

"Dugan!" Pistis called.

The red head looked up. His face was expressionless.

"Be alert. If we have ever needed a scout, its now."

Dugan shrugged. "That's why I'm here, isn't it?"

A slight crease flashed on Pistis's brow then he turned toward the trail. "Let's go."

The squad lined up but Cleato still sat under one of the trees. Con turned toward him. "Cleato, you comin'?"

Cleato nodded. "I will be around. For now, listen to Pistis. He knows where you are to go and what you are to do. If you need me, I'll be close. But I must search another part of this wood. Other soldiers are here that may need me."

Pistis raised his hand and the squad marched into the darkness of the wood.

Chapter 23

The forest was mostly of Oak with some Elm mixed in. The trees formed a thick canopy about fifteen feet off the ground. The branches appeared to be gigantic beams and the thick cover a solid ceiling. Very little light filtered to the ground, creating twilight at midday and a deep, purplish semi-dark in the mornings and evenings. When night fell, it was total darkness for no moon or starlight could penetrate the smoke and the leaves together.

There was no underbrush—the trees greedily soaked up all the life from above. Only molds, moss, and fungi lived on the forest floor. Even at the brightest of the day, dark shadows filled the forest. An army of Raiders could be a few feet away and the squad would have walked past them in ignorance.

Pistis led them on a narrow path that wound around the giant trunks. They lost sight of the mountains. The ground remained flat, or rising so imperceptibly that none of them could see it. The trees blocked their view within a few hundred feet in every direction. There was nothing to indicate progress except more and more rough-barked giants.

As the purple light closed in on them on the first night, Pistis raised his hand. "We'll camp under this tree. It will get very dark soon, so settle in quickly."

Beatrice began to collect sticks. Pistis shook his head. "No fires. Cold camp. We can't afford to announce our presence in this wood."

Beatrice dropped the wood and trudged back to her pack. Pistis reached into his and grabbed a wafer. "Your supper," he called to the squad, holding up the wafer. They all nodded and dug in their own packs for the small wafers that had been issued back in the City.

Dugan set his pack down away from the rest and sat down on it. There was just enough light left for Con to see the disgusted look on his face. Con picked his pack up and walked over to sit next to him. Dugan looked up.

"That uncle of yours is crazy. He's gonna get us killed. You know that, don't you?"

Con shook his head. "C'mon, Dugan. He's been here before. We ain't. Give him some trust."

Dugan rose and picked up his pack. "Yeah, I thought that was the way it was."

He trudged further from the group and dropped his pack again. Con returned to the main group.

Rusty walked over to him as Con was munching his wafer. "Con. Be careful."

Con glanced over his shoulder at Dugan. "Of him?"

Rusty shook his head. "Naw. He's jest a sorehead but, if'n I ain't wrong, he'll come around when the action starts. Naw, I seen somethin' an' it scared me."

Con looked around the almost black camp. "Today? In the forest? Why didn't you yell?"

"Warn't today. It was back on the last hill top—you know, when we was singin'?"

"Rusty, you couldn't have seen nothin' from there. That was five days ago."

"Didn't say I saw it in my eyes, now did I?" Rusty snapped. "Sometimes it is near impossible to talk to you. Why don't you hush up and listen?"

Con wanted to argue again but he held his peace. Rusty's obtuse ramblings always got around to the point sooner or later.

"I seen it in my mind's eye. I've done that afore. Cleato says that the C'mmander sometimes gives us things that way. That's why I want you to be careful."

"You think it was the Commander?"

Rusty nodded. "Sure enough. An' what I saw scared me, as I said. Seems, I saw you trussed up with ropes and thrown over the back of a horse. Saw it plain as day."

Rusty stood then. "Got to get to my pack. See you in the mornin'"

Con stared out into the darkness. Tied up and thrown over a horse. It didn't ring true in his own mind and he dismissed it. He lay back on his ground sheet and pulled the pack under his head. Morning would come soon.

The next day's march was the same. The twilight world, the dampness, the ever-present toadstools and fungus started to take a toll on the team. Dugan straggled, then the others slowed down. Patrol discipline broke down. Pistis had to put Rusty on the point and take the rear himself to keep the squad bunched.

At dusk, Pistis rushed forward and pointed the squad close to the bole of a tree. When they had all dropped their packs, he stood for a moment, then turned to Rusty. "I think a hot meal is in order. Get some sticks—nothing big, just a few one-inchers or so.

"Beatrice, meat and wine."

Rusty jumped up and started collecting sticks. Beatrice smiled broadly and started to dig in her pack. Sarah joined her and sorted the things Beatrice removed. Dugan and Con helped Rusty.

"A small fire, Rusty," Pistis cautioned. "Just enough to cook the food."

Con approached his uncle. "Ain't you afraid of whatever is out there in the forest?"

Pistis nodded. "But I am more afraid of this squad's morale. Sooner or later the enemy will find us. We can't afford to face him with these dreary attitudes and long faces. We would be defeated before we began."

Pistis stared around, obviously concerned. Then he turned back to Con. "I think I would rather face him sooner with a contented, disciplined squad than later with five individual, disheartened soldiers."

Pots and pans banged. With that sound came the murmur of voices—the squad was talking again. Even Dugan moved close to the group and helped. Beatrice fried the meat. Rusty began serving the plates and goblets. Again, Beatrice grabbed two plates and two goblets. She walked to where Pistis sat and handed him his food. Then she plopped down along side of him. He smiled at her.

"Thank you, Beatrice. You have been treating me extra special."

Beatrice tried to hide her smile behind her hand, then grinned broadly. "Got to take care of the leader, you know."

Pistis reached over and patted her on the head. "Well, I appreciate that." He turned to his meal.

Beatrice's face fell and she looked down at her plate quickly. It was dim but Con thought he saw redness climbing up her neck. At what, he could not fathom.

At the end of the meal, the only light in the forest was the glow of the coals from the cooking fire. Pistis walked toward it with a handful of soil. Beatrice groaned. "Oh, come on, Pistis. Can't we enjoy the glow for a few minutes. They will burn themselves out within an hour."

Pistis glanced at the glowing coals, then around the forest. "Ok. Gather 'round. This may be the last fire we see until we get to the Dragon's gates. And that fire won't be near as pleasant."

Pistis sat down. Beatrice moved close to him. "Tell us about the Citadel. You've been there?"

Pistis nodded. "I think Cleato will tell you about the Citadel when he is ready. Let me tell you about the gates. There is a tall, stone wall that juts out from the solid rock of the barriers. It is about ten feet thick and at least twenty feet high."

Con shook his head. "More like fifteen feet thick. And it has parapets all along it."

Pistis stared at him across the fire. The rest of the squad turned to stare at him. "Tell us more, Mr. Ataxia," Pistis said, an amused look on his face.

Con stared at the ground, trying to recreate the picture of the wall in his mind. "Well, it runs from the East Barriers to the West Barriers. Of course, it is very close to where they come together to block the south end of the Valley. But it is still a long wall. The parapets have archers in them. And they have arrows with rags wrapped around the ends. There was a barrel in each parapet and a lamp. I think the barrels had some sort of oil—like the oil you get from peanuts or from linseed when you press them. Only it was pretty dark. The lamps were lit, even though it was daylight. I figure the guards dipped the rags in the oil, then lit it from the lamps before shootin' the arrows."

No one spoke. Pistis stared at him. "And the gate?"

"I don't remember much about the gate except it was huge and made of wood."

Pistis shook his head. "How do you know that?"

Con looked up. "Oh, yeah. The gate had big parapets on either side. An' there were four or five guards in each one."

Pistis's mouth dropped open. "You've been there. Or the Commander has given you extraordinary knowledge."

"I been there."

Dugan leaned over to him. "When? You been in trainin' with us ever since you joined."

Con started to answer, then shut up. To tell them how he knew would be to admit his sojourn with Fourberie—his dabbling with the dream smoke. To tell them would be to admit that he had been in places and done things that no soldier should ever have been or done.

Sarah was next to him. His friends were all around him. By telling them the truth, he might loose them. By not telling them, he would arouse their suspicions—now that they knew he had knowledge that he could not possibly have. He regretted having opened his mouth at all.

Steeling himself, he said, "When I first started hunting for a way to free my father, I was told that following the Masters would get me the power I needed. I tried that for a while."

Dugan stood up. "You smoked the dream smoke, didn't you?"

Con looked around at the staring eyes. He looked cautiously at Sarah. She was looking at Dugan. Con nodded. "Yeah, I smoked it. And I traveled. I traveled right to the Citadel and had a fight with the Raiders right there. That's how I know about the wall."

He looked down at his toes poking through the tips of the sandals.

Dugan walked away a few feet. "A traveler. And a smoker. Man, and this guy is our swordsman." He threw up his arms and walked to the trunk of the tree. He leaned on one hand, facing away from the squad.

Sarah looked off into space. Rusty refused to meet his eyes. Beatrice grabbed her pack and peered into it, rearranging things. No one spoke to him.

Pistis stood. "Con, this was before you joined the Commander?"

Con nodded. "About a year."

"Do you still think that the way to find your father is through the Masters?"

Con snorted. "'Course not. The Commander is the only way to defeat the Dragon."

Pistis nodded. "Does the Commander still blame you for smokin' and travelin'?"

Con thought for a minute. "No. I don't believe he does. Else, why would he give me this sword and this armor," he swept his hand down his chest. "I mean, he give me this breast plate. No, I don't think he blames me at all."

Pistis looked into the eyes of each soldier. "Then why should we?"

Rusty nodded and smiled. "Ah, Con, I wasn't blamin' you. I was jest thinkin' of what I did afore the Commander took me in. Weren't the same as you but it was some pow'rful bad stuff. Stuff I ain't sure I'd want to tell ya'll about."

Sarah's face reddened. "Yeah. I think Rusty has a point. I may not have been following the Masters but I had my own problems." She moved closer to Con and slid her arm under his.

Beatrice, still searching in her pack, smiled and giggled. "You ain't gonna hear about my past."

Dugan stomped back to the group. "You gotta be kiddin' me. Have I been put with a whole squad of rebels?'

"C'mon, Dugan," Rusty laughed. "You mean you ain't done nothin' yer ashamed of?"

Dugan's freckles disappeared in the redness of his cheeks. "No! Of course not. How can all of you sit here and brag about your cavorting." He turned away, then spun back, obviously very distressed. "Of course not."

He grabbed his pack and stomped off into the darkness.

Pistis threw some dirt on the fire. "Get some sleep. It will be a long day tomorrow." It might have been the shadows cast by the dying glow of the fire, but the creases in Pistis's brow seemed extra deep and wide.

In the morning, Pistis set them in marching order. "Dugan. Take the point."

Con looked at him but Pistis ignored him. "Sarah, right flank but don't go out more that five yards. Beatrice, left flank. Same for you. Con, take the rear, but keep close."

Pistis waved and they began to march. He caught up with Dugan and whispered something to him. Dugan's head snapped around to look at him, then he drew his sword.

Pistis fell back and they marched off. Within a quarter mile, the trees thinned. Dull, silver-white sunlight filtered down to the forest floor. In the splotches of light, brambles and small bushes grew. Within another quarter mile, the size of the standing timber diminished and long stretches of underbrush filled the spaces between the trunks.

Dugan stopped. His hand flew up in the air, then he kneeled. The rest of the squad dropped to the ground. Pistis crawled up to him. Dugan pointed toward the brush on their right. It was about twenty feet from the path, the area between filled with tall grass. Pistis whispered something. Dugan nodded, then ran into the brush, his shield pushing through, making a way. Pistis rose to one knee and waved the squad forward. As each came, he pointed at a spot on the ground and whispered something.

As Con approached, he saw the squad was laid out in a semi-circle in the grass, Rusty on one end, then Sarah. Beatrice was just moving into a position—far from Sarah. Pistis pointed at the end of the semi-circle. "Get there quickly, then lay down on your stomach. Wait for my command."

Con moved off swiftly. Pistis crossed the circle and lay down next to the brush.

Dugan screamed. The hair on Con's neck stood up. He started to rise, as did Beatrice. Pistis waved them back down.

Dugan screamed again. "No, get away. Get away!"

There was a crash in the underbrush. Dugan tore loose of the grasping branches and burst into the center of the semicircle. He ran in a panic, his sword trailing hanging loosely in his right hand.

"Get away!" he screamed again.

Dugan slid onto the ground, turning onto his belly and laying the sword out in front of him. He filled the open position in the circle.

Two creatures ran from the thicket. They stopped in the grass—barely able to see over it. They were three feet tall or so. Each could not have weighed more than fifty pounds. Their skin was pink and hairless. Their heads were round and bald. The only clothing they wore was a wide leather belt slung from shoulder to waist. From it hung a short, slender scabbard. There bodies reminded one of a human but their faces quickly changed that impression. Wide, thick lips curled back over glistening, needle-like teeth, giving the impression of a perpetual, evil grin. Their ears were long and pointed and their noses were pushed up like the snout of a pig. High cheekbones and elongated, slanted eyes gave them an amused look.

The daggers in their hands contradicted that. There was no amusement there.

"Up!"

Pistis rose from the ground and moved to close off the beings' retreat. The rest the squad jumped to their feet and quickly surrounded them, sword points aimed low at the little people's chests.

When Dugan rose from the grass, his sword point out, the little people squealed and spun around. Pistis thrust out his sword, almost touching the taller one. That one squealed again, like a pig at slaughter, then threw up its hands and dropped into the grass. The other one spun from side to side, slashing with its dagger. When it saw the six swords did not waver, and that there was no escape, it plopped down onto the ground next to its fellow. Both of them flicked their daggers down, so that the points stuck into the ground. The handles buzzed like angry insects as they vibrated back and forth.

The taller one smiled its needle-filled grin at Pistis, "S-s-sooo, Pisssstissss, you haf visssited our foressst again. Didn't you get enough the lasssst time?"

Pistis remained mute, his eyes watching the two intently. Con opened his mouth to answer but his uncle shook his head. Reluctantly, he snapped his jaws shut.

The smaller one started to move toward Rusty. Rusty dropped his sword tip in response. The being slid to a stop and retreated, its hands up and out.

It turned suddenly and lunged toward the hole between Dugan and Beatrice. Beatrice gasped, waiting a split second too long to bring her sword around. The pink creature ducked inside Beatrice's sword point and rushed at the opening, trying to break clear. Beatrice, in reflex, reached to grab the being. Pistis yelled but too late. The beast sank its teeth into her arm. Beatrice screamed and snatched her arm back, getting raked by the teeth for her effort. The beast started running again.

Dugan reacted quickly. He whirled low, his sword straight out. The blade leaped forward. The tip sliced into the calf of the fleeing being. A horrible shriek burst from the beast and it fell to the leaves, clutching at the wound, which spurted bluish fluid.

All eyes turned toward the skirmish. The larger beast reached down and scooped up its dagger and lunged toward Rusty. It leaped, arms and feet extended, like a cat attacking its prey. Rusty's eyes returned to the beast in mid-air. He froze. Con screamed and dove forward, swinging his sword in a wide, overhead arc.

The sword slammed broadside into the body of the beast. The pink being slammed into the ground, sprawling on its belly. With flailing legs, it wriggled back, away from the soldiers. Rusty chopped with his sword. It struck the ground and sunk in several inches but missed the rapidly retreating being. Con swung at it, edge first. The small being screamed and crawled on hands and knees further from the soldiers, back into the center of the circle.

On its feet again, it spun and ran toward Con. "You die!"

Con, settling finally as a swordsman should, lifted his sword point to gain the leverage, then flicked the point at the hand that held the dagger. He caught the knife behind the guard and with a twist of his wrist, sent it flying through the air. The beast stopped and stared at its empty hand, bewildered.

Its sloped eyes found Con's. He noticed that the color was purple flecked with green. "You are gooooood," it hissed at him. It plopped down onto the wet leaves and put its hands on its head.

"Bind them."

The team turned at the deep baritone voice. Cleato stood on the trail holding two silk-like cords. He was beaming. "Con, take this cords and bind that one. Dugan, this one."

Con took one and tested it. It appeared to be little more than uniform decorations, but when he tried to break it, he could not even cause it to stretch. Quickly, he bound the being on the ground while

Rusty held his sword close to its neck. Con looked up from his task to see Dugan binding the other while Sarah threatened it with her sword.

Dugan finished tying off the beast with a flourish. He stood and turned to Cleato. "What will we do with them, Cleato?"

"We will leave them here. We can not let them go for they will tell the Dragon we are here and that we are strong."

"Who are they? Better, what are they?" Con asked, examining them closely. The beings followed him with their eyes, the expressions on their distorted faces transmitting the hate they had for him. "They certainly don't look like Dragon Raiders."

"They are not, Con," Pistis answered walking up to stand next to him. "They're in this realm but they're really from the other side of the tunnel. They've existed in both realms for centuries. Some call them the little people, others pixies. There have been many stories, but for centuries upon centuries, they've been owned by the Dragon and have been used by him to guard this forest. They're formidable foes, having captured many who would have escaped the enemy except for their vigilance." He turned to look at the whole squad. "You've done an excellent job today."

Cleato nodded. "Yes, you have. No more than I expected you could do, though, when you work as a unit."

The taller one, apparently the leader, looked up at Cleato. "S-S-Sooo, Lord Cleato. You think theesss are good enough to enter the citadel," the smaller one hissed at him. It looked the squad over, its eyes returning to Dugan twice. Its next remark, it addressed directly to him. "You can't, you know. The dragon issss too sssstrong for you. The five of you jussssst barely captured usssss. How will you fight the Raidersssss?"

The beast laughed. The squad recoiled under the ridicule; its confidence melting away like snow on a warm spring hill.

Cleato laughed. "Be quiet, Qird. Your lies will do no good for your master, little slave."

Qird's eyes narrowed. "The little people are slaves to no one, Lord Cleato. You know that."

"I know that you sold yourselves into slavery centuries ago and now lie to yourselves to protect your pride. But, enough. We will leave. You will stay."

With that, Cleato nodded at Pistis. He picked up his pack and walked toward the road. The squad did likewise.

Chapter 24

The squad fell into line. Cleato lifted a bottle out of the pack and walked over to the captives. The pair wriggled in their bonds and tried to slither on the wet carpet of leaves. Qird hissed.

"Not on us-s-s, Cleato. Ev-hen you woult not be s-s-sooo cruel."

"Not on you, Qird, but around you. I'll not apply it to you until you've asked for it."

The beast shuddered. "That won't happen in your lifetime, Cleato. I am of a free people. I won't submit to you again."

Cleato nodded. "I know that, Qird. Never-the-less, it is available." He popped the cork stopper from the small-necked bottle and tipped it over. Thick, red fluid poured from it—as red as blood. Con glanced at Pistis with the question.

"It is blood," Pistis announced to the whole squad. "it is the blood of a lamb."

Cleato poured a solid, unbroken ring of blood around the beings. Both Qird and his companion pulled their legs up, away from the ruby colored ring, and held them with their arms.

"They are secure now," Cleato said. "They could otherwise have slithered away even though bound. Now they will be held until we release them."

Beatrice stepped forward. "What power does the blood of a lamb hold, Cleato?" Her voice quavered and she rocked her injured arm in her free hand.

Without answering, Cleato pulled her arm out straight and held the bottle over it. A single drop of the blood fell onto her arm.

The fluid spread quickly. Beatrice gasped and tried to pull away. Cleato held her securely. "Does it hurt?"

Beatrice shook her head. "No, I was surprised at its warmth."

Her eyebrows shot up and she yelled, "Look!"

The ragged wounds closed. The skin knitted, leaving red lines where the gashes had been. New pink skin grew in from the edges, covering the redness and replacing it with a healthy pink glow.

Cleato raised his hand to the questions that began to pour from the squad and said, "Suffice it to say that all the power of the Commander is available in this blood: to hold the enemy; to heal the wounds he inflicts; to dissolve the bonds that he uses."

Con eyed the smallness of the bottle with alarm. Cleato shook his head. Laughing, he said, "It is not the size of the container, Con. It is the power of the contents."

Cleato brought the small flask over to him and uncorked it. High in the neck, the red liquid sat. Con looked up, his brow pressed together.

Rusty came up behind him and laid a hand on his shoulder. "We ain't on the other side. Remember?"

Cleato checked the two prisoners once more. When he was sure they were secure, he turned to Pistis "Set the squad in marching order. And noise discipline is once again necessary."

The little beasts yelled as they left, "You can't beat him. He isssss too powerful for you."

The squad marched off smartly, heads high. They never looked back at their captives.

They marched into the thick wood again. The eternal twilight descended then thickened into the purplish pre-night of the late afternoon. Night approached, although to Con it was yet early. Through the thick leaves patches of sky, deep gray as during a snowstorm, glowed.

The darkness increased the danger of the path. Roots ran across it at ankle height. Wet leaves clung to every grade. Then Cleato's light appeared at their feet.

The shadows engulfed the whole forest. Nothing outside the ring of foot-light was visible. Cleato pushed on, searching first to one side, then to the other, as if looking for a specific spot. Finally, he grunted and stopped. The rest of the squad closed up to him.

They stood at the intersection of two paths. The one they followed was narrow and ill defined. The other was a broad thoroughfare. The leaves and grass were beaten down as if by the passing of regular traffic. Cleato moved down the main road twenty yards then dropped his pack.

"We camp here tonight."

Dugan grumbled, "This is not a good place. Others obviously use this road and we will probably meet them."

"That is correct, Dugan," Cleato answered while setting up a piece of canvas to act as a shelter.

"Then why-the-sam-hill are we camping here?"

All the rest followed Cleato's lead and set up shelter halves to protect them from the morning dew. Dugan stood on the road, unmoving.

"I asked why are we staying here?"

Cleato looked up at Dugan and sighed. Pistis's voice cut through the darkness, "Dugan, set up your camp. When we need to know, Cleato will tell us."

Dugan stared obstinately at Pistis, then his shoulders heaved in a shrug. He trudged onto the grass and dropped his pack.

Cleato walked over to Dugan. He spoke softly. None of the others could hear. Dugan grunted. Cleato spoke again. Again, the reply was a grunt.

Beatrice prepared the meal. In addition to the wine and meat, Cleato broke out a loaf of unleavened bread. It was warm and fresh. The sweet and chewy dough melted as Con bit into it, releasing a honey and spice flavor. Con moaned and rolled his eyes. "This is great. Why haven't we had it before?"

Cleato smiled. "There was no need before. Now we have to be as one."

Beatrice swallowed her first bite. "What's it have to do with being one?"

"The loaf makes us one. All who eat of it are saying they will join together and work for the Commander—will, in a sense, be one with him. If we are all one with him then we are one with each other."

Dugan sat away from the group, seeming to pay no attention. He sniffed at the bread, then laid it down untouched.

After the meal, Rusty went to douse the fire. Cleato stopped him. "Let it burn tonight, Rusty. We may need it later."

Dugan looked up sharply, a disgusted look passing over his face. He rose and returned to his own tent.

Cleato nodded at Pistis. He grabbed his pack and walked down the broad lane into the darkness.

"Get some rest. We may have company before the night is out," Cleato said.

"Do you mean the enemy?" Rusty asked.

"We will see," was the only answer.

Sleep would not come for Con. He lay awake, looking up into the blackness, aware of his companions by their shuffling and wheezes. The fire was only coals and Cleato did not seem inclined to stir it up.

Con heard footsteps and leaned on one elbow to look. Someone moved quickly on the main path. A man ran up to the glowing fire and began to put on some small twigs. It was Pistis, back from his walk. He nodded toward Cleato. "They come."

Cleato smiled. "I know, Pistis. I know."

"Do we rouse the troops?'

Cleato nodded his head. Pistis ran to each lean-to and shook the inhabitant.

Cleato suddenly sat upright. He leaned to one side and stared into the darkness as if he'd heard something.

Something shuffled in the leaves down the main path.

The noise came plainly, shish-shish—shish-shish. Con got on his hands and knees and crawled to the fire, intent on smothering it. Cleato reached it first and, instead of smothering it, added dry leaves and larger sticks to what Pistis had started.

"What are you doing, Cleato? They will see the flames."

" I want them to. This is not the enemy."

The rest of squad came to the fire, swords drawn. Cleato moved to the middle of the path, in plain view. Dugan came last to the light—his sword still sheathed.

The noise on the path came again, much closer. It was obviously someone or something walking in the thick carpet of dead leaves. Nothing was visible, for the fire blinded their eyes to the slight glow of the forest. Beyond the small circle of flickering, yellow light nothing existed.

The squad, almost unconsciously, took up a defensive position. Sword points came to the ready.

The noise grew more distinct. Con made it out to be the slow, shuffling steps of several people. He looked to Cleato. No command, no suggestion, no direction came from him. He stood in the middle of the road and looked into the darkness, his head shaking and a sad, almost pitying, look covered his face.

Pistis stood on the road, in front of the squad, a position he would not normally assume in battle. He seemed to be as confused as the squad.

The noise grew louder. Figures, distorted by the wavering light and the moving shadows, tramped toward them. As they closed on the fire, they showed themselves to be men; normal size—normal proportions—normal men. Sarah gasped. Beatrice, on his other side, moaned.

The six men and women who approached stopped fifteen feet away. Their arms were across their faces as if unused to the brightness. Their clothes were tattered and ripped. Holes gaped at the knees and elbows and the rest were in shreds. The men were unshaven and all were unkempt.

The thing which had caused the girls to moan, though, was not these outward things but the hollow eyes—eyes that sank back into their heads—eyes ringed with dark circles—eyes that cried out in pain and fear—and hunger.

One of the group, an older man with silver-gray hair ventured forward a few steps. Ignoring Cleato, he looked toward Pistis. "You are soldiers?"

"We are."

"Thank the Commander's Father!" the man moaned, signaling his group forward. They trooped to the fire, past the squad. The squad dropped their sword points and stared. Pistis waved his hand at them and they all sheathed their swords.

Con walked over to the fire and sat down across from them. They sat close to it, appearing to be exhausted and cold. Each warmed his hands near the flames, grabbing for the heat as if they'd not felt it for a long time.

"Are you hungry?" Beatrice asked.

"You have food?" the leader asked eagerly. Then a frown crossed his face, "What would soldiers be doing this far into the Dragon's realm?"

"We do have food," Pistis answered. "Your people look hungry. Perhaps we should feed them first. Then we can discuss each other's purpose in being here."

The rest of the newcomers looked pleadingly at the leader. The leader, still frowning, nodded once. Beatrice rushed to the pack.

Con studied the man. He was short and fat. His long silver hair straggled about his head, greasy and filled with pieces of bark and debris from the forest. His clothes had a good cut and, although they were torn and tattered, the quality of them was plain. His shoes were of the finest leather and looked as if they once had shone with a high polish. Now, they were scuffed and dirty.

Looking at the rest of the group, he saw a similar cut to the clothing and the people. Back in the City they were of the upper crust, living the best of life. He could not fathom what they were doing here.

Beatrice prepared a meal of bread and wine. The small group looked at it strangely as if they did not recognize it as food. A few twittered and laughed when it was given to them.

"It is food," Pistis said. "Eat it."

A thin, white-haired woman, with square, thick glasses held onto her head by a silver chain around her neck, spoke, "It may be food to you, young man, but we've never eaten any of this sort. John," she turned to the leader, "do we eat this?"

John examined the bread, turning it over in his hands. He sniffed the wine. "It is pretty crude stuff. But it won't hurt you, so long as you don't make a habit of eating it. I think that we'll be offered nothing else in this camp."

Rusty's look clouded and he snapped, "It's the same as we eat. It won't do ya' no harm. Might do some of ya' a heap a' good."

"Oh, don't be insulted. We meant no harm. If this satisfies your needs we certainly would not want to interfere."

Another of the group sniggered. Con heard one whisper to another, "Do you believe they really eat this?"

The other returned his comment, "Yes, but the real surprise is that they like it."

Both sniggered behind their hands, but continued to eat.

Con, his anger flaring at the insult, leaned forward to correct them. Pistis's hand fell on his shoulder. "They are our guests."

Con, still angry, looked to Cleato for support. The big man was not in camp. He stood out on the road, immobile and silent. Con got up and walked out to him.

"Cleato, d'you hear them? How do you treat a bunch like this?"

"With patience, Con, with patience."

"I'd like to treat them with the tip of my sandal."

Cleato laughed. "Me, too. Sometimes." He paused. "Go back to the fire. They will tell you some things you should hear."

Con returned to the fire. He heard the last of Rusty's comments. "...then on to the Citadel ta free us some captives."

The leader of the other group shook his head. "No, you'll never succeed there. You can't do it. You see, those people want to be there."

He shook his head slowly. "No, you'll never convince them otherwise. We tried several times."

"We will convince them once we defeat the Dragon."

"Defeat the Dragon!" The group stared wide-eyed into the darkness.

Their leader stared open-mouthed for a full ten seconds. One of the men with him shouted, "You aren't strong enough! You don't stand a chance."

"Look, youngsters," their leader said, dropping his voice down as if he was afraid that someone would overhear. "We fought the Dragon, or we tried to. He is powerful. Very powerful! Stronger than anything I've ever met. We went against him with a whole battalion of troops. We are the only ones left. No, youngsters, don't be so foolhardy."

Sarah and Con exchanged glances. Rusty cleared his throat and stared at Cleato. The big man remained silent, watching the road.

Beatrice asked, "Where are your swords?"

"Yes, I see you have big swords. And very sharp, from the looks of it. But so did we. They may have not been as long as yours and perhaps they were less sharp...." He paused, a pained look, almost as of guilt, passed over his face. "But we had them," he said suddenly, defiantly, "and we had to drop them in the midst of the battle and flee. They weighed so much we couldn't run fast enough with them in our hands."

Dugan walked out of the shadows and into the conversation, "Did you have Cleato with you?"

"Cleato?" Each of them looked at the other. "Of course we did. We have Cleato with us no matter where we go."

Con glanced at Cleato. The big man stood impassively, but when Con's eye caught his, he shook his head once.

"Do you mean," Con said, "that Cleato marched with you. That he directed you in battle and you still lost."

"If you mean that he actually was there, standing next to us—of course not! That never happens anymore. That hasn't happened for centuries."

Sarah jumped up then, laughing. "Hasn't happened for centuries? Why he's standing right there." She pointed her finger at him and the whole group turned to look.

Instead of acknowledging Cleato, they looked up and down the path.

"Where?" the fat leader asked, turning back to Sarah.

Con answered him. "Do you mean you can't see our leader?"

The visitors glanced back and forth at one another. Their leader looked first at Con, then to Pistis. "Are you one of those groups?" he asked, his eyebrows arching.

Pistis smiled, "Yes, we are."

The visitors got to their feet as a group and backed off from the squad. They gathered together on the road and edged away.

"Well, we appreciate the hospitality but we must be going."

"Goin'?" Con asked. "But it's pitch dark. You'll stumble and fall and just get yourself more lost than you already are. Stay until mornin'."

The visitors ignored Con and continued to edge away.

"And why is it that you are leaving us?" Pistis asked.

John started to answer, then stopped. His eyes roamed up and down the length of Pistis. "Don't I know you?"

Pistis shrugged. "I suppose you could. I've been around the Regiments for a lot of years."

Beatrice came over to him with her pack. "Pistis, I have a little of the bread left. Should we give it to them for their journey?"

"Pistis!" the little lady exclaimed. "Of course, you are that rebel, Pistis Trueblood. I heard you babble at a staff meeting one time. Languages! Talking directly to the Commander. Posh!"

John nodded. "Pistis Trueblood. Well, now I know what you people are. Yes," he turned to his people, "they're Dragon worshippers, folks."

He turned back to Pistis. "You stay away from us. We're leavin' this land and there is nothing you can do about it."

Beatrice tried to hand them some bread but they winced away. Slowly, they edged out of the light. When they separated themselves from the squad by twenty feet or so the leader turned his back and ran. "Every one for himself," he yelled over his shoulder as he disappeared into the darkness.

His followers, who had been watching the squad, turned in time to see their leader disappearing. With a shout, they ran after him, tripping one another in their haste to depart.

Con started after them but Cleato called him back. "They will not listen, Con. Let them go." He sounded sad and hurt but resolute.

The squad seated themselves in the dying glow of the fire. Dugan seated himself across the fire from Cleato, as far as he could get from him.

"I knew this was a fool's trip," he mumbled.

Cleato seemed to endure a sharp pain, but he said nothing. Beatrice looked at Dugan with a questioning frown. "What is that supposed to mean?"

"We can't defeat the Dragon."

"Of course we can, Dugan," Sarah said. "Cleato is with us. And he says we can."

"A fools trip!" Dugan yelled at her. "You heard those people. Cleato was with them, too. And they were a battalion strong, not just a squad of fools."

"But Dugan," Rusty argued, "these people didn't even recognize—no, they couldn't even *see* Cleato. There's the differ'nce."

"What difference?" Dugan yelled.

Con turned to Cleato. The big man winced at each of Dugan's words. "Tell him, Cleato."

"Cleato!" yelled Dugan, "Cleato! That's all you people ever say. Can't you make any decisions on your own?"

"He won't hear me anymore, Con," Cleato said quietly.

Dugan ranted. "A bunch of fools. That's what you are. Those soldiers going off there have more sense than you will ever have."

With that, he grabbed his pack and started up the trail.

"Dugan!" Con called and started after him.

Dugan whirled around. His sword appeared in his hand and he slashed at Con, sinking the edge of the sword into his buckler. Con threw himself to the left, slipping on wet leaves and landing an his back.

Dugan looked down at him and snorted. "You. The great swordsman. Just a smoker and a traveler making himself up to be somethin' he ain't. I ain't forgot how you tricked me in that first fight so's you could make a fool of me in front of my girl."

He spun toward Pistis. "Had it all worked out between you two, didn't you? First he makes me the fool, then you come in with your wheedlin' flattery and steal her from me."

He threw down his sword and rushed into the darkness, pursuing the other group.

On the leaves lay a book—Dugan's manual. Con grabbed it, calling to Dugan. No answer came back from the darkness except his own echo.

Con returned to the fire. Sarah and Beatrice stood together, hugging each other, shocked looks on their faces. Rusty stared into the blackness—silent—woeful. Pistis paced back and forth. Cleato stood impassive again, back to the fire, searching the darkness around them.

"Get some sleep," he said, almost in a monotone.

"Now, wait."

Pistis stood next to the fire, hands on his hips. "What kind of accusation was that? Where in the world did he get the idea I stole his girlfriend? Who was his girlfriend, anyway?"

Beatrice spun toward him. Her fists jammed her hips and she stared him in the eye. Pistis recoiled from the angry look. Then she stamped one foot and growled, "Errrrr-uh!"

With that, she spun around and marched toward her shelter.

Pistis stared around wide-eyed. "What was th...?"

Cleato smiled. "Pistis, you discern the plans of the enemy well. But you sure don't know women. We are going to have to work on that."

Sarah grabbed Cleato's arm, tears on her cheeks. "Cleato, we've lost Dugan. We must do something."

"I'll care for him, Sarah," the big man said, looking down with a kind smile on his face. "I'll take care of him. Remember that I told you before we might lose some. Don't be concerned. I'll guide him back to the City. Perhaps there we can reclaim him."

Sarah nodded and turned to the fire. She kneeled and began putting things back in Beatrice's pack. The firelight glinted off a tear as it streamed down her cheek.

Pistis stood where Beatrice had left him. He looked at his hands, flipping fingers out and back on each as if calculating something. Then he stared at the dark lean-to where Beatrice had retreated. Then, back to his hands. His face was a mask of confusion.

Con and Rusty went to Cleato. He glanced at them and smiled. A sigh escaped his lips and he said, "It always hurts when one deserts you like that. It shouldn't hurt anymore, after all the ones who have done it, but it still does."

"What will happen to Dugan?" Con asked, searching Cleato's face.

"Right now, it is unsure. We will not give up on Dugan. When this mission is over we will find him."

Rusty patted him on the back then turned and went to his shelter. Con remained next to Cleato, staring out into the darkness with him.

"What happened?" he asked.

"To Dugan?"

"Uh-huh," Con said, "Why did he run?"

"He didn't run, Con. He could not accept the rebuke I gave him and has brooded on it ever since. He had been looking for an excuse to leave us. I knew this group would give it to him."

"You knew? Then why did you pick this place to stop? Why didn't you hide from them?"

"You are not thinking clearly, Con. If Dugan had gone further with us he still would have been ready to leave us. Had that urge overwhelmed him while we were in battle, he may have been killed and he probably would have gotten one of you killed. As it is, he is not lost to us, only protected. And we are protected from his weakness."

Cleato turned and stared into the darkness. Con, too, became quiet. Finally the exertion, the silence, and the peace of being next to Cleato overcame Con's desire to remain alert. He returned to his blanket and slept.

Chapter 25

He sat up. Leaves fell from his face and a wool blanket dropped to his lap. The early morning dew covered him and a slight, chill breeze brought a shiver to his body. Sleep gripped his eyes and his mind, so he wrapped the blanket around his shoulder and huddled down for a few minutes.

Around him there was only blackness. He turned toward the camp, looking for Cleato. No one stirred. The fire was only darkened coals barely glowing in the predawn blackness. Con shuffled to it keeping the blanket around his shoulders. He threw on a few twigs.

The fire caught quickly. Con rubbed his hands over the small flames. Someone shuffled in the leaves behind him then touched his shoulder and whispered, "Good morning." Sarah leaned over and kissed him on the cheek.

Con started to answer when Cleato's bulk loomed out of the shadows. "I have been up the trail a few miles. It is clear now but there is no time to lose. We must start quickly. Get Pistis for me, Con. I'm afraid the confusion of last night has dulled him a bit."

Con glanced at him, concerned, but Cleato smiled.

Con hurried to do his bidding. Sarah grabbed at loose objects on the forest floor and threw them into the waiting pack. There would be no warm breakfast that morning.

Pistis staggered up the fire, trying to stifle a yawn. "I'm sorry, Cleato. I had trouble getting to sleep last night."

Cleato bent over to gather wet leaves. He said, "Understandable. Now get the squad ready." In the faint light, Con could see a grin on Cleato's face.

As Pistis went to wake Rusty and Beatrice, Con got close to Cleato. "What is up with my uncle? I see that grin on your face a lot when talking with him now?"

Cleato cocked his head to one side. "Hmmm. No, I don't think you need to know that yet. Let me tell you though, Con, so that you will remember this later: The Commander will give his soldiers what they really desire—even when they don't know that they desire it."

Cleato dropped the leaves on the fire, then walked away. "Get 'em in line. We must move quickly."

Con stared, trying to figure out what that meant. How could one desire something and not know that they desire it? That didn't make any sense.

Cleato handed out small wafers of the bread they had had the night before. "Eat them. They'll do you as much good, though they are not as tasty."

As soon as the squad gulped down the small ration, Cleato trotted away. The squad fell into line and ran with him. Pistis took the rear. Beatrice and Sarah jogged in the middle of the group, bracketed by Rusty and Con.

The trail was rough. Many roots, larger than a man's arm, stuck into it, forsaking the soil for the most part and forming a series of ankle high snares. Cleato seemed to glide over top of them. The squad didn't. All their attention was spent on keeping their footing.

Within two miles, the giant trees dwindled, replaced by small, thin trunks, bent in grotesque shapes. Cleato picked up the pace. Beatrice grunted then gasped. "Cleato, I must rest."

The big man stopped and looked at her. He hesitated for a moment, looking first back over their shoulders then up the trail. Nervous, but satisfied, he nodded his head and signaled for the squad to be seated. They stood in place and bent over. Rusty's breath came in quick gasps. The girls breathed deeply through their mouths but, otherwise, seemed to be in good shape. Pistis's chest heaved in and out but he still breathed through his nose. He did a few knee bends and stretched one leg, as if it had bunched up on him.

Cleato trotted down the trail, looking into every opening in the forest, peering around trees and even up into the branches. The squad plopped down onto the leaf-covered grass. Con watched for a few minutes, then regained his feet and went back to check their back trail.

No one seemed to be on it.

Cleato returned and signaled them to stand. Con shifted the pack on his shoulders while the others stood slowly.

Cleato waited for a moment, letting them get settled. Then he spoke, "I am pushing you very hard. It is necessary. Our friends from last night have set the two beasts free and they have gone to report. We will have visitors of an unfriendly nature very soon if we stay here."

Sarah gasped. "Do you mean that Dugan set those creatures free after what they tried to do to him?" Her tone changed from shock to anger as she spoke.

Cleato shook his head, "Do not blame Dugan. He is not sure of what he is doing now. The ones he joined considered them harmless."

He put his hand on Sarah's shoulder. "Do not waste anger on him or them. We will need all our wits about us to get out of this." He looked each in the eye to emphasize the point.

Cleato jerked suddenly, then looked back down the trail. His eyes narrowed and he listened intently. Con cocked his head but could hear nothing.

Beatrice whispered, "They're coming. I can hear them."

Con strained to hear but only the rustle of the forest was discernible to him. He glanced at Sarah. She shrugged and shook her head.

Beatrice was adamant. "I can hear them," she said. "They are coming, and quickly."

Again silence ensued. Cleato finally spoke, "She is correct. And look to her now. She is now your scout."

Cleato moved off the trail to the East. "Quickly, Children. We must be off this trail when they come. Run quickly."

He pointed at some cliffs seen dimly through the thin forest. Beatrice took the point and, holding her scabbard to her side, ran as fast as she could. The others fell in behind her. Con tried to take the rear but his uncle pushed him on. "I need to be here, Con. You stay in close contact, though. I may need your sword."

"Do not wait for me," Cleato yelled after them. "I'll catch you."

As Con left the scene, Cleato pulled a bag from his pack. He tore it open and dusted the whole area with a fine, grayish powder. When it was gone, he stuffed the bag back into his pack and ran after his squad.

Con ran easily, remaining several yards behind the girls. Rusty slowed after the initial surge and showed signs of slowing more. Con moved up closer.

Feet clomped the mossy ground behind him. As Con turned to see, Cleato caught him and ran by. He regained the point position, then slowed slightly. The squad matched his pace and followed him as he turned them slightly toward the face of the cliff.

The forest thinned. Small trees, their trunks thin and bent, pushed toward the sky. Bushes grappled with them for the best sun and soil. Boulders and jagged rock ledges, bare of soil, reared out of the ground. A different land—drier—rougher. They were climbing the mountain range—that bare, black barrier that had blocked their view of the East for so long that they had forgotten it was there.

Con glanced back over his shoulder. Already they had climbed above the forest floor. He could see clearly the abandoned path as a scar on the land. No one followed.

Ahead, the sides of a cliff loomed up from the grassy slope—fifty feet of shear rock, dominating everything. It was scarred by the wind and erosion but without apparent break. Cleato ran straight at it.

Right up to the face of it he ran—the squad struggling and wheezing behind him—then he veered off to the left, and ran along the bare rock face. Ahead of them, behind the brush that had grown or been blown up against it and hidden by a fold in the cliff, the rock face split. In the split was a trail that went up and then back. Cleato entered the notch without slowing down. The squad followed.

The narrow trail followed the notch up into the rock, hugging the right side and rounding the bulk about fifty feet away. Cleato disappeared around the bend. Rusty also made the turn and the girls struggled up the trail halfway to the goal. Con stopped and glanced back before beginning the climb. His uncle struggled about fifteen feet back. His face was red and he was gasping for breath.

"Son," he called as he approached Con. "You got to take the back. I can't. I wouldn't be much good in a fight."

Con nodded and shoved him in front of him. Then he stopped him again and pulled off his pack. "I'll get this to the top. You get yourself."

Pistis started to argue, then glanced at the steep trail. "I'll do for you, sometime."

Con nodded and slapped him on the back.

He waited until Pistis began to climb, then looked back down the trail. He neither saw nor heard anything. With that, he turned and followed his uncle.

The trail was paved with loose rock and shale. After only a few seconds, Con's breath came in chunks, gulped down and blasted out. His legs pumped, cramping with exertion. He weaved slightly and had to push off the rock face with both hands. The desire to stop, to rest a minute crept up on him, beckoning him to ease off the strain. He rounded the bend. Ahead of him was a steeper climb of about twenty feet. The trail turned again to the right.

His uncle's feet disappeared around that bend. The others were gone already. Con pushed on, gasping for breath.

The trail topped out on the rock just beyond the bend. The rest of the squad lay about on their backs on the smooth, sloping rock gasping, their arms spread out and their mouths wide. Loud wheezing filled

Con's ears. Cleato lay calmly on his belly close to the edge of the rock, overlooking their approach.

Con dropped the pack next to his uncle. Pistis nodded, still wheezing for breath. He dropped his hand onto the pack and nodded again. Con moved up close to Cleato, puffing through his nose, trying to control his breath. His head was close to the rock and each breath raised a small cloud of dust. Cleato smiled and patted his back.

Through the forest the trail was visible as a dim line on the surface of the grass. Con started to speak but Cleato raised his fingers to his lips. They lay side by side staring across the half-mile.

A sound, like baying hounds, drifted on the breeze. It was like baying hounds, but something was different, something strange and foreign. The faint sound, growing louder by the second, awoke memories in Con—memories of winter nights as a child when the wolves circled the house, hunting for meat—any meat, even that of a small child—when the dog cowered in the corner and growled deep within its throat in fear and humiliation—when his father ran to close all the shutters and stood in the center of the room with his bow in his hand and an arrow nocked—when Con lay in his bed, before the fire, shaking, cringing at the fearful sound of the hunters' voices.

Con strained to see them but the dense forest covered the trail. Cleato had picked the perfect place to rest—as he usually did. His choice of observation points was probably the only places in the whole forest where they could see their back trail far enough to do any good.

The baying grew louder. It became clearly distinguishable from that of a normal dog—or a wolf—or anything else in nature. There was a ferocity in the call, all out of proportion with any natural hunter. It reacted not on his ear but on his soul, driving fear, like a hot poker, through his mind, quickening every nightmarish thought he'd ever had. What followed them was more than he had faced before. What followed them was vicious, wicked—powerful.

The hounds rushed out of the dense woods at full lope, noses to the ground, mouths opening and closing but out of synchronization with their sound—adding an unreal quality to the scene. They passed the ground where Cleato had spread the powder. Like acrobats, the dogs flipped into the air, clawing at the sky, then back onto the grass, still clawing. They tore at their snouts with flailing paws.

The baying stopped. Whining cries, like a dog in pain, echoed across the distance. They ran into the grass, scraping their snouts on the ground and rolling over and over.

"What is it, Cleato? What has caused them to lose the trail?"

Cleato smiled briefly. "It is nothing but dust."

The rest of the squad, recovered from the exhaustive run, crept up alongside of them. Sarah asked, "But they've been following our trail for a day and there has been dust before."

"Not like this dust." He smiled again. "It is not the dust, but where it came from. This dust was collected on the streets of the upper castle. It has not really hurt them. The smell of it was recognizable at once and they could not stand to have it on them."

This did not make a lot of sense to Con but he refrained from asking. The hounds recovered as they spoke and sniffed around the trail, carefully avoiding the dusted area, wincing away when they blundered into it.

They were strange dogs. Their color was a pale, sickly white. They were long, sleek. Their snouts were stretched out and their overall appearance was like that of a greyhound. But there was something wrong.

Con shuddered. He remembered the wolf-like beast he had seen during the mind trip, the one that had attacked him. A cold, hard knot formed in the pit of his stomach.

One of the dogs below them stared at the hill. Con ducked. The fear in him said this beast was looking directly into his eyes as had the wolf-beast that day. The coldness in the pit of his stomach spread throughout his body and he shuddered again.

"They have found us," Beatrice said.

Cleato nodded and said, "We must go quickly. I do not want to defend this place. Come quickly up into the Barriers. They will not follow there."

"Why is that, Cleato?" Rusty asked.

"They are not permitted," was his only answer.

Cleato slid back down the rock to a flat area. The rest of the squad did likewise. "I do not believe they have actually seen us but they have sensed our presence. It will not take long for them to figure out our location. We must run quickly but stay together. We must have no stragglers."

Chapter 26

The trail ran between large boulders. Cleato herded them onto it then followed, protecting the rear. Pistis took the lead. Con dropped back to run alongside Cleato.

"What is it they want, Cleato? Why do they seek us?"

"They are of the Dragon. His hounds, so to speak. Hounds, but not unintelligent. They may wreak havoc among us with no direction from him. And they aren't always hounds. The way you see them now is good for trailing so they use it. When it is more convenient to walk on two legs they will do that. If the shape of a tree will allow them to perform their mission then they will be that. Always, though, they have the head, the canine head."

Con remembered the beast of his dream again and shuddered, for it had been one of these, maybe even one of the same ones who followed, that had attacked him. He felt nauseated. His legs grew weak, yet with all his strength he wanted to sprint away. He glanced back over his shoulder, the whites of his eyes flashing.

"That is their food, Con."

Con turned his head to look at Cleato, not knowing his meaning at first. Then he caught it. "My fear! Of course. He wants to make me fear. The attack on the woman was to make her fear, to panic."

"Correct. They induce fear, like no other being. Then they feed on the energy of it. To defeat them you must capture that thought, control that fear, defeat it."

Con nodded. He grappled with the unreasoning part of it, the pure panic that gripped him every time he saw or thought of the beast. Cleato patted him on the back and sped up.

Con picked up the pace also but Cleato waved him back. Yelling over his shoulder he said, "Stay in the rear. I must take the lead and guide us to an opening of which I know. Do not straggle and do not let the others get behind you."

With that he opened his stride and quickly overtook the girls and Rusty. Con lost sight of him as the trail began to twist between the big rocks.

Cleato led them through a maze of trails in the broken landscape. He ran between boulders where his shoulders scraped the sides and climbed small rocky slopes that seemed to lead to blank walls. Each time a trail appeared that carried them up—up into the high Barriers.

The sounds of the squads rasping breaths echoed off the rocks. Con's lungs ached and his legs weighed a ton. The girls slowed down more and more. Rusty, suffering more than the girls, dropped back giving place to both Sarah and Beatrice. Pistis held his place directly behind Cleato but fell further and further behind the big man. At each turn, Cleato waited for them, waving them to him, urging them to greater effort. Con slowed a little to fall farther behind them.

They ran on a five feet wide ledge that hugged the sheer rock wall on their left. To their right, the mountain dropped away in shear cliff. Sharp, pointed rocks lay fifty or sixty feet down. The wall curved slightly to the left, hiding the trail ahead by its bulk. They ran on, seeking only to stay with Cleato.

Around the bend, the trail entered a notch between two rock walls and climbed steeply to another plateau about thirty feet above them. The slope was littered with broken shale and small rocks, as if at times, it was the bed of swift stream. Cleato stood at the top of it urging them on. He disappeared into the rock face on the left then reappeared to urge them again.

Cleato yelled to them, "Quickly, children. This is the last leg of the run. Through here we enter the domain of the Commander. The Enemy is not permitted in it. Come quickly!"

The girls perked up at the news and struggled up the slippery slope. Rusty dashed up the first few feet, then slipped onto all fours. Still he scrambled, kicking small rocks and dust up with each flailing movement. Wheezing breaths ripped through his open mouth.

Loud baying sounded on the trail behind them. The hounds were close—only a few hundred yards—no more. Their cries changed to shrill screeching as if they too pressed hard to reach the squad before they got to the cave. Con stopped and listened through the gasping of his own breath.

They were close. Too close. Rusty would never make it. His steps were labored and he slipped back every other step, just too tired to lift his feet over the loose footing.

"Pistis!" Con screamed.

His uncle stopped near the top of the notch. He turned to look back. Con stood at Rusty's feet. He grabbed Rusty under his left arm and lifted him. The little man tried to rise but slumped back down, exhausted.

Pistis's eyes grew wide. He glanced over his shoulder but Cleato had already entered the cave. His eyes returned to the trail, listening to the hounds. "Sarah. Beatrice. Into the cave."

The girls struggled to the cave entrance and bent over struggling for breath. Pistis shoved them both deeper into the darkness. He turned and leaped back onto the slippery surface and scrambled on his back to Rusty.

"We have to get him up. He can't..."

Con stopped, for his uncle reached down and pulled Rusty onto his shoulders. Without a word, he started back up the slope. Each step brought out a grunt of pain and effort but he slowly made his way up the steep incline.

Con turned to follow but the sound of the hounds stopped him. They were close, just around that bend. Before Pistis could get halfway to the cave, they would be on him, pulling him down, slicing at his throat with their drooling jaws. And Pistis would have no chance to pull his sword.

Con turned to face the trail. He leaned over, gasping in air as quickly as he could. The hounds were close, only tens of feet behind them. He drew his sword, still breathing hard, and scrambled back down to solid footing.

He stood where the path first broadened. It was only five feet wide—too narrow for a good swing of the sword. The path was only visible for a few feet. If the beasts quit calling he would have no warning of their attack. He smiled. Of course, they would have no warning of his presence, either.

Con bent his knees, leaned forward, and thrust the sword out in front of him. Then he waited.

The sounds died. Silence enveloped him like a wave, making his own labored breathing sound like the roar of wind. The tip of his sword wavered as the fear and tension gripped his heart.

From behind him, Pistis called, "Con, no. Cleato said to run, not to fight. Come quickly."

A pale, lean body rounded the corner, charging at full speed. Con lifted the sword point. The things lips were drawn back over sharp, gleaming teeth in a deathly grin. A low, vicious snarl poured from its chests.

Through his roaring fear and the growls of the beasts, Con barely heard Cleato calling, "Retreat, Con. Retreat. I will protect you. Retreat."

Too late. The lead dog leaped. Con swung his sword.

The beast swerved in mid-air. Its impossible maneuver avoided the singing steel edge but the point struck hard in its side. It went down in a heap, biting at the wound on its rear flank, coming to a stop against the left wall. Con hauled on the flying blade and reversed its travel. The other beast dropped onto its haunches and skidded. Con reached out for it, but the blade whistled over its head.

The downed beast leaped up. The other set itself in a low crouch and edged forward, still snarling. Con back peddled, his sword weaving in front of him. *Two of us could have handled this*, he thought. *I should have called another back.*

"Yes, you should have," one of the beasts said. "But you didn't, little soldier. So now you are ours."

The sound of the beast speaking shocked Con, then he remembered Cleato's statement that they were intelligent.

Fear snagged his breath again and his heart pounded wildly in his ears. Con could not rely on them doing what a brute would do. He had to out think them as well as outfight them. He swallowed hard and twirled the hilt of the sword in his hands. "Well, come and taste, dog head."

The beast he faced stopped and its eyebrows raised. Then it smiled again and chuckled.

Con ran at the one on his left, swinging suddenly and wildly with his sword, yelling the battle cry of the Militia—the name of the Commander. The beast scrambled backward, avoiding the flashing blade. A voice screamed in Con's head, "The other one. Watch the other one."

Seeming to ignore the advice, Con ran harder, still swinging the sword. Then he dug in his cleats, turned, and chopped his sword down in an overhand swing. The sword flashed out, seeking his enemy, singing as its edge sliced the air. The second dog, leaping at his exposed back, squealed as the edge whistled toward it.

The sword rang as it sank deep into the skull of the dog-beast. The thing fell with a thud. Pale, green fluid gushed from the wound in a putrid stream, then slowed to a dribble. The air filled with the smell of rot—as if a casket, two months old, had been opened.

Con yanked his blade free. He turned quickly, recovering his balance in time to see the other beast crouch for a leap. He leapt to his left, getting above the beast on the trail. He brought the tip of his sword around to face the beast—then ran at it, again screaming out the name of the Commander.

The beast's ears flattened. It snarled in surprise at the tactic. With scrambling feet, it fled backward, straight toward the edge. Con screamed again and rushed it. The back legs slipped over, scraping against the vertical rock. The front paws dug in, but continued to slide, its nails screeching like chalk on slate. The snarl changed to a whine as the beast looked over its shoulder at the rocks below.

Con kicked at its muzzle. The thing's head snapped back and tooth chips flew away from it. It squealed again, then snarled, slashing at him with its broken fangs even as its front paws slipped two more inches. Con leaned back and kicked so that the hobs on his shoes caught the beast in the snout. Blood flew beneath his foot and the beast flew backward, over the edge. A few seconds later, a sickening thud rose from the rocks below.

Con slumped to the ground, sucking his breath noisily.

They were dead. They were both dead!

He turned to kick the body of the first one off the cliff, also.

The body was gone.

He jumped to his feet and searched the small area with his eyes. Only the greenish wet spot remained. There were no tracks. No drag marks. No foot prints. It was simply gone.

An echoing laugh reached him. Con spun, trying to find the source. A second laugh joined the first, seeming to come from over the ledge. Con peered over the rim.

Two large, winged creatures with pale white bodies glided on the wind. No broken dog body littered the rocks below. The winged creatures—thin and pale—flapped their wide, feathered wings, rising toward him. Their strange call echoed up the cliff face,

They were fifty feet from the cliff and just below it. Canine heads hung from the bodies. Canine ears pricked at the sound of Con's gasp. Canine eyes searched him out. They were the beasts—still with chipped teeth and crushed head. They were the exact beasts he had just killed.

Con rushed up the slope. Falling on the loose shale, he dropped his sword. It clattered down the slope, stopping ten feet from him. He looked at the top, still twenty feet away, then at the sword. A jeering laugh from above caught his ear. The beasts circled above, ready to drop on him.

They were eagles with dog's heads. Their pale-white, feathery wings spread out fifteen feet. They raised and lowered slowly, beating great quantities of air with each stroke, lifting the beasts higher and higher.

Pink tongues lolled out. Saliva dripped from glistening teeth. Thin legs kicked and quivered along their sides. They were dog legs but they ended in the talons of an eagle—long, curved, deadly.

Up the hill he struggled, slipping and tripping on every loose rock. With one hand, he pushed off, scrambling desperately. The edge of his shield caught on a rock tip, tripping him. He yanked at the shield but it was caught on something. In a panic, he pulled his arm from it and left it where it lay.

He ran again, but fell, ripping his legs and hands bloody on the sharp rocks. Fear crawled into his belly and out his arms and legs, robbing them of strength. The two beasts who could not be killed hovered above him, laughing hideously at his futile struggles with the rocks and stones of the slope. His thought was the cave. He had to get to the cave or die.

He had to.

One of the Dog-birds called to him, "You can't make it, little soldier. Why don't you just stop and let us have our fun. Come. Fight us. We want to see you do it again. And, again. And, again. We have eternity to fight you." It shrieked in delight.

The other one clucked it's tongue. "Oh, Zerfon. Don't be so ignorant. He's mortal."

The first one yelled, "Oh, that's not fair. He gets to kill us over and over."

The thing dropped down to the trail between him and the cave entrance. It glared at him. "But, we only get to kill you once." Then it smiled again. A hideous laugh filled the air, or his mind. Con couldn't be sure anymore.

A movement above him caught his eye. The gray sky was suddenly crisscrossed with brown squares, expanding, growing. Something thumped over him, around him.

A net!

He struggled to get out from under it. It tangled like a live snake around his arms. He pushed it away. The heavy ropes wrapped around his feet and his legs, growing tighter with each movement. He stumbled. The net gripped him harder. He fell face down onto the sharp rocks. The ropes tightened, threatening to strangle him in their constrictor-like hold.

Shadows passed over him, moving shadows that closed in around him. He screamed. His body jerked and writhed. His eyes went blank, seeing only white, then red, then white again. His heart raced, threatening to burst. Like a hammer, his pulse beat against his temple. Light failed. He was gone—dying—dying of fright.

"That's what they feed on."

The voice came to him like a bolt. He looked around but there was no help there. Just the net, forcing him into the rocks.

He held his breath, forcing himself to quit jerking and struggling. Slowly, the scene came back in focus. He was alive. He was still whole. With an effort, he forced himself onto his back and started breathing again, slow, controlled breaths.

Above him, his attackers circled, screeching out their victory. Each extended its taloned feet, hanging on the air currents, ready to drop. Con grabbed the panic that rose in his chest and forced it to quiet.

There was an angry screech from above him. The two beasts hovered for a second longer then waved at someone to his side.

Something struck him on the side of the helmet. His head bounced off the rock and his ears rang. Above him, thick lips, heavy whiskered jowls, a head with no neck, sprouting directly from broad, powerful shoulders appeared. The upside down mouth leered at him.

Raiders.

The face laughed and disappeared again.

"It *is* the little farmer!" a voice said from the same direction. "The Dragon will be pleased."

Coarse laughter broke out from several spots around him. Large hands gripped him from both sides and lifted him to his feet. They stood him up on the broken ground and wrapped the net tightly around him. Five of them leered at him, large and muscular, and armed with the double-edged spears he had seen in the square, so long ago.

"A great swordsman." The largest one jeered, "Where's your skill now?

A hot answer rose in Con's throat but he choked it back.

"Cat got your tongue, Farmer? Or are you afraid we'll cut it out if you show it?" The Raiders all laughed again.

The slights to his courage stung, but he again held his peace, awaiting the right opportunity to answer.

The Raider frowned deeply, its flexible face distorting completely from the action. It leaned close, holding the point of its spear close to Con's throat. Foul breath, smelling of onions and garlic, watered his eyes. "Are you such a coward that you can not even speak to the men who defeated you, human? Grovel before us and perhaps we will let you live."

Con glared back. "I defeated myself, Donkey Hooves. You had nothing to do with it."

The beast jerked back. Its face turned bright green. With a loud growl, it slashed the spear point at his chest. The spearhead clanged against Con's breastplate. Con was thrown backward onto the rocks.

He landed on the chain mail and bounced once. Expecting to find himself without breath, Con was surprised at how gentle the fall had been. The realization struck him with as much force as the Raider's blow. Although securely captured—by his own panic and disobedience—he was unharmed. He still wore his armor—and his armor would continue to work, even in the midst of his disobedience and foolishness.

The beast raised its spear above its head, holding it in both hands. "Now, beg, human. Beg or I'll spill your ugly red blood right here on these rocks."

Con tensed his body preparing to roll to either side.

There was a crash and the Raider flew forward, landing on top of him. The spear hit the rocks well above his head and glanced away. As the heavy beast rolled off of him, a deep, growling voice boomed out, "If anyone tries to kill the prisoner before we return him to the Dragon he will answer to me."

A large man-dog stood above him. It was one of the beasts he had fought, the one whose head he had wounded. No longer a birds or a dog, he wore the body of a man—but the head was the same that he fought and wounded. The other walked up behind the first, also in the shape of a man, holding a large knife. The two of them faced the group of Raiders, standing on the other side of Con.

The second one spoke, its words distorted by the broken and missing teeth, "If you have any arguments, Zorn, take them up with my mistress."

He twirled his knife in his fingers as he spoke and flipped the tip of the blade in a circle. The faces of the Raiders became rigid but they did not answer.

The dog-man looked at Con, "Donkey Hooves. Good name for them, human." It laughed a high squeaky laugh, then reached down and hauled Con to his feet.

"They are animals—beasts of burden, really," he said, nodding at the Raiders. He pulled the net tight about Con once more. "No intelligence, just brawn."

The Raider leader, Zorn, glowered at the dog-men. "You watch your tongue, Dog-face. I am still an officer in the Dragon's service. You may have his ear now but in a few millennia it may not be so and I will have command of you once more."

"Perhaps, Donkey Hooves, but for now, you do as I say. So go and prepare a mount for this human that we may return to the Citadel tonight. I do not wish to spend more time with you and him than I have to."

Zorn turned abruptly and stormed off, his hooves striking the stones with such fury that sparks flew from under his robe.

The dog-man returned his attention to Con. "You fight well, Little Farmer. But you did not have a chance. Once that coward, Cleato, left you, you were ours for the taking."

The dog-man busied itself examining Con's fallen shield. It did not touch it but stared at its construction. "Always amazes me how something this flimsy can hold up so well."

He turned back to Con. "Yes, it is a shame. You really do fight well."

The other dog-man stared hard at him, looking for something. Con remained quiet and passive. Finally, the dog-man slapped his leg and walked up to him. "Good! You have been trained well. You may be fun, yet."

He placed the hilt of his weapon on Con's chest, insuring he touched no part of the armor, then shoved. Con fell backwards, unable to keep his balance in the tight bonds. He braced himself, expecting another rap on the head. Instead, he fell into the arms of the second dog-man. The first beast lifted his legs and they carried Con out of the notch to the trail.

Chapter 27

A large, shaggy quadruped lumbered around the boulder on the narrow path. A Raider walked in front of it, leading it on a halter. The thing, looking like a bloated horse, had clumps of brown material matted in its hair. As it got closer, the powerful stench of fresh manure let Con know what the material was. He was thrown across the back of it, landing on his doubled fist bunched in his stomach. He grunted hard.

The animal turned clumsily on the narrow path and walked onto the ledge. Beneath Con, on the rocks, lay a book—a tattered, dog-eared manual that had been the most powerful weapon in the Valley. Con grunted again, this time from internal pain.

The beast clumped onto the narrow ledge. Con's head brushed the rock face and he felt himself slip toward the abyss behind him.

"Hey! I'm slipping."

Only laughter answered him. Con reached through the ropes of the net and dug his stiff fingers into the hairy coat. He shoved, knocking his head against the rock again and slipping back. He clutched desperately at the hair and once again forced himself over the back of the beast. Laughter broke out again.

For hours they traveled, first down out of the hills and then through the big woods. Con's fingers ached, then numbed. Finally he lost all feeling in them. They arrived at a large road and turned south again.

Shadows gathered around him. Con raised his head as far as he could, bending up almost off balance, to see. The dark form of the Western Barrier Mountains stood out against a light, dusky sky. The mountains were close, no more than a few miles away. They had to be on the main north-south road nearing the very southern end of the Valley.

"Halt!"

The beast stopped. Strong hands grabbed Con and pulled him down to the ground. Unfeeling, his feet slammed into the ground. His knees bent and he tumbled onto the gravel of the road. With what freedom he could manage, he wriggled his hands and fingers—driving tingly ice cycles through them. He flexed his ankles, finally feeling life come back into them.

The Raider who had pulled him down cursed, then pulled him roughly to his feet again. He cuffed him on the side of the head with an open hand. Con fell back to the gravel.

The Raider grabbed the ropes and yanked up straight. "Stand up, human. I'm certainly not going to carry you."

Con balanced on his still, unresponsive feet and legs. With a slight movement of his head, he tried to see what was around him, why they had stopped. The Raider saw him and laughed. "You worried about where we are, Little Farmer?"

He picked Con up and turned him around. Con recoiled from the sight. The Raider laughed wickedly.

They stood not fifty feet from a high, stone wall. It was made of rough-hewn blocks, ten feet square. The wall itself was three blocks high. Con had to bend his head back to see the top. The road ran up to a double gate that stood twenty foot high and twice that in width. It was made of large, uniform, wooden planks, fifteen inches across.

Huge iron hinges supported the gates, three to a side. The pins of the hinges were on the outside, although the hinges were mounted to the stone frame and hidden by the closed doors.

Two raiders grabbed the loose end of the net wrapped around Con and pulled. He fell hard. They continued to tug, turning him over and over. Finally, he popped out of the net and sprawled in the dust on his belly. One of the Raiders pinned him to the ground with the end of his spear and other forced his arms behind him. They bound his wrists together with thin leather cords.

Someone grabbed his bound hands and lifted him to his feet, wrenching his shoulders. "Walk, Little Farmer."

Con stepped with his numb legs but fell over again. One of the Raiders kicked at him. Its hoof struck his buckler. The blow jarred him several inches, but when he breathed again, there was no pain.

Con got to his knees. One of them grabbed his wrists and lifted him again. "Walk, you puny human, or I will kick you all the way to his majesty."

He walked, tentatively at first, but with more confidence—and pain—as his legs came to life.

Boldly, the Raiders marched to the big gates, calling out for them to be opened.

Nothing happened.

A Raider, the one called Zorn, pushed Con up against the big door then yelled, "Open it, you dunderhead. We have a prisoner for his Royal Majesty, the Supreme One."

"How do we know you aren't a spy?" a squeaky voice asked from behind the gate.

"A spy? Why you idiot, can't you see who I am?" Zorn growled. His brow wrinkled deeply and he cast a suspicious eye at the gate. "Paxorn? Is that you?"

"How did you know my name, spy?" the squeaky voice asked.

"Paxorn, you stupid fool, this is Zorn. Now open that door or I'll have you sent to a post at an Army convention so that you can report on the contents of the speeches."

The gates slowly opened. When a crack appeared, the movement stopped and Paxorn peered out. The doors were twelve inches thick. Paxorn must have recognized Zorn for the doors swung wide and he snapped to attention alongside them.

Paxorn was a small, wiry looking biped. His facial features were almost human but were long and drawn out as if they were made of wax and had gotten too close to a fire. He wore spectacles and the arms that came out from his robes were long and thin. In his hand was a clipboard. All sizes and shapes and colors of paper stuck out of the clip.

"It *is* you, Zorn. I couldn't be sure. The sentries report that a large band of soldiers roams the countryside, destroying our men left and right. The Dragon is in a fit, ranting and raving and throwing anyone whom he dislikes into the pit. It's a real mess in here."

"Shut up, you fool. Can't you see I have a soldier with me?"

Paxorn adjusted his glasses. "So it is. And a puny one also."

"They are all puny, Paxorn. You'd know that if you'd quit changing the roster so that you always get these gate jobs. Now get out of my way. I must bring this one to his exalted Highness."

Paxorn swung the gate open and Zorn shoved Con inside. The rest of the squad followed.

They entered a large square, completely paved with flagstone or something like it. Bordering the square were old buildings in varying states of disrepair. They all were covered with lichen that gave them a faint green color where the grime had been rubbed off. Overhead, the thick, sulfurous smoke seemed to hang right at the top of the spires.

Several alleys spread out from the square. All were dark. One large street led off directly opposite of the gate. It was wide and lined with two story, stone buildings made of the same stone as the wall. These buildings were in good repair and were scrubbed clean.

Several humans walked in the square. Behind, or in front of, each of them walked a Raider or another being from the Dragon's service. The humans were all bowed over with large, hairy shoulder packs that seemed much too heavy for them. Zorn shoved Con out into the square.

Off to Con's left, a man tripped, landing on his knee. He rolled on the ground, holding the damaged leg and crying out. The large brown pack fell and rolled away on the slimy pavement. The guard ran at the man, screaming and poking at him with a pointed stick. The man slapped at the stick and slithered away, crying and pleading. Finally, the man heaved to his feet and ran. The guard screamed and tripped him again, then poked him in the back with the stick.

The man struggled up to his feet, standing on one leg. He put his hands out toward the brown, hairy pack he had been carrying. To Con's utter amazement, the pack grew two legs and a toothy mouth, then ran to the man and leaped into his arms. The man put the thing on his back.

The pack, which looked like dirty laundry wrapped in a buffalo hide, withdrew its legs then sank its teeth into the man's neck and clung there. The man grimaced at the pain and arched his neck but did not cry out. The Raider behind him poked him sharply in the buttocks with the pointed stick, drawing blood. The man stumbled off in the direction he was headed, limping heavily.

Con shuddered.

Behind him a sneering laugh broke out. "That's what you've got coming, little farmer. As soon as the Dragon selects the proper burden for you."

The Raider shoved him hard. Con stumbled forward across the square, into the wide thoroughfare. They traveled for several blocks without a word.

A group of ten humans, bunched and herded like sheep by four dog-men, stood on the side of the road. They stared hard at Con—the only human present without a burden on his back. The dog-men barked at them, and bared their teeth. The humans, looking like sheep in the presence of wolves, crowded closer to one another. One of the dog-men shook his head. He called to the Raider escorting Con.

"You got to teach them everything again and again. What did the Commander ever see in this animated dirt?"

Zorn swung his spear out to point at the dog-man. "Watch the way you throw that filthy name around, Porgon. If the Dragon hears you using it, you'll join your sheep there."

The dog-man waved the warning away. "The Dragon's got more problems than a few mouthy servants, Zorn."

He turned back to the humans. "No, you idiots, like this." He cupped his hand and yelled at Con, "You ain't no soldier. You ain't nothin' but pig dung. Get a burden, you pile a' manure."

He turned back to his charges. "Can't you humans remember nothin'. I just taught you that ten years ago?"

The humans clung to one another, throwing fearful glances at each of the dog-men around them. Porgon, the one who had spoken to Zorn, snarled low in his throat, then slashed at the nearest human with his fangs. The human jumped and shrieked. The others tried to move way.

As Zorn and Con moved up the street, Porgon finally got the humans lined up and they began to yell at Con. "Pig dung! Get a burden!"

Zorn stopped and looked back, his free hand on his hip. He shook his head. "Pitiful, Porgon, Pitiful."

Porgon shrugged. "You can't play a symphony on a squeeze box."

In front of a large stone building with a street level entrance, Zorn grabbed con's bound hands and yanked back. Pain shot through Con's shoulders and a short exclamation escaped his mouth.

"In here, human," the Zorn said, indicating the door to their left.

Con turned and stepped up on the stoop. The door was partially open and the Raider shoved him hard. Con lost his balance, crashed through the half-opened door, and fell face down on the wooden plank floor.

The occupants of the room all turned and stared at the noise.

There were four beings in the room, none of them human. All of them had arms and legs. Three of them had human-like heads, much like Zorn. The other had an eagle's head on its shoulders. All of them were dressed in a similar uniform, which appeared to be the dress version of Zorn's.

"What is that human slime doing here?" the one with the eagle head asked from behind a broad, wooden desk. "And, by the Dragon, where is its burden?"

Zorn went to the desk and performed what Con took to be a salute, though it looked like he was stabbing himself in the heart with his left hand.

The one behind the desk asked again, "What is this human doing in here, Zorn? That slimy, little thing should be at work."

"Begging the Captain's pardon, but this one is one of the raiders which I single-handedly captured out there in the woods. I had orders to bring any of that group directly to his Royal Consumption."

The officer behind the desk stood and looked at Con. The rest of the officers in the room gathered around, murmuring.

"Strip him," the eagle said. "The dragon will not want to see him in that armor."

Zorn looked uncomfortable and made no move to comply.

The officer seated himself and returned to his paperwork. Zorn remained standing in front of the desk.

The officer looked up. "I told you to strip him of that armor. I'll not take a prisoner to the Dragon with his armor still on him."

"Uh, Sir?" Zorn said, looking nervously from Con to the desk. "May I have a word with you?"

The officer snorted, then signaled Zorn to approach. Zorn whispered in his ear for a minute, gesturing toward Con and pointing at each piece of armor. As Zorn spoke the eyes of the officer grew larger and his face lost the angry look. When Zorn finished he asked out loud, "Is that the truth, Zorn?"

Zorn nodded. The Captain called the other officers over and a hasty, whispered conference ensued. There was much gesturing and the tone sounded angry. Then one of them reached for a book and started thumbing through it rapidly. Zorn looked at Con and raised his eyebrows in a "you know how it is," gesture from one common soldier to another. Con almost laughed.

Finally they seemed to arrive at some sort of agreement. The book was closed and they turned toward Con.

"Take off your armor."

Con smiled and shook his head.

One of the officers leaned close to the eagle and whispered something. The eagle spoke again, "If we untie your arms will you take off your armor? We want to bathe you in preparation for your meeting with our king."

The lie came smoothly, but it didn't cover his obvious nervousness. Con was sure. They could not touch his armor. Only he could take it off.

"I'll not take one item of it off by my will. If you want it, take it off yourself. As for your king, I'd feel more comfortable rolling in cow dung than bathing before meeting him."

A large, hairy fist slammed into Con's jaw. He fell backward and lay still.

Zorn leaned down and picked him up. Con swore the big Raider was chuckling under his breath. He set him on his feet squarely then slapped him again. "You'll not talk of his Exalted Excellence in that manner again, human, or you won't make it to the meeting. Now strip off your armor as the Captain said."

Con stared at him but did not move. So long as he had something they could not touch, he had power.

The officers had a conference again and finally set Con in a chair on the side wall. Everyone went back to its job. Con was ignored.

Two hours passed. Out the open door, darkness fell. People passed by with torches, still trudging with burdens on their backs, still being driven by the relentless guards.

No one appeared to notice or care for Con. He assumed they had called for some higher official to handle the problem. Con studied the situation, trying to find a way to escape.

He sat in a chair opposite the door. Nothing was between him and the opening except a few Raiders. These came and went, changing position constantly. As long as they kept working the way they were, he could not reach the door. He watched and waited.

A shout came from the street. It was unintelligible to Con but it caused a stir among the officers in the room. The ones working at desks jumped up and ran to the window. The ones milling around the floor ran up behind them trying to climb over them to see what was going on. No one was left to watch Con and no one was in front of the door.

Con rose from the chair. No one looked around. He scanned the room again. No one watched him and no one was near enough to stop him. He took a step.

The commotion outside grew. Shouts and screams pounded in through the open door and window. The guards beat their charges with the pointed sticks, clearing all of them off the streets, making a clear path. Con took two more long steps.

No one looked around. Their attention was riveted to the window.

He stepped again, close to the door. Another step and he would be on the street running. His heart pounded and his muscles tensed for a run to the outside.

Zorn screamed. Con dove for the door. A large, hairy body knocked him aside. Con spun, regained his balance, and charged for he door. His hobbed sandals landed squarely in the back of Zorn, who still lay face down on the wood.

Zorn howled and rolled over. Con's legs flew out from under him and he fell hard backward on his pinned arms. He rolled over and drew up his knees but something heavy smashed into his back, pinning him to the floor. His face bounced off the dusty wooden planks.

He rolled his head to one side and coughed out dust and the blood that trickled from his bruised nose. He had failed.

"What is going on?" someone growled.

The hoof came off his back and he heard what sounded like logs falling on the wooden floor. He looked to the side and saw all the officers on their knees, their heads bowed to the floor. He rolled onto his back.

Standing above him was a tall, dark, rather handsome man. At least, he appeared to be a man.

He was dressed in a dark, brown robe, with a high cowl, richly embroidered with strange geometric shapes. The robe extended down his whole body and dragged on the floor, completely covering him. His skin was light, almost white. His eyes were very dark and hidden deep in the shadows of the cowl. He had high cheekbones and an aquiline nose.

His arms were folded in front of him, each hand clasping the opposing wrist. They were long, thin hands—an artist's hands. The skin on them was milky white, almost translucent. The fingers were long and supple, moving all the time that Con watched.

All in all, he was a very good-looking being.

Con guessed from his captor's adulation that this was the Dragon. If he'd met him on the street he'd have never guessed. Con had built in his mind a picture of a creature obviously evil and as ugly as his actions. This being that faced him was nothing of the sort.

The being asked again, sounding almost bored, "What is going on?"

The Captain rose. "When we sent word that we had the one you were after, your Royal Excellence, I had no idea that you would come yourself. We are not prepared to greet such as yourself. Please forgive us, your Highness."

"Is that why your men are on the floor playing with a human, Captain?"

"Oh, no, Sir. The human tried to escape, but due to our quick wits, he was recaptured just before you arrived, Oh Great One."

The Dragon raised his hand and pinched the bridge of his nose. With a slow shake of his head, he mumbled something unintelligible. Then his hands flew up and he yelled, "Am I condemned to this place with all idiots? Why did only the stupid ones follow me out of the mountains?"

The whole group looked sheepish and said no more.

"Get him up, that I may look at him."

Zorn jumped to his feet and lifted Con up, pulling his arms almost out of joint. He set him directly in front of the Dragon. The tallness of the man was an illusion. He was actually no taller than Con himself—no larger—certainly no stronger. If Con's arms were not bound, he felt he could throttle this man, and be gone before they could react.

The Dragon fixed Con in his stare. Con's confidence melted away. The power he saw staring at him was bested only by that which he sensed coming from Cleato. This one would not ever fight Con. He had no need to. This one could destroy Con with just a thought.

"So you come to my realm, Ataxia, to steal my property and harass my subjects." The Dragon lisped a little as he spoke.

Con did not answer. He knew that to enter a conversation with this man would be to lose any sense he had left. The danger of it flooded over him and the fear of the power he faced knotted his stomach.

"Answer me, farmer!"

Con held his peace. The Dragon snorted. He turned to the Captain and demanded, "Why is he still dressed in this awful armor? I told you to strip him when you found him."

The Captain looked bewildered and frightened. He hemmed and hawed and looked to each of his subordinates. All of them avoided his eyes, suddenly finding something of extreme interest on the ceiling or floor.

The Dragon yelled impatiently, "I want an answer."

"He won't take them off, Sir," the Captain yelled, his hands flying out to the side.

"He won't take them off?" the Dragon yelled again, flipping his cowl back to reveal a full head of dark black hair combed back and parted in the middle. "He won't take them off? Then why haven't you taken them off for him?"

"But, Sir, it says right here in the manual that we...."

The Dragon waved him silent. "I know. I know. I wrote the blamed thing."

The Dragon turned to Zorn, "Untie him. I don't think we will get any more trouble from him."

Zorn untied the bonds on Con's arms. The blood rushed back into his numb hands and wrists causing pain to shoot into his fingertips. Con rubbed them.

The Dragon turned to Con, "Take your armor off so that we may care for your wounds. We are not barbarians like you humans, you know."

"I have no wounds," Con answered.

"None that you know of, anyway. Take off that silly armor and let us examine you, to be sure. After all, when we turn you back over to the Commander, we do not want him to think we mistreated you."

Con's heart leaped again. The thought of being freed had not occurred to him. What if there were prisoner exchanges? His mind raced. Perhaps he should cooperate. That might speed the process. He reached for his buckle subconsciously. The Dragon stared hard at him. Alarms went off all over his mind. With a lot of effort, Con pulled his hand from his buckle and dropped it to his side.

The Dragon snorted and slapped at Con's face. He turned away. "It is the helmet. I can't penetrate the helmet."

The pressure to undress disappeared. Con blew out in relief. The Dragon had deceived him so easily that he had not even realized what was happening. Fear once again rose in him—fear and respect for the Dragon's power.

"So, little farmer, you won't undress for us, now." The Dragon's face grew crimson. His hands shook visibly.

The Dragon turned quickly, the robe flowing out away from him as he did. He headed for the door, causing his subjects to fall over themselves to keep from being trampled. He snapped as he went out the door, "Take him to the dungeon. When he is ready to take off the armor bring him to me. Until then ignore him.

"And bring his father to my castle. I want him close to me."

Chapter 28

He was deep below the Citadel. Two hours before, the last light had been cut off by the slamming of the heavy door at the top of the stairs. Darkness surrounded him. Silence, except for the tinkling sounds of running water, filled his ears. The air was cool and moist, like a wet towel.

His fingers reached absently for the wall on his right. A rough, slime covered surface met them.

He had not seen much of the cell as he was thrown in, but from what he did remember, it was like half a teacup on its side. At the center, and close to the bars in front, it was seven feet high. It rounded down to the rear of the cell where it met the floor. In the back, against the wall, was a stone bench, where he sat. There was nothing else, not even a place to relieve himself.

With a heavy sigh, he stood. His head bumped the ceiling. He crouched and stepped further out.

Able to stand erect, he reached out, his fingers extended. They brushed something. He stared hard, willing himself to see the object. The blackness gave no hint. He took a small step forward and reached out again. Round, hard, vertical poles, about an inch in diameter met his grasp. They were solid all the way to the ceiling and within four inches of one another. He followed them down to the floor, where they penetrated the floor.

The sound of running water was louder. He reached through the bars and patted the floor. Water splashed under his fingertips. He pushed his fingers into it. It was cold, about three inches deep. It ran in a gutter about four inches wide. The water had a metallic smell. He touched a drop to his tongue. It was slightly bitter—and tasted of iron—no worse than the well water on the farm.

He edged himself along the bars until he felt the side wall, then followed it back to the bench. On the other side of the bench he followed the wall back to the bars. There were no more than fourteen feet from side to side. Con felt his way back to the bench and slumped back onto it.

He sagged—in body and spirit. The adrenaline was all gone. Reality took its place. In the darkness of a cell, well below the Dragon's Citadel, he once again contemplated the future—or lack of it.

He was at a stalemate with the Dragon. His enemy could not disarm him anymore than he had already done to himself. He could not free himself. His shield and sword were gone, thrown away when he needed them the most. Cleato and the squad were on the outside and did not even know where he was. The words of the dog-man on that slippery slope came back to him. They had eternity. He did not. All the Dragon had to do was wait. Con would die of starvation or disease soon enough.

Disgusted, he yelled, "I am finished."

His voice echoed back at him from the cave walls. Laughter seemed to echo with it—jeering, evil laughter. Con drooped. his face in his hands.

He lifted his head to the darkness again and shouted, "Why?" The echo changed it from a cry of anguish to jeering mockery.

The words of the defeated regimental soldiers came back to him. "You can't defeat the Dragon," they said. "He is too strong."

He had felt so much confidence then—so much that he mocked those people in his own heart. Truth prevails. They were free, back in the City. He was trapped in the Dragon's dungeon, having proven their statement.

"Why?" he yelled again. "Why am I lost, who was doing your work? Why aren't they lost and I free?"

The words rolled around the cave in a thousand reverberations. The word "free" echoed back over and over again as if a score of onlookers shouted it.

He lunged to his feet in anger. His helmet smashed into the rocks above. Searing pain knocked him back to the bench.

He rocked on the stone bench holding his head, waiting for his ears to quit ringing.

Someone called, "Con."

He took his hands off his ears. Only the ringing was there. He laid back on the bench.

His name sounded again, "Con."

Whoever called spoke low or was far away. He sat up again and listened. Again, it disappeared. All he heard was the roaring of his own blood. He relaxed again.

"I will never leave you. I will never desert you. Trust me."

The voice came lightly to his mind, then it was gone.

He called out, "Is that you? Are you here?"

Nothing. He listened, trying to quiet the thudding in his chest. No answer came. The only sound was the water tinkling in the gutter.

Con stared at the bars in the front of his cell. He did that for several seconds before he realized that he could see them. He rubbed his eyes and looked again. They were not plain but the wall behind them was lighter than it had been. He blinked his eyes and rubbed them with the heels of his hands.

It was so. He could see the bars. The wall of the dungeon was shining.

He heard a scraping knock, as if a piece of wood had hit the rock wall. He stood and walked to the bars. There was definitely illumination. He tried to thrust his head through the bars but they were set too close.

A song mixed with the tinkling of the water—barely discernible from random notes of the flow. A voice.

No it was just the water.

No, it was a voice—or a musical instrument.

A voice. He could hear a voice. Not the words. It blended too much with the subterranean sounds of the dungeon, but it was a voice, growing louder with each passing minute.

The voice grew stronger and the light became brighter. Details of the floor and walls were plain.

The passageway to his right brightened. He caught a snatch of the tune and a few words. It was a battle song of the Army, one sung by the Regiments as they paraded.

A soldier in this place! Joy ran through his heart. Tears welled up in his eyes. He exploded, "Here! I'm here!"

The singing stopped and the sounds of the footsteps on the rocky floor ceased. A scratchy, old voice called, "What was that?"

Con yelled again, "Here, I say. I'm over here in this cell."

There was silence for a second. Then the shuffling footsteps started again. "Of course, you are. Where else would you be?"

The light grew brighter against the wall, then like dawn in the valley when the sun explodes over the tops of the barriers, the hallway burst into brilliance as a lantern rounded a corner and pointed straight down the passageway. Con retreated back into the darkness of his cell, covering his eyes with his arm, squinting to see past the pain. The bearer burst into song again as he traipsed toward Con's cell.

"Onward, Soldiers, onward. Till the victory's won," he sang. Then he hummed a few bars, dribbling off to silence. In a few seconds, he sang out again. "Onward, Soldiers, onward." The singing stopped and an old voice said, "Got to remember the rest of that."

Con's eyes became more accustomed to the bright light. He stepped to the bars and looked toward the singing. An old man, dressed in rags, with sandals on his feet shuffled along the hall. His hair was white and stuck out all over his head. He had a growth of bristly whiskers, also white. A wooden bucket suspended on a leather handle was in one hand and a lantern in the other. The leather of the handle was thick where it attached to the bucket, but worn thin where he gripped it. The lantern was made of sheets of thin, beaten metal with a large port through which bright, yellow light poured. It was fueled with some kind of oil, the smoke of which poured from the top. The old man was stooped over, as if the pail was more than he could carry. Yet when he set it on the ground he did not straighten.

"You're my rescuer?"

"Your rescuer?" The old man chuckled. His toothless mouth gaped idiotically. "My goodness, no. I'm your feeder, boy."

Con's stomach dropped.

"Here. Eat your meal." The old man reached into the bucket and produced a bowl of bread and a cup of wine.

The wine had a bitter smell. Con sipped it, then spat it into the gutter.

"This is no good. It is laced with something."

The old man shrugged his shoulders.

Con smelled the bread. It smelled as it should. He bit and chewed. The texture turned to slime and a taste, as of mildew, spread through his mouth. He spat it out and set the cup and bowl on the stone floor.

"They are both adulterated with something putrid. I'll starve before I eat that stuff."

"You will starve before you get anything else in this place, boy. You better eat what's in front of you. The Dragon don't supply no sumptuous meals for his prisoners. And he don't care if you don't like it."

The old man stood directly in front of the bars, glaring at Con. His toothless mouth was closed so tightly that his long, hooked nose reached for his chin and his lips were forced out around it. He stuck out his chin belligerently. His breaths came in snorts, blowing through the gaps made by the edge of his nostrils against his upper lip.

Con turned and walked back to his bench, leaving the bowl and cup on the floor next to the bars. The old man looked down at the food—then back at Con.

"Ain't goin' to eat it, huh?" he said.

"No, I'm not. He mighta' captured me, but I ain't his slave. I won't eat this garbage."

"All the other captured soldiers eat it."

"I ain't other soldiers."

They remained silent for several minutes, staring at one another.

"You really ain't gonna eat it?"

Con didn't answer but lay back down on the bench. The old man stared at him.

Con closed his eyes. He really didn't want the old man to leave with the light, but he was not going to eat the polluted food either.

"Phutt!"

Con opened his eyes. The old man stood close to the bars. He pursed his lips and tried to signal Con again. The only thing that came out was, "Phutt!"

Con sat up on one arm and looked at him. The old man waved at him. "Come here. Quickly! If I stay much longer at this cell," he jerked his thumb over his shoulder, "*he* will wonder."

Con went to the bars.

The old man signaled Con to lean forward. He put his lips close to Con's ear and whispered, "I believe you really are a soldier. We get a lot in here that don't last the first day. They normally eat this stuff right away—then they're lost. Yer right. Got somethin' in it. But I think you are the one I was placed here to see."

Con drew back and looked at the old man. No longer were the eyes dull nor did the mouth hang open like an imbecile's. His voice was sure and his bearing firm.

"A long time ago I was captured. I've stayed, and stayed true to the Commander." The old man looked away. "'Cause I got a mission. I was given this a long time ago and told to give it to a soldier—a real soldier, one who will fight. I believe you are the one."

The old man handed him a small package. It was wrapped carefully in oil cloth and appeared to be very old. Con took it and looked at it closely. It was a book. He started to unwrap it but the old man placed his hand over it. "Not now, soldier. Wait until I'm gone. I got to have time to get away."

"But you'll take the light. How will I see it?"

The old man chuckled. "You'll know what it is, even in the dark."

He backed away from the cell then, and picked up his burdens again. "I'll be going now. Use it well, son. I've given a life to get it to you."

Con looked at the book and realized what he had. He looked back at the old man and nodded, "I'll do it, old man. I'll do it. Thank you."

"Thank *you*, soldier. I am finally free of this place. I can go home."

The old man hobbled off, bent over once again, looking more worn out than before. Before he turned the corner, he stopped and looked back. "Son, I'll see you at the gate. Don't fail me." Then he scooted around the corner.

In the dimming light Con returned to his bench, fingering the package.

The darkness closed in once again. The cell bars and the wall across the passageway faded and disappeared into the blackness. The sound of the old man's singing died away. Con sat in the quiet—waiting, wondering.

His fingers explored the package. He pulled on a loose edge then stopped. When he opened it, he would need to use it. Simply to possess it would invite battle in the Dragon's realm. He had already lost that battle once. His fingers found the seam and rested there.

"The choice is still yours, Con."

The voice startled him. In the silence of his thoughts, the voice was loud and booming. He listened closely.

"You may open that and fight or you may hold it as the old one did in anticipation of one who will."

Con stared at the package. Inside him the fighting fervor he had felt back on the cliff rose. The fear of the Enemy melted away with the realization that the Commander had not deserted him. The urge to battle grew.

"But why'd you leave me?" Con asked quietly.

"I didn't," came the answer.

"But you let me be captured, to be thrown in this darkness without my weapons. I thought you had given up on me."

"You threw your weapons away in the battle. You disobeyed Cleato and stood to fight before I was ready for you to do so. If I had turned the whole squad to fight to save you I would have lost them. Should I have sacrificed them for your pride, Con?"

He knew what the Commander said was true. His head hung down as he contemplated his actions.

"You are right, Sir. I deserve this."

"What you deserve is not the question now, Con. What you are to do, is. Will you fight for me again, or will you wait?"

Con stood slowly, moving out from the wall. "I will fight."

"Do you believe that we can defeat the Dragon? Just you and I?"

Con was staggered at the thought—then, remembering the power of the Commander, he answered without reservation, "I believe you can defeat the Dragon with or without me, Sir."

There was a chuckling in Con's mind. "You are right, Mr. Ataxia. And you are ready. Unwrap the Book."

Con removed the wrapping and let it fall to the floor. In his hand was a small book, much smaller than the training manual that he knew to contain the sword.

"What's this, Sir? It's too small to be a sword."

"Con, from where does the sword come?"

Con was about to answer, "the book", when he realized that that was not true. He answered, instead, "From you, Sir."

"Then what difference does the size of the book make? So long as that training manual I gave you a long time ago has been written within you, you will always have the potential of having a sword. This little portion that you hold in your hand is enough to draw it out. Reach for it. Now!"

The command came like the snap of a whip. The little book grew suddenly in his hand and he felt the familiar hilt in his palm. Fire sprang out of it and lit the cell like the sun. In the midst of the flame the two-edged blade formed and firmed. When it felt right he swung the blade in a wide, fast arc and yelled a battle cry. The blade roared as it cut the air, throwing the flame all around him.

He ran to the front of the cell. The door remained closed and locked. The voice said, "Touch your sword to it."

Con laid the tip of his sword on the lock and the door sprang open with the scream of ripping metal. The sound echoed up and down the passageway a hundred times, bouncing off the walls, rattling the stone. Con ran into the passageway.

The voice came again, "Look in your cell."

Con looked. Lying on the bench was his shield, or one exactly like it. He went in and picked it up.

"Don't throw it down again. You will never be safe without it from now on. You have committed yourself to a life of warfare in my service. The Enemy knows he cannot defeat you with guile and craft. He will try to kill you at every turn. Keep your shield with you."

Con stared at it. The shield had always been the least liked of his armor. He always thought of attack. The shield always spoke of defense. The Commander's words, though, sobered him. Although he had never really needed it in battle before, he hefted it securely on his left forearm and strode from the cell.

"Now, to your right and up the steps. The Enemy knows you are loose and he knows you are dangerous. Beware!"

Con ran. Though the rocks were covered with green mold and water stood in puddles everywhere, the hobs of his sandals dug into the cracks, the seams, and the bare rock face itself. It was as if he ran on good, solid soil.

An opening appeared on his left. The stairs. Although nothing but a black hole greeted his eyes, he plunged into it, climbing rapidly up the stone treads.

The flame of the sword grew dimmer. Less and less of the passage in front of him was visible. Con shook the sword several times. Nothing helped. It grew dimmer by the step. He stopped and watched it go dark.

The darkness wrapped around him, cloaking everything again. He saw nothing in front or behind. Then, at his feet, a glow spread out to light the stairs. It glowed brightly and the step before him was plain. He stepped up. The light moved up another step. For each step he took the light took one also. Con continued his climb, at a walk now, careful not to outrun the light.

Above him the sound of dozens of hooves clanging and clacking on the slick rock resounded off the walls. He lifted the sword, a grin spreading across his face. Now he would meet the enemy on much better terms. He swung the sword over his head.

Sparks flew as the blade bounced off the stone of the passageway.

"Hmmm," he mused. "This is not the place to face a group coming from above me."

He climbed three more steps. On his left appeared a shallow closet or an alcove, perhaps thirty inches wide and as many deep. The sounds of hooves grew louder. They would be on him soon. Con slipped back into the alcove.

The sound of hooves grew to a din. Dark figures passed in front of him. None stopped or gave indication of sensing him.

He waited.

The din continued down the steps. Con stepped forward until his shield was even with the edge of the closet. The sounds below him was like that of a herd of goats clamoring down the side of a mountain, hooves striking rapidly on the solid stone—growing further away with each click and clack.

He stepped out. Above him, the sound of a single set of hooves rang on the stone. He grinned. Whatever lagged behind would taste his steel. He stepped back into the alcove and raised his sword over his head. He placed the shield between him and the opening.

A shadow loomed before him. Con chopped the blade down hard. He felt the jar of contact. The sword sliced through a helmet, into the being, driving itself through the head and into the body. The being collapsed onto the slippery steps and started sliding. A clamor, like a thousand pots and pans, rose as its armored body tumbled and bounced along the steep steps.

The same putrid smell that had come from the wounded dog-man filled the air. Con gagged, almost dropping his sword as it pulled loose from the body. He turned from the smell and ran up the steps. The light jumped ahead, illuminating three or four steps. Behind him, hoots and shouts echoed up the damp walls. The clatter of hooves stopped, then began again at a slower cadence.

Con ran for minutes, climbing the narrow, steep steps. The foul, humid air burned his throat and made his lungs ache. His thigh muscles knotted at each step and his calves tightened.

He passed through a narrow arch, three feet wide, onto a flat landing. The stairs went up from the landing a quarter turn away through another narrow arch. Con stopped and caught his breath.

The sound of pursuit burst on him as the beasts rounded a corner further down the stairwell. Con threw himself against the wall to the left of the arch. His right hand held the sword above his head and parallel to the wall.

The sounds grew. Con steadied himself and tensed his muscles. The little room lit up. A head thrust through the opening, twisting from side to side. Con swung the blade as hard as he could. It crashed down onto the Raider's thick neck. There was a hissing sounds as the blade sliced into the flesh. Con lifted it and struck again in the same spot, cutting through cleanly. The head flew into the landing, bouncing on the floor with a hollow thunk. Two eyes stared from the disembodied orb in apparent surprise. The body crashed to the floor, then slid back down the steps. The lantern, having bounced on the dusty stones, rolled to the edge and followed the Raider down the steps.

There was a yell from below. Someone issued commands, but in a language Con could not understand. He heard the clatter of hooves just below the opening. Con jumped directly in front of the arch and thrust his sword point out. The rushing beast, just looking up from scooping up the bouncing lantern, impaled itself on the steel, its mouth and eyes popping open in surprise.

A squeal, like that of a pig at slaughter, pierced Con's ears. He wanted to drop the sword and cover his ears from the terrible sound. As his grip loosened, the beast dropped the lantern and grasped the sword blade. It tugged as it fell, almost ripping the blade from Con's grasp. Instead of letting go, Con shoved, then yanked the blade back. The beast fell backward with an angry screech, its fingers severed by the keen edges. Its fall, and the momentum given it by Con's final thrust, shoved it into those that followed and they all bounced down the steps in a tangle. Con kicked the lantern after them, and ran up the steps.

He was sure he had not killed them all (he wasn't sure he could kill any of them) but his last attack made them wary. As long as they followed slowly he could make it to the top.

After several more landings and two doors which flew apart at the touch of the sword, Con stood before a large wooden door with a small barred window high in the center. No landing preceded it. He rose on tip-toe and peered out.

The smell was refreshing. The air of the citadel was rank and humid, but it certainly smelled good from inside the dungeon. He breathed deep, gathering strength, watching the outside for signs of the enemy.

Beyond the doorway was a wide alley. Fifty feet further, the alley opened onto a large street. The alley was dark but the street was lit by what appeared to be torchlight. No one was visible, neither beast nor man.

Perhaps the alert was only in the dungeon and the Dragon could not believe that one soldier could make his way out. Or perhaps the Dragon's men were preoccupied. Or perhaps it was a trap. Con stood for long minutes debating in his mind. He remembered with a jolt that there was pursuit behind him and he touched the sword to the doorknob. There was a pop and the door swung open. Con stepped out onto the pavement with his sword at the ready and shield in front of him. No one challenged him. No one showed himself.

He walked slowly down the alley, expecting an attack at every moment. He swung from side to side, constantly looking into the dark corners. Tension pulled the tendons in his neck, causing the muscles to tighten and ache. His sword arm stiffened as he held the sword at ready.

Nothing happened.

Halfway down the alley he turned back to the door. Finding a large wooden pole laying in a garbage heap next to the door, jammed it into the door, effectively locking it.

He turned, sword at the ready, and advanced up the alley.

Chapter 29

Con crouched in the shadows of the alley and surveyed the fifty foot wide, stone paved street in front of him. The light, coming from blazing torches set in sockets in the rock building face, revealed only empty cobblestones. Across the street there was open land, a park or field. The darkness yielded no other information. The whole scene reminded Con of the street on which he had been led to the Citadel.

Con waited in the shadows, shifting his weight nervously from foot to foot, eyes flicking between the road and the door at the rear of the alley. Scrapes and clicks, all normal night sounds in a city, caused his ears to prick and he swung from side to side, listening. His sword stayed at the ready. Unsure of his next move, he waited for some sign or indication of direction.

Marching feet echoed in the alley. He swung around to face the door. It was still closed. He swung back around. The noise came from the street.

The cadence was quick, a double time at least. He crept to the edge of the alley and poked his head out to look. No one was on the street. The sound grew sharper, yet the echo masked its direction.

The alley was in the middle of a block. The building on his left was a large stone structure several stories high.

It had tall steps made of granite blocks that led out to the edge of the road. Their bulk blocked Con's view.

On his right was another stone building, not as tall as the other. It, too, had steps but only a few and not reaching out into the street. Con withdrew deep into the shadows.

The clicks grew sharp. He flattened himself against the wall, placing the shield between himself and the street. A platoon of hoofed beasts passed in formation, running at double time. They all were in battle gear and carried spears with half moon heads. Their leader ran along side of them, calling cadence. None looked into the alley. Con let them get well past his position.

The voice of the leader was lost in the echoes of their hoofs and the sound receded again to the sharp click of their hooves on the stone. Con crept out of the alley, looking both ways. The squad was already disappearing into the gloom. He waited, wondering what to do.

He stared at the sky as he thought, breathing deeply. The night sky had no stars, only an inky, uniform blackness. Only—it wasn't uniform. The sky was lighter on one side of the city.

Dawn!

Alarm jolted him. The darkness had been an ally. The light would start the business of the place once again and would reveal him to all his enemies. There would be no hiding. He must find the gate to the Citadel quickly.

The lighter sky was to his rear as he faced the road. That meant the road ran north and south and to his right would be the main gate. He studied it for a minute, then turned north on the road and started to trot. He stayed next to the building, letting its shadow hide him.

No other footsteps save the light click-click, click-click of the platoon in front of him broke through the night. His own sandals produced a slight squeak but nothing else. No lights lit the buildings. No doors opened. The torches, fewer now, burned with a bright, yellow light, producing amber splotches on the black stones

The outline of the curbs and buildings grew sharper as the sky lightened. The street became visible to him—and he to anyone on the street. He slowed and dodged into an alley. His eyes swept the still dark, filthy place for any hiding place. He shook his head. There was no place.

His only hope of staying free was to get out of the Citadel. Gathering his courage, he darted out of the alley and jogged toward the gate.

The road was straight. Far in the distance was the dim shape of a large, white building blocking the roadway.

The light grew stronger as he ran. He dodged into a convenient alley and searched the street before venturing out again. His fingers wound tightly around the hilt of the sword. Sweat trickled down his temple and into the corner of his eye. If discovered, he would have to fight his way to the gate.

He stepped back into the street and turned again to the north.

He jogged forward, studying the road. Then he smiled. It was not a large building straddling the road but the wall. More importantly, it was the gate. He picked up his pace.

With a struggle, Con slowed again, saving his breath. He did not want to meet a squad of Raiders breathless.

There had been a large square just inside the gate he had been brought through. Pistis had said there was only one gate in the wall—so it had to be the same one. That meant that Con would have to cross that same open area to get out of the Citadel—a sobering thought. All through the square, large bodies of men moved about in formation.

Con ran forward, bent over, dodging from stoop to stoop, keeping something between him and the gate. A lone runner, armed as he was, was sure to draw attention if spotted—attention he did not want.

Behind him he heard the click-click of a running platoon. He ran hard to the next alley. With his shield in front of him, he waited for the Raiders to pass.

A platoon of Raiders ran by. They were in the same battle gear as the previous platoon and ran in the same fashion.

When they cleared the opening, Con rushed to follow but to his surprise, the leader called a sudden halt. The big beasts stopped, their chests heaving. The leader yelled at someone, apparently standing on the steps of one of the buildings.

"Get back inside, human. Get inside or I'll run you through."

"But what's happening? My guard didn't show up this morning. I don't know what to do."

"Shut up and get inside. There is a disturbance at the gate. When we take care of it we will be back for you. Now get inside."

"Is it the Army? Have they come for me?" the voice from the steps yelled.

"Yes, human, they've come for you. But don't you worry. We won't let them take you." The leader laughed wickedly, then threw something. It struck the stone front of the building and rattled on the pavement below. "Now get back in there or I'm liable to turn you over to them."

A door slammed. The leader snorted, then called his platoon to attention and started them off at a run.

Crouching, Con ran for the next stoop. When the way was clear, he ran to the next alley and dodged into it. In this manner, alley to stoop, stoop to alley, he continued until he stood at the entrance to the square. He knelt next to the wall and surveyed the area.

From that location he could see the gate plainly, as well as its defenses. A squad of six Raiders stood at the base of the door around a large spoked wheel. The wheel was attached to a shaft that entered a large wooden box. From the top of the box came a chain that extended up to a pulley system, then back down into the top of the box. From the pulley system ran large ropes out to the edges of both gates.

The beasts at the wheel were trying to fit a thick wooden pin into the mechanism. It appeared to be too large for the hole.

Con realized, quickly, that it was a lock. With that pin in place, the spoked wheel would not turn. If he was to get out of that gate, that pin had to be kept out of that box.

The Raiders struggled with the pin, shoving and hammering, but it was jammed. Even from that distance, Con could see the curl of a shaving on the side of the pin jamming it in the hole.

The rest of the square bustled with activity. Squads and platoons entered the area from all the side alleys and streets. As fast as the beasts entered the square they were redirected by an officer to some defensive position. Con watched to determine where they all were.

The numbers astounded him. Everywhere he looked Raiders or guards marched. There seemed to be several legions at the Dragon's disposal.

On either side of the gates, stone steps led up to the top of the wall. The corners of the buildings blocked Con's view of the wall farther down but apparently there were more steps. The officers directed the squads in both directions down the wall. Beasts climbed the steps on both sides of the gate, filling up the parapets.

On top of the wall sentries lit arrows from flaming pots and shot them at something outside the gate. The newcomers joined them as they arrived in position.

From the response of the Dragon's forces one would surmise that a whole army faced them at the gate. Yet, only the ones near the gate fired their arrows. That meant it was a small force which attacked. His heart leaped. There was only one small fighting force in the area.

Con watched the activity, reevaluating his mission. Up to then, his concern had been to get out of the Citadel. His friends, though, were just then trying to get in. Now he could see his purpose in being there at that time. He smiled and stood, dropping his sword to his side. Yes, that was what he was there for.

As Con watched, the square cleared. A bad tactical error was taking place. The Dragon's forces were all sent to the wall. None were left at ground level to protect the gate. The six men at the gate were reduced to two as the beasts assigned there drifted up the steps to watch the battle. The square was clear of Raiders. Con gathered himself. He stood with the shield in front of him and his sword up. He marched out into the square. With each step he expected the yell of hoarse voices and the challenge of a guard.

No one challenged him.

No one called.

The two guards at the gate stood, backs to the square, and stared up at the parapets. Con saw the wooden pin had finally been driven into place. One yelled something up to the ones on top. The noise drowned his call. He yelled again—and again.

Con broke into a trot. Fifty yards to go. They still looked up.

Twenty yards. The one on the left, who had been calling, threw his hands up in disgust and turned away. The other continued to look up. The one who turned kicked at a stone, still not seeing Con. Con ran harder, trying to get to them while he still could surprise at least one of them. Ten yards to go.

The guard looked up. A look of surprise, then alarm, then terror gripped his features. He hit the other on the back and yelled. The other turned and saw Con. He grabbed for his sword. The first cupped his hands and, looking at the top of the wall, yelled.

Con lifted his sword high above his head and yelled, "For the Commander and Cleato!"

The two separated quickly leaving Con with two targets and two directions to defend. Con expected that. He continued to rush toward the center of them then stopped and spun backward with his sword straight out. He stooped, bringing the sword around backhanded at the beast on the left. His spin took him out of range of the beast on the right and put the other one in a bad defensive position. It gave ground.

The sword tip missed but Con had separated the two so that they could not work in unison. He stood quickly and rushed the second beast, letting the shield on his left arm protect him from the one who had retreated.

This beast gave ground, back-pedaling quickly. It blocked two of Con's slashes but ruined the edge of its short sword doing it. Its face went ashen as the sword swung at it over and over. It made no attempt to attack but continued to move backwards away from the sword.

That was bad. Con did not want to move that far in one direction. He lost contact with the other beast. His back was open.

The beast he was attacking glanced behind Con. Con turned quickly left, his sword slashing at whatever was there. Before he saw anything, he felt a blow on his shield. Then his sword bit into something soft.

Con pushed off with his shield and pulled back on the sword. Something grunted and he heard a heavy metallic thud. When the weight left his shield, he stepped back. The beast lay on the ground, a green fluid pouring from the wound in its side.

He swung back to fight the other Raider but it was gone. Con ran out into the square. A Raider climbed the steps, yelling at those on top.

Con ran to the gate and peered out through an open portal. Standing a hundred yards away, with shields raised above their heads, was the squad. Pistis and Rusty stood in the front. Beatrice and Sarah faced each side. Their raised shields formed a solid covering for the squad. Flaming arrows rained down on them, covering them and the ground around them with porcupine-like quills.

The flaming rain continued but the Enemy did not drive them off. The squad, though, did not advance. Con ran back to the gate mechanism. He put his shoulder to the rim of the heavy wheel and shoved. It rolled a few inches then jammed on the big pin.

The pin was twelve inches thick and six feet long. It was stuck solidly into the wooden box and through a hole in the rim of the wheel.

Con laid down his shield and sword. He wrapped his thick arms around the beam and heaved.

Nothing happened.

He stooped and put his shoulder under the log. With a loud groan he lifted, feeling the wood tear his flesh.

Nothing moved. The beam was locked in place.

He stepped back, sweating and panting. The squad was under fierce attack. He was in mortal danger. The escaped beast would return soon with reinforcements. Yet he could not move the pin.

He yelled again and pressed his body against the unyielding beam. He groaned and pushed. He strained until the blood in his ears pounded painfully through his head. His face glowed with sweat and blood.

The beam held.

He dropped away from the beam, spent. The beginnings of panic gripped him as he looked back at the steps. The sound of battle was just as strong, yet he thought he heard the rapid, clicking beat of hoofs on stone.

"Where's your sword, Con?"

The voice came as a shock. He had been so wrapped up in his own attempts to open the gate he had forgotten about the Commander and his weaponry. He remembered the warning the Commander had given him back in the cell.

He grabbed up his shield and sword. Seven Raiders ran down the last few steps, spears and swords at the ready. At the head of them was the Raider he had driven off.

They spread out in a half circle, eyeing their fallen comrade and the armed soldier in front of them. They did not advance.

Con raised his sword. There were too many of them for him to attack. If he were in the right defensive position he might stand a chance against them. The problem was, if he retreated to a good position then the squad would be lost. He had to get the gate open.

Deciding quickly, he ran to the pin and hacked at it with the sword. The edge of the sword bit deep. Con twisted it when it hit and the wood split. He hacked again from another angle. A chip the size of his hand flew out. Quickly he chopped again.

"Hey! Stop that." One of the beasts advanced, angrily waving its spear. Con stopped hacking at the wood. He turned back toward the beast. The Raider stopped at the sight of the hot steel blade and, glancing at the body on the ground, backed up to its companions.

Con returned to the pin with fury, spinning back only when the Raiders found the courage to close in again. Each time they retreated, yelling hotly but avoiding the steel. With a final hack, the pin broke and fell out of the hole in the box. Con shoved the piece in the wheel and it too fell to the ground. He whirled to face his enemies again and with his free hand spun the wheel.

It whirled. He hit it again. The wheel picked up speed and began to whistle. Ponderously, by inches, the big gates swung out.

As the gates opened, a bright light flooded in. It poured through the crack like a raging torrent, pulling the doors apart, tearing at the supports. The chains and ropes buzzed around the pulleys like a swarm of angry hornets. Smoke poured from the seams in the big wooden box and the wind in the wheel spokes groaned out a protest at the unaccustomed speed and power. The beasts on the square turned and ran shrieking.

Suddenly, the air was filled with flying bodies. Raiders, guards, and flying creatures threw themselves off the wall and thudded hard into the pavement. Most rose and limped off. Others lay still, green fluid spreading on the stones around them. The steps all along the wall were filled with black streams of the Dragon's legions trying to get off the wall and back into the Citadel.

Through the gate ran Pistis followed by Rusty, Beatrice and Sarah. Con ran to them, his sword and shield flung to the sides, his arms opening to embrace them all. Sarah got to him first.

"Con!" she yelled as she dropped her sword and shield and threw her arms about his neck. "I thought you were lost! I thought you were lost!" Tears streamed down her cheeks.

The others gathered around him and clubbed him on the back good-naturedly. They all yelled so that Con could not understand any one of them. It didn't matter. The real message was plain. He that was lost was found. He that had strayed was again in the squad.

Chapter 30

Cleato walked through the gate. He picked up Sarah's sword and shield and handed them to her. His gentle frown was rebuke enough. Sarah took up the weapons and looked at the ground. He patted her shoulder. "We'll have time for reunions when the battle is over, soldiers. Con has gotten us through the gate. Now, let us accomplish our mission."

Sarah put her sword in her shield hand and hugged him again. Beatrice kissed him on the cheek and Rusty hugged his shoulder. Pistis smiled proudly and patted his back. "Well done, Con. Now, let us free as many as we can."

Con nodded at him and Pistis formed them in a battle line across the entrance, standing an arm's length apart on each side. Cleato said, "Forward!" and they marched off.

Cleato was not dressed in armor. He wore the same hooded garment as when Con had first seen him at the gate to the City. The hood, though, was pushed back. As they began to march, Cleato raised the hood, hiding his head within its folds.

Con expected a pitched battle all the way to the Dragon's throne. The legions, though, were in retreat all along the front. Only a rear guard, running just behind the fleeing army, showed any semblance of order.

Cleato ignored the ones still streaming from the wall. They headed out of the square in all directions, staying as far from the squad as possible. The main body of the enemy continued to retreat directly up the main boulevard. They would not retreat forever—if only because, sooner or later, they would retreat into the Dragon himself.

Two blocks in front of them, the rear guard of the Dragon's army passed through a stationary group of beings. Their details were vague but, at least one hundred strong, they stood stock still in the center of the road, facing the squad.

Con lifted his shield and set it on a comfortable place on his forearm. He gripped the sword, opening and closing his fingers until it felt just right and the edge was at the correct angle to his wrist.

Something was wrong with the enemy force. It did not prepare properly. Then Con saw it. They were not Raiders; they were humans. They did not carry weapons either. The only thing they had were their burdens. The humans stood in the middle of the road, snarling at the soldiers.

One stepped forward and cupped his hand to his mouth. "Go away. We don't want to hear your nonsense. Go away and leave us alone."

The rest of the group murmured. Heads nodded in the group and fists shook toward the squad. The whole mob stepped forward.

Con stepped out to take up a prime battle position. Pistis called him back.

"Not you, Con. You haven't been trained for this type of warfare. Let Beatrice and Rusty take the lead. You fall to the rear. Do not attack any of the humans with your sword. That can only be done with a certain skill. We came to save them, not destroy them."

"But they will destroy us if we don't stop them," Con replied, unsure of his course.

"Nevertheless, we came to save them. Let Rusty and Beatrice use the sword. You save yourself for battle with the Raiders. You will have plenty of opportunity yet."

Con dropped to the rear with Sarah. Rusty and Beatrice ran ahead to meet the crowd of angry humans. They sheathed their swords and raised their hands.

The human crowd stopped, unsure. "Leave us alone. We don't want you," the leader whined as the pair got closer. The Raiders in the back growled out orders but the people milled about. Two of the Raiders entered the crowd and whipped the ones close to them, driving them forward. A deep roar like a clap of thunder sounded from the rear of the squad. Con turned. Cleato's eyes flashed. The thunder came again.

The Raiders looked up wide-eyed, as if they'd heard their own doom. Pistis signaled to Con and Sarah. The two of them walked quickly toward the crowd, swords up. The Raiders retreated out of the group.

Pistis called them back. "That's good enough, for now. Let Rusty and Beatrice work."

Rusty held his hands up to get the crowd's attention. They quieted down and Rusty began speaking to them. Con did not pay attention to the speech. He, instead, searched the rooftops for a trap and scouted their rear with his eyes.

The Raiders on the other side of the crowd retreated. A large gap opened up between them and the humans. The humans stood still, engrossed in what Rusty spoke, oblivious to the retreat of their captors.

One of the humans walked forward. Rusty took out his sword and swung it deftly at the burden on the man's back. The blade cut deeply and surely, separating the burden from the man, yet not touching the man's flesh. The burden shrieked and fell to the ground. The foul smell that emanated from all of the wounded beasts permeated the area. Many in the crowd gagged and retched.

The burden lay still on the stones. It was like a large hairy tick, the kind that attacks dogs in the field and bloats itself on blood.

The man straightened up to his full height. He placed his hands on his lower back and stretched, laughing and nodding at the others.

As he stretched his chest out, Rusty struck. The sword sliced into the center of his abdomen, just below the rib cage. The man fell backwards to the flagstones, pulling free from the blade as he hit the ground. Con yelled and ran forward.

"You've killed him!" someone in the crowd yelled.

"You've killed him. Why did you save him just to kill him?"

The crowd became restless and the murmuring turned ugly.

Con stood over the man, sword up. The restless ones calmed, staring at the broadsword facing them. The rest of the humans gathered around and stared. As they looked on, a fearful murmur rose in their midst.

"He's not dead," Rusty said. "He is not dead. He has just been set free from a bondage he didn't even know the enemy had put on him. Each of you must be set free from that bondage."

The man on the ground stirred, then got up, his face bright and alive. His eyes danced. He looked around like a child seeing the world for the first time. Beatrice took him by the hand and led him back to Cleato.

"Who is next?" Rusty yelled.

A woman stepped timidly up. Before she reached him, Rusty whipped the edge of the sword at the burden. It fell from her, shrieking as it did. With his backhand swing, Rusty pierced her heart and she, too, fell dead-like to the pavement.

Chapter 31

The woman rose from the ground like the first man. Beatrice led her back to Cleato and Rusty called for another. The crowd of humans rushed forward, jostling each other to be next in line. Rusty hollered and yelled to get them calm but nothing helped. The prospect of liberty from the burden on them drove them.

Pistis watched for a few minutes then said, "C'mon Con, Sarah. Let's straighten this out." They walked into the midst of the crowd, directing them into order. The sight of the three soldiers standing stern and calm in the midst of them and the sight of the Raider's "blood" yet on Con's sword sobered those close to them. Outside of that calm harbor the sea of people stormed back and forth, still trying to get ahead of one another.

As Rusty and Beatrice got control, Pistis nodded to Sarah and Con. "Report back to Cleato. I think he has something for you. I'll maintain whatever calm we've got here."

Cleato ignored the approaching soldiers. Instead, he stared up the street at the distant Raiders. He said nothing for a few minutes, still gazing up the boulevard with a pained expression on his face. Then he said, "We will leave them soon. The battle is not yet won, although we have accomplished one of our objectives."

The Raiders waited patiently a few blocks away. Con glanced at Sarah with a question on his eyebrows. Sarah shrugged.

"Cleato," she said, "haven't we done well? We've set free over one hundred prisoners."

"You have done well. But do not count your victories so quickly. Those are not waiting just for us." He nodded at the Raiders.

Con glanced at them. They seemed unconcerned with the happenings among the prisoners. They stood around, not in battle formation, but lounging, as if waiting for something.

"What do they wait for, Cleato?" Con asked.

"They wait to see what we will do, for one thing. To see if we will be satisfied with our success and retreat with our freed humans or if we will advance. But they have another reason for waiting so near."

Cleato's voice dropped and he seemed to sigh silently. Con and Sarah again glanced questioningly at each other.

More received their freedom. The crowd waiting dwindled to half then a quarter. The crowd of freed men grew again and again. Each newly freed person was brought to Cleato. He spoke to them quietly and privately. Some listened intently; some acted as if they didn't hear him; some were so excited that nothing sank in.

When only a few were left, Cleato leaned over to Con and said, "Watch the crowd now. See what they are doing."

On the edge of the crowd a few individuals gathered. Most of the people still hugged one another or stretched to their full height in shear joy of being able to do so. The other few did neither. They stood talking, murmuring among themselves. They glanced up the street at the Raiders and then at the pile of burst and bleeding burdens lying on the cobblestone.

Realization of what they were doing gripped Con's gut and he started for them. Cleato restrained him.

A tall, dark man, thin from his many trials in captivity, drifted to the side of the street. His eyes switched from side to side, watching the others. The small group from which he had come watched him closely.

Suddenly, the thin man burst from the crowd and ran down the street to the Raiders. Rusty saw him and yelled, but the man ran harder. When he arrived at the laughing Raiders, he threw himself on the ground in front of them. One of the Raiders lifted him up roughly and threw him back into the pack. Another picked a burden up from a stack next to them and fitted it on the neck of the man. His scream shook the stones of the buildings. It pierced Con's heart the way Rusty's sword had pierced the captives.

"Why?" Con cried.

"It is unbelievable. But it happens always. Some return to the Dragon immediately. Some wait."

Con looked at Cleato with disbelief. Cleato continued to stare at the crowd, waiting.

Rusty and Beatrice walked among the group who had drawn away. They talked with each one. All seemed calm.

Rusty went back to the other crowd.

Another ran down the road toward the Raiders, then two more. Within minutes half of the people who had been set free ran down the street and fell in front of the Raiders.

The Raiders laughed. Three of them walked out toward the squad, stopped and raised their hands toward Cleato, one digit raised. Then they all laughed and returned to the prisoners.

There was the flash of hooves in the dull light. All of the Raiders kicked at the prisoners and poked them with the sharp sticks. Screams of pain and terror came back to those who had held still. Blood flowed down the cobblestones. Two of the returned prisoners fell suddenly and did not rise. The Raiders kicked them several times but got no reaction.

The burdens on the fallen prisoners released their hold and returned to the stack. The Raiders laughed aloud so that the freed ones could hear. None of them moved.

"These will stay," Cleato said. "Some of the ones who ran we will again capture and set free. They will perhaps stay free then. Some will now die under the treatment of the Dragon and they will be lost to us. Some will return to the Dragon no matter what we do."

He sighed loudly.

"Rusty, stay with the freed ones. Lead them back to the gate and prepare them for the march out. Feed each one the Bread and Wine. Do not give them meat yet, for their stomachs will reject it. Be gentle, but keep them moving. We must get them out of the Citadel.

"Pistis, gather your squad. We march on. Any more captives we will send back with Beatrice. Our objective is to get to the Dragon's seat. There, Con, you will find your father."

Sarah and Con started to walk forward, toward the Raiders. Cleato, shook his head. "Come here, children."

They returned. All four soldiers gathered around their leader. "We will be entering a battle greater than any you have had to date. You will be tested sorely in endurance and strength. Each of you take this."

He handed each of them each a small vial.

"It is wine," he explained, "new wine. When you need it, use it."

Con placed the small vial in his buckler and hefted his shield and sword. Sarah moved beside him. Pistis and Beatrice lined up next to her. Cleato stood in the rear.

There was a flash of light from behind. The squad spun around, swords up. There, they faced Cleato. No longer covered in a robe, he stood in golden armor. He stood like one of the giant oaks of the Kleinmensch Forest—large, solid, and unmovable in the worst wind. His arms were like the thighs of men and his thighs were like the trunks of those oaks. He had on a golden helmet that caught every ray of the dull sun, amplified it and broadcast it back into the dullness of the Citadel. Golden rays shot from it and exploded against the dull walls around them. His broad shoulders supported his massive breastplate—a breastplate that must have been beaten out of a hundred pounds of the most precious gold. Its brilliance was only matched by the gleam of the helmet.

His buckler was one-inch thick leather, supple and pliable, moving with every move of his body. Yet, it appeared unbroachable. The worst weapon the enemy could hurl at him would not split that belt. Finally, the soles of the sandals on his feet were at least two inches thick. They spread under his weight and gripped the stones with no compromise. Where he tread with those, he owned. There was no dispute, no slipping away.

Con noticed something he had not seen before. On the ankles of the big man there were deep scars—pucker marks, like something rough and wide had pierced them. They were similar to the marks on his wrists that Con had seen the day he had joined. He looked on in wonder at those holes, again asking himself who could wound this soldier.

Cleato stared over the heads of his soldiers. He raised a sword that was four times as large as the ones in the hands of his troops. Its edge gleamed with keenness, catching the golden rays of his helmet and breast plate and shooting them off like sparks in all directions.

Con stared, his mouth hanging open. The rest of the squad did also. Their swords clanked as they dropped the points onto the stone of the road. Only Pistis remained alert. He grinned from ear to ear.

"My Lord," he said and dropped to one knee. His sword he laid across that knee. His shield he lowered to the ground next to him.

Con saw his uncle's obeisance and did the same. The other two simply stared.

Confusion and fear broke out in the Raiders ranks. Ten of the Raiders formed a rear guard and set themselves across the road. The rest drove the human prisoners down an alley.

The squad advanced to within half a block. The Raiders formation broke and retreated two more blocks, reformed and stood as before.

"They seek to make us rush or to turn. Ignore them," Cleato said. "They will not fight us until they are forced."

Block after block they used the same tactic. They never allowed the squad to get closer than half a block. They did not want to fight. They only wanted to keep track of the squad's position.

The buildings got taller. Instead of the two story, rough stone houses which had surrounded the square they found themselves dwarfed by four and five story buildings of polished stone. Ahead, higher buildings lined the street.

His gaze was drawn up by the increasing height to the highest of all the buildings, towering above the roofs in the distance. At the same time he heard Sarah gasp.

It towered over the rest, dwarfing them. It was ten stories high with a five story high large pointed spire mounted on it. The face of the building gleamed like a polished jewel even in the dull light from the overhead smoke. The spire appeared to be wooden, or something similar, and painted to match the stone of the building.

"It is the Citadel," Cleato said, noticing the enthralled look on both faces. "It is the seat of government here. And it is where we will find the Dragon and your father, Con."

"But it must be defended by the best troops and legions of them," Sarah gasped out.

"It is well defended. And you will have the battle you've desired. It will be difficult but with perseverance you will succeed."

They were within a block of the large square on which the Citadel was situated. The Raiders rear guard disappeared around a corner.

"What ever happens, keep pushing toward the Citadel. Do not get stopped in a fight. Cut, slash and push forward. If you get tied up with the underlings you will never get to the Dragon. Do not try to use finesse. Fight to get through them, not to defeat them. Depend on your armor to protect your rear."

Cleato's pace picked up until they were at a double time. Con and Sarah both lifted their swords high and broke into a run. Pistis and Beatrice yelled out the Commander's name and charged forward.

They rounded the corner running. Cleato raised his hands, signaling a halt. All of them stopped except for Beatrice. She charged directly into the line, hacking and slashing, yelling all the time. Quickly, she was surrounded. One of the beasts, slashed with its claws at her exposed legs.

Beatrice screamed. Blood spurted from the wound and ran down her leg in a steady stream. She fell.

Pistis, on the right flank of the squad, screamed and charged forward. "No. NO!"

He slammed into the circle of beasts around Beatrice, hacking and slashing. He fought like a madman, hitting the beasts so hard that limbs, green blood, and heads flew from the tip of his sword, slamming into the faces of the ones who were next to feel his steel.

Cleato pointed at the battle. "Into it, my soldiers. Free Beatrice—then onto the Citadel!"

Cleato ran at the bunched beasts, raising his sword high over his head.

Con screamed out a loud battle cry and ran toward the group Cleato had indicated. He heard Sarah's high-pitched yell from alongside him. The beasts surrounding Beatrice melted away. The whole of the Dragon's army retreated, leaving a gap between the crazed swordsman standing over his downed comrade.

When the last beast backed away, Pistis dropped to his knee and cradled Beatrice. Her face was pale and her lips were set in the thin line. Sweat beads covered his forehead and upper lip. Pistis hugged her up close. He kissed her forehead.

Her eyes popped open and she smiled slightly, fighting the pain of the wound in her leg. There was a sparkle in her eye. "Man, what a girl's gotta do to get your attention."

Cleato laughed. "And what do I have to do to get that type of intensity out of you?"

Pistis looked up, redness tingeing his ears and cheeks. "I..."

Cleato waved him away. He reached down and touched the wound on Beatrice's thigh. "This will be fine in a few minutes. Pistis, stay with her until she can fight. Then follow on."

He stood. "Con, Sarah. Onward. And don't let them stop you."

Between them and the entrance to the citadel was two hundred yards of lawn and garden. Right then, it was a garden of grotesque life forms, slithering enemy soldiers, and Raiders. They all were armed and they all faced the depleted squad.

Con screamed and ran straight at the front line. The beasts on the front tried to retreat but were thrust at the singing steel by the press from behind. Con hacked at the first of them, cutting into them just as he had cut into the log. He swung and yelled over and over.

From all around him blades swung at him. Blow after blow reigned on his shield. Blades of swords and spears slammed into his breastplate. Pointed weapons struck at his midsection. The buckler absorbed each thrust and deflected the power harmlessly. His helmet protected him from the clubs that got past the shield and landed on his head. Though some of the blows slowed him, none of them harmed him.

As much as his armor held, theirs didn't. With every hack, thrust or slice, he cut into them. With single blows he lopped off arms, hands, hooves and talons. He struck at dog-heads, cows, snakes, eagles, and every other conceivable shape. For every foe that fell around him another stepped forward.

He realized he was not moving forward and, remembering Cleato's instructions, climbed over the bodies of the victims of his blade.

He no longer saw or heard Sarah. Over the heads of the enemy horde, Cleato's head bobbed, moving steadily toward the citadel. No one fought him. They all tried to get out of his way. What impeded him the most was throwing the enemy out of his path so he could walk.

The smell of battle sickened Con. Each blow of the sword brought the nauseating stench of the beasts' blood. The flagstone under his feet was covered with it. It oozed between the stones, advancing like thick, green mucus. It stuck to the bottom of his sandals and squished out when he stepped.

"Forward, Con! Forward, Sarah!" Cleato's voice came from the front. Con looked for the big man but he was too far away. He redoubled his efforts and, although his breathing was ragged and labored, he swung the blade faster and harder, pushing with his shield to get through the crowd. Behind him bodies lined the flagstone, looking like the wake of a ship cutting through a sea of beasts. In front of him, the endless sea waited.

He groaned. Weariness plagued his arms and chest. His wrist became weak. The blood lust that had driven him wore thin. Exhaustion weakened his sword. The insurmountable and ever increasing odds drove him to despair.

His pace slackened. He held his sword from biting into those that faced him. Laboring for breath, he stopped, barely holding his sword tip up.

The beasts in front of him backed off, forming a half ring around him. They leered at him. They were fresh, having sacrificed their comrades to wear Con down. Their weapons came up as Con's went down.

"Did you think you could really defeat us on our own ground, little farmer?" one of the snake-like beasts hissed. They all laughed.

"Cleato brings many of you fools here to die," a dog-man said. "One would think you humans would get wisdom and have nothing to do with these fools-errands."

Con tried to lift his sword back up but he had no strength left. The beasts saw it and moved closer. Death, hate, malice flowed from their eyes and mouths. With a groan, Con lifted the sword and made a half hearted swing at them. They jumped back and laughed.

The circle closed around him. More beasts ran to join in.

From a great distance he heard, "Forward, Con! Forward!"

He could not respond.

He let the sword point rest on the flagstone. The ground beneath him was covered with the blood of the beasts he had killed.

Soon, he thought, **it will be mine.**

He straightened himself up to his full height.

Determined to die like a man, he lifted his sword again. Something jabbed his stomach from underneath his buckler, irritating him. He snatched at it, anger for the irritation mounting him. His fingers closed on the vial Cleato had given him before the march.

Con grinned—remembering the wine in the forest, and on that first night. The beast in front of him, a thing with a human body and a cat's head, lifted its spear and backed up a step. Its feline eyes narrowed in suspicion at the sudden change in the soldier.

Those behind it pushed it forward. "Attack that dirt ball, Gord," one of its friends yelled.

Con shifted his sword to his shield hand, raised the small bottle to his mouth and pulled the cork with his teeth. There was no more than a few ounces of liquid in the vial but he gulped all of it. He dropped the empty vial and took up his sword again.

His stomach burned as if a hot poker had been shoved in it. The burning radiated out to his limbs. A feeling of power washed over him and the fatigue drained off him like water after a shower.

He knew he could win.

A growl started deep within his chest. He lifted the sword back to the ready and the growl became a blaring yell, "The sword of the mighty King."

The beasts closest to him panicked. His yell and sudden resurgence broke their line and they stumbled on one another in their attempt to get out of his reach, shoving over their comrades who could not yet see the enraged, battle-crazed soldier in front of them. Panic washed over the whole legion as Con moved forward. The area in front of him slowly cleared as all the beasts tried to escape.

Con ran forward, slicing into the beasts within his reach. Over and over he cried out, "The sword of the mighty King! The sword of the mighty King!"

Beasts flew, crawled, and ran to escape him. Sarah, too, had been surrounded but the panic had spread that far and beasts were running over one another to get away. The area in front of her cleared as Con watched.

"What happened?" she called.

"The wine. I drank the wine," he yelled, gesturing at her buckler.

She patted the buckler and her eyebrows shot up. She removed the vial and quickly drank the contents. Con watched the transformation, seeing what the enemy had seen when he had downed the wine a few minutes before.

Sarah stood up straight—no, more than that. It was as if inches were added to her height. Her face glowed. Her arms radiated power as she hefted the sword and began to swing it in wide arcs.

Her face took on the most change. Her eyes had drooped with fatigue. Now, they shot fire. Her jaw had sagged in despair. Now it was firm and square. Sarah was ready to move to battle.

The square was clear in front of them. They ran toward Cleato and the Citadel—and the only remaining group of Raiders with any semblance of discipline. These stood directly in front of the large doors.

Cleato was almost up to the Raiders. Con saw the consternation of the group, which obviously was the palace guard, at the approach of the big man. They did not want to face him.

The Raider officer barked out orders. The lines quieted and their weapons came up. Cleato stopped, standing directly in front of them, separated by fifty feet. Con and Sarah ran to catch up.

The Raider officer called out, "What do you want here, Lord Cleato. It is not time for you to be here."

The officer obviously was nervous, but he spoke with as much authority as he could muster.

"I am not here to destroy this place, yet. Nor will I take your authority for a season. But you have captured where you shouldn't have and I have come to retrieve what is mine."

The officer stood his ground but his men wavered. The crowd of beasts that had retreated edged in slightly—more to get a better view than in threat. Con and Sarah stood alongside of Cleato and waited for his instructions.

The Raider officer spoke harshly over his shoulder. A noncom walked in front of the Raiders and struck a few who had broken ranks. The platoon returned to attention.

The voice of the officer quavered as he tried to speak. His jaw clicked shut.

He rose to his full height and stuck out his chin. "I can't let you in."

"You can not stop me," Cleato answered, laughing a little.

"That is true, Lord Cleato. And if you desire you will walk over me. But I will not leave this place to you or your slaves."

The officer pointed at Con and Sarah with his sword point as he spoke. Then swung it toward the open square. "Or those."

Pistis and Beatrice walked up to stand next to Cleato. Beatrice appeared pale but her eyes said she was once again a soldier.

"Plazark, you were a good soldier," Cleato said, a wistful look on his face. "You should never have joined the rebellion."

"And you were ever a good commander, Lord Cleato," the officer said, also looking wistful. He seemed almost to want to lay down his sword and bow before Cleato but he firmed again. "But I did join."

The wine still throbbed through Con and the energy it gave demanded an outlet. He stepped forward, "Let us attack, Cleato. If they will not yield, we will force them out of the way."

Pistis snapped. "Back in line, Con. You don't know what you face." Con was beyond listening. The blood lust was in him again and he wanted battle. He walked toward the line of Raiders.

Sarah looked at Cleato, then at Con, confused and undecided. Finally she settled on Cleato and moved over close to him.

The officer spoke again, "Your humans are always so impetuous, Lord Cleato. You know that if he comes close I shall destroy him."

"You don't have the power to destroy me, Donkey hooves," Con said.

The Raider just smiled and lifted the skirt of his uniform to reveal normal feet. Con stopped.

"So you are not a goat. I will still fight you. I have the power," Con yelled, lifting the sword.

As he did, the officer lifted his sword also. A crackling light flew from the point and struck Con on the chest. Con staggered back and fell at Cleato's feet, blinded. A boom of thunder deafened his ears.

Sarah kneeled down and cradled him. Con groped with his hand to find his sword and shield, both of which he had dropped when the bolt hit him.

"What happened?" he whispered to Sarah, still blinded but getting his hearing back.

Sarah didn't answer. Cleato spoke. "You have taught him a lesson, Plazark. You will do no more. I have spoken."

The officer started to answer but a loud, sizzling sound, like water bring thrown in a hot frying pan, interrupted him. The sizzling continued for a few seconds. Then silence.

Con's vision returned. He rubbed his eyes and looked around. He lay on his back in Sarah's arms. She sat on the ground. Her folded legs supported him. Cleato stood over them. No one else was in the square except Pistis and Beatrice.

"What happened?" Con asked.

Sarah stared at him with her mouth hanging open. She looked up at Cleato, then back at Con, her mouth still open but no sound coming out.

Pistis leaned down and took Con's hand, pulling him to his feet. "Are you all right?" he asked.

"What happened?" Con repeated, looking around the empty square.

Sarah stammered. She choked and coughed, then found her tongue. "Cleato, waved his hand and they were gone!" she exclaimed with wonder. "They just disappeared. Sizzled!"

Con looked at his leader and back at Sarah, who stood again agape. Cleato just said, "We are close."

Sarah continued to stare open-mouthed at Cleato and at the empty square. Con grabbed his armor and followed Cleato to the big doors. Pistis walked up behind him.

They were large, arched affairs with ornate carving in the wood. The knockers were heavy, burnished brass and the door knob appeared to be gold. The doorframe was made of polished stone that gleamed white like the rest of the building.

Con stood before the door wondering how to get in. Cleato stood next to him, quietly. Sarah still stood on the flagstone staring around.

The door cracked open.

Con jumped back. He lifted his sword over his head to prepare for a quick, powerful swing when the attack came.

A low, throbbing squeak came from the hinges as the thick, wooden door made its ponderous swing out.

The quietness that accompanied the slow opening was worse than the whole past battle. Con's nerves drew taut, his breath caught in his throat and the muscles in his arms twitched in anticipation. Whatever beast attacked them would be the worst, he was sure.

The door opened all the way. Something stood just inside the door, out of the light. It did not move.

Con dropped the sword point to a defensive position, the chance for a surprise chop at an attacking foe lost. The being in the doorway still did not move.

"Con?" the being asked, bewilderment pouring out with that one word.

Con dropped his sword point and looked closer. The shape of the being was familiar, the voice almost like his....

"Father!"

"Con, what are we doing here? Wait, I remember. The Dragon!"

Incor Ataxia looked around suddenly, ducking down. "He's here, Con. I saw him. They brought me here from the Market."

Incor looked at Con again, puzzled. "But how did you get here so quickly?"

"It has not been quickly, Father, It has been over a year since they took you."

"A year? Nay. It has been only hours since they got me here."

"A year." Sarah said, finally recovering from her shock.

"Who are you?" he asked, turning to Sarah and then to Cleato.

"There is no time now," Cleato said. "We must be going. Con, the point."

"But aren't we going after the Dragon? We came to fight him."

"It is not time yet," Cleato said, shaking his head. "I am not ready yet to end things."

Con shrugged. His desire to get his father home was just as strong as his desire for battle. So he turned to Pistis. "The point, Pistis?"

Pistis nodded. Incor stepped forward. "Pistis?" He turned the soldier to him and looked him hard in the face. "Older. Thinner. But…" Tears weld up in his eyes and overflowed onto his cheek. "Oh, Commander. It is you."

Pistis smiled and nodded. "Hello, Incor."

"Pistis, the one I threw out of my house. Pistis, the one I said I would never again allow to see his sister or her children."

Pistis continued to smile. "That is all in the past, Incor."

A tear ran again down the rough looking man's cheek. "Pistis, you came with my son. How do I -?"

Pistis turned toward Cleato. "Not me, Incor. Him." He pointed at the man walking across the garden—a big man but dressed in a robe that covered him from head to foot, with a hood that hid his handsome features.

Pistis nodded at Con. "Take your father to Cleato, Con."

Con started to move toward him but stopped. "No, I think that would best be done by the one who first tried to introduce them." He swept his sword toward the big man.

Pistis nodded. "Incor?" He tilted his head toward Cleato.

They walked across the green grass. Cleato turned, flipped his hood back, and smiled at the approaching pair.

Chapter 32

They marched quickly out of the square and down the street. Rusty waited for them three blocks from the gate.

"I have fifty-five freedmen waiting at the gate. All opposition has ceased but we must move quickly."

Seeing Incor, he smiled and slapped Con on the back. "You did it!"

"No, he did it," Con said, nodding at Cleato.

Rusty nodded agreement, still smiling broadly. "By the way, Con. There is a bent, old man—says he is a soldier—standing at the gate. I tried to get him in with the freedmen but he said he would not go until he saw you."

A stooped figure stood at the gate, weaving back and forth, hand raised to shade his eyes as he stared at the approaching figures. Con raised his sword—the one supplied by the old man—in a salute. The old face burst into a grin, then the figure turned and walked through the open gate.

The freedmen were just inside the gates. Cleato placed Con and Sarah on one side of them and Beatrice and Pistis on the other. The freedman walked out between them.

As the first approached the portal, the ground shook lightly. Black storm clouds formed over the spire of the Citadel. Lightning bolts played among the clouds, outlining then in their brilliance.

Con stood in the gate and hurried the freedmen out. Peals of distant thunder vibrated their chests and. the ground reverberated below their feet.

"He is angry," Con said as Cleato came close.

"Yes, he is angry. More than that, his pride has been hurt. Five soldiers entered his realm, set free his prisoners, destroyed many of his hordes and are now escaping. His ego is damaged. It will take many lies to soothe it."

Con glanced back at the storm. The violence of the storm threatened to tear the spire from its mounts. Con remembered the clean, handsome-faced features of the Dragon and shook his head.

"It does not seem possible that he has caused all this."

"This and more," said Cleato, staring along with Con. "And more to come."

They herded the last of the freedmen out of the gate. Cleato grasped the big knocker and pushed the door closed. Its mate followed. They walked away into the field of tall grass outside the wall, kicking at the arrow shafts that still protruded from the ground like porcupine quills. Rusty, Sarah, and Beatrice had the freedmen sitting in formation. They passed out the bread and wine, provisions for the long march home.

A vicious, howling wind ripped down from the mountain slopes, screeching in fury. The shields and swords, which had been stuck in the ground, clanged over into the grass. Thick, bloated clouds appeared over the mountains, then rushed down on them, covering the dusky sky from East to West in seconds, deepening the smoky afternoon gloom to darkness. The wind slashed at them with daggers of ice-cold rain.

The wind's force sucked the breath out of Con's throat. Freedmen and squad alike were knocked onto the grass-covered ground. The freedmen cried out in terror and cowered in the tall grass, hiding their eyes behind folded arms.

Lightning cracked around them, over and over, bolt after bolt only seconds apart. The thunder rolled over them like a solid sheet. Con pushed to his knees, leaning into the wind to keep from being blown over. Rusty lay on his back, holding onto his helmet. Sarah and Beatrice crawled on their bellies among the people trying to calm them.

Only Cleato stood.

He stood rock still above them. Not even his cloak moved in the fury of the wind. The wind screeched and howled and the rain pelted at them. He remained unmoved, dry, calm. He stared purposefully at the wall.

High above the gates, on the parapet, stood a lone figure. Around him was blackness. His hands moved up and down, conducting his orchestra of wind, rain and lightning. Thunder roared as he pointed; lightning leaped from his outstretched hands; the wind swirled and battered at them, following his flowing arms.

Yet, for all his commands and power, no bolts fell among the company. Hail bounced heavily all around them, yet none reached the humans. The driving raindrops stopped suddenly, just short of the group, and fell on them as a gentle mist.

All the power of the Dragon was diverted and redirected around the humans. The only part that affected the people was the deafening and frightening roar.

Con put his foot under him and pushed up. The wind reversed suddenly and hit him in the back like a giant fly swatter. He fell hard on his face.

He lay for a minute then pushed himself up to a kneeling position again.

The people screamed and cowered down. The Dragon, up on the wall, laughed loudly. The wicked sound was carried by the roaring wind to all their ears.

He shouted at them, "O-him has dared to insult me with you humans coming into my city. 0-him, I may not be able to destroy you yet but I can and will crush your putrid little dirt balls; crush them till their blood irrigates my fields."

The Dragon roared in wicked laughter and cast more lightning at the frightened humans. Cleato stood still, staring up at the Dragon perched on his aerie. Bolt after bolt crashed their way. Each one deflected harmlessly, though with an ear-splitting roar.

Cleato raised his hand and shouted, "Hush!"

The wind cut off so suddenly that Con fell on his face. There was dead silence all around him—an eerie, total lack of sound. He raised his head. The clouds had split directly above them. Blue sky was revealed as the smoke rolled back. The small sounds of whispers and gasps of the people, still lying in the grass, grew to exclamations and cries.

Con rose to his knees, then to his feet. Rusty and Pistis stood up next to him. Sarah and Beatrice climbed to their knees. They all stared at the devastation around them. They were centered in a circle of grass that looked much like it had when they walked out of the gates. Outside of that ring there was only the charred remains of the field.

The blackness of the burnt grass was broken place after place by the brown of fresh dirt, turned up by the frustrated lightning. Con counted twenty-five scars within one hundred yards of them. He whistled softly.

The freedmen cowered in the grass, more afraid of the silence than they had been of the storm.

Cleato stood with his hand still raised. The Dragon looked down on them from the parapet, his hands gripping the stone in front of him. An area of blackness persisted around him but everywhere else there was light.

Cleato spoke, his voice deep and commanding, "You have challenged me too often, Lu-for. And you have threatened my humans enough. If you want to test your strength then we shall."

The Dragon reeled backwards. He reappeared slowly, "I am not prepared for a battle with you, 0-him. You have destroyed all my forces."

"The battle is between you and I, Lu-for. It has been that way since the beginning."

Lu-for backed away again from the edge. No answer came.

"You are, as always, devious and oblique in your ways. But do not fear. I am not ready to burn this valley with fire…yet. So you escape for another time. But because you have challenged me…."

Cleato spoke no more. The ground rose, then fell under their feet and they stumbled. A series of waves spread out from Cleato's feet, raising and breaking the surface of the ground as if it were a pond into which a rock had been hurled.

The waves broke on the mighty block wall with a crashing groan. The stones of the wall screeched as they raised and fell and swayed back and forth. A blast split the air and the wall opened up in a gaping crack from bottom to top. The granite blocks near the top, tons in weight, jumped up and down, left their appointed places, and thundered into the undulating ground.

The whole wall buckled and swayed as if it were a wild beast unhappy with its rider. The ground lifted and dropped again and again. The Dragon was pitched forward into sight then backward and hidden again by the blocks of the parapet. As the wall began to crumble, a black creature rose on pale wings from where the Dragon had stood. A blood-curdling scream tore from its throat and it flew quickly into the city, angling toward the white spire.

The ground swells subsided. The wall stopped its gyrations. The noise of destruction ceased and near silence returned to the field. The wall moaned and grated in an unseen movement. Up and down the length of it, the tortured cry sounded. Slowly, almost as if the blocks floated on the air for an instant, the wall careened to the ground, falling inward, away from them.

The ground jumped and shuddered as the heavy blocks struck. Dust flew up in great clouds and drifted on air currents away from the group of humans, obscuring the whole city from their view. All along the wall, as far as Con could see, there were no two blocks left together.

"He has fled," Cleato said, finally. "We will have no trouble from him—for a season anyway."

"Let us attack now, Cleato," Con urged. "While he is weak, we will destroy him."

"Your courage is only matched by your ignorance, my friend," Cleato responded, laughing a little. "No, it is not time. And the destruction of

Lu-for, the Dragon as you call him, involves much more than you can imagine. For now, we will let him be.

"Head up our party, Con. Pistis, set them in marching order. Sarah and Beatrice, take the sides of the group. I will cover our rear. Rusty, you march with them, caring for them."

"The direction, Cleato?"

"Straight up the road, Con. Straight up the road."

Con started them off. Cleato stood his position and watched them go. He turned to the Citadel again. His powerful eyes picked out the dark spot against the gray, dusty sky, circling the tower.

"Soon, Lu-for. Soon"

About the Author

L. Robert Pyle lives with his wife of thirty-one years in Wichita, Kansas. They have traveled extensively throughout their marriage having lived in Delaware, Kentucky, Texas, and Kansas as well as a few years in Germany and Korea. He has been an elder in the Body of Christ for many years and serves, currently, in a local Wichita church. Trained as an engineer, a scientist by nature, a manager by vocation, and a Christian by Grace, he utilizes all of his extensive background and experience in writing for the Church.

9 780595 183029